The Illumination of Alice J. Cunningham

Lyn Webster

DEDALUS/HIPPOCRENE

Published in the U.K. by Dedalus Ltd.
Langford Lodge, St. Judith's Lane, Sawtry, Cambs, PE17 5XE.

ISBN 0 946626 39 1

Distributed in the U.S.A. by Hippocrene Books Inc,
171, Madison Avenue, New York, NY10016

First published as a hardback in 1987
First paperback edition 1989

Printed by The City Printing Works (Chester-le-Street) Ltd.,
Broadwood View, Chester-le-Street, Co. Durham DH3 3NJ.

A C.I.P. reference for this title is available on request from
the British Library.

For my mother and father.

CONTENTS

CONTENTS

The Prologue

Now it so happened that in the cold, wet springtime which preceded that heatwave summer, Alice, our heroine fell ill. In fact she fell very ill indeed, with a temperature which peaked to a hundred and four Fahrenheit at times, a cough of such ferocity that it bounced her upright in her bed, and a delirium which turned her nights into a phantasmagorical picture show, wherein, it seemed, the forces of good and evil battled for control of her soul. She was not at all sure which side won in the end because on some nights, when the fever was at its worst, she felt that she — the Alice J. Cunningham she had known for some thirty years so far — had been altogether wiped out, annihiliated by the great, hot, waves that flooded into her and swept away all the cherished, familiar bits of being that she had hung on to for so long.

It was just the usual bug of course, which everybody had that year, which for some reason had decided to savage the robust and rosy Alice while it left frailer people comfortably sipping Ribena in front of afternoon television. For Alice it was a melodrama: her bed rocked, she felt she would surely die of the terrible discomfort which would never let her sleep. In consequence she talked to angels, gods and goddesses, saw her future children by several possible fathers run before her eyes, embraced her dead brother, found again her lost father, spent hours arguing for her life in gloomy courts of law. In the morning she knew all this for the fantasy and hallucination it was, easily dispelled by Radio Four, a cup of tea and a few spoonfuls of tinned rice pudding. But she did not get better. The antibiotics did not work and the night-mare fantasies became more violent, more harrowing, more real.

It came to the point where Alice realised she had to get better or give in. But she did not know how. She fought and pleaded for her life at night but didn't win. The forces which had set themselves against her were too strong for her. There must be another way to survive, and she must find it soon! She was, it must be said, more than a little frightened.

Then one night, when she was getting quite near the end of her strength, she dreamed a dream which she had not dreamed since she was a very little girl. In it she stood in an enormous black cavern somewhere under the earth, and saw before her, hanging in the void, a great, glittering crystal shape. It hung, pointing both upwards and downwards, turning imperceptibly in the air with awful authority and menace. A voice spoke and said, "Alice, unless you manage to do the impossible task, your mother and father, your brother, your grandmother and your uncle, will all be utterly destroyed. You must, you *must* do it . . . " Alice shivered with absolute terror, and knew in her heart that she was not capable of doing this dreadful, impossible task (in the dream she was quite clear what it was although she could not remember when she woke up) and that the cruel judgement would certainly be visited on the people she loved.

But this time, twenty five years on, Alice was not quite so afraid. "I'll do it!" she said, "if you'll tell me what it is and how to begin. But I'll forget, I know that I'll forget, when I wake up, and then the punishment will happen all the same . . . " "No," was the reply. "No — it doesn't matter that you'll think you have forgotten. We will lead you along the path you need to follow. If you give us your promise now then that's enough — we'll make the arrangements that need to be made, don't worry . . . " And Alice fell into a dark, empty sleep and when she woke up in the morning she felt rested and refreshed and her fever did not return again. The crisis was over, and within ten days she was back at work.

She had lost a stone in weight (which was not serious as she was a buxom woman), stopped smoking, acquired a flinty sparkle in her eyes, and a raw, spongy patch at the bottom of her lungs, which would flare up sporadically for the rest of her life.

She did not remember the dream of course, although later on things were to happen which would *almost* remind her, and make her remember that there was something difficult and dangerous that she had to do . . .

But I jump ahead of myself. We must go back to the rainy Maytime that followed Alice's convalescence, when her old schoolfriend Maria, five months pregnant with her wayward lover's child, came to stay . . .

PART ONE: The Camp

"With all its eyes the creature-world beholds
the open. But our eyes, as though reversed
encircle it on every side, like traps
set round its unobstructed path to freedom."

R.M. Rilke
Eighth Elegy from the
Duino Elegies

"There is no death — everyone knows that,
It is insipid to repeat!
But what is there — let them tell me that.
Who's knocking?
Everyone has been admitted.
It is a visitor from inside the mirrors?"

Anna Akhmatova
from *Poem Without a Hero*

CHAPTER ONE

The Opening

CHAPTER ONE

The heatwave summer had not yet arrived. The dark, wet spring dragged on into a stormy May, into which the hot day on which the 'event' happened dropped like a piece of paradise. Swarms of wild flowers, of which neither Alice nor Maria knew the names, flew past as they drove lacka-daisically into the countryside for a picnic. The car windows were closed because of Alice's hayfever, but even so atoms of sparkling air bashed themselves against the barriers, shouting at the two women to rejoice. They did not. Alice's arms were braced rigid on the wheel, her eyes staring into vacancy. Periodically she sighed. Maria, with her hands self-consciously crossed over her swelling stomach, cast dazed eyes out on the flashing colours of the verge, being careful to avoid looking up at the sky which was so ostentatiously flushed with ecstacy.

"It's too hot," said Alice.

"I've got a headache," said Maria.

"But I suppose we should be grateful," added Alice.

"To whom?" rejoined Maria morosely.

"Actually I do believe in God in a way," said Alice after a pause. "Not an old bearded man of course — more a principle of meaning. But then I think I always did, it's just that I pretended for ages not to because it wasn't ideologically sound. Thank God we're old enough not to care about that any more."

"Mmmm" said Maria as if she didn't really agree, or found the quality of the thought beneath her notice, or else wasn't listening.

Alice felt irritated and wished she could have a cigarette, but remembered that even if she hadn't given up she couldn't have had one in the sealed-up car with a pregnant Maria. This made her feel even more irritated.

"Why are you pregnant anyway?" she asked with false mildness and genuine curiosity. To her surprise Maria turned and looked at her properly for the first time that day. Alice noted that her face was tired and puffy, faded like the face of a mother of three who had sacrificed everything, not the face of a whiz-kid psychiatrist with a first book on feminist psychotherapy already in its second printing. Her eyes smarted with awkward love for her friend but she thought it was hayfever and rubbed them crossly. After a long time Maria spoke.

"I could say it was an accident, but I can't really let myself get away with that."

"Is it definitely Philip's?"

"Yes, I'd stopped sleeping with Alan for a while just in case."

"In case what?"

"In case I got pregnant."

"I see. Some accident!"

"Oh, in a way it *was* an accident. I didn't mean to stay that night. I'd just popped in to drop him off a book he needed, but the household was celebrating something — someone just resigned their job I think — and there were bottles of wine around . . . so I stayed, got a bit drunk, fell into bed, and of course I didn't have my cap with me . . ."

"But you didn't mind really, if it happened?"

"I know, I admit it, it's true. And someone said to me just that morning what lovely eyes he had and wasn't I tempted to have his child."

"Is he pleased?"

"A bit titillated. Quite pleased really. I've promised not to ask him for any money."

"That's outrageous!"

"Why? It was me who wanted a child, not him. The relationship's not that committed."

"Yes, but, as my mum would say, if we left it up to men to want children the human race would die out. I think they should be held responsible as a sex, never mind as individuals!"

"You're naive, Alice! It's one of the few ways men can assert their independence nowadays. And anyway, I'm earning a good salary and he's on the dole. It doesn't make sense to make him pay. As long as he babysits."

As Maria passed once again into what Alice thought of as a cow-like reverie Alice felt gingerly for the aching tooth of her own misery and waggled it gently to keep her company. What would *he* be doing now? Either something stupid or something brilliant no doubt. How bitter that someone so beautiful, so radiant, elegant and clever, so full of chutzpah and joie de vivre, should also be a creep, a creep who would pull Alice towards him with one hand and push her away with the other. How cruel that Alice should have her first experience in thirty years of sexual failure, sexual rejection, from the man with whom she had been hopelessly in love for a long year now. And yet, and yet, and yet maybe it *could* still work, if she was prepared to sacrifice, and be patient and learn to give and give and give and expect nothing in return . . . But that did not sound very much like the behaviour of the Alice she knew and rather liked.

"Sex," she said out loud, "what a shame we can't do without it."

"I like sex," said Maria defiantly.

"Oh, I know, I know! So do I. But it's never just a matter of sex. All sorts of things stick to it. Like men,"

"You could always try women."

"I've told you before — I like women far too much to want to go to bed with them."

"A cheap phrase, Alice. You're scared. You'd enjoy it."

"Don't you tell me what I'd enjoy, you little bully. Being pregnant hasn't mellowed you much I see!"

Maria rustled in her bag and brought out an orange. She stuck her nail into it and its impudent odour fizzed into the car. They both giggled. Alice forgot her hayfever and opened the window. The outside jumped joyfully in to embrace the inside and the little car shot like an arrow into the dark heart of the smiling green countryside.

★   ★   ★

If you had been the elf who was sitting in a certain high beech tree that day you would have seen the two of them sprawled beneath you, abandoning themselves to the shifting, rustling shade of the big tree as they rarely did to men, and, in Maria's case, other sorts of lovers. Alice lay on her side, in odalisque position, her chin propped on her hand, squinting upwards at the sun as it glittered at her through the leaves. She was wearing a nineteen forties crêpe dress bought in an Oxfam shop, which strained somewhat against her full breasts and wide hips, obliging her to ruck it up at the waist and undo buttons at the neck to allow the sun more easy access to her pale, freckly flesh. The elf thought she would have looked better naked, but did allow that her long and shapely arms and legs swam gracefully in the waves of lush green grass as she wriggled herself into the best sunbeam catching position and reached for another sandwich from the plastic bag.

She was feeling mildly erotic and mildly anxious. She tugged absently at the browney blonde hair which sat like a floppy mushroom on the top of her head gripped in an elastic band, as if it were somehow possible to order its unruliness. Her crystalline green eyes (her only un-odalisque-like feature — they were the kind of sharp, accusing eyes which made people turn away from her if she stared at them too long, which she often did) were ringed with red from rubbing at the pollen-irritation. She stared into the distance, her mouth set in a glum pout, as if resisting an unspoken suggestion that life was not so bad really.

Maria, her yellowy skin already turning honey-colour in the sun, lay flat on her back, immobile and neatly arranged as a corpse on a slab. She was built on a different scale to Alice, several sizes smaller and deftly and econom-ically designed to instruct mankind and to please him. For Maria was both clever and exquisite — her mother having been a tiny, flower-like Indian doctor. She was also, it must be said, ferocious in argument and rigorous in intel-lect, so that she was, on the whole, admired rather than desired by the men she encountered. But now she was asleep and dreaming that her mother came like the witch in Sleeping Beauty and cursed her child in the womb. "You have to pay tribute to the mothers first, my pretty!" she cackled. "And you know that that means blood, means blood, means blood . . . " Maria had read a lot of books about the triple goddess of the moon and the semiological meanings of menstruation, so that nowadays her dreams often had the feel of seminar illustrations. Good academic that she was, she was already filing this one away for use in her next book which was to be about the myth of the satis-faction of motherhood.

However, it should be mentioned that in a layer of

dreaming *beyond* this one (of which Maria was not aware) her five month old *male* foetus screamed and screamed at her with dreadul, absolute, demanding rage and tore at the walls of her womb with precociously developed finger-nails. When Maria awoke she would feel strange bands of soreness around her middle.

The elf was particularly enjoying the rhythm of Maria's body: the delicate curve of her translucent eyelids, which curve as it washed down her body became her breasts, her swelling belly and her neat and shiny apple knees. Why make them any bigger? he thought approvingly. The small ones fit in very well with my countryside, while the big fidgety ones upset the flow a bit. Then he fell to ruminat-ing on the boringness of human woman. Why did they not dance or sing or tell each other stories? Why did they just lie there like puddings in his carefully tended landscape? He thought that he would shake some dewdrops down onto the sleeper's nose so that she would wake up and make conversation. What use is a human being to me, he thought, without some conversation?

Maria sat up abruptly.

"Funny," she said, "it feels cold now, and just a minute ago it was hot."

"Hmmm," said Alice, not feeling cold at all and pouring herself another glass of wine, forgetful of the fact that she was driving. Maria was not tempted. She was the sort of person who had willpower, never put on weight, and passed exams easily. She shivered again.

"All right," said Alice, "Let's go, but let's have a walk in the woods first. It seems a shame to waste the sunshine."

And let it be remembered, lest in the main body of the story it seem that Alice is the one with the imagination, that had not Maria, the intellectual, registered that cosmic blast of coldness which Alice could not feel, then the two of them would not have got up just then and moved through the door that was opening, just for a moment, and would perhaps have closed again had they lingered any longer on the grass.

So, the vague disconsolateness, the itchy malaise which had affected them both all day turned into a restful melan-choly as they entered the dark wood. And strangely enough, instead of striking chill after the open sunlight, the woodland air seemed warmer on their faces. This time it was Alice who noticed the change, but she said nothing for fear that Maria would have a scientific explanation for it.

An underwater stillness ruled in the wood, and the trees arched high over their heads, sighing in a wind that was only palpable at their high level. Alice reflected that it was more of a grand, ancient forest than a wood, the kind of place you feel you've visited in another life, but another life when you lived in a fairy tale and met unicorns and medieval knights. Maria felt as if something cold and heavy was pressing down on her heart. Her ribs ached and she was fearful that something was going wrong with the baby, her little girl, already named Dorothea after the heroine of her favourite novel, 'Middlemarch'. For a moment they both shared a sense of the wood as an awesome, dangerous place, and had they followed the subtle impulse to flight that ran through both their nervous systems at that moment then they would have turned round and walked back to the car as fast as their legs could carry them. But Alice said:

"Oh, it's the bluebells!" And they both felt that the sensation of deep heart-chill which had touched them must have been triggered by the icy odour of the flowers.

At the end of the avenue of high trees they came upon two stone gateposts which marked the beginning of a drive which looked as if it was still in use. And yet there were no car tracks on the path up which they had just come.

"How strange," said Alice. "I wonder where it leads to. There must be some kind of old manor house up there."

At that moment Maria distinctly felt herself turn and walk back along the path which led out of the wood, saying that she was tired and wanted to get home quickly and lie down for a while. But actually she was walking with Alice in the opposite direction up the drive and, as her friend had predicted, a big, Victorian building was swimming into view.

"Alice," began Maria, "I'm feeling very tired, and I really think we ought to go . . . "

"It looks inhabited," said Alice, crunching intrepidly up the gravel pathway to the door. "Perhaps they'd let us sit down inside for five minutes and give us a cup of tea," she continued, peering through a ground floor window. "It feels like some kind of nursing home or rest home . . . I can see a consulting couch through the window."

Maria was about to assert her wishes to go home more forcefully when a young woman in a nurse's uniform materialised from round a corner and smiled pleasantly at her.

"Hello, can I help you at all? Are we expecting you, or were you just calling on the off-chance?"

"Oh, we were just walking actually," flustered Maria who hated being welcomed anywhere on false pretences," and we didn't realise this was a private drive or we wouldn't have come up it."

"My friend's not feeling very well," interrupted Alice boldly, stepping unembarrassed from the flower bed, "and we were wondering if there was somewhere we could sit down for a few moments, and have a cup of tea . . . "

"Of course," smiled the sweet nurse, "there's a canteen where it's cool. Come with me and I'll show you where it is."

She led them off round the back of the house, through a kitchen garden that smelt revoltingly of hot cabbage, through a glass door into a long corridor with cream walls and a glistening brown floor. The place smelt of hospital disinfectant, but it made Alice think of school — the long, brown corridor they walked down every day to prayers and the stairway they clattered up afterwards, with its dark green tiles and the big, sombre board on the wall with the names of all the head girls dating back to 1893 in golden letters on it.

That morning when suddenly she had looked down on her own tousled head as it bobbed up the stairs with the other girls and thought in amazement: '*That* is *me* down there? *That* one? That bouncing little girl with precociously developed breasts? Alice Cunningham, Form 2a of Putney High School for Girls? Just that? Me? Now? Oh, oh, oh . . . ' and felt giddy and sick and overwhelmed and unreal, like looking in a mirror and seeing yourself looking in a mirror seeing yourself looking in a mirror . . . or writing the World, the Universe, the Galaxy, Infinity — and stepping off the edge there and wondering where you were if anywhere and . . .

"Yes," the nurse was saying, "it is a rest home really. A place where people come to get away from it all, be safe for a while when things get too much for them."

'A place rich people come to to pretend to have nervous breakdowns,' thought Maria tartly, but Alice was not listening. She was looking out of the windows into the gardens, which reminded her of somewhere too, a place she had known a long time ago, or was it perhaps just that they had been used as a location for a television play she had seen?

In the canteen, which was small and windowless, they drank stewed tea but Maria did not feel better. In fact she turned a gluey yellow colour, said she felt sick and had pains in her stomach like period pains and she thought they'd better find a doctor straightaway, if there was a real one on the premises . . .

Alice felt a convulsion of dreadful excitement in her bowels. Things were taking a dark turn again. She knew her little god-son (she guessed Maria's baby would be a boy somehow) could not survive rude expulsion into the world at five and a half months, but she suspected that the idea of spontaneous abortion was his and his alone.

"It's no fun being an abortion, kid", she told him, as she ran along the corridor to find a nurse. "Now that you've come so far you might as well go through with it. If you really can't stand it once you're here you can always arrange a cot death or being smothered by a cat. But you'll have to go through the birth pangs anyway, even if you come out now, and I promise you, after that, nothing can ever be quite as bad again. OK?"

The angry baby churned himself at her: "You'll have to do better than that," he growled. "My mother is an idiot, that's bad enough. But a feminist as well — it's impossible! She'll spoil me rotten when she finds out I'm a boy, and I did want to try and be a real human being this time round!"

"No," thought Alice, "he's right. There are enough spoiled brats in the world. If only Maria didn't feel so guilty about being clever and beautiful and well off then she wouldn't have to go around doing good to people all the time!"

By this time they were wheeling Maria to a side-ward

where she was laid down and examined by a doctor. Alice sat in the corner feeling dazed and heavy-eyed. The erotic self-awareness she'd experienced earlier had not abated. She felt a strong, unruly desire to take her clothes off and roll her hot, naked body in some long wet grass. However, Maria left dozing in the side-ward, she wandered out into the strangely familiar garden and sat herself respectably on a wooden bench.

There her conversation with the angry foetus struggled to bring itself up into her consciousness disguised as anxiety about her friend, but failed. Instead she found herself tormented by trying to remember where she had seen this particular garden before . . . or even when she had *been* in it before. Of course, it was impossible that she had actually *been* in it, unless in a dream of some sort, but that was a far-fetched and daft idea. She ruled it out.

It was a garden which combined classicism with juicy abundance, so that, while there was a fountain in the centre, surrounded by geometric flower-beds planted with well-pruned roses, there were also wild corners and bowers where big, heavy blossoms swung and honey-suckle trailed languorously over the old trellises and mossy walls.

"Perhaps it seems familiar because it's archetypal," she thought, having, of course, read C.G. Jung. A bumble bee zoomed through her field of vision, so close it almost bumped against her nose. "Z-z-z-idiot!" it said. She jumped up and wandered into a particularly sensuous, bowery corner and stood there, with her nose pressed into the honeysuckle. A wave of warm, golden energy flooded through her, soaking her from the loins upwards in its electric glow.

"Hah!" she thought angrily. "What the hell is it that I'm trying to remember? What is it that I'm meant to do?"

The honeysuckle pollen was floating down into her lungs and suddenly she coughed, a deep scratchy cough which jarred the bottom of her lungs. And she remembered, just for a split second, her illness and the nights of fever and coughing, and the dream, and the promise, and the impossible task, whatever it was . . .

"Silly, silly!" she admonished herself. "I'm so silly at the moment. Everything upsets me. Everything seems to have a meaning which I can't quite get at . . . and I just can't concentrate . . . you'd think I was the pregnant one and not Maria . . . "

But there was no chance of Alice being pregnant. "I'm cold," he'd said, Lewis, the man she was in love with, at half past three in the morning after she had drunk three whiskies and he had smoked three joints, and he'd wrapped his arms about himself like a kid at the swimming pool, and hugged himself and shivered violently. She had been about to get up and go. Although it was clear that each of them wanted to go to bed with the other (for drastically different reasons, she thought grimly now) there had seemed to be no way to cut through the adolescent intensity of their conversation and get there. But now she went up to him and rubbed his arms to warm him up. It was true that his flesh, his brown arms with the long white-blonde hairs on them, was chilled. She rubbed his arms and his back. Then it was easy for their mouths to bump into each other so that they could kiss and clasp and rub their cheeks fiercely, embarrassedly together. But she should have spotted that already something was going wrong.

"Tell me about the first time you fell in love," she said. His eyes were filmy, concussed. He wasn't looking at her.

"I will," he said, "I will tell you everything, everything . . . "

She was taken aback by his vehemence, by the unseemly haste with which he tore off his clothes, the trembling vigour of his embrace, the fluttering, childish excitement with which he touched her skin and squeezed her breasts.

But when she let her fingers travel down his body and come upon his penis it was small and flaccid. Never before in the twelve years of her sexually active life had she been to bed for the first time with a man who didn't have an erection. She was flummoxed.

"Look at me a minute, will you?" she said.

He groaned and turned his eyes in her direction, but he would not really look at her.

"Don't let's go to sleep yet, eh?" he murmured. "It's so lovely . . . "

"But Lewis," she said, "I want to talk to you!"

"Oh no!" he growled, his mouth falling wet against the pillow.

"Do you think men and women really are very different in their sexual behaviour?" she asked him timidly, trying to frame her distress in a safe abstraction.

"Oh yes, oh yes" he said as he pulled away from her and curled himself up in a ball facing towards the wall," not just different . . . irreconcilable, quite irreconcilable . . ."

She lay for a moment, rigid with shock, then sprang out of bed and got the first bus home.

And yet, and yet, she was still in love with him. Whenever she saw him she wanted to put her hand up and touch his icy, silvery hair, the kind of ashen-fair hair that has dark green shadows in it and makes you think of meadows, twilight and outdoor love-making. Although he gave me nothing, she thought, not even the most basic gift that a man can give a women — his penis in her vagina — I have to admit that beauty like his gives of itself, without trying or doing anything . . . I am grateful that he exists even if I can't have him . . . But is that so sure? Maybe if we tried again, in more favourable circumstances . . .

As Alice came to herself the sun broke through the clouds and burnt her in a sudden, furious Mediterranean outburst. She went and sat in the shade. There, it was too cold. Is there no escape at all for me? she thought.

★ ★ ★

By six o'clock she was feeling irritable and hungry and wanted to go home. But Maria was still yellowish, the whites of her eyes lilac in the cold light of the hospital room.

"She can't be moved," said the nurse. "We may yet save the baby if she rests and stays quite still."

Alice reviewed in her mind the tedium of walking back to the car on her own, driving home down the motorway, and coming back next morning for Maria. She would be home by eight which would give her plenty of time to get ready for the party, which Lewis might be at. She could ring Maria first thing in the morning to see how she was and . . .

"Don't leave me, Ally." A small voice came from the person in the bed. Alice flushed with shock. Maria had not called her by that name since they were seaweed together in the school play.

"Of course not" she said huskily. "Are you scared?"

"I don't want to talk about it, but I don't want you to go away."

"You'll be all right, kid. It's probably the heat or maybe the paté in those sandwiches was off . . . I'm sorry I made you walk all that way."

"It's not that. I know I really could lose the baby. Did I tell you I was going to call her Dorothea?"

"Yes, you did. But actually I think it's going to be a boy. Then what a responsibility, eh?"

Tears stood in the corners of Maria's perfect almond eyes, the eyes of a houri that had somehow found themselves in the body of a Marxist-feminist.

"It's all right, Alice, you don't have to talk to me. You're not exactly brilliant at saying the right thing in this sort of situation, so why don't you go and get something to eat. You must be hungry by now."

In the dark grey canteen Alice ate egg and chips. There was no-one else in there except a man in brown overalls who sat with his back to her. She badly needed a cigarette. Perhaps the man in brown would give her one, or sell her a few to see her through the night. But as she prepared herself to put the proposition to him, he rose abruptly and swung round to face her as he left the room. She felt as if a bucket of icy water had been poured all over her. Her body thrummed, outraged. His eyes were a light, uncanny grey and they had jumped at her, issuing a command. When he was gone she found that she was trembling.

"It was not sexual," she told herself. "At least not in the usual way. It was as if he'd been sent to *push* me, to tell me to get up and get on with it. But what's 'it'?"

She got up and went out into the garden again, half-expecting to see him there. But there was nobody about and only the plish-plashing of the fountain to be heard. She went and trailed her fingers in the water. Her whole body wanted to join them, but the fountain basin was not big enough to take it, unless she wound herself around the central stem like a snake . . .

"This is boring," she thought. "I have no book to read, no cigarettes, no alcohol and I can't go to the party and maybe see Lewis . . . there's no-one to talk to even . . .

28

Why am I here? What am I waiting for? Why did that man look at me so peculiarly? And what can I do to stop Maria's baby from aborting himself?"

Alice sat and waited for something to happen, for someone to come and tell her what to do. Nothing happened and nobody came.

★ ★ ★

The next morning Maria felt much better and wanted to go home. The doctor said that was all right, as long as she stayed off her feet, because she had an incompetent cervix and needed to be stitched. The little nurse with the sweet smile, whose name had turned out to be Lily, offered to give them a lift to their car. Alice felt deeply relieved to see the purplish nightmare hues of the previous evening being washed away in the sensible gaberdine-grey clarity of an ordinary rainy day.

They left the nursing home by a different entrance which took them via a different drive to an anonymous suburban street. Alice was surprised. She had not thought they were so close to the outskirts of a town the day before. She was even more surprised when the suburbs soon gave way to blocks of higher, somehow *central-European* looking buildings, amongst which were a few little shops doing half-open Sunday business.

"Where the hell are we?" she asked. "I didn't know we were anywhere near a town round here. I thought we were miles from anywhere."

"Oh, it's not a town really," said Lily evenly.

"What is it then?"

"No — its a kind of camp I suppose you would call it really."

"A camp?"

"A sort of extension of the principles of the nursing home, which is a kind of reception centre for the whole place. It's a place where people can live — a sort of holiday village only you're not on holiday . . . it has a lot of lovely features . . . a lot of people are very fond of these old buildings, with their wrought iron lifts and all . . . "

Lily's mélange of schoolgirl vagueness and holiday brochure hype was beginning to get on Alice's nerves.

"But has it always been here? How big is it? Who knows about it? Is it on the map? Do people come here voluntarily? Lily, isn't this a rather long way round to our car?"

Lily braked smoothly and reversed round a corner so that they were parked in the gloomy shadow of the high apartment blocks.

"I can't answer your questions. I'm not qualified. I was just told to take you into the camp and find somewhere for you to stay, that's all."

"But we don't want to stay! We want to go home! We can't just hang around in your holiday camp! Oh, for goodness sake, just take us to the car."

"That's just it. I can't. There isn't any way back to your car from here."

"That's ridiculous! Of course there's a way back! There's the way we came. You just take us back to the rest home and we'll walk from there, OK?"

Lily unfastened her seat belt and turned round so that she could see both of them as she spoke.

"Look," she said in her nice, comforting voice, "you both chose to come here. It was quite easy for you. Some people make big sacrifices to get in. But once you're here there's no question of going back again, to *there*. It's like my Aunt Lettie says: 'that way lies madness', thinking of 'out there' all the time as if it were some special, wonderful place. You know it isn't, don't you?"

Alice felt a bubble of panic form in her solar plexus and start to rise. 'So this is where the silliness has brought me, is it?' she thought.

"This can't be real," she said, "This can't be happening?"

"Sometimes," said Lily, with a voice that was gaining in authority by the minute, "the usual rules do not apply. They are only the usual rules after all."

A stone dropped into the space that was waiting in Alice's heart, a clean suffocating stone, and there was no moving it out.

"Is everything going on out there as usual?" she asked in a quiet voice, "Or are we outside of time?"

"I've told you, I can't answer your questions — all I can do is take you to my sister's apartment. She's away at the moment. You can live there for a while and acclimatise yourselves. All right? Shall we go on?"

Alice's will to resist flickered, and then went out. Maria was staring out of the window, her lips a little open like a baby's waiting to suck. She said nothing and didn't appear to notice what was going on. Her foetus floated quiet as a goldfish in his amniotic sac. He knew his weapons must be held in abeyance for a while.

★ ★ ★

When she saw the room in which they were to live Alice experienced a delicious, dry tickle of excitement in her belly, like the feeling you get from the first few gulps of champagne before the dopeyness hits you. It was the kind of room she had always wanted to live in: big, high-ceiling-ed and white-walled, with long windows which reached to the floor and looked down on a lively street four floors below with a café, a newsagent and a lady selling flowers in it. It was not the kind of street you would find in Leeds where Alice lived — it had rather a flavour of Warsaw or Paris, or the part of New York you see in Woody Allen films. In one corner of the room there was a double bed, with screens round it bearing the faded pattern of an eighteenth century hunting scene where Diana and her hounds pursued an effete and incompetent-looking Acteon. Otherwise there was little furniture except a wounded old sofa draped in a Persian rug and a kitchen table with two hard chairs. In a cubby hole which was something between a cupboard and a small room they found a shower and hand-basin (Alice thought immediately how unpleasant it would be to be locked in there and vowed never to take a shower when she was on her own). The toilet, which they had to share with the other people on the floor, was outside on the landing.

As soon as Lily left, Maria slumped down on the bed and closed her eyes. Alice pulled off her friend's shoes and pushed her between the clean white sheets.

"You rest," she said, "I'll go and fetch the car."

"But she said we couldn't get to the car from here!"

"I'll try anyway. It's too early to give up."

"But supposing you can't find your way back?"

"Maria, I won't abandon you, I promise! Just sleep a bit

and don't worry."

Alice's head was hot and muzzy. What she really wanted to do was lie down on the bed beside Maria and fall asleep. But she knew she must not. 'Must keep awake,' she instructed herself, 'keep awake and focus on something. Mustn't go under. Mustn't accept their limitations. Mustn't forget . . . '

But already, as she was stepping out of the apartment block, the street was striking her as deadly familiar. She might have lived there all her life — it was so ordinary, beloved and comfortable. Inside the newsagents opposite, where she went to buy a map, she was assailed by presences from her childhood — lucky bags, pink shrimps, cut-out dolly books and Fry's chocolate cream — slyly reminding her of her first erotic fantasy as a child: of taking a bar of 'Five Boys' chocolate from the counter and slipping it under her dress while the man wasn't looking. There had been a new, prickling, bursting sensation in that place between her legs. She had felt ashamed and thrilled and giddy with secret power. She had not taken the chocolate — it was enough to know she could do if she wanted . . .

"Do you have a map of this place, please?" she asked the otter-sleek shopkeeper.

"A map?" He scanned her with eyes full of sympathy and sweetness so that she squirmed and cast her own eyes down. "We don't sell maps here, dear. They're not necessary."

"I'll have a bar of that anyway," she said pointing to the Fry's Chocolate Cream. "But why are maps not necessary? I'm a stranger here. I need to know my way around."

"Our streets," he explained, still holding her with his hot, affectionate eyes, are all laid out in a spiral. If you follow them inwards you always get to the centre. If you follow them outwards, to the periphery. There are many little alleyways, ginnels which link up the main streets, and provide a short cut if you're walking, but it's just impossible to get lost. It is a most intelligent, elegant design. Why no-one else has thought of it beats me."

"OK, but how do I get *out* of this place? My car is parked on the other side of the wood in which the nursing home — I mean, the reception centre — is situated."

"Again, 'out' is not a word we find necessary here. We don't need to go 'out' to get things, to see things. We have everything we need, *inside*. Don't you see?"

"You may," said Alice politely, "but I don't. I don't have my mother or my house or my job or my friends in here."

"You don't know that. You haven't looked."

Alice was beginning to perspire. She felt caught out, wrong-footed. None of this needed to have happened, if only she'd paid attention when there was still time, if only she remembered . . .

She stood at the shop doorway, looking out into the now sunny street. Her mind was dissolving and streaming out into the sunshine with the motes of dust.

The man spoke.

"There is someone who takes an interest in the outside. He has a junk shop in the old quarter. I shouldn't tell you about him — it will not make you any happier to see him, but I can see you will be restless until you realise there is no hope. Of getting out I mean."

She thanked him and slipped outside to eat her chocolate under his canopy. Its supersweetness made her teeth smart. Now she had a choice: either to penetrate towards the centre and find the junk shop, or head outwards towards the periphery to find the rest-home and the car. She decided that the outward trip would be the least dangerous and most helpful — going inwards seemed to imply a kind of resignation, even fascination which she did not want to allow herself to feel.

For an hour she marched outwards along the main road, following every short-cut alleyway as she came to it. It was hot and hazy but there were few people about; it was as if everyone was indoors eating Sunday lunch or having a siesta. She tried to remember whether it had been Saturday the day before, in the other world, but she couldn't. It already seemed far away, vague, irrelevant.

Then she became aware of an intensification in the traffic, mainly of heavy lorries, and turned the last, lazy sweeping bend to find herself at the end of the road. There was a high stone wall and in it a big archway through which the heavy lorries were thundering. Beyond she could just glimpse a pale green and rust coloured plain, which looked very much like an 'out there' landscape. There was no guard on the exit, but neither was there any pavement. She would have to wait for a safe gap in the traffic. She waited.

The stream of grey, dirty lorries seemed never-ending, but as she watched, half-transfixed, she noticed that there was a kind of rhythm to their passage — five lorries, a little gap, seven more, then a bigger gap, just long enough to slip through, as long as she didn't trip up under the archway and get crushed to death.

Heart hammering, she counted the lorries out and after the seventh without a break had passed, she flung herself through the archway. Now she stood in a wasteland of railway cuttings where the road stretched on beside a derelict railway line as far as the eye could see. This must be the no-man's land, she thought, which buffers the camp from the world outside. I suppose I should just kick off and walk across it . . . But she was frightened by the expanse of meaningless space and therefore felt quite relieved when one of the lorries skewed off the road and stopped beside her. Even if it were the police, she figured, or the security men, she might learn something about the nature of the place which would be useful next time round.

But the man who leant out of the lorry's cab was rosy-cheeked and smiling and wore a grubby orange knitted hat on his head.

"Where are you going, gal?" he asked.

"I'm trying to get to my car. It's on the outside. On the other side of the reception centre. I've got to get it urgently because my friend is ill. Can you help me?"

The man narrowed his smiling eyes.

"We none of us go out there nowadays, you know. I don't think it's possible. But we can take you as far as that centre place, and drop you off. We're on the outer peripheral run and we pass it on our way . . . jump in!"

She found herself sitting between two men in the cab, the orange-hatted one, who seemed to be in his early thirties and had a snaggle tooth in the corner of his mouth and an older man who was still and serious and kept his eyes on the road and his big, powerful hands on the wheel. There was no conversation after the first 'hellos' and Alice quite liked that. There was some very agreeable odour permeating the cab — something like scented tobacco or spices or newly cut wood. It soothed and lulled her so that she sat back relaxed, feeling cocooned, looked after, safely on her way.

Then the younger man, who sat on her left, put his hand on her leg, just above the knee and began, gently but firmly, to push her dress up. She put her hand down to push his away just as the other man took his left hand off the steering wheel and put it on her other leg, in the same position as his mate.

"Please!" she said, but even as she heard her own voice echo in the sweet-smelling cab she could feel the warmth of the blood that was pumping round their bodies flow deliciously into her as they pulled her legs slowly open and slid their hands up the inside of her thigh. Her heart hiccuped and she felt the same thrilling, *wrong* excitement she had felt in the sweetie shop of her childhood. They began to palp and knead the tender skin at the very top of her thighs. The sun beat in through the big windscreen filling her head with light and her body with voluptuous golden-syrupy sweetness. She could feel the plump lips of her vagina softening and opening. She thought: 'This is terrible. I can't let this happen. I mustn't. . . . '

The smiling one spoke.

"If you're in a hurry we can go in the bed compartment just behind us. We needn't stop. So you won't keep your friend."

He removed his hand and pulled her towards him, unbuttoning her dress to fondle and expose her breasts.

"Oh!" he said. "Look at that! Beautiful, beautiful . . . " and he turned her round by the shoulders to show his friend. The older man nodded politely and smiled for the first time — a kind, approving smile, before turning his eyes back to the road.

They were soon in the bunk behind the driving seats, and the man wasted little time in penetrating her, filling her with slow, easy thrusts that hit her right back in there where all the waters meet. She wanted the steady, rhythmic thrusting to go on for ever, but, after a couple of minutes he stopped, withdrew himself and changed places with his mate at the wheel. Alice could not but be grateful: the other man's penis was that bit longer and thicker, and instead of moving in and out, he moved it round and round, stretching and stimulating the walls of her vagina until she was gasping and crying out in helpless ecstacy. She finally came as he changed his movement and thrust into her for the first time. As she came she thought of Lewis and how she had never come with him. But she fell asleep immediately afterwards and remembered nothing else until she was awakened by the smiling man and handed decorously out of the cab. The drive of the reception centre hung before her like a black hole, sucking in all the light that was still effervescing in her body.

"Hope you find your car," said the older man.

She suddenly recalled that neither of them had had an orgasm.

"Can I do anything for you before I go?" she asked awkwardly. "You've been so kind."

"No, no," said the young one, throwing back his head and laughing rumbustiously, "We're in training at the moment, we're not allowed to waste our vital energies."

"How very curious" said Alice, "Not like the world I'm used to. Not one little bit."

They started up their lorry and it lumbered off the grass verge into the road.

"Call us if you need us," shouted the smiling one. "We'll stay in touch, don't worry, now we've found your frequency."

'Now they've found my frequency?' thought Alice, confusedly remembering the rhythm of the lorries through the archway and the rhythm of the fucking she'd just enjoyed and wondering if it were anything to do with that.

'Were they joking?' she asked herself. 'Were they making fun of me? Yet there was no cruelty or coercion. I wanted it all to happen. I enjoyed it . . . but what was in it for them?'

As she started off down the drive her own juices trickled stickily down her leg. She did not feel like the heroine she was trying to be. She felt like a fallen woman. She felt ashamed of herself.

She reached the main building and skirted carefully round it until she found the back entrance, where they had lingered the day before. She looked down between her breasts and saw her little gold medallion, with her dead brother's photo in it, jumping and quivering against her heart-beat. 'What am I frightened of?' she thought. 'It will be plain sailing from now on, nothing can really go wrong . . .'

But supposing she not find the car? Supposing she found the car but could not find her way back to Maria? Supposing she wandered out of the wood and saw two women lying under a tall tree — a big fair one and a small, dark one? Supposing she saw *herself*? She had seen a science fiction film on the television recently where a man bumped accidentally into his earlier self while in a time warp and they both dematerialised from the shock . . . on the other hand, supposing she got back to the car and found Maria sitting in it waiting for her? Supposing, as she was about to leave the grounds, she was stopped by a nurse and found out she was a patient there, a crazy person, suffering from delusions . . . ?

But she knew she wasn't mad. Her consciousness was normal, lucid. Her perceptions were not particularly vivid or intense. The house looked real enough. It was solid and did not change shape or nature, or gain in windows or immensity, between blinks or glances, the way dream houses often do. It existed apart from her. After all, she had gone away from it and come back again, to find it exactly as it was.

She had read lots of stories about worlds parallel to ours, or intersecting with it, worlds on the other side of the mirror, worlds which blinked on as ours blinked off, worlds of anti-matter, dream-worlds, archetypal worlds. She had even visited such worlds in daydreams or in sleep. But why had she got stuck in this particular one? Got stuck in it in what seemed to be waking consciousness? What had caused this strange disjunction? What were the laws of nature of this side of the fence? All she knew was the 'usual rules do not apply.' So, could she just walk out? Would her car be waiting for her in the lay-bye on the single-track country road somewhere in the Vale of Bowland?

She turned round resolutely and walked down the path which had led them to the house. She passed the gateposts and walked down the avenue of high, arching trees which took her out of the wood. She looked across the field of young corn to the meadow where they had had their picnic. There was nobody there. From the picnic spot to the car was a brisk five-minute walk. The punishing heat did not bother her — triumph was rising in her breast and she felt like laughing and bounding along from joy and relief.

And yes — there was the car, on the other side of the hedge, glinting in the sun as if it had been sweating with anxiety about her return. Perhaps Lily, the little nurse, was a practical joker . . . an agent for a kind of cosmic candid camera, whose object was to make a holy fool of you!

Yes, there was the car, with the cassette player lying on the back seat, along with two copies of the 'Guardian' and a half-full bottle of Vimto. These parts of her had remained loyal, patiently waiting for their mistress's return. Chaos had not come into her universe. The centre had just about managed to hold.

It was then that she realised, rummaging amongst the notebooks and chewing gum and library tickets and ten pence pieces for the parking meter and other things that clunked and tinkled against each other in her bag, that she had left her car-keys behind in the room.

★ ★ ★

CHAPTER TWO

No Turning Back

CHAPTER TWO

When Alice got back to the room its atmosphere had changed completely. Warm early evening sunshine slanted in the windows making a luminous puddle on the bed where Maria sat cross-legged, tranquilly reading a paperback. There were yellow flowers on the formica-topped table, groceries, including a large bottle of wine, on the shelves, and the damp, sweet odour of tobacco hanging in the air.

"Who's been smoking?" Alice asked sharply.

Maria pushed a tin towards her.

"Me. Have one. Roll ups. I used to smoke them — remember? — years ago. It just seemed like time to start again."

"But you're pregnant!"

"In moderation. I just wanted to. Here, in this place."

"You're feeling better?"

"Much, much. Lily came round and we went out shopping. Have some wine. I'll make us something to eat in a minute."

"Playing houses. Very nice! But is it worth it? We'll be gone tomorrow."

"Ah, you got the car?" A trace of disappointment showed on her face.

"No, but I got to the car. Then I found I didn't have the keys with me. Buggery and damnation, I thought. But nothing strange happened on the way — or not very anyway — the usual rules did apply. I think Lily may be stringing us along."

"Funny really. I've got to quite like it here. I suppose I was hoping we might have to stay a day or two."

"I tell you it's a terrible bleak place, Maria! The buildings are so close together! There's no space anywhere. It's so claustrophobic, and the streets all go in this spiral pattern."

"I know. Lily told me. The trams are marked either 'inwards' or 'outwards' and that's that — no complicated numbering system. But you're right — space is the one thing they're not keen on. Apparently it's not considered to be 'necessary'."

"A word they use a lot. And yet there are some good things. I met these two blokes today . . . " but as she spoke Alice realised she could not possibly tell Maria the truth about what had happened . . . "and they were really kind and helpful . . . took me right up to the reception centre in their lorry. Anyway, tomorrow, if you're feeling all right, we'll get a taxi and go straight there . . . we'll be back by lunchtime."

"So there's nothing mysterious about this place after all?"

"It would seem not. Are you disappointed? I suppose I am. Strange though, that it wasn't on the map."

"Well, the Vale of Bowland is such a vague sort of area. People down south haven't heard of it at all. Maybe it was marked and we just didn't notice. There'll be a simple explanation for it, you can be sure of that."

★ ★ ★

They went to bed early, but Alice could not sleep. She lay on her side, guarding Maria like a truculent lioness. She was angry with her because she liked the camp and wanted to stay. Part of Alice felt the same, but it seemed to her an ignoble part, and she wanted to suppress it. She watched her friend as she slept, curled up into a tiny, neat ball beside her in the bed. Her liquorice-black hair hid her face; only the full, slightly pouting lips showed. Who would believe, looking at her now, how steely, determined and brave she was; how stubborn, irritating and bold!

They were nine when they met. Maria came up to Alice in the playground and said:

"Are you getting tired of being good? Because if so, and if you'd like to start being bad, you can join in with me."

Alice accepted the offer, because it was true, she was beginning to feel uncomfortable with the good girls who up till then had been her friends. She thought it very perspicacious of Maria to have spotted her potentiality for badness. Perhaps it was because they both had foreign mothers who embarrassed them on open days.

However, the badness referred to was not very scientifically evil. It consisted mainly in persuading other little girls at their middle-class prep school to give up making camps in the shrubbery in favour of playing at escaping from prisoner of war camps. Maria, though small, was tough and fierce, quite capable of terrorising girls older and bigger than herself.

She was also clever, but careful to conceal this at school, only allowing the occasional perceptive English teacher to guess at the depth of her abilities. She was considered scruffy, troublesome, a rebel. Alice, on the other hand, enjoyed the status that being a sunny, talented all-rounder afforded. In consequence she was never punished, while Maria was always going and coming back from repeated 'last warnings' in the head-mistress' study.

Then suddenly, in the sixth form, they switched roles. Maria became hard-working and serious, took to hitching to Stratford at weekends with a boring girl known as a swot, to see Shakespeare plays and go on country walks. Alice, meanwhile, discovered sex (well, not *sex* but heavy petting) and CND, and style, and Bob Dylan and how to tell lies to her mother so as to stay at all-night parties, and consequently began to treat her schoolwork with disdain. She was going to be an artist anyway, so it was all irrelevant. Maria, on the other hand, was educating herself in Marxism. They grew apart, found other best friends, and even began to dislike each other. Their only shared passion was the film of Jean Luc Godard. They would skive off from domestic science on Friday afternoons and meet up in the foyer of the Classic cinema to look out for an avant-garde old lady who would vouch to the suspicious box-office woman that they were eighteen even though Maria only looked fourteen and they were both in school uniform.

In the end they were helplessly united by their outcast status. They were both a bit 'odd' and could find no-one to produce scurrilous magazines or subversive school-plays with except each other. But they frequently came to blows. Their classmates would always remember the day Alice poured a bottle of milk over Maria's head in the sixth form common-room and how the two of them rolled on the floor like a couple of bundling kids until Alice sprang up with a scream and a set of purple teeth-marks in her neck.

It continued to be so. They disapproved of one another. Maria considered Alice to be a self-indulgent scatter-brain who lived in a squalid twilight world of afternoon sex and hand-to-mouth contracts to make idiotic, impractical clothes. Alice, on the other hand, found Maria's world cold and half-hearted. She hated visiting the communal house in Sheffield where Maria lived, with its fortnightly house meetings, cooking rotas and vicious tom-cat, who sprayed democratically in each room in turn and couldn't be castrated because it would be interfering with his sexuality. She also disapproved of Maria's philosophy of non-possessive, non-mongogamous sexual relationships, which meant, in practise, that Maria had two regular male lovers who weren't supposed to mind about each other and as many female lovers as she felt was necessary.

Maria's pet hate was what she called 'Alice's sloppy emotionalism', by which she meant that Alice cried in films, prayed in cathedrals and was rapturous on mountain sides.

"You are a mystic, Alice, but not a real one," she announced crisply one day. "You use your mysticism as an escape, an obfuscation, to throw people off your tracks. And that's all wrong. Mysticism isn't meant to be an evasion of the harsh realities of life. Quite the opposite in fact."

Alice ignored her and went on visiting synagogues and catholic churches, starting but not finishing courses in Yoga or Tai Chi, and even secretly teaching herself how to read Tarot cards.

But now she was paying the price for her belief in other realities: she was in one! Mind you, so was Maria, who had done nothing to deserve it.

Alice finally fell asleep and dreamed she was a ship, a full-sailed galleon, bringing Persian carpets to London from the Orient. She skipped over the little billows, her heart light and carefree, secure in the knowledge that she was a fine ship with a fine cargo, doing just what a fine ship should be dong in a rich and reasonable world. But as she skimmed she suddenly remembered that she had no Captain — she had left him behind, dead drunk on brandy in a dockside bar. And although she could sail very well on her own without him, her sense of rightness was gone, quite flown away, and her timbers creaked painfully as she set her course towards that cold country that was her destination in the darkening north.

★ ★ ★

Next morning Maria remarked that it would be a shame to leave the camp without once making the journey inwards, to see what the centre was like, the old quarter of the spiral town.

"We can get a tram in, and a tram out again to the periphery. Why not, eh?"

Alice had not been on a tram since auntie-visiting days in Glasgow, when her younger brother had cried and refused to mount the great reverberating monsters. Now she yearned to do so and felt there could be no harm in delaying their departure by a couple of hours, given that they now knew the route to the car to be unproblematic.

At first, all they could see from the top of the tram, which was a cinnamon and cream double-decker, were the usual Central-European apartment blocks, interspersed with tiny public gardens and the odd dusty chestnut tree. The sky, when you could glimpse it, was darkbright and thundery, like the face of a feverish child. Then the tram debouched suddenly from the cramped streets and headed over a viaduct under which there was a much bigger open space than they had hitherto seen in the camp. They saw a giant swimming-pool in the shape of an amoeba, which had waves running up and down it like a miniature sea. They passed, at their own eye level, an artificial mountain of yellow sandstone bricks, with people toiling up it or rock-climbing on its steeper inclines. The area all around was covered with lush green grass, bright wild flowers and wilder, tropical-looking foliage.

"A sort of pleasure park, I suppose," said Maria.

"Everything is little," remarked Alice. "Everything fitted into the smallest possible space. A pocket-sized Lake Distict, ugh!"

But as they progressed towards the centre the atmosphere gradually changed. The sunshine seemed warmer, more Mediterranean. They passed a delightful little square where chairs and tables were set out under awnings and the smell of meat grilling over charcoal drifted up to them. The buildings were getting older now: there was mellow red brick, flintstone and granite, and the Gothic facade of what they took to be a university, because groups of young people were hanging around outside.

Beyond the university the tram stopped for good, and they were at the entrance to an open market, which seemed to mark the centre of the camp. It sold fruit and vegetables and imperfect chain store pullovers just like the market of any English country town, but there were also booths for fortune-telling and palmistry, and stalls offering theosophical books, precious stones and magical instruments. The odours of spiced cooking and Turkish coffee made with cardomom were everywhere. Again, there was a strange sense of familiarity. Alice 'knew' for instance that there was a second-hand bookstall specialising in poetry near the other entrance to the market and she 'knew' how to get to that other entrance. There she found and bought a copy of Anna Akhmatova's poems, in translation, but with a dedication written in Russian on the flyleaf. All that she could make out of it was the word, 'cecmp' — *sestre*, which, she remembered from 'O' level Russian, mean 'sister'.

She stood leaning her back on a warm brick wall and flicked through the book. She read:

"The world transformed itself for just an instant.
The wine was strangely altered on the tongue."

and thought: 'Is it the wine or the tongue that are altered? Or both? Or neither? And who was the 'sister' to whom the book was given? A real sister or a friend who was so close that she could be called a sister? Or was it given by a man who loved the woman he was giving it to like a sister, not a mistress? As Lewis loved her maybe, if indeed he 'loved' her at all . . . '

"Alice!" Maria's voice was as crisp as a bite into a tart green apple. "Shall we go?"

Instantly awake, Alice looked around herself guiltily.

"Sorry," she said, "but wait! There's a shop around here somewhere, run by a man who's interested in the outside . . . shall we look for it while we're here?"

But she realised now that the wall she had been leaning

46

on belonged to a circular pavilion, with arches all around offering access to an arcade which seemed to run through the centre of it. In the dim interior she could see shops with illuminated windows. She took Maria's elbow and wheeled her round into the arcade.

"All right?" she asked as they proceeded, arm in arm.

"On the brink," said Maria. "One foot in sea and one on shore, as it were."

The shops they passed all looked equally inviting. One sold Persian carpets, another embroidered lampshades, a third tea, coffee-beans and incense, but the one that made them linger longest did not look like a shop at all, but more like a window onto somebody's back room.

The room reminded Alice of her Scottish grand-mother's kitchen, with its old black range, spice chest smelling of cinnamon and cloves, and ever-ready pot of tea stewing on the hob. A copper kettle burbled over the flames. Ranks of tea-caddies and decorated biscuit-tins waited on the mantelpiece for their turn. A mellifluous old radio whispered low from the corner and a game of chess stood half-finished on the table. There was no shopkeeper in sight.

Alice stood irresolute at the door.

"Do you think everything's for sale?"

"I suppose so. But it looks so complete and perfect."

"And so *warm*."

"Well, let's go in and find out, shall we?"

Maria pushed the door. A bell jangled. Alice hesitated. Somehow she felt reluctant to enter. Maria turned, as if to draw her in, but her face was pale and startled, her features subtly distorted, as if she was under water. Alice stepped in quickly after her.

The vibration hit her instantly. As certainly as a swimmer steps into a swimming-pool, she had stepped into a vibration! It grabbed her by the shoulders, the hips, the collar, anywhere it could get a grip on her, and shook her mercilessly; up and down, round and round, juddering and jarring her until she felt her brain must have jumped loose in her skull and her legs lost their moorings in her pelvic girdle.

With something that she thought must be her will she attempted to fling herself further into the shop, out of the zone of furious oscillation. For a second a terrible crushing pressure bore down on her from all sides and she felt herself shrink to pinhead size and prance indignant on the tiled floor like a clothes-peg doll. Then, just as suddenly, she expanded and her giant being filled the whole room, bouncing weightlessly off the walls like a pig-balloon. Then she was through. She stood, catapulted, steadying herself on the mantelpiece, looking down on Maria who was crumpled, shivering, on the hearthrug.

"Jesus wept!" she breathed. "What was that when it was at home?"

"Tcha!" choked Maria. "Something that didn't want us in, that's for sure!"

Alice helped her up. The kettle was boiling furiously on the fire, its lid rattling from the pressure of the steam.

"I suppose we might as well make a cup of tea," she said.

The radio was no longer playing. There was a still, underwater atmosphere in the shop very like the one they had noticed in the wood. Daylight hardly penetrated.

In the glow of the fire and the tinted glass lamps they could have believed themselves in an old lady's parlour in midwinter Leeds. They settled down comfortably in the fireside chairs and waited. It was all right now — there was all the time in the world, time to drink scented tea from the translucent china cups and eat the ginger snaps and garibaldis laid out for them on a plate.

The man might have been watching them for quite a while before they noticed him.

"Good," he said, "you've made yourselves at home. Pour out a cup for me, will you?"

Alice and Maria stared at him without speaking. He was not what they had expected. His straight black hair with silver streaks in it was pushed rakishly back from his brow as if he had just been playing tennis or cricket. But his elegant cotton pants and shirt were dove-grey, not white, and his pale, quite young-looking face did not look as if it often saw the sun. He turned from one to the other of them, smiling courteously and took up the cup of tea which Alice had fumblingly poured for him.

"I am at your service, you know," he said.

"Do you know who we are then?" blurted Alice.

"No. Not yet. Or rather, not exactly. But I will soon, won't I?"

"What do you mean?" asked Alice suspiciously.

"Don't be suspicious! I just meant: no doubt you'll tell me who you are, that's all."

"I just thought . . . maybe the newsagent . . . maybe the people at the reception centre . . . oh, I don't know . . . that maybe the word had got round . . . that we were here I mean . . . "

Alice stopped. She was rambling. Her mind seemed to go cloudy as soon as she tried to use it. It was fine and clear though as long as she did not try to think. She coughed in embarrassment, hard enough to hurt her lungs, and the image of something crystalline flashed before her eyes. Her mind felt clearer now. The man looked at her and looked and looked and looked. His eyes held her steadily and would not go away. Her cheeks burnt and she reached up to fiddle with her top-knot.

"We managed to get past your strange security device," said Maria brightly. "It was very unpleasant though. Is such a thing really necessary? If someone had a weak heart they could die from the shock I should think."

"It's not my idea, I assure you. The authorities insist. They only let me operate on sufferance. But if people are keen they do get through. But now, ladies, enough of the light conversation. How can I help you?"

With that he put down his tea-cup and went to sit behind an elegant miniature writing desk. Under the glass lamp his black and silver head glittered like a wet stone in moonlight. Alice thought he looked as clever and alert as a snake waiting for the right moment to jump on and swallow a mouse.

"We want to get out of this place," said Alice baldly.

"Really? But why? Doesn't it interest you at all?"

"It's not that. Yes, it's interesting, but we've got things to do. At home, you know . . . " Alice trailed off, infuriated by her own vagueness. Somehow reasons and justifications slide off her tongue before she could get it round them, and plopped down in shameful puddles at her feet.

"What *is* this place anyhow?" interjected Maria, who still seemed to retain some intellectual focus.

There was a long pause while the man stared at a point

between their heads, as if listening for instructions from the unseen world as to how much he could tell them.

"It's a place," he began suddenly and incisively, "where the worlds meet, are gathered and contracted. It offers certain opportunities. Certain limitations also. Otherwise it is a place like any other."

"But is it real?"

"Wrong question."

"Can we get out of it?"

"Stupid question."

"Why are we in it in the first place?"

"Because you wanted to be. You looked for it and found it. Good for you."

"This is silly," said Alice miserably.

The man shifted himself in his chair, and took an oval-bored Turkish cigarette from a box on the desk. Alice sensed a change of gear. He was going to try again.

"Do you remember a book called 'The Lion, the Witch and the Wardrobe'?" he asked. "Perhaps you read it when you were children?"

Alice remembered. Sitting on the grass in the apple-orchard, Miss Wharton reading out loud in her flat, gruff voice. Those with no breasts yet (which means nearly everyone except herself and fat revolting Janey) can take their tops off. It is very hot. Heatwave Summer of '61. Alice sits at the back with Maria, fulfilling her 'bad' role, flicking cherry stones at the neck of fat revolting Janey who tries to ignore them and be good. Alice is feeling wilful and angry. She does not like being one of the two in the class to have to keep her dress on, and she doesn't like the book. It frightens her with its frozen people and wicked uncles, talking beasts and puddles which drop down into other worlds. Besides it's babyish and stupid and not *true* . . . She wishes the bell would go for break, even if that means soon handwriting which she hates and at which she is very clumsy . . .

"Oh yes!" Maria speaks, her voice sparkles, delightful, and the room glows. "It was wonderful! It was my favourite book. I can still remember bits of it so vividly."

'Hypocrite! Liar!' thinks Alice. 'We *hated* it. Don't you remember? We were above fairy stories then. We liked realistic stories of adventures you could actually *have*! Not like the rest of the stupid girls in our class. We were *superior*. Don't you remember? Silly cow!'

"Well," the man was saying, "this shop is like the wardrobe in that story — a kind of gateway. You go through it, and you are in a different place. It's like — say you're in a car on a hot day, going along a motorway, and you keep falling asleep and waking up again. Think now! Where do you go when your mind blinks off for a few moments? What's going on? Even in a fraction of a second's sleep you go somewhere, don't you?

"Are you saying that we've been here before then, in our sleep? asked Maria. "Is that why it seems so familiar to us?"

"You *are* here," says the man. "That's the important thing. Now you must tell me what I can do for you. I can't offer anything unless you ask for it — those are the rules in this place."

"Can't we stay for a bit then, Alice?" Maria asks in the ardent voice of a child who wants to linger in an amusement arcade. "So that we can find out a bit more about the camp?"

"But you've never been interested in this sort of thing before," says Alice crossly.

"There's not point in arguing about it," says the man. "It's doubtful whether you'll get out now anyway. It's probably too late."

"But I did get out yesterday," protests Alice. "At least I got to my car. Only I'd forgotten the keys."

The man bursts out laughing. A harsh, braying, unnatural sort of laugh. Alice is paralysed by the strange sound. She wants to get out of the shop and be in her right mind again. She doesn't want to hear any more of this brain-distorting nonsense. She . . .

No-one is speaking now. They sit in awkward silence. Alice feels sleepy and begins to dream of hot countries, desert breezes, crystalline seas in which big amber-eyed fish swim.

The man speaks finally.

"One thing I can tell you: you won't get 'out' as you call it by going back to your car and climbing in and driving home. Even if you take your keys with you this time. There *are* ways out of this place, but you'll never find them by going back. You have to go on, through . . . however you want to put it. I tell you this without you asking me. I shouldn't but I have. Now, go away and do what you must do."

* * *

"It's a confusion of levels really," said Maria. They were walking through the wood on their way to Alice's car.

"What do you mean by that?" asked Alice grumpily.

"It's happening all the time in mental illness — confusion between the physical world — normal reality that is — and the world of the imagination. Internal fatnasies begin to be projected outwards. They become as real, if not realler than the outside world."

"And where does patriarchy come in? I thought all your theories had to do with patriarchy." Alice was feeling needled by Maria's cool and wanted to annoy her if she could. Sensibly Maria ignored the provocation.

"There's a sort of break with the general consensus of reality," she continued, "an emotional decision to make and to live in a different world from other people."

"And this is what's happening to us, you think?"

"I didn't say that."

"But, there's two of us. You can't share an imaginary world can you? Unless of course we're not actually sharing it. And I'm in yours and you're in mine, or something."

"Well, we *did* share a lot of reality in our childhood. But actually this is all irrelevant. So far, we have no real evidence that this is anything other than a normal, physical, geographically situated *place*. There may be some strange people in it, but so what? Here we are, walking to the car, unimpeded by metaphysical obstacles of any sort."

"I suppose so, but . . . " Alice felt as if she were letting go of something beautiful and fascinating which Maria wanted to consign prematurely to the rubbish bin. She was aware that this sort of moment had happened very often in her life: she had relinquished her sense of something 'rich and strange' for a bald, drained, *sensible* ment-

52

ality with no magic in it.

"You're just trying to reduce it all to sensible dimensions! You're trying to make everything normal and rational! But I don't want you to! I'd rather go on living in wonderland, I really would!"

"Living in wonderland?" queried Maria coldly.

"You remember! Miss Pickles in biology. Whenever I went off in a day-dream she'd say, sarcastically, "Look girls, Alice is in wonderland again!' "

"I don't remember that. I was in the same set as you for biology and I don't remember that."

"You don't remember because you were concentrating so hard on your bloody work! You'd decided to be a doctor that year, so you reformed and started working. Don't you remember *that*?"

"I remember you coming top in the exam in spite of never paying the slightest attention to the lessons. That was before you decided to give up thinking and become an artist, if I remember right."

"You call that thinking? What we used to do in biology in school?"

"You call that art? Those eccentric garments you spend all your time in making and getting paid a pittance for?"

"I have to earn a living," said Alice, wounded into plaintiveness. "And there's no point in me having delusions about 'being a painter' is there? Everyone wants to be an artist these days and none of them have got a bloody thing to say!"

"But Alice," said Maria, halting in exasperation, "you *do* have something to say. You *do* have ideas. You *do* have intelligence. It's just that your powers of concentration are so terrible! I think you must be the most self-indulgent person that I know!"

Alice hitched her loose, blousey dress up over her belt and fingered the belt thoughtfully. It was her brother's boy-scout belt, and she had stolen it from his drawer the day after his death, before his girlfriend Polly could get at it. Polly had not known him as a hectic five year old or a dazed and dreaming fourteen your old and therefore, did not deserve to get the belt. She had not known, as Alice had, since she was quite a little girl, that he was soon to die. No-one expected his illness and death, except Alice. It was one of her flashes of useless, treacherous knowledge, knowledge which could not be passed on but would stick in her throat until she gulped and swallowed it. Now, thinking of her brother, she turned to Maria, to ask how *she* remembered him, but then recalled that they were fighting, and moved abruptly on.

The two women walked in silence, out of the wood and across the field to the spot under the tree where they had eaten their picnic just two days before. From there they had only to follow the field edge round until they reached the car. Maria was the first to spot it, the sun glinting on its dull blue roof, but her exclamation of triumph was cut short: the car was not alone. Leaning over its bonnet, immersed in an activity which could have been reading the paper, rolling a joint or playing pontoon were two men in khaki uniform. Soldiers evidently.

"What level of reality are *they* from then?" asked Alice dryly.

"They could be negative animus figures — cruel, aggressive males, often found in the dreams of women who have not yet achieved any degree of psychological autonomy. On the other hand, they look pretty real to me . . . "

They retreated swiftly behind a hedge. At which point, the two soldiers straightened up, put away whatever they had been playing with, and made a tour around the car, looking about themselves with eagle-eyed acuity, swinging their guns carelessly from their shoulder-straps.

"I think they're waiting for us," said Alice, feeling a wretched, long-waiting knot in her stomach unbind.

"What can we do? Wait until dark and hope they go? Or go up and face them and try to drive the car away?"

"If they are animus figures," said Maria slowly, "then we should confront them. Only by doing so can we reintegrate the split-off energy they represent . . . "

Suddenly they heard the heavy rhythmic thump-and-rustle of bodies marching somewhere close to them. Alice looked round and glimpsed a flash of metal through the branches of the hedge.

"Get down and keep quiet! They're coming this way!"

Crouching behind the thornbush, their hearts jumping, they made out a group of about ten soldiers, thudding around the field towards them, on the other side of the hedge. In the centre of the party, roped together, they could glimpse two or three women, stumbling along, out of rhythm with the marching men. As the party passed, horrifically close, they could hear the women's fast panicky breathing and a racking sob coming from someone at the back of the party. In response to this the soldier behind her swung his machine-gun up and thwacked her across the bottom with it, making her stagger and lose her footing for an instant, so that Alice and Maria caught brief sight of her flushed face, before she righted herself again.

It was only when the sinister party had disappeared into the wood that Maria spoke, in a whisper, as if they could still be overheard.

"Did you get a look at the woman at the end?" she asked.

"Not really. But I saw that she was tall and had fair hair falling over her face."

"Alice!" breathed Maria ferociously. "Don't prevaricate! It was you! That woman the soldier hit was you! I know it was."

"Yes." said Alice briskly. "Me. Me if I had gone up and confronted the soldiers I suppose. I wonder if you were in the party too."

Maria shuddered.

"What a dreadful sort of warning! Is that 'you' we saw just now as real as you are? What do you think?"

Alice did not know. Her heart was fluttering. 'Fear is not very different in its symptoms to sexual arousal.' she was thinking, 'Perhaps all this is a punishment for my adventures yesterday in the lorry.

"If this whole area is a between-worlds," she began carefully, "then she — the other me I mean — exists on another plane that intersected with ours for just a moment, and now it's leading away into quite a different dimension. What happens now is no concern of ours."

But even as she spoke she felt the stinging stripe across her buttocks where her other self had so recently been struck.

★ ★ ★

CHAPTER THREE

Looking for the Beloved

CHAPTER THREE

That night in bed Alice, to comfort herself, began to think of *him*, Lewis. Normally, nowadays, she forbade herself the dreadful pleasure of going over their meetings, non-meetings, encounters and avoidances, of remembering moments of contact and of rejection, of playing round with the jigsaw pieces of past and possible futures to see if anything thrilling might come out of it. But tonight she felt some basic trust had been broken, a pact she had made with the world a long time ago, when she was a little girl, and had been crushed to nothing in a great indifferent fist. Therefore she was free to do exactly as she wanted, even if it were a hurtful and self-destructive thing.

Spitefully she dug around for the most distressing memory. It was not hard to find. A friend had talked to Lewis at a party and asked him what he thought of Alice.

"Alice Cunningham?" he had said, looking deep and significantly into the friend's mild eyes. "I am very fond of her. She's very stylish, very original. But she's such a *big* person, don't you think? I mean, when you're with Alice there's room for nothing else inside your field of vision. She fills the frame from side to side. A wonderful woman, but altogether just a bit too much. Don't you agree?"

The friend had agreed for the sake of appearances and filed away every word to repeat to Alice later on. Not from malice, but because she thought Alice was too good for the 'stuck up' Lewis, and hoped to break her friend's obsession. Alice, however, although bruised and winded, was not finally put out of her misery. She hated especially the bits about being 'big' and 'original' . . .

But now she was sweating in her half-sleep and turned to find a comforting memory with which to tranquillise herself. Yes . . . she could see him fighting his way across a crowded bar towards her, holding his beer up high above his head, but still it would splash down on him and the people he was shouldering out of the way, and he laughed and joked with them as he came, but ever with his eyes on her . . . then, taking her arm, steering her into a quite corner, laying his head in her lap like a unicorn in the old story, murmuring: "Alice, do with me what you will . . . why are you so difficult to find? Why do you always run away from me?"

But that memory, she realised suddenly, was of a dream. And although Alice claimed she gave her dreams quite as high a status as her waking life, this was partly affectation. She did not *really* believe that, deep down, Lewis thought that way of her . . .

In the morning she woke up full of common sense and indignation.

"We can't be held here against our will, you know," she told the sleepy, grey-faced Maria, "I've decided to go to the police station and find out exactly what's going on. If they want to arrest us, let them do so, and tell us what the charge is. If not, they can jolly well let us get back to our car and away from this place to our ordinary lives."

She set off through a humid, sunny morning, the streets smelling of Dettol, garlic and diesel oil, the cafés breathing out beer and coffee, the fruit-shops ripe peaches and the news-stands a dizzying mixture of fresh newsprint and tobacco. There came once again to her that pernicious sense of familiarity and belonging. She tried to shrug it off, but she felt her pace slackening, her face smiling at old ladies standing at bus-stops. She knew, if she was not careful, she would soon collect acquaintances, roots and reasons for staying in the camp.

She marched resolutely towards the police station, looking neither to the right or to the left. She wished Maria was with her because Maria knew how to handle authority; she was cool and steely and gave them no quarter, while Alice tended to be nice and conciliatory and was therefore often outwitted. However, no-one was going to stop her today; Maria was unwell again, not with the threatened miscarriage, but with what she suspected was high blood pressure. They must get home again, soon.

The police station was an elderly, decaying tenement with tiny dark windows and a hand-painted sign on the door saying 'Please use entrance round the back'. Alice was alarmed; it seemed that law and order could not have much of a priority in this place. As she stood feeling baffled and uncertain, someone touched her on the arm — a young woman with a scrubbed, shining face and big, bulging, light-coloured eyes that pulsed and fluttered as she looked into Alice's own.

"Can we help you at all?" she asked with emphatic warmth.

"Who is we?" countered Alice politely.

"We is the women of the women's house — it's just here." She pointed to the tall, red-brick mansion which stood next to the crumbling police station. Alice could feel the warmth of the place reaching out to her, smells of baking, babies, women's cosy muckiness. She was sorely tempted to go in. There would be tea, roll-ups, toast. Her sisters would look after her. Instead she spoke dryly to the friendly girl.

"Do you know how to get out of this place? The camp I mean?"

"Get out? Oh, we don't bother ourselves about that. It's not really necessary. We're in a kind of inner exile here. We're very happy. We've got everything we need."

"No men allowed?"

"We're not doctrinaire. We don't like them sleeping on the premises, but even that, sometimes, if they miss the last bus home . . . anyway babies have to be made somehow. We accept the realities of life."

Alice knew the girl. She had met her as a patrol-leader in the Girl Guides, a chairwoman in the W.I., a lesbian social worker in the Gay Rights Centre.

"I'm sorry," she said (she knew one must always apologise to this person for not being helped by her) "but if you don't know the way out you're no use to me. I have no interest in staying."

She smiled and turned away and passed through a ricketty green gate into the back-garden of the police station. It was a rank and weedy yard where rampant mint fought with tom-cat for ascendancy of odour. The cat probably responsible basked on a dustbin lid.

Gingerly she opened the back door and found herself stumbling down some steps into a long, dark, low-ceilinged room which she could sense immediately was full of people. As her eyes got used to the low light she realised that they were all women, and all in some degree of pain or distress. One woman was actually in a wheel-chair with one leg in plaster and a bandage over her eyes. Only her mouth showed and it was a thin line turned down at both ends in a grim imitation of a child's mouth in the moment before it bursts into torrents of tantrum-tears. Next to her sat a tiny, scraggy, yellow-complexioned woman who held her Players No. Ten just an inch from her lips, as if frightened that it would be snatched away from her, and trembled like a freezing dog. Over in the furthest corner a plump women with beautiful, voluptuous auburn hair was sobbing loudly. The scene was both grotesque and pitiful. It reminded Alice of the breast-clinic she had been sent to once by her GP, with what turned out to be a harmless patch of eczema under her nipple. As the waves of misery that were pulsing round the room hit her she felt the tears rising to her eyes.

'Alice!' she said severely to herself, 'you've got to learn to control this facile crying mechanism. It really doesn't help at all, just blurs your vision. Now, breathe deeply and stay cool!'

She made out a small grey-haired woman scribbling purposefully behind a big desk in the far corner.

"Excuse me," she said, having tip-toed in between the ranks of suffering women, "Can you help me? I don't need any kind of complicated assistance. I just need to talk to someone for two minutes. A matter of directions. Terribly simple, honestly."

The little woman stopped and stared at Alice with the same intensity of purpose she had been putting into her scribbling. Her eyes were grossly magnified by spectacles so that they loomed largely at Alice like creatures with their own vitality.

"Well, I'm sorry, my dear, but the sergeant is doing the best he can. It would cause a riot if I were to let you jump the queue now, wouldn't it?"

Turning and finding a multitude of anxious, angry eyes fixed on her, Alice had to agree that it would.

"But listen," she said, moving her face close to the little woman's to avoid playing the whole scene to the gallery. "Can *you* help me then? I'm in a desperate situation."

"Everyone here is in a desperate situation," said the little woman sternly.

"Yes, I know, but I'm different. I don't *belong* here. I

only want to know how to get out of this camp and get home, and then I won't give anybody any further trouble."

The woman took off her glasses, and with her surprisingly penetrating naked eyes, surveyed Alice candidly.

"It's true," she said, "you don't have the look of a run-of-the-mill victim. Mind you, you do look as if you might be given to bouts of sentimentality."

"That's true," said Alice quickly. "I confess it. But does that mean that all the women in here are victims of some sort of crime?"

"Of course. They have come here looking for redress. The poor sergeant is quite overworked and overwhelmed by it all. You see," and here her tone became almost confiding, "women — and I say this because I am one and I'm in the same boat as all of us — women are very keen on *justice*, and, in the same breath, *fairness*. But the trouble is — as my mother used to say — 'justice is always done but not necessarily in such a way that we can see it being done'. But here, you see, justice has to be seen to be done, and that's the sergeant's headache."

At this moment, rapt as she was in the woman's argument, Alice felt moved to turn round abruptly as if someone has just called her name. And sure enough behind her stood another elderly woman, short, stout and sour-looking, wearing a pulled-down pudding-basin hat, whose feathers had been sticking into the nape of Alice's neck. She stood, planted next to a bulging paper carrier, her feather now jabbing aggressively up Alice's nose.

"You've got a kind face, darling!" she announced in a loud, hoarse voice. "She's got a kind face, hasn't she?" she continued, looking around the suffering women for support. 'Which means, naturally, that she's a fool! Now listen girl, I've got to tell you something: don't you be fooled by their patheticness! Don't you be fooled by that little-boy-just-wet-his-pants look they put onto their faces. Don't be led astray by pity. Your pity can lead to your own destruction, and *then* who will you be sorry for?"

There was a murmur of assent from the waiting women. Alice smiled embarrassedly and shifted back so that the feather could not have such easy access to her nose. The fat little woman shuffled forward so that her weapon found its mark again.

"You see," she continued in a hectoring tone, "it's a *lure*, a *seduction*, a last merciful gift given them by God to stop us from finishing them off completely. Oh why, oh why do we believe their lying eyes? Why did the good Lord give them such soft and speaking eyes and such evil, evil hearts?"

Alice felt a polite good-girl smile hover on her lips. She felt that what the woman was saying was largely true, and yet she knew she did not want to inhabit *that* world, the world where it was true, for the rest of her life. As she looked at the plaintive, wounded faces of the women in the room she had her familiar feeling of belonging and yet not belonging. 'I'm always swinging between the worlds', she thought.

"I am a fool, you're right," she said out loud.

The fierce woman jerked her feather up and away from Alice's nose at last.

"I know," she retorted ungraciously. "And so are all the rest of them here. And they know it too. I come in every day to tell them. But do I get any kind of sensible, rational response out of them? I do not. And yet I come. And yet I feel it is my duty."

"I have to remind you, Minnie", spoke up the receptionist, "as I do every day, that this is not a feminist seminar room, but a police station, and if the former is what you're looking for you'd be better off next door."

"Feminists!" snorted Minnie. "You call that lot of overgrown girl guides, feminists?"

While the argument was continuing in this vein Alice thought she might as well leave, so walking backwards so as not to be thought rude, smiling placatingly all the way, she did so.

Outside the ingratiating sun which seemed to prevail always in this world continued to bash down. The garden smells were even more ferocious and the basking cat had got up and was staring coldly at Alice. 'And disapprovingly,' she thought, 'everyone in this world disapproves of me.'

At that moment she heard the door spring open and someone clattered noisily out of it. It was the little receptionist, whose bag had fallen open scattering car-keys, library books and sandwiches all over the grass.

"I'm so glad I caught you," she stammered eagerly as Alice helped her to gather her things together, "Because Minnie's taking over so that I can have my lunch-hour, so now I can talk to you in my proper person so to speak, not as a paid employee of our glorious law and order institution. Look, get into my car with me, I'll drive you to the place I think may be the exit, not that that's an end so much as a beginning, but with luck it's not actually a step in the wrong direction, as my endearingly pessimistic mother used to say."

Alice found herself hustled into a small, rudimentary car-like thing, more a grown up version of a soapbox than an automobile, that catapulted itself off down the road with most impudent alacrity.

"Calm down, calm down now, chonka!" said the little woman as she attempted to throttle the creature back, "don't show me up in front of the visitor from other times and spaces, *please*. I race at the weekends, you see, so it takes me a bit of time to get used to normal driving sometimes."

Alice was nonplussed. She coughed, remembered with regret that she had given up smoking and thought how nice it would be to have a fag.

"Yes, of course," said the little woman, "there's a pack of Turkish in the glove compartment. Help yourself and light one up for me, will you?"

"What a funny place this is!" said Alice, allowing herself to relax into wonderment and sighing as she lit both cigarettes causing the car to fill suddenly with smoke.

"You call it a place!" countered the little woman heartily. "It's more a state of mind, but when states of mind are shared by lots of people I suppose they tend to become places. Tell you what, though — that waiting room is driving me crazy."

"Yes, it's not a pleasant place."

"Minnie's right, of course, but they won't listen to her. It's revenge they want, you see."

"And you?" asked Alice, "What are you doing here? And what's your name — we haven't even got round to that."

"My name is Lettie, short of course for Laetitia, not that I've ever in my life been called that. I'm here," she paused and shot Alice a smile of such intensity and candour that she felt herself blush from the warmth of it, "I'm here — I've been here all my life nearly — because of my mother. I was lonely without her after she came. I was only a little girl at the time. She had suffered terribly you see, in Warsaw during the war. She lost everything. What she saw then, she said, was too terrible to tell me, so I imagined, and what I imagined was too terrible to tell her. She came here to escape her memory."

"My mother was Polish too," said Alice. "She was just a child when she came. And she never really suffered. My father used to say that that was her problem."

"I think she felt too exposed in the world," continued Lettie. "There were too many parks and commons and big gardens in London. Too much space. We used to stand on the edge of them and look. I wanted to go across, but my mother always made us go round. Anyway, *here* no space is wasted. She liked that."

"I see," said Alice, baffled by this idea of fear of space and yet remembering her own feeling of terror when she had seen the wasteland on the other side of the archway, the first time she had tried to escape.

Alice looked out of the car windows for the first time, and saw that they were entering the busy approach road which led to the exit-archway.

"Lettie!" she exclaimed, "I've been here before! I don't think you can get out this way!"

"Wait!" said Lettie, tucking the tiny car into an alleyway that turned off just before the archway, "I have my own theory of how it's done. No, don't get out, they'll spot us. Just watch the lorries going through from here."

"But everyone we meet, the man in the sweetie shop, the man in the Victorian curio shop, they all tell us it's impossible to get out. Last time we tried the soldiers caught me and took me away with them." She remembered the hot tears splashing down her cheeks as they'd pushed her through the cornfield into the wood. "It was obviously a warning!" she ended melodramatically.

"Soldiers!" said Lettie scornfully. "It doesn't do to pay attention to the soldiers! That's one thing I've learnt:

never to believe what they tell you, no matter who *they* are. Nothing is necessarily and always so. Now turn round and look! Watch the lorries going through that archway, and tell me how you got through the other day."

"I just waited for one of the longer than average gaps and jumped through. Quickly. I was scared. I could easily have been crushed to death!"

"But that's it!" said Lettie excitedly, "you've spotted it already — a gap, a space! They can't get rid of them altogether. So it *is* possible to get through."

"But there's the wasteland on the other side. They'd be bound to pick you up walking across that — there's nowhere to hide at all."

"Ah, but don't you see?" said Lettie, whipping off her glasses in excitement, "if you do it right, then, when you get to the other side, the wasteland won't be there! If you prepare yourself by holding the moment in your other life you want to get to very firmly in your mind, and if you jump across the gap, still holding it, then when you get to the other side you'll be *there*, in your other life, not *here* in the camp. There is no wasteland really — it's just an optical illusion!"

"How, though," asked Alice, "do you choose your moment? Must it be a moment from the past which you know well? Or a moment in the future which you hope is going to be?"

"I'm not sure," said Lettie. "I haven't tried it out myself, for fear of not being able to come back. But I would have thought what the moment was wouldn't matter terribly, because as soon as you get there you would forget being here so if you chose some moment from the past you wouldn't remember the future as you lived it, so to speak . . ."

"But then, when you come to the moment in your life where you ended up coming here, to this camp, wouldn't you choose to come again, and end up caught in a vicious circle? Like a hamster, going round and round on one of those wheel things in a cage?"

"I don't know for sure, but I don't *think* you'd live your life in the same way again, because of the knowledge you'd got here, even though you probably wouldn't consciously remember it. So you wouldn't end up at the same coordinate point in time and space, and everything would end up differently.

"This place — this camp — is a branchline — it's not a mainline world at all. But once you're in it it's very difficult to leave."

"Gosh," said Alice, who had been fighting for the last five minutes an inclination to pass into a daze.

"Would you like to try it?" asked Lettie briskly.

"Try what?"

"To jump the gap back onto the mainline."

"Well, look, I would do, but I can't today, because I haven't got my friend with me. She's back in our room being ill. I'd have to go back and get her and persuade her that it's possible to try — and not too dangerous."

"But these things can only be done by individuals, you know. You may not be able to take your friend with you."

"Then I won't go."

"Such loyalties may not be kind in the long run . . . but, I forget, I am not one to talk. I have not tried myself. My memories of the outside world are very dim now, you see."

"But listen!" Alice was thinking well now. She sometimes did, in between the daydreaming and the dazes. "We could do it, the three of us together. We could make up a moment in the future with all of us in it and come here and jump together, and we'd all wake up safe and sound in the real world! We could sort of carry you along with us. What do you think of that?"

Lettie looked at Alice as if she were not looking at her, but at a very big person standing just behind her whose bulk was casting dark shadows into her eyes, making their pupils dilate enormously.

"It might be possible," she said, "but my lunch-hour's nearly over and we haven't even had our sandwiches yet. We'd better start off now and eat them on the way back, or I'll be late."

She put her distorting spectacles on, turned the car round and headed them back to town.

★ ★ ★

When Alice left Lettie outside the police station she was

rattled, jarred and jumbled. She also felt guilty, as if she and Lettie had been up to something unclean together. Lettie seemed to feel this too, because she avoided Alice's eyes while they were saying their goodbyes.

Now Alice felt like getting drunk and smoking lots of cigarettes, so with that in mind she set of in an inward direction, thinking to find a pleasant café where a woman on her own could sit and drink unmolested. As she walked big drops of rain began to fall and the skies darkened, so she jumped on a tram and slumped in the back seat, staring out of the window, feeling desolate.

The tram was passing one of the charming little court-yards with chestnut tree and café in it (one of the most seductive features of life in the camp, thought Alice), when it slowed down and stopped in a traffic jam. Alice's eyes fell onto a couple of men who sat talking animatedly at one of the outdoor tables, even though the big spots of rain must have been soaking them. The man facing her was gypsy-dark and had the kind of hairy chest that invited a medallion. His companion was fair and leant forward right across the table, talking fast and vehement, a dark sweat stain spreading over his white-shirted back. It was the kind of back that Alice liked — sturdy yet flexible, with a deep channel down the centre where the backbone runs.

As the tram moved off Alice craned her neck to get a look at the face of the sweat-stained talking man, to see if it was as nice as his back. The face that she saw was unmistakeable that of Lewis Jarman, the man she was in love with in the other world! She sprang up from her seat and clattered down the stairs, managing to leap off the tram as it slowed down to turn a corner. She raced, cursing her high-heeled espadrilles, back to the café, to find that they were no longer there. 'Damnation and buggery,' she thought. Then it occurred to her, as the warm rain began to trickle down her neck, that they had probably just taken shelter inside the cafe.

The interior of the café was not so charming as its exterior. The door opened straight onto a bar with a row of silent men sitting up at it and beyond that were a few un-cleared tables stretching back into an inner sanctum. There was no sign of Lewis or his companion, but Alice hitched herself up onto a bar stool anyway and ordered a glass of brandy.

"Does anyone here know the two men who left a minute ago?" she asked the assembled company.

The men stared at her and made the faintest negative grimaces that they could without completely ignoring her question.

"One was dark and swarthy, the other a bit smaller, fair and good-looking."

The face of the man nearest broke into a sly grin at this and she wished she had not used the words 'good-looking'. It seemed to have introduced a sexual element into the atmosphere. Then she noticed that all the men had lowered their eyes and were staring at her chest. She guessed without looking that the rain had made her dress stick to her and that her nipples were standing up. She finished her brandy quickly and slid off the stool. A young man at the other end of the bar did the same thing.

"Hang on," he shouted over to her. "I know where the blonde guy lives. I'll take you to him."

Once outside she saw that he was very young, with pricked up hair and hard black eyes.

"What's it worth for me to take you to him?" he asked.

"I'm sorry, I haven't got any money with me." Alice kept her arms crossed over her chest and her eyes fixed firmly on his chest.

"I don't mean money. You know what I mean. I felt the vibes you were giving out in there."

A crazy idea that she owed the male sex one for her joy-ride of two days back coursed through Alice's mind, but she ruthlessly suppressed it.

"Nothing doing. I'm not that bothered about finding him."

She expected the boy to curse her and go, but he hesitated.

"All right then. Come round here for a minute though." He pulled her round the side of the café so that they were leaning up against the chestnut tree and hidden from the road. "OK. You give me a feel of your tits and I'll give you the address."

The brandy had warmed Alice. The boy's easy reduction of his terms made him seem unthreatening.

"If you give me a cigarette as well as the address you

can."

Unsmiling he slid a No.6 from a packet in his top pocket and handed it to Alice. Then, expertly, he undid the top three buttons of her dress and reached in to squeeze her breasts. Alice shut her eyes, biting her tongue to stop herself enjoying it too much. She had forgotten how much she liked having her breasts fondled.

"Big girls like you should wear a bra," he said. "Walking around like that, you're giving every boy ideas."

"The address," said Alice coldly, removing his hands and buttoning up her dress.

"He lives in that big apartment block with the swimming pool in the basement. Where all the nancy boys go. It's on spiral seven. You can't miss it. There's a mermaid statue on the side."

Without being asked he gave Alice a light for her cigarette, and escorted her back to the front of the café. She felt strange — strong, capable, and corrupted, as if the boy had made a present to her of something of his rough vitality when he had touched her breasts.

★ ★ ★

Spiral seven was not far away, only a couple of turns of the snailshell, easily short-cut by a ginnel which snaked round the back of some Victorian cottages. Alice walked inwards from spiral eight, looking up to spot the mermaid. When she first floated into view it was like finding an old friend: the jaunty, upwards-curving breasts, the supercilious smile, the backwards-blowing locks sent an exuberant puff of ocean air scudding into Alice's heavy heart.

The place was called the 'Aquarium' and from the outside looked like the kind of Victorian office block that looms in the streets of Manchester or Leeds. Inside, however, Alice was at once enveloped in hot, steamy air, a languid oriental atmosphere which reminded her of the Harem of the Galatai palace in Instanbul. The marble floors and blue-and-white tiled walls of the corridors were warm and wet to touch, glittering with beads of condensation. The people she passed were all either wrapped in white towels or dressed in bathing suits and their murmuring and giggling seemed to come from a long way off even when they were very close to her.

She padded down a wide marble staircase and came, quite suddenly upon the swimming pool. The moment she looked at the dancing blue water, drowsiness hit her and she wanted to throw all her clothes off and slide into it. A few indolent young men were playing at life-saving one another, their yelps and squeals echoing round the dirty glass dome above them through which some melancholy daylight filtered.

Alice walked carefully round the edge, curbing a desire to slip and fall in, and followed the gurgle of running water into the Turkish baths. In the first room she encountered two enormous odalisques lying on their sides facing each other, one peeling a grapefruit, the other de-seeding a melon. Round the corner an oiled, naked boy was doing rapid press-ups on the tiled floor. Alice shook her head like a dog to clear her mind.

A young man in white shorts and vest padded past her carrying a pile of white towels.

"Excuse me," said Alice, skidding on the wet floor as she moved to stop him, and landing at his feet with a cruel bump, not too painful to one who had such a well-covered bottom as her own.

"Sweetheart, be careful!" he murmured, helping her up with exaggerated gallantry, and she was relieved to recognise him as the sort of homosexual who adored women and really wished he was one.

"Sorry," said Alice, used to tumbling and therefore not embarrassed by it. "I just wondered if you could tell me where I might find a chap by the name of Lewis Jarman. I know he lives here but I've no idea how to find his room."

"Darling, I'm not very good at names, but if you can describe the gentleman to me, I might be able to help you."

"He's average size," she said, "well-built with a very beautiful back. But the main thing is his hair — very fair, ash-blonde you call it. You can tell it's natural because it's much darker underneath."

"I think I know your man."

"The other thing you'd notice is that he has hazel eyes, but one of them has a patch of blue in it."

"I know him! I have had the pleasure of massaging his body, professionally only I'm afraid, and if you come with me I should have his room number in my book."

"What sort of place is this?" she asked as she followed him to his cubby-hole.

"Rich man's paradise, sweetheart. The likes of you or I couldn't afford to live here, but every amenity's provided for the gentlemen."

"No women?"

"There are some concubines around. But no women live here permanently, or they're not supposed to. But I mustn't sound cynical — I love it. These little rich boys like to keep themselves in good condition."

He found Lewis' room number for her and she set off through the baths in the direction of the main staircase. As she entered the shower room she was forced to spring out of the way smartly to avoid being drenched by water from a hose-pipe aimed by two men at a buxom naked girl who ran screaming round the room trying to avoid it. Water ricocheted everywhere until they finally trapped her in a corner and played the jet hard all over her body. Alice hesitated for a moment, thinking a sister was being tormented and that maybe she should step in and rescue her, but she caught sight of the helpless pleasure on the girl's face and left the room immediately.

The rooms and apartments in the place were all ranged off the three galleries that surrounded the swimming pool.

She rang the doorbell of number twenty-five and at first there was no response. Then the dark man she had seen at the café appeared.

"I'm looking for Lewis," she said.

"Ah!" he smiled graciously. "Come in. Will you just wait in here one minute while I finish a 'phone call and then I will be free to talk to you."

She was ushered into a bare and formal bedroom, everything in shades of white or cream or oatmeal. By the window stood an old-fashioned fifties dressing-table of the sort she had had herself when she was a little girl — a kidney-shaped body with three rounded mirrors which you could arrange, she remembered, in such a way as to see your own profile.

She sat down and picked up a brush to tidy her hair. As

usual it was a fruitless task. She looked at herself in the mirror and hated what she saw. Her pulled-up hair sat on her head like a flaccid pickled mushroom. Her breasts sagged into her belly. She looked sweaty, tired and dazed, like a collection of rough sketches done one on top of the other but never put together into a proper portrait.

She decided to try the mirror trick — sometimes then you could catch a glimpse of yourself as others saw you . . . She leaned over to adjust the side mirrors in order to achieve this and her hand brushed against a photograph.

It was a smudgey polaroid. In the foreground a bright ball of hair, presumably the back of someone's head — probably Lewis'. In the background a thin, dark woman, dressed in black underwear and holding a whip in either hand. The woman smiled menacingly, but there was something unconvincing about her menace. The photo had obviously been taken for a laugh. Alice turned it over. On the back was written: 'Happy Birthday. I wish you the fulfillment of every fantasy. Bill' Who was Bill and who was the photo destined for? For Lewis or for the dark lady? If Lewis, then what was his relationship with Bill, who was perhaps the man he shared the apartment with. Alice felt sick and frightened, like a little girl who finds a pornographic book in her mother's drawer and wishes she hadn't looked. She felt her innocence radiate out around her as ridiculous as her unruly hair. Alice knew the photograph was a joke and not a joke.

She looked up and saw the dark man reflected in the mirror. For a moment they watched each other silently. He was very beautiful, in a league of beauty far above her own, with his curling dionysiac hair, his black maidenly eyes and his light, perfectly balanced body. But most of all there was his smile — a warm, entrancing, infinitely understanding smile.

She turned and faced him. He saw that she held the photo but merely intensified his smile.

"This is Lewis' room, as if you didn't guess! Disgustingly tidy, isn't it. I'm afraid he's out at the moment, but he'll be back for the party tonight. Why don't you come back then, and have a few drinks with us? Just tell them at the door that you're a friend of Lewis' and Bill's."

Alice laid the photo down on the dressing-table.

74

"I'm very nosey," she said. "I'm sorry — I shouldn't have looked."

"It was one of my pathetic attempts to cheer him up."

"What's the matter with him?"

"He's a very troubled soul, don't you find?"

"Yes, yes I do. And difficult to help."

"Are you by any chance his sister?"

"No, just a friend. Why do you ask?"

"There's a likeness. Something in the eyes — the expression of the eyes maybe."

"Oh." Alice was used to people commenting on her eyes, not always favourably, but it hurt her badly to remember Lewis's.

"You're beautiful too," she said, "and no doubt clever. You must make a dazzling couple."

"He's not gay, if that's what you mean. Neither am I for that matter. Polymorphously perverse — yes, homosexual — no."

Alice did not know what to say. In spite of Bill's kind words and charming smile she felt him critical of her abundant femaleness. Her yeasty presence was an affront to the spare, masculine room. She rose to leave.

"I'll be back tonight," she said politely. "If you'll just tell him Alice called."

★ ★ ★

CHAPTER FOUR

Confusion-Psyche Fluttering her Fan

CHAPTER FOUR

When Alice got back to the room she found that Maria was feeling much better, which meant, of course, that she would have to be asked to the party. Alice was not happy about that because she knew she was going to smoke and drink a lot and probably behave in a wild and extreme fashion which she would have preferred Maria not to witness. Moreover, Maria was in one of her grown-up and sensible moods.

"I'll just come for an hour or so to see the people," she announced crisply. "Then I'll come home and go to bed. Don't worry, Alice, I won't cramp your style."

They got ready in their different ways. Maria washed her face and under her arms and put on a clean tee-shirt under her maternity dungarees. Alice rummaged in Lily's sister's wardrobe and found some velvet shorts and the top of a grown-up sailor suit, which she wore with her wayward hair deliberately tangled and frizzed out and a lot of nineteen fifties existentialist-beatnik make-up.

"I always liked white faces, black eyes and pale lips," she said as she painted herself. "I only regret I was too young to do it first time round."

Maria folded her arms and frowned. She had been ready for twenty minutes.

"I don't know why you bother with this sort of tedious adornment ritual. You look much nicer without make-up."

"Nicer to you, but not to me," riposted Alice tartly. "And I don't know why you don't wear something other than those boring dungarees. I don't know why you feel the need to conceal the fact that you're a woman . . . "

They rumbled on a while. They had had this argument before, many times, and once, Alice had emptied a colander of wet lettuce over Maria's head, in response to which Maria had banged her so hard on the nose that it bled for five minutes afterwards.

But Maria, although scrub-faced, was not a killjoy, and she admitted to experiencing a frisson of excitement as they crossed the threshhold of the Aquarium and the moist, soft air kissed her for the first time. The cocktail bar, to which they found themselves directed, was deep in the basement, white and bleak like a ship's engine room, throbbing with the bass beat of the music from upstairs. The barman was the Turkish bath attendant, now wearing a bow-tie and Brylcreem, but little else except a pair of silk running shorts.

"You found him?" he purred. "I'm glad. It doesn't seem fair that we should always get the prettiest ones."

"That's kind of you , but I think that you may have him anyway. He seems to be sharing a flat with a glittering person called Bill."

"Oh, Bill's harmless enough. Poor boy is just too pretty for his own good. Spoils them really, don't you think?"

"Don't ask me, ask her!" said Alice, indicating Maria at her side. "She's the beautiful one, and she spends all her time trying to make herself ugly."

But Maria had gone to sit primly in the corner with her alcohol-free banana daiquiri. By now, although they were unfashionably early, a few other guests had begun to drift into the bar. They were mostly young men with perfectly windswept hair and soft pullovers slung round their shoulders, but there were a few women, with brown backs, pert breasts that hardly jiggled as they walked, and eyes that avoided looking at anything except each other and any young man who showed signs of being titillated by their epicene charms.

"They're all strangely sexless," murmured Alice, sucking the plastic mermaid which had been sticking in her drink. "They don't look as if they sweat or have armpits or every suffer from unwanted facial hair. Who are they? I've never seen people like this before."

"Except in adverts," said Maria. "Perhaps they're the people who do the modelling for those?"

"They might be of a different species to ourselves. And look how they don't see us! You'd think they might be just a little curious about two people so different from themselves."

Alice's heart started bouncing decorously against her chest wall. This must mean that Lewis was near. The bouncing became more violent and she began to wish she had not come to the party. 'Why did I choose to live in exciting times?' she asked herself. Lewis and Bill walked in.

Everybody shifted their positions slightly to get a view of them, and Alice noticed that the atmosphere suddenly acquired a charge of lustrous energy. She studied their backs. Bill was the taller of the two, and willowy; he went in beautifully at the waist so that his buttocks could swell and flow down melodiously into his long, straight legs. But Lewis's back radiated a kind of turbulent vitality which made everyone in the bar feel more alive in their skins. He could not stand still. The muscles of his back, his neck, his arms and legs were all the time in a flux of slippery movement, as he explained, gesticulated and held forth to his friend. Alice's eyes were particularly caught by the tender place at the nape of his neck where his astonishing hair ended and his radiant skin began. She longed to go over to him and kiss it. As she looked he put his hand up and lovingly caressed the place himself.

'Wanker, wanker, miserable, beautiful wanker!' she thought.

"I suppose we ought to go over and say hello," she said out loud.

"So that's *him*," said Maria, who had never met Lewis before. "No, let's wait and see how long it takes them to see us. It'll be good just to watch them for a while."

Alice laid her hand lightly over her now painfully beating heart and took another cigarette from the packet she had bought.

"How do you know which one he is anyway?" she asked sharply.

"He's the one with the bleached hair. The other one's too straightforwardly god-like for you."

"It's natural, his hair! He doesn't bleach it. It's the sun. The sun loves him and makes him beautiful."

"Well, he's certainly got something about him, but I fear it may be simple, basic narcissism! His mother told him he was wonderful and he believed her. A common syndrome."

"Oh, come on, it's more than that! He does have a rare talent, an undeniable skill. He knows how to get people going, he knows how to touch a nerve . . . "

81

"What *does* he do?" Maria interrupted in the terse, no-nonsense voice she used normally to combat sloppy think-ing in her students.

"He's a photographer. But also a writer, a journalist . . . and he writes poetry. Which gets published . . . "

"A dilettante you mean?"

"No, more a sort of Renaissance man. He's really good at what he does, Ria, he's good at everything."

"He may be good at everything, but is he *good*? Why do women idealise men so? Have you slept with him?"

"Once. It wasn't very successful. But it could be. I know what his problem is — he finds it difficult to make love to a woman he respects. It makes him embarrassed about his sexuality."

"You know his problem do you? So he's a lame dog! Hero and lame dog. Delightful combination for today's self-immolating woman. Oh Alice, I wish you'd learn to leave all that alone!"

"But if we leave them alone, Ria, who will have them?" asked Alice earnestly. "What will become of them?"

"That's what will become of them," said Maria shortly, flicking her eyes up towards the bar. "They'll find each other, play with each other's little willies and do very nicely thank you. It's what will become of you you should be thinking of, my girl!"

Lewis, having completed his absorbing explanation, turned round to scan the people in the bar. His eyes soon fell on Alice, and without even a beat-pause for ambiva-lence he dived towards her, smiling like a gracious king.

"He*llo*!" he said, his voice reverberant with affection and admiration. "Alice, you look wonderful! Like a lioness lurking in her den."

"This is Maria," said Alice awkwardly, casting her eyes down to protect herself from his appalling radiance. "We've known each other since childhood. She is my old-est friend." Maria and Lewis's eyes locked together in a moment of perfect antagonism then Lewis swung himself down next to Alice, poked his face close to hers and just stared into for five seconds or so.

'I think he does love her, how surprising,' thought Maria. 'But not in the way she wants him to. No good will come it. What can I do?'

"What are you doing here anyway, Lewis?" Alice was asking breathlessly, fumbling for yet another cigarette to cover her agitation. "I didn't expect to meet you in this place."

"I live here. Didn't you know?"

"But this is not the flat of yours I've been to in the past."

"What I mean is — I live here when I'm *here*."

"You mean you come here often?"

Lewis squeezed her knee.

"I have to. It maintains my sanity. Do you think I could survive out there without this place? This is where I get all my best ideas."

"You mean you can move in and out of here freely?"

"I'm not sure 'freely' is the word. But I can move in and out. It can be done. There's a price to pay of course, but we won't talk of that here . . . this is your first time, I suppose?"

"It is — at least I think so. We didn't mean to come. We sort of stumbled in, and now we can't get out."

"Don't worry. You'll get used to it. It has innumerable advantages."

Suddenly Alice remembered a poem of Lewis' she had read and learnt by heart:

'The dark bridge at dusk
Will you meet me there?
I'm trying to say something
Only sayable in silences . . .
Come to the bridge at twilight
The bridge of blood and air . . . '

"Poetry . . . " she said softly.

"Yes." he replied. "It comes from here. Mine and most other people's."

"Does that mean then . . . that we can talk here? Properly, I mean. Say things that can't be said out there?"

"Yes, yes, all that and more. But later. I must go now. I have to meet some people. I'll see you in the big room at twelve o'clock, OK?"

He left abruptly, leaving a strong, earthy odour hanging in the air behind him.

"They say you can always tell a devil by his smell," said Maria.

"But this is a sweet smell, not sulphur and brimstone."
"Maybe he uses scent to cover the odour of decay."

★ ★ ★

Alice felt sick with excitement and certainty, like a little girl at Christmas. She knew something was going to happen. It was all going to be finally resolved. She felt light and irresponsible. She knew she did not have to do anything, except get mildly drunk — or very drunk. It did not matter — she could drink as much as she wanted and the adrenalin foaming and fizzing through her body would keep her lucid. But not too lucid. She was looking for that precarious, dangerous condition which she called to herself 'being-on-the-edge', that vertiginous sense of height, depth, space, possibilities, when you knew that one wrong step would take you over the brink and into the void.

The party intensified around them, but they could not join it because people ignored them, looked through them while waving to someone at the other side of the room, and brushed past them carelessly as if they were not flesh and blood which could be bruised, or at least offended. Alice grew angry — she was not used to being ignored — but Maria pacified her, pointing out that it was useful to be invisible for a change and able to stare at people for long periods without them noticing and brushing your eyes away. They wandered into the Turkish baths. Half-naked people and sometimes very nearly naked people who had stripped down to their tasteful underwear drank champagne and pretended to massage each other.

In the 'big room' which Lewis had mentioned, which was lined with mirrors reaching up to the ceiling, people were dancing, sometimes with other people, sometimes, in reflection, with themselves. Small groups were having conversations which sounded like snatches of 'actuality' for a film, being picked up by a hidden microphone.

"Sometimes I think that this melancholy is an American invention," an ageing man in white was saying to his suave, concave-cheeked companion.

"Quite," replied the latter. "Left to our own devices I don't think we would feel any guilt at all. The old world has always taken decadence for granted. The new world behaves as if they've just discovered it."

It was ten to twelve. Maria left. The rendezvous with Lewis was close at hand. At the back of her mind Alice held a sense that the reason she had been brought to the camp and to the Aquarium was specifically and solely to find Lewis, to meet him in a special place, a special atmosphere where their essences could speak unfettered by ego, where problems like her over-ardent personality, his fear of making love to women that he liked would dissolve. There was something (albeit a disturbing, even menacing thing) in the atmosphere tonight which meant that the truth, whatever it was, would have to be spoken. Alice walked slowly, with all the dignity of knowledge, into the big room.

She felt her life organise itself and swish into the room behind her like a big, powerful tail. Lewis was still rapt in conversation with Bill, his fair head dipped as if in obeisance, listening with complete absorption to what the other man was saying. It felt improper to interrupt them but the tail lashed and made her bold.

"OK, Lewis, it's time for us to talk!"

He turned his face slowly towards her and she felt his warmth trickle through her like honey through a piece of bread. Bill touched him lightly on the shoulder and said he was going off to buy a bottle of wine. Lewis said nothing and eventually dropped his eyes away from Alice.

"Out there," began Alice, "it was never possible to really talk. I suppose our egos got in the way, I know mine did, but now, can't we — I mean, shall we be able to be completely honest? To tell each other what we really feel."

"You're very intense, Alice."

"That's just my personality."

"No, I think you really are."

"And you too. Maria spoke about corruption."

"Yes, I suppose it's nearly done. Soon I won't be fit for human consumption."

"I don't want to consume you."

"Then you are a rarity amongst women, devoutly to be praised."

"No! No, I'm not."

"What do you want of me then?" His eyes took on a different look — empty, childish, sly.

'He is frightened of me,' she thought, 'but why don't I say that? Because he'll only deny it, and here we ought to tell the truth?'

"I'm frightened," she said. "I'm frightened because I feel this connection between us and I don't know what it is."

They found themselves dropping down onto a low settee. His head fell onto her shoulder. He began to stroke the velvet surface of her thigh.

"You look strange tonight. Amazing. I've never seen you look like this before."

"Ambisexual?"

"Yes. An Edwardian boy-child. A straw boater and you'd be complete . . . innocent, you look innocent, and yet infinitely corruptible . . . "

"Yes," she said quickly. "You see right. I have done something recently which you would not believe of me."

"What have you done, Alice?" his face jumped into a sharp focus of interest. "What have you done that I wouldn't believe of you?"

She knew she must not tell him, but she wanted to, to create a bridge between them. A bridge of corruption.

She heard herself say:

"I let two men in a lorry fuck me."

But she did not say it. She looked back at him. He lifted his eyes dreamily from her leg to her face and smiled a faint mischievous smile. She found it almost unbearable to watch him. He was a part of herself from which she had been mysteriously disjuncted.

"Go on, tell me what you did!"

She sat and stared down at her shoes. Her knees shone stone-white and skeletal through the black tights. Alice could see Lewis' face saved and not-saved: saved he had a beard and ruddy whiskers, his violent, forceful being was refined into a steady, low-burning flame; unsaved his eyes had faded from hazel to that too-light green that Alice called cold-hearted green his cheeks had clapped in prematurely and had a hectic, peachy bloom. She shivered at her vision.

He was very close to her. It was a habit of his, when talking, to sit so close and put his face so near to hers, that often, by the time he had finished the conversation, he was

86

sitting more on her seat than on his own.

"I can't tell you," she said finally. "But anyway, it's probably nothing compared with what you've done in your time."

She felt him swing away from her on a wide arc which took him over cold seas the like of which she had never known and probably never would know.

He had once described to her a scene from De Sade's 'Sodom and Gomorrah' where a little boy was flayed alive, covered with honey and exposed to a swarm of bees, which, he claimed, had particularly revolted him. But Alice could not rub from her mind the sense that he revelled in the image, that he was fascinated by it, that he was watching out to see what effect it would have on her. 'Yet if I'm not prepared to keep him company in hell, what use am I to him?' she wondered.

"Let me stay with you tonight!" she said suddenly. "Please! Let's give it a chance. Don't you want me to?"

"To be honest, it might be better if you didn't. Do you mind?"

"Oh, please let me stay!"

"If you really want to . . . "

"But you don't want me to!"

"It's not that, I'm just so tired. And I'll be even tireder later on. I've had so many late nights recently."

"Lewis, I think I've *got* to say!"

★ ★ ★

There was none of the intensity and excitement of the time before. He went straight into his bedroom, she to the bathroom where she stood, shivering in front of the mirror, wondering whether to stay or go. She looked good. Her skin shone and her hair had fizzed out in the steamy atmosphere into a halo of fair curls. She looked, she thought, like a crumpled button-hole rose that had been cast off but still retained its odour, its pathetic prettiness even though there was no-one around to admire it any more . . .

She could not believe that he did not want her to stay. She could believe that he was frightened — that was all right — but *reluctant*? That was impossible. She washed herself cursorily. Now she had got this far she would have to stay. She decided to shut her thinking faculty down: 'I'm doing what I'm doing. I'm going on instinct even though it goes against all reason. If I'm doing wrong then it's surely only me who will have to pay.'

She took her clothes off in the living room. It seemed indecent and presumptuous to undress in front of him in his bedroom. She presented herself there already naked and found him cuddled up in bed, as if well on the way to sleep. 'At least he's not turned away from me,' she thought.

"Can I turn out the light?" she asked.

"If you want to."

He sounded surprised. Did he not realise that she did not want to be bothered by his beauty?

He was kissing her with tenderness. Their legs were interlaced, his tongue was in her mouth. If his body felt a bit limp, a bit wound-down, she could understand that. He had drunk and smoked a great deal. He was tired and she was asking for a lot.

She was glad she could not look at him in the darkness. She couldn't see whether he was paying attention to her or not. His fingers were moving very tentatively over neutral areas of her body, plucking at the skin. 'I wish he would *take hold of me*! Until he takes hold of me I can't take hold of *him*.' She ran her hands up and down his body — nothing flawed at all — no pot belly, no goose pimples on his bottom, no spotty back, no dirty neck. 'It would be better for both of us if he were not quite so perfect,' she thought.

Eventually she couldn't help herself. She wormed her arms around him and hugged him very hard. He responded by disengaging himself, getting on top of her and pushing his penis in. It felt erect but not very hard. He started moving rapidly up and down. Alice sailed far away, up high and looked down on the scene beneath her. It was clear that he was trying to bring himself as quickly as possible to that condition of frenzy where who or what it is doesn't matter any more. Already his hands on her shoulders were pressing too hard, were digging painfully into her flesh. Already she was clamped immobile. Already she was getting angry. Already she could not feel.

"Stop it, Lewis! This is all wrong, all wrong!"

"No, no, it's OK," he panted.

"No!" she shouted, pulling herself sharply out from under him. "It's no good. I'm sorry. It was a mistake!"

He did not make it difficult. He did not reproach her, just lay beside her, still as a dead man, hardly breathing at all.

"Oh God," she said, "I'm so sorry."

He said nothing.

"You didn't really want to do it, did you? We shouldn't have. And now I've done what it's absolutely not right to do."

He put his hand down under the bedclothes as if to feel the degree of his tumescence.

"It's all right," he said. "Don't get upset."

"But *why* won't it work between us, Lewis? It so nearly does and then something stops it."

"It's simple," he said finally. "We're not in love with one another. Neither is there a proper degree of lust between us. You know I am screwed up about women, Alice . . . "

He continued but she had stopped listening. 'We're not in love with one another' was enough. She *was* in love with him. She had thought he knew it, but now there seemed little point in telling him. She felt herself falling backwards into time as if she would find there a moment when she could stop and choose another, not this hopeless and desolating path.

Instead she found herself suddenly in a very quiet place where there was nothing but the smell of the future and of the past. The smell and then the sounds . . . A child was screaming and screaming in a deep cellar, screaming and screaming, but nobody came. If somebody ever did come, she knew they never would be let go of . . . Then she was plunging through layers of warmth, layers of ice, layers of corruption and of innocence, plunging down to the bottom of Lewis' soul. Or was it her own soul?

Down here everything was clear. The future they could have together was hanging immanent in the air. She could see the mechanics of it, the wheels and pulleys that would drive the motors of their desire, their union, and the inevitable tearing away and repudiation of each other which would end the sequence of events. She could see how his terrible need would pull her close to him, would enthrall her at the start, fill her full of love and pity, then would begin to frighten and appal her; how she would struggle to pull him out of the dark cellar in which he screamed and screamed unheard and bring him up into the light of ordinary, human day; how he would resist her, knowing that it was in that very dark, loveless place that the roots of his brilliance were nourished, where they absorbed the magic liquor which fuelled his desperate, creative drive.

She saw herself trying to 'help' him, to balance him, humanise him, do for him what countless generations of self-sacrificing women have done for countless generations of lost men, and she knew that, eventually, inevitably, he would come to hate her for it. Alice shuddered. Where did this terrible knowledge come from?

He was asleep when she returned from that place, the odour of her own perdition in her nostrils. His breathing was heavy, his skin hot-cold to the touch. Gently, gently, so as not to wake him, she disengaged herself from his half-hearted embrace and moved herself to balance on the edge of the bed, out of his orbit. Now she was experiencing a novel kind of despair — she had got what she wanted and found that it was not what she wanted. She saw his unhappiness, his inability to take what he needed, she understood what would be required of her if she wished to be his woman, his partner, his helpmeet. But there in the place in herself where she should have found a latent capacity for sacrifice, for giving and not counting the cost, she found instead a hard, sheeny kernel of pure selfishness. She did not want to save him. She wanted to save herself. This knowledge was devastating.

Her chest ached. Her heart pushed against it and wanted to burst. Waves of something worse than mere misery found her out and broke over her. So this is what I really am, she thought. Rejected. Rejecting. A cold-hearted creature. Not me the phoenix dying in the flames. I embody the victory of the sensible over the noble, and I can't bear it.

When the dawn came it sucked the warm darkness from the room and laid bare its bareness. His clothes lay in a livid little pile on the floor. The thought of their recent contact with his warm, vigorous, unhappy body broke her heart. She closed her eyes and let the next wave of grief break over her. 'I must go,' she thought, 'there is no place for me here.'

CHAPTER FIVE

Who's Knocking?

CHAPTER FIVE

Alice moved through the streets quick and light as a phantom. This was no ordinary dawn. The sky was icily bright and yet the high buildings which lined the way were still soaked in darkness. It was if it were day and night at the same time or as if the camp were trembling on the border between light and dark, flickering backwards and forwards so that the eye saw both and neither.

She had never found walking so effortless. The couple of miles which separated the Aquarium in the centre from their room on the outskirts passed in the twinkling of an eye, and soon she was bouncing up the five flights to their floor two and three steps at a time, a feeling of power and ease flowing through her.

Maria was not in the bed, though her clothes were draped tidily over a chair. Alice banged on the toilet door outside on the landing. No response. She flung open the door to the cupboard bathroom. Maria was curled up in the corner. No, she was not curled, she was bound with ropes into a tight bundle, and another rope gagged her mouth. Blood was pumping from stab wounds all over her body.

Alice catapulted herself out into the hallway. Just above her nape there was a heavy, drowsy throbbing. Her vision scrambled for a minute, as if the world were muddling itself up to confuse her. 'This *cannot* be happening', she told herself, 'I don't accept it, I don't accept it!' Then, in the gap between one shuddering breath and the next one, she *realised* — she had been expecting it! All the way home, all the way up the stairs, the frightful image of Maria in the bathroom had been flashing behind her eyes, in some ante-chamber of consciousness, just waiting for the right moment to burst forth into the main auditorium and shriek its terrible news.

Trembling, she pushed open the door to the room again. Maria was sitting on the bed in a ragged jumble-sale nightie cutting her toe-nails onto an old copy of 'The Guardian' they had brought with them.

"Hello," she said. "I couldn't sleep. I had such an awful dream."

Alice sat down on the bed beside her. The thumping, scrambling chaos in her brain was gradually subsiding.

"Go on," she said. "Tell me about it."

"Well . . . I went straight to bed when I got home, and straight to sleep. But at some point in the night I was wakened by a terrible banging at the door. I was terrified, I didn't answer it. Then it got worse, louder, I could hear people throwing themselves against the door, trying to break it down. I jumped out of bed, trying to think of somewhere to hide myself, and went to put on the light. But it wouldn't go on! and *then* I remembered. I remembered that I was dreaming. Because I read somewhere that not being able to switch on the lights is one of the surest signs that you're in a dream, not in reality. So! So since I knew I was dreaming and they couldn't really hurt me, I went over to the door and opened it. There was a polite little boy outside who handed me a package and disappeared without a word. By that time I was nearly on the point of waking up, so it was difficult to find out what was in it. But I managed — just — to pull the paper off, and there inside was a beautiful, shiny knife, a dagger really, with a long, sharp, pointed blade. Then I woke up."

Alice realised she should tell Maria about her own experience, but a powerful lassitude swept over her, her tongue felt heavy and reluctant to move. "I think it was a clue," she said.

"A clue?"

"Yes" she continued, "I'm beginning to get the feel of this place! I'm beginning to work out the rules. I think what you have to do here is to *pay attention*, to notice all the big things and all the little things which might be relevant to working out why we're here and how we can get out. A knife to me has all the right qualities for a clue."

"A clue from whom?" asked Maria in her 'eminently reasonable' voice.

"I don't know. A clue from this world to us, telling us how to get out of it perhaps."

"But what is this 'world' that we talk about? I'm beginning to get so used to it, I feel almost I've always lived here. I'm beginning to forget what life was like outside."

"But don't you see? That's why it's so important for us to keep awake, not to forget where we came from!"

"Well, just at the moment, keeping awake is the last thing on my mind — I want to sleep and I'm going to."

The terrible lassitude swept over Alice again. This time the undertow of the wave dragged sharp stones and pebbles over the soft ground of her being, producing an acute and nauseating pain there which made her want to moan out loud. But Maria was lying back on the bed, her eyes shut, a soppy, peaceful smile on her lips.

"I'm glad you're back, Ally. I think I'll be able to sleep now."

'She hasn't even asked me what happened with Lewis,' thought Alice. 'But of course, I forget, she is nurturing that awful child. What a shock she will have when he's born a boy, and how dreadfully and disproportionately she will love him! But they will at least have each other, however parasitic their relationship, while I shall have nobody because I can't love.' She lifted her head and saw it was black night all round her now. 'I must be asleep and dreaming,' she thought, 'dreaming of the void.' But the black air was soft, moist, warm on her cheek. It sailed into her lungs easily, seemed to like her and want to comfort her. She stood up and leaned forward into it. It held her. She took a little jump off the ground. She was lifted, buoyed playfully up till she was swimming smoothly in the air. 'This is wonderful,' she thought. 'How come I've never done it before? When it's so easy and so delightful. . . ?' As she drifted down through the black, kindly void her consciousness left her and whatever adventure she had there we will never know because when she awoke at midday the next day she remembered nothing.

She had only been properly awake for a couple of minutes before the pain and humiliation of the night before jumped out and bit her. Her heart fluttered. Her mouth tasted sour. Her eyes ached. She went out to the newsagents opposite and bought herself another packet of cigarettes.

Sitting at the formica table she munched stolidly through a bowl of cornflakes. Maria was out shopping so she could cry now in peace if she wanted to. A lump filled her throat so that it was hard to swallow the cornflakes.

She took them back into her mouth and chewed them finer. 'I really am very sensible,' she thought, 'I shall never not be able to eat.'

After breakfast, still holding back the tears and trying not to think about the previous night, she opened the only book she had with her — Anna Akhmatova's Selected Poems. She looked through the photographs of the poet's face: when young so fine, aquiline, arrogant; when old so fat, ordinary, magnificent.

> 'My love is constant,' so he told me,
> And laid his hand upon my dress.
> How far they feel from a caress,
> These hands that touch but do not hold me.
>
> Thus one may stroke a cat, a bird
> Look some trim circus rider over,
> These eyes remain amused but sober,
> By gauzy golden lashes blurred.

'Yes, yes,' thought Alice, 'oh *yes!*' These early poems, you could slump down and rest upon them in such delicious melancholy — like the poet herself in that photo where she reclines on a settee, insolent, angular but voluptuous, in a big fisherman's pullover, staring out her fate with heavy-lidded eyes. By that time they had stopped publishing her poetry, her ex-husband had been executed, her son was about to be taken away to the camps. She was going to be hungry, she was going to be homeless, she was going to be rejected by the man she loved, but she was going to find her *real* voice, her *real* task right in the midst of all this suffering and brutality . . . '

Alice had quite forgotten her own misery in the excitement of reading Akhmatova again. She flicked through to the end of the book to find her favourite poem, the long, rambling 'Poem without a Hero', the poem written in a code which the critics had never managed to crack, dazzling, frightening, absolutely elusive. She turned to the notes in the back of the book and found a quote from a letter Akhmatova had written to a friend about it.

"It kept catching me unexpectedly over and over, like fits of some incurable disease," she wrote. "It could happen anywhere — at concerts, on the street, even in my dreams, and I could not tear loose from it."

'Sounds like the camp', thought Alice. 'Maybe it's a poem about the camp. Maybe she came here too and wanted to write about it afterwards in a way that only those who had been here would understand.' She scanned the first lines excitedly, looking for clues and confirmation.

The words were mysterious, yet she felt she knew what they meant. But just as soon as her mind formed a concept to hang onto and look at, the meaning ran away from her, turning back into itself, biting its own tail like a dragon. She read on.

> "Is it you Confusion-Psyche
> Fluttering your fan of black and white,
> Are you bending down to me;
> Do you want to tell me in secret
> That Lethe is now behind you,
> And you breathe of a different Spring.
> No dictation — I can hear it myself;"

Now *this* made sense, this was coming through clearer. 'Confusion-Psyche' is the phantom of Akhmatova's dead friend, Olga — temptress, dancer, actress, femme-fatale — who is trying to speak to her from beyond death, but without a body has only the psyche to live in and the psyche's confusing, dazzling, ever-changing forms to communicate with. The poet does not know if it is her friend or merely a creature of her own imagination who calls her . . . and is not sure that there could be a line drawn between them anyway. Now Lettie had said that the camp was not so much a place as a state of mind that was shared by a certain group of people! Wasn't the room where Akhmatova awaits her phantom New-Year guests, where everything is constantly changing —

> "And the walls moved apart for them,
> Lights flared on, sirens wailed,
> And the ceiling bulged like a cupola —"

— wasn't this room the same kind of place as the camp? Wasn't Akhmatova's vision of the Devil who gatecrashes her party of the same order as her own hallucination of the previous night, of Maria murdered by the torturers?

'Yes!' thought Alice. 'The poem *is* in code! But what is the key to unlock it?' She had a feeling that the poet wanted her to find it, to understand, that her presence was pushing out through the words on the page, ballooning them up into Alice's eyes, trying to burst through into the *now*. Alice strained to hear, to see, to *sense* the real meaning of the poem. She tried not to breathe, not to move, not to break the spell. And *yes*, there *was* a voice speaking, speaking fast and rhythmically, not in English, not in Russian, but in . . . *thought*? The meaning of the poem reverberated around the room, inside and outside Alice. Some rigid barrier which had kept her from the truth of before was broken down and everything was flooding in . . .

She gasped and pushed her cornflake bowl away from her in panic. This was just too much! She shut the book sharply and looked around the room. The light in it had turned golden. It was dense, cloudy, like a saturated liquid on the point of precipitation. Something was surely about to happen, some great event, something was being manufactured in the room! She shifted her eyes onto the potted primrose which was sitting on the table. It was trembling. Something was going on around the table, something was ebbing, fizzing, dancing, puzzling about! She shook her head to clear it but it would not be dispelled. It was as if she had entered a dimension just half a degree out of sync with the usual one, so that the room was the same room and yet subtly different. It was as if she was catching the room in the act of *making itself up*!

> "The world transformed itself for just an instant,
> And wine was strangely altered on the tongue
> . . ."

She sat, hardly breathing, poised like a princess in an incandescent palace, until the prickling sound of a key in the lock announced the return of Maria from the shops.

"I think I've got it," she said, as Maria began unloading tins and bags of fruit onto the table. "From Akhmatova, just now. Poetry is a kind of code, you see, saying what can't be said in any other way. Saying that the thing that you and I have been waiting for, the great event of liberation, *isn't going to happen*! And that's because it's happening already! The primrose is trembling on the table, but it's not trembling on the brink of something — its existence is itself the brink! Do you see? Just like the camp. Does it exist or doesn't it? How do we get out of it? Well, they're all the wrong questions really. I can see that now, and . . . "

"You're saying that the camp is just a state of mind?" interrupted Maria. "Well, I've worked that one out too actually, without benefit of mystical poetry."

"Yes, yes, I mean that, but a lot more too. I mean that every place that exists is just a state of mind, but we can't see it, we think that places are outside us!"

"All right then. You mean we're in the camp because of a *failure* of the imagination?"

"Not exactly," said Alice lamely. Maria's formulations sounded so convincing, but she was absurdly sure they were not quite *right*. Now her vision was fading. She was standing on a magnificent sandcastle, triumphing, but all the time mechanical waves were rolling in and washing it away.

"It's as if," she began slowly, "we're spinning and yet we're also standing still, and while we're spinning we're seeing all sorts of people and things and landscapes. But while we're standing still, which is happening at the same time as we're spinning, we only see *one* set of people and things, *one* landscape. But the trouble is that the standing-still part doesn't know it's spinning. And the spinning part is not aware that at every point it spins around it's also standing still. It's what's meant by the conscious and the unconscious. It's why we're big and small people at the same time."

"Does Akhmatova say that?" asked Maria, frowning.

"No," admitted Alice, "I just thought of it. It explains the camp though, doesn't it? It's one of the standing still spots I was talking about, and we're separated from all the other standing still spots by a sea of spinning . . . do you see?"

"So what do we do to get back to our usual standing still spot? Swim?"

Suddenly Alice felt so angry with Maria that, had she not been pregnant, she would have hit her.

"I think you like it here," she said bitterly. "I think you deserve to be here, to stay here. It's a world entirely suitable for pregnant marxist-feminist- rationalists!"

"You're quite right — I don't think it's so bad at all," said Maria calmly. "It's you who's always going on about having to get out."

"I just can't *bear* it here!" said Alice with an intensity that shocked her. "And I'm going back to talk to that man in the shop. We were stupid last time, we wasted our opportunity."

Maria stood by the table, arranging the tins she had bought into a neat line. Her dungarees hung neatly on her small shoulders and fell neatly over her neat bump. Her black Milly-Molly-Mandy hair framed her neat, set face. 'She looks like a toy person,' thought Alice scornfully, 'and she's deliberately avoiding my eyes because she knows it's wrong to cop out.'

She felt a cord going out from her own belly into Maria's and she felt her own turbulent energy leaking out through it, sucked by the voracious monster-baby in Maria's womb. 'I must cut myself off or we are both lost,' she thought suddenly.

"I must go now, Ria. Time's running out, I can feel it."

"Don't go, Ally! It's dangerous!" said Maria with desperation, "It won't do any good. We'll just have to bide our time until they let us out."

"They won't *let* us out, it doesn't work like that."

"I don't want to be on my own at the moment, I'm still not feeling too good!"

But Alice was already trying on her dusty espadrilles, snapping her hair up into its floppy mushroom, wiping last night's black make-up from under her eyes with tongue-licked finger. Neither of them said anything until she was half-way out of the door, and then it was Alice who spoke.

"I just think it's necessary," she said. "I can't explain. I won't be very long," and left.

· ★ ★ ★

When she reached the shop it was shut. A blaring neon light lit the exquisite interior, making it look tawdry, vacuous and artificial, and there was clearly nobody within. She turned away, deflated, and noticed how the arcade seemed desolate and sombre now. There were very few people about; hurried and furtive, they walked past her with their eyes cast down, their arms clutched tightly about their chests.

She traversed the empty market place and headed towards the massive turretted building they had guessed must be the university. On closer examination it was less welcoming — the thick red walls rose sheer and unbroken up to third-floor level, where small, barred windows were visible, and as she skirted the corner looking for its entrance she came upon a long, straggling line of women leaning wearily up against the side of it, bundles and carrier bags propped at their feet. She walked down the line, squinting covertly up at their faces, but she need not have worried — none of them paid her any attention at all. Then she came upon the back-view of a figure that she thought she recognised — a black dress that hung straight down from square, still shoulders, barely touching the body, a headscarf tied peasant-fashion, black with violently pink roses. Alice hesitated, pretending to fiddle with her espadrilles, and saw the woman ahead of this one in the queue turn and talk to her. Her face was puffy, mottled with eczema, her eyes danced like creatures tortured on hot coals. With a jolt Alice realised that the building must be a prison, the women wives and mothers waiting to hand in food parcels for their men.

"Can you describe this?" the agonised woman asked the black-clad one.

"I can," the other answered evenly. Alice straightened up in a flash and laid her hand on the still woman's shoulder.

"Excuse me," she said, "but are you the poet? Are you the poet, Anna Akhmatova?"

Now she could see the eyes as the woman turned to face her. They were lighter than in the photographs, reflecting the dry, dusty quietness of the street surrounding them.

"I am."

"But you were older before."

The poet did not reply, just raised her eyebrows humorously.

"Can you tell me how to get out of this place?"

"I can tell you how I would get out, if I wanted to. I *have* told you. In the poem. But each person must find the way for himself."

"You're not talking Russian," said Alice in amazement. "And you're not talking English with an execrable accent, like it says you did in the books."

"I'm not talking anything," said the poet, smiling an ineffable, crackling smile, "it's all in your imagination."

"It isn't!" said Alice as hotly as a little girl.

"Well done!" said the poet gently. "I'm glad you see that."

"But how can you be here, now?" asked Alice, bewildered. "I know now that anyone living can turn up here, but the dead? You died back in nineteen sixty-six."

The poet smiled again but this time the smile burnt at its edges and the skin on her face turned paper-thin and seemed to be dissolving in the flames.

"I live in the real, not the calendar twentieth century," she said.

Alice felt a drumming at the place just above her nape, very like the throbbing which had accompanied the scrambling experience of the morning. This time it would not go away but gathered in intensity until she was confronted with its origin — a cavalcade of enormous, heavy lorries hammering down the street towards them, obliterating conversation. For a moment they just stood and watched the monsters as they thundered past, then she felt her arm taken and she was pulled down so that her ear was level with the poet's mouth. Alice struggled to hear what Akhmatova was trying to say to her, but she could only pick up odd words and phrases — "patterns . . . dangerous . . . only *apparent* complexity . . . symbols *not* things . . . don't be fooled . . . opacity . . . "

'Why don't we just wait until the lorries have passed by?' she thought with a spasm of irritation. But there was no sign of the cavalcade ending and the poet seemed to feel a sense of urgency because she reached into her bag and drew out a scrap of paper on which she scribbled something quickly before stuffing it into Alice's hand.

"Go, *go* now," she said, pushing Alice quite forcefully away from her. "Go, before they find you and pick you up, you stupid girl"

Alice did not want to leave the ambience of those dry, bright eyes, but she found herself walking speedily away, back along the line of dejected women and then down a narrow alleyway which led towards the centre of the camp. As soon as the roar of the lorries had died away and she felt safe, she slackened her pace and studied the piece of paper that had been thrust into her hand.

The handwriting was very crisp and clear.

"Find the visitor from inside the mirrors" it said.

Alice was disappointed. She recognised the quote. It was from "Poem without a hero." But she had hoped for some simple instruction such as 'go to the central tram station and ask for Jim' or 'drink peppermint tea and sleep on your right side for a week and you'll wake up back home.' She never tired of hoping for magical formulae. But more poetry? Who the hell was this "visitor from inside the mirrors"? How did you recognise a looking-glass person? Was he or she part of herself? An alternative, left-handed self? Or was the line not a clue but a mischievous poetic conceit, a joke, designed to make her buckle down and accept the reality of the camp as her own?

No, it had more resonance than that. She remembered how, as a child, she had stared and stared into the mirror, longing for the glass to melt and let her pass through to the other side. She knew, of course, that you could pass the barrier easily enough 'in the imagination'. But that seemed a poor substitute for doing it 'in reality'. 'Imagination' was just something that cropped up in English lessons and in art, where the teacher might congratulate you for having it. Her mother on the other hand had always told her that she had a lot of it, but that it was the 'wrong sort'.

Imagination? Was the "visitor from inside the mirrors" to be found in the world reached only by the imagination? The denigrated, guiltily visited secret realm that Alice had tried so hard since childhood to 'grow out of'? She felt a thrill run up from her clitoris to her heart. She felt that she was right or, if she was not then, that being wrong would be exciting.

Quite soon, near the market, she came across a humdrum little park, guarded by a low brick wall. As soon as she walked into it Alice noticed a stillness, a scintillating shimmer in the air which seemed to make everyone who came in walk slowly and fall into silence. She lay down on a small space of parched grass near a bench from which two very aged ladies were watching a massive black lad doing some training exercises. The combination made Alice feel safe. She closed her eyes and for a moment lay listening to her heart.

It banged violently against her breastbone for a while, then quietened and seemed to float off into space, a vast inner space inside her chest. She felt big, like a blown-up doll, and light, floating about in that interior space. Then suddenly but naturally she was in her old bedroom at home, sitting at the kidney-shaped dressing table, staring at her thirteen-year old self. Her wayward, golden-syrup-coloured hair, just liberated from pigtails stood out around her ruddy face in a not-yet fashionable tangle of kinks and curls.

She looked into her own eyes and her own eyes looked back at her. A sister inside the mirror, who lived properly and well.

"I would like to meet you, sister," she said.

"Come and join me then," said the sister.

The room beyond the mirror looked cool, translucent, as if it were under water, deep, cold water which would stun you, chill you to the bone.

The sister held out her hand.

"Come on," she said, her voice ringing like a bell.

Alice put her arm out and the sister pulled her through. Now they were in one body, but she knew that they could still talk to each other if they wanted to. Sure enough the air was thicker in there and buoyed you up easily so that you could bounce and float around like a spaceman. Or you could walk about like a normal person if you chose. It was cool too, but with a kind of 'alive' bracing coolness that made you feel immensely strong and easy in your skin. Alice was enjoying herself, and she was about to try turning somersaults in the air, but then she became suddenly aware of the hot sun on her face and that she was lying on the grass in the park once more.

She blinked and went under again almost immediately, having checked that her guardian angels were still doing their duty round about. This time she was in Lewis' bedroom, but she was staring into the mirrors of the kidney-shaped dressing-table again. Bill was watching her from the door, his lip curled in a mild sort of sneer. She brushed her hair unworried. Then Lewis was there too, in the corner of the room, also in the mirror. His eyes caught and hooked into hers and she was sucked easily through to the other side again.

Bill was gone. She and Lewis were on a beach somewhere. It seemed to be late afternoon because the sky was thundery, the air hot and heavy on the skin. A few feet out, in the dead-calm sea, floated a great viscous bank of seaweed. Alice shuddered as she imagined it wrapping itself around her legs. Lewis had on some tattered blue trunks and was sitting at the edge of the waves, dipping his feet in the water. Her body was slippery and wet, as if she had just come out of the sea.

She put her hand into the runnel of his back and pushed it gently up to rest around his neck. His skin was clammy, almost slimy to the touch, like a dead fish's belly.

"We've certainly missed our chance for good this time round, Alice" he said.

"I don't think I can bear it!"

"Bear it? You'll do more than bear it! It's a lucky break for you."

"Lewis, I know you're a wounded soldier, but wounds are meant to heal, you don't have to go on bleeding for ever!"

"And you're the wounded healer, are you, Alice?" You're the one who'll bring me back to health?"

"I love you, Lewis. I can't say that in the ordinary world, but it's true, I do. Surely love can heal the most terrible wounds!"

"Oh, I'm far too far gone for that. Ridiculous woman, have you any idea how rotted and rotten I am? You were put on earth to be a clown, Alice, a circus-rider, an entertainer of the troops, not to spill your blood for the sake of a lost soul and imbecile like me. Do you want to go against the instructions the great maker has stamped all over your packaging?"

"But do *you* love *me*, Lewis, that's the point?"

"It's not the point at all, Alice."

"But I want you," she said, "I want you!"

"I don't like being wanted."

"But you need me!"

"I only need you if I want to be saved, and maybe I don't want to be saved!"

A kind of horror was shadowing the sands. Alice wanted to run away as fast as her feet would carry her, but she knew that Lewis was waiting, waiting for it to come.

"Let's go," she said, "something's calling us, let's go."

"It's calling you, not me. Go on, follow! I'm staying."

Then she was walking away, away from the water, over the sand-dunes, someone was waiting, she had to get home . . . She turned round and saw Lewis still sitting, with bent head, at the water's edge. 'They'll come for him soon, I suppose' she thought, 'but I'm not going to save him, I've hardened my heart.'

She woke up. The park was deserted, her guardians were gone. 'I've just been asleep,' she thought crossly. 'Although I *was* somewhere . . . but there was no 'visitor', only Lewis and me, and some horrible seaweed . . . and something terrible just about to happen somewhere . . . but I can't remember, the experiment's failed! It's all just illusion, delusion and rubbish. There isn't any reality behind it, there isn't any kernel of essence at the heart of the world — only tinier and tinier reflections of my own stupidity and cupidity . . . '

Lewis' back curves away from her. He is clenched up in foetal position protecting his soft parts. The dark, sticky hairs at the nape of his neck. The glitter of long blonde hairs on his arms. His cold, tidy room. His beautiful friend. His exciting, despicable life. The child who screams at the bottom of the well, screams and screams until he's sick and falls asleep and wakes to scream and scream again.

'I must stopper my ears,' thought Alice. 'I don't want to hear that sound any more.'

CHAPTER SIX

The Visitor from Inside the Mirror

CHAPTER SIX

"But Alice, who is sending us these clues?"

Maria was standing on the table, reaching up to white-wash the walls. Alice was lying on the bed drinking cider from the bottle and smoking a cigarette.

"It's not that I think a *person* is sending us the clues . . . anyway, what's with the nest-making activity? It's not worth painting the walls, we won't be here by the time he's born."

"You never know — we might! And what do you mean by 'he'? But never mind that, I've been thinking and I'm sure we could just walk out."

"We've tried that."

"But we went for the car, and they were guarding it. And there was that woman prisoner we saw, who looked like you . . . that freaked us out."

"I thought we thought it *was* me."

"Well it couldn't have been, could it? Anyway, I think if we just walked out, without bothering about the car, through the archway and across the wasteland, that we'd find ourselves back on that main road again. We could hitch a lift to Sheffield, borrow another car and come back and fetch yours. With some heavy support if necessary. What do you think?"

"I've told you. It's not just a physical thing, this camp. It doesn't abide by the usual rules."

Maria clambered down from the table and laid her paintbrush carefully on the newspaper.

"You say so Alice. But I've seen no evidence to prove conclusively that this is the case. Certainly there are certain rather self-consciously created symbolic structures, like the spiral road system and the trams going inwards and outwards, but symbolic or not, it all seems perfectly physical. Someone made it all up, that's all."

Alice finished her cigarette, picked up the paintbrush, made one meticulous stripe along the wall, and stopped.

"You'd like to stay here, wouldn't you? And have me looking after you? For the two of us to live on here, with the baby, eh? Not do anything, just stay here, suspended in time and space, with every excuse for not *doing* anything. Well, I can't do that, I've got to get out soon. I've got things I must get on with."

"Like what?"

"Like the giant wall-hanging of the Greenham Women."

"You've been planning that for ages."

"Well, now's the time."

"Why wasn't 'now' the time before?"

"Because I had to do all those bloody draw-string trousers and baby dungaree things to get money, that's why! Because my bloody car broke down and I couldn't get round the outworkers to pick the stuff up to make the money to fix the car and so on. God, you're really getting on my nerves today. Why are you being so infuriating?"

"I'm just questioning your assumptions."

"You're not! You're accusing me of playing at being an artist!"

"Alice, why should I do that? I like your work, at least I think you've got definite potential — I just wish you'd get on and *do* some instead of squandering your energy making cheap clothes for unemployed vegetarians and having hopeless obsessions for awful men."

Alice said nothing. Her temper had risen and fallen without paroxysm. Maria was right. She always found the energy and enthusiasm to do things only when massive obstacles were thrown in her way. And perhaps her impatience was keeping them in the camp more firmly than Maria's acquiescence.

The tiny, big-bellied Maria painted on impassively, her shiny hair pulled sensibly back into a rubber band. She was as sweet and perfect as a ripe glossy hazelnut that you would never dare to crack open and eat. But Alice knew that the shell of composure was made of standing waves of pure fright.

"I'm at a loss, frankly Ria, I'm really confused . . . Sometimes I look at something — it could be quite ordinary, like the crack in the plaster on the toilet wall — I look at it and suddenly I see a streaming, as if the air in front of it were wobbling, and then the wall itself is streaming and wobbling . . . and the blackness in the crack is luminous and melting . . . as if things were making and unmaking themselves at every moment, and you see, that makes me feel as if this whole place were not quite solid, as if it's connected up to our eyes, our brains in some strange way . . . "

Maria was standing stockstill, listening, but not to Alice.

"What's that?"

A faint clamour reached them from the street below, a throaty, rhythmic chanting, which came quickly closer as they listened. Alice went over to the window, pulled up the sash and stuck her head out. Maria did not move.

"It seems to be some kind of protest march," she reported. "Banners, posters, the usual sort of thing. Funny though, they all seem to be men . . . "

"Soldiers?"

"No, just ordinary men . . . hang on, shut up and let me listen, see if I can make out what they're shouting for."

Alice watched the procession make an untidy halt outside their building. Two men with red armbands were trying to orchestrate some ordered chanting.

"Out, out, out!" she deciphered. "Women *out, out, out!*"

"Women out?" she repeated. "What on earth do they want women out *of?*"

"I know," said Maria quietly.

"Jee*zus*," said Alice, "do you know what they're carrying? The wankers! A giant prick! They've made a giant prick out of papier-mâché or cardboard or something, and they're carrying it through the streets, waving it about under our noses. What a cheek!"

"Out, out, out, or we'll come and get you out," shouted the men and Alice saw two of them race into the café opposite and emerge dragging a struggling girl, to shouts of approbation from the rest.

"Christ," said Alice soberly, "this isn't funny. What are they doing? What do they want?"

"I know what they want. They want us, and revenge on us."

"But why? What have we done to them?"

"I'm frightened, Alice. I know what we've done."

Alice left the window and joined Maria, who was crouching by the gas fire. Maria stared into the fire but pointed to her stomach.

"This — what do you think this is? *This* is what we've done. Where's the father of this eh? Not around, is he? Do I ever mention him? Hardly ever. I wouldn't be surprised if he was out there too, chanting for his baby. Don't you see, Alice? We've taken their children away. We've taken ourselves away. We've made them small and unimportant. We're not even frightened of them any more. They can rape us, kill us and still we're not frightened. But they're trying to put the fear of God in us now — they're trying to get us back again!"

The chanting thickened and swelled into the drubbing beat which is usually the prelude to action. A muffled voice barked an instruction and there was a spatter of laughter and a clatter of dispersing feet.

Then a crisp knocking at their own door.

"Don't answer it!" gasped Maria as Alice started automatically to her feet.

A male voice spoke:

"Let me in. I won't hurt you. Let me in."

Neither of them breathed a word or moved a muscle.

"Look, let me in quickly! It's for your own good. If you don't open I'll come in anyway, I've got the master-key — oh, no, blow, I haven't — well, anyway I've got a knife and I'll pick the lock."

Alice began to move towards the door.

"No!" whispered Maria vehemently. "Don't! He's bluffing. Don't let him in!"

Alice froze where she was. They listened helplessly as the lock was efficiently picked. The door opened very gently. A big man in green workman's overalls walked in. His ruddy, freckled face turned this way and that as he examined the room and themselves. In his right hand was a dagger with a long tapering blade. He slammed the door shut behind him with his foot, then strode to the window and looked out. He watched the mob for a few seconds and then moved away from the window, laughing quietly to himself.

"It's all right," he said, slinging the dagger carelessly down on the table, "they won't touch you if I'm here. Have you got anything to drink at all? I'm incredibly thirsty."

114

Alice fetched the half-empty cider bottle and gave it to him. He flung his russetty, leonine head back and swigged it. They both watched him closely. Maria was thinking he looked wild and unpredictable, probably a psychopath. Alice was recognising him: it was the younger of the two lorry-drivers, the gap-toothed one who had been wearing the woolly hat the first time they had met. Alice was captivated; she had always thought that people whose hair and eyes were the same colour must have magic powers, and now she knew it to be true. Maria thought he looked unnatural, like a red-brown albino. He spoke again.

"My name's Gene. G-E-N-E, Gene. My mother deliberately gave me a bi-sexual name in case I grew up homosexual. She was an early bohemian and free-thinker. I'm the caretaker here. It's just one of my jobs. I heard your call and guessed what the trouble was. You haven't got anything to eat, have you? I forgot to have breakfast this morning and now my stomach is giving my gyp."

Alice fetched him some bread and cheese from the cupboard and Gene set about making himself a giant sandwich.

"What's going on out there? What do those men want? What will they do to the women they capture? What's that giant phallus about?" she asked, all in a rush.

"Oh, it's just something that happens every now and again. The lads get restive. They come out looking for women. Spare women, that is. They won't touch you if you're attached to someone. If you aren't they whip you away . . . "

There was a rata-tat-tat at the door. Gene leapt to his feet.

"That'll be them now. Don't worry — let me do the talking."

They heard him explaining: "yes, there's two of them, my girlfriend and her cousin from the other side of town. She's pregnant, come in to go to the clinic. Yes, she's married — her husband's a driver on the peripheral run. You can check if you like. OK? Good day to you, bye!"

He came back and crouched down by the fire with them.

"You have to be accounted for, you see. Not that they'll check. Might do if I was a smaller bloke, I suppose. But I made sure they didn't get a chance to get a good look at you. That's not a good idea, because if they like what they see they can get persistent."

Alice looked into his sleepy, russetty eyes and saw that he remembered their encounter. A hot blush suffused her whole body and a subtle throbbing started up in her vagina. He flicked his eyes away in a gentlemanly manner.

"What would they have done to us, if they'd got us?" asked Maria anxiously.

"Don't know exactly," replied Gene, fumbling in his overalls for tobacco and setting about the making of a roll-up. "Better not to know really. Maybe nothing so terrible. It's just that everything has to be in order in this place. Women must be accounted for, otherwise they get up to mischief, so they say. So they allow these bands of men to roam around and hoover up all the stragglers. You would have probably been assigned to someone, each of you. It's considered to be a social duty, to belong."

"How horrible!" said Maria.

"Oh," said Gene sleepily, "there are worse fates." His eyes picked up Alice's again and she knew, had Maria not been there, they would have been sucked towards each other and ended up copulating on the floor.

"But what about you?" asked Alice, fighting the waves of vigorous sexual longing. "What are you doing in a place like this?"

"What's a nice boy like me doing in a rum place like this?" He giggled and rumpled his hair. His eyes flickered and seemed to turn inward. Alice watched him carefully — there was an edge of intelligence in his manner which he wanted to conceal. It was as if he must protect himself at all costs from something sharp in him which had hurt him badly once.

"Well . . . which version of the truth shall I tell you? The most dramatic or the most boring? I'll start with the boring one. I'm just a caretaker, a night-watchman, some-times a driver on the peripheral run, a marginal being if you like. They need a few people like me in here to do the jobs that no-one else will do, so I'm tolerated, although I don't exactly conform. In the outside world I was a sort of rebel, not a very impressive one — a self-styled outsider, a drug-taker who reached the brink, turned back and didn't know what to do with himself having given up the idea of glorious self-destruction, . . . I can't say I'm happy here, but at least I know the ropes, I know the rules. There is no 'unknown' so there's nothing to be frightened of. Mind you, I sometimes hanker after being scared again, to know that tingle of fear that gets you by the balls and makes you feel alive, no matter what else it brings."

"Do you want to leave? Do you want to get out?"

"What for?"

"You mean you came here of your own free will?"

"Of course. Didn't you?"

"I suppose we did. But once we were in we couldn't get out, we were trapped."

Gene folded his long legs under him and stood up. He yawned.

"There's no point in discussing it. You'll learn that. Words, words, words . . . I came here to escape them. To lead a simple life, and that's what I'm doing. I don't know what you wanted, but no doubt you've got it, so what's the problem?"

Alice stared at him in amazement. She did not believe a word he was saying, but she also knew that he did not think he was lying. He stood there, a living contradiction, a fine man who claimed to be a coward and a lackey, but who was not one, whatever he said or did.

"Don't go," she said impulsively, a lump rising in her throat and sticking there so that her voice was oddly deep and resonant. "Maybe we can help each other. We *must* get out of here soon, before the baby's born. You know the place well, you know the ropes — you just said so — together we could make it, I know we could!"

"There's no point," Gene answered roughly, "that's a fool's game, a delusion . . . "

"That doesn't *matter*," Alice heard herself say with tremendous force. "I've been a fool all my life and I know that doesn't *matter*."

Gene would not look at her now. He stuffed his tobacco into his overalls pocket and stood towering above them, diffident and empty.

Alice tried to find her way back into his eyes, but he wouldn't let her.

"In other matters," he said gruffly, "I am available to you at any time. Just call me like you did to-day. Goodbye, and take it easy."

He was out of the door before she could think of any way to stop him.

"What a hero!" said Maria with heavy irony.

"Trouble with you is you don't know a good man when you see one," responded Alice bitterly. "You want men to be like women, but he can't help being big and strong and making the air sway when he walks through it. And why shouldn't he carry a dagger? After all, it came in useful, it saved us from a pretty dubious fate."

They both realised at the same moment that the dagger was still lying on the table where Gene has slung it.

"Is it the same one? The one the boy gave you in your dream?"

"It's the same *type*, I have to admit that. It's not the same *dagger*, though. The other one wasn't real."

"Was the dagger that came back to haunt Macbeth real?" snapped Alice. "Huh, anyway this is sophistry — you'll have to accept now that the dagger is a clue. We must be meant to use it in some way."

She picked it up and pressed the point against the end of her thumb. A tiny bubble of blood appeared.

"It's sharp all right," she said. "Useful for self-defence if those hyenas come back. Not that I could use it on them I suppose."

"I could," said Maria vehemently, "I could and would."

There was a quiet knock at the door. When she opened, Alice found a small girl planted outside, with dusty black hair, a very dirty face and round black eyes like pontefract cakes.

"My name is Masha," she said with haughty gravity, "and I have brought you this. I'm to wait for a reply."

The child handed her a piece of paper.

"Would you like a drink of milk or a biscuit or something?" asked Alice awkwardly. She knew little of children except they had to be fed and watered often.

"No thank you," said Masha politely, squinting up at her severely with one black eye. "I've got to go straight back. It's urgent."

Alice unfolded the paper.

'Lewis is in danger,' it read. 'You can help. Come to the

shop in the arcade. Ask for Anaxa. Please. Anaxa.'

"Who's Anaxa?" asked Alice.

"My mother," said Masha with emphasis. "We are of Russian origin. Russian-Armenian. I am three-quarters Russian. My mother is half Russian."

"But Masha, how can you be more Russian than your mother?"

"Because my father was a whole one," answered Masha smartly. "But this is wasting time."

"I'll come with you now. Just wait till I find my shoes . . ."

'I have always wanted,' thought Alice as she tied up her espadrilles, 'to have an adventure of this sort. Now it's happening I just hope I don't muck it up.'

As an afterthought she picked up the dagger and put it in her shoulderbag, folded in the old copy of 'The Guardian' they had brought with them from the outside world.

* * *

This time the door of the shop was flung wide open, the interior was discreetly and cosily lit and a young couple stood arguing over an Edwardian tea-set. The proprietor, who had been so sombre and meaningful before, lounged on a chaise longue in a floppy orange shirt with beach umbrellas on it, drinking lager from a can. He nodded pleasantly at Alice, but did not speak to her.

"Where's Anaxa?" asked Masha in the stentorian voice of little girls, who will grow up to be headmistresses.

"She's upstairs lying down," said the proprietor. "There's no-one with her. You can go up. Not you, Masha, the lady, I mean. You're to stay down here and help me for a while — there's those red beads need threading . . . "

Alice passed through the back of the shop and started up the stairs. They were steep and narrow and got creakier as she neared the top, the fifth floor, where Anaxa's room was. Her door was painted black and there was a peep-hole in it. Alice did not feel that she was being watched, so she paused to draw breath and try to pick up some sense of the atmosphere she was plunging into. It seemed to her that there was a terrible silence behind the door, the silence of dead-drunk sleep or narcotic trance, so she was taken aback when it suddenly sprang open and she was confronted by a creature vibrating with life and bright attention.

For a few seconds they just stood and stared at each other. Alice, stunned by the complete absence of any expression of welcome or greeting, felt herself devoured, ruthlessly sucked up into Anaxa's great black eyes, and could hardly find the strength left in herself to suck up any impressions of her own. She tottered slightly and Anaxa moved back to let her in. Without speaking she showed her guest to a low, rumpled sofa. Then she stood quite still in Alice's line of vision and let herself be looked at for quite a while.

She was one of those women irresistably attractive to men and often positively repulsive to women. Her hair was black, dull and dusty like a blackbird's wing, her face was stone-white, her lips red and her dark eyes ringed with smudges of kohl. Her skin was clammy, luminescent, as if she had not washed for a day or two, and she wore nothing but a flimsy Chinese dressing-gown which was ripped all down one side so that some scrawny ribs and a blue-shadowed flank were visible. Around her neck was a heavy silver chain and another chain of the same sort was wrapped around one grubby ankle. She could have been anything from sixteen to forty years old, and she held herself in front of Alice with perfect stillness until the latter's eyes had had their fill. Then she smiled, a wicked, piratical smile, that revealed a mouth full of small milky teeth, of which one of the front-central pair was missing. Alice gulped a big draught of air down into her belly and sighed. She was utterly disarmed and fascinated, and also, very faintly but surely, scared out of her wits.

"You'll have some tea and whisky." It was a command not an invitation. The voice that spoke it was husky and hit a note that resonated uncomfortably somewhere in Alice's pelvic region. While her hostess disappeared into the shadows to fetch refreshments Alice looked around the room. A heavy throat-catching incense was burning, which just about managed to drown the smell of sweat and sex that hung in the air. The windows were masked with heavy lace cream curtains so that the atmosphere was crepuscular although it was only mid-afternoon. By the window was an enormous low bed covered with cushions and rugs in all colours of red and pink and orange. The floor was carpeted with more cushions, rugs and cast-off items of clothing, all in shades of red or gold or black.

"It's like being under water being in here," said Alice.

"I don't like the daylight very much. I like to keep my skin white."

"Oh," said Alice faintly.

"I shall be frank with you," said Anaxa, setting a large tumbler half-full of whisky and a tiny glass of Russian tea in front of Alice, "I am not yet impressed by what I see of you. Your outline is too blurry for my liking, but of course it's likely that you'll tighten up with use."

There was a silence while Anaxa drained her own glass of whisky and poured herself another, and Alice, flushed with wounded irritation, wondered if she should just get up and leave.

"Listen, don't mind me," Anaxa began again. "I don't mean to be insulting. I don't mean that I don't like you when I say I'm not impressed — it's something quite different — you'll see when I begin. Have some more whisky — there's no need to be sober for the moment, is there?"

Anaxa lit a cigarette and lolled back on the bed, curling her waxy-white legs up under her.

"Lewis is in danger," she began, "and since you could say that it was us, you and I, I mean, who drove him to it in our different ways, I thought that we should get together and try to save him. It's not allowed of course, but I don't care a fig for that, — I've already had just about all the come-uppance I can have — but I can't do it on my own. It can only be done if you are willing. What do you say?"

"Well, I'd really need to know a lot more about it," said Alice, hearing her own voice sound staid and sensible and hating it. "I mean, what kind of danger is it exactly that he's in? How do you think that I can help you? How did you know who I was or how to get hold of me?"

"He talked about you once. You sounded powerful. Which is why I was disappointed when I saw you just now. Then I asked Thomas — he's the man who keeps the shop downstairs — if he knew you and he did. That sealed it. I knew you were the one for me. Oh, and I did the cards — a fair woman came up. I'm looking for a warrior, you see. That's something I can't be myself. You understand?"

"No." But looking at Anaxa's white, much-used body nestling amongst the cushions, she suddenly did. "What are you anyway? Are you a prostitute?"

Anaxa betrayed no repugnance at the suggestion.

"Not exactly. I have no objection to doing it for money, though it has to be a lot. But there is usually somebody who's willing to keep me, so I don't have to go out and look for it. I like sex. I prefer to do it just for the sake of it, not for money. My real gift is that I have no shame. I find out what they really want, what it is they've enacted in their deepest, darkest fantasies, and I give it to them."

Alice remembered: the dark woman with the whip. The photograph on Lewis's dressing-table. She shrank from making the connection, but it was inescapable: Anaxa was that woman, that degraded and degrading woman.

"You see, I'm what they call a man's woman," continued Anaxa. "I know them, I manipulate them, I understand them, I forgive them. Nothing is alien to me. That's an anathema for you of course, the modern woman" — here there was a note of derision in her voice — "but then you know very little, you work always from your head, not your guts, your heart."

"So what's Lewis's thing then?" cut in Alice harshly, wanting to bring a fresh hurt crashing down on her head, to drown the nauseating pain already there.

"Nothing unusual," said Anaxa easily. "He needs there to be some pain. His own, someone else's, doesn't make much difference."

"You mean he's a sado-masochist?"

"Big words for little things."

"Does he pay you?"

"He did at first. Then I wouldn't let him. That's when the trouble started. Oh, Alice," Anaxa uncurled her white limbs and reached out for the whisky bottle, "don't you see what happened? You, his sister, his Beatrice, his pure angel, you turned out to want his body too. You wanted fucking. And why not? You are a woman not a plaster saint. And I, his whore, his angel of despair, I wouldn't take his money. I began to love him. Between us we've squeezed him, driven him out of his hole into the wilderness, cut off his escape routes, pushed him to the brink of desperation!"

"Just because, in our different ways, we loved him?"

"You find it disgusting?"

"I don't understand. This whole world is strange to me. It feels . . . evil."

"Good. I'm glad you feel that, it shows you have some powers of discrimination. Lewis doesn't. He doesn't *know*. He doesn't know about where things lead, the inner connections. He is frightened, but deep down he thinks that it will be all right, that there is no price to be paid. He's like a child who thinks all will be forgiven, that his mummy and daddy will take care of everything. And so he throws himself away! If we don't go to pick him up, no-one else will, he will drift out of our reach."

"I'm sure he doesn't *want* us to help him."

"So? It makes no difference. We can do it just the same. Now I must get ready. Drink more whisky while I am dressing."

She stood up and slid off her dressing-gown. Her body was silvery-white, soft, so soft that Alice felt if she poked her the impression would linger in her flesh. She fished amongst the debris on the floor and pulled out black tights, a black leather skirt and waistcoat. Slowly she put them on, concentrating totally on the act of dressing. Alice knew it would be wrong to speak to her now. Finally she sat down on a stool and began to paint her nails silver.

"You remember the party at the Aquarium?" she began. "I heard that you were there. Did you notice anything strange about it?"

"Only that everyone ignored us."

"Yes, of course, they would. And you should be glad they did. On the surface it was an ordinary party, wasn't it? A few gay men, a few sexy-games, booze, dope, fancy dress — the usual circus. That was all that you would see. But the party was going on at other levels too. Other things were happening of which you knew nothing. The party was an opening, an opportunity, a market place for all the worlds, where you could, if you knew the right people, the right words to say, buy any sort of experience, an entrée to any sort of reality you wanted."

"If you were willing to pay the price?"

"Exactly," said Anaxa. Her muddy eyes clarified and sparkled for a moment. "Now, some people are safe in such places. I am. I move between the levels, but I have my boundaries, my safety-nets. I can smell the worst dangers and avoid them. Masha keeps me anchored. I have to come back for her. And besides, I have few appetites myself, except for alcohol. You, on the other hand, were protected by your innocence. Not that it couldn't be corrupted . . . "

"What was being bought and sold at the party I didn't see?"

"Better not to know. Better not to think of it. But now, to business! You are a warrior, albeit an incompetent one. Are you prepared to kill?"

"Kill whom?"

"Not Lewis. Whomsoever it might be necessary to kill in order to rescue him."

"He is held prisoner then?"

"I don't know. I only know he has disappeared. After the party, after the night he spent with you. There are not many places to run to in this camp — I have my suspicions. We will find out tonight. But once again I have to ask you: are you prepared to kill?"

"I don't know. I've never been asked before."

"You must do it for Lewis, for love of him. Without hope of course of possessing him or pleasing him. And you must remember, if you do not kill when it is necessary, then you yourself will be destroyed. It's not something to be undertaken lightly. I only ask you because I believe you *are* a warrior, because I *see* you are one, in spite of the blurry edges. Are you prepared to do it?"

"I don't know," said Alice again, her bowels quivering with fear, excitement or arousal, she didn't know which. "And I don't know that I do love Lewis any more. I had decided to give him up, forget him. What you have told me about him makes me feel even more that way. It disgusts me, upsets me . . . "

"Don't go on. I don't want to hear your explanations. I only want to see your actions. Listen, tonight I am dancing in a club — a bit like the Aquarium, a between-worlds sort of place. If you come I will know you have decided to do it. Then my dance will help you understand. You see, sometimes I dance pure and beautiful" — here she rose and shimmied across the room — "like a temple dancer, dedicating my power, my sexuality to God. Then sometimes, I break the bowl and I dance like this" — here she put her arms above her head and propelled herself back across the room by way of vigorous pelvic thrusts which nearly caused her breasts to jump out of their tight bodice. "That's to show them the way to hell. But I only *show*, I do not drag them there. Those who understand know *all* my dance is sacred. Those who do not presume I am a common whore. But I just do my job, something which must be done. Messengers are needed to run between the worlds, and I am safe in these dreary wildernesses, I never lose my bearings. And you too will be safe, if you stay with me. It is the best place to find news of Lewis too. I have a mole in there who will take us to him."

Anaxa grew abstracted as she spoke. Alice sensed she was already drifting away to somewhere other, or perhaps it was just the effect of the alcohol . . . she drew her stool up in front of an oval mirror draped with red and gold scarves and heavy silver jewellery and began painting her eyes. Alice watched closely, being interested in the art, but soon found her eyes floating off Anaxa, into the gloomy, twilight room. The dark air shimmered in the mirror, not knowing whether to go or to stay, like water in a sunlit swimming-pool, which invites you to dive into it and be lost forever. Yes, the air was like water; if you passed through the glass and got there, through to the other side of the mirror, you could surely swim and float and fly . . .

The visitor from inside the mirrors? 'It is Anaxa of course,' though Alice. 'Now I have found her, I suppose I must do whatever she says.'

* * *

CHAPTER SEVEN

The Lost Boy

CHAPTER SEVEN

Alice sat in the night-club and thought about Lewis. Around her parties of businessmen loosened their ties and drank champagne with hostesses in cut-away swimsuits and spiked heels. She sat on her own at the prominent front-row table where Anaxa had placed her, in the sailor-suit which Anaxa had instructed her to wear. In her bag was the dagger, still wrapped in the old copy of "The Guardian". She sat on her own with her legs neatly crossed and a crisp expression on her face which she was borrowing from Maria. She sipped orange juice and thought of Lewis.

She shuddered. Her hands were icy although the club was very warm, steamy with odours of alcohol, richly perfumed sweat and sexual stirrings. She did not want to feel for Lewis, it was not sensible. She had decided she must cut herself off from him or be destroyed.

But tonight her 'common-sense' decision seemed to have become irrelevant. She was in a hell of tumbling, tumultuous passions and pains, all detached from their owners and originators and waltzing around blindly like drunken phantoms at some hideous occasion of debauchery. 'I can't bear it,' she thought. 'I can't bear to love a man who has nothing to give me and I can't bear to abandon him. I can't bear to live in a world without him, and I can't bear to give my heart up to be broken on the wheel.' A wave of panic rippled through her — if only she could cry, but she was sitting at a table in a public night-club and she couldn't. But the ripple gathered power and rose into a tidal wave of agony, towering over her, just about to crash down upon her head . . . Then a voice spoke out within her. "Wait a minute, Alice," it said. "Before you let that tidal wave break over you. Have you ever thought of trying an experiment? Why don't you just stop bothering about what you feel and try paying attention to the world out there? It's not *necessary* to waste your energy in terrible suffering you know. Suffering is entirely optional. Then you might be able to relax and do whatever it is you have to do."

Timorously Alice relaxed her body. The nightmare wave fell back short of her and fizzled away. She was left feeling empty, sad, but dry-eyed and oddly calm. The glorious vehemence had gone. A glow remained. She looked then for the terror, the apprehension. It was still there but had concentrated and hardened to a razor's edge of steel upon which perilously and yet securely her consciousness was resting. She took a deep breath and looked around her. A few curious eyes tried to meet hers but she swept them away and carried on looking. A plump, motherly hostess, ridiculous in the scanty uniform but there doubtless to cater to those appetites greedy for great scoops of milky flesh, caught her eye and came up to her.

"You all right dear? Waiting for someone, are you? I can sit down with you for a couple of minutes if you like. You don't have to buy me a drink or anything."

"I'm OK," said Alice, feeling the tears flood back into her eyes at the woman's kindness. "I'm a friend of Anaxa's. I've come to see her dance . . . " but the brave soldier could not hold out any longer; fat, hot, babyish tears began to trickle down her cheeks. The hostess sat down and fished a tissue out of her cleavage.

There was an abrasive jingle-jangle from behind the bead curtain on the stage, and, as Alice looked up, mopping her tears, Anaxa stalked out onto the platform and stood staring unsmilingly into the audience. She stood, her knees slightly bent and her bare feet apart, moving her eyes round from one group to the next, skipping Alice, but otherwise leaving no-one out until she had stared at and subdued every person in the room. Then she began, very slowly, to move her hips, in a subtle, flowing sideways movement which gradually gathered momentum and rocked her into more vigorous action, swirling her pelvis around into bowls, garlands, figures-of-eight, flicking her hips up and out, shimmying and shuddering her belly, all the time watching the punters, fixing them with a cold, haughty, impersonal stare. To Alice this was most strange — she had expected the performance to be stirring, erotic, but it was actually chilling! Anaxa swirled, turned round and round on her own dead centre, hinting at depths, channels, funnels and tunnels which would lead deep down to realms of endless pleasure, but she was hinting and denying, yielding and then barring the way, conveying her own ecstacy but pointing out in a none too subtle way that it required no-one else to arouse or satisfy it.

Then the dance changed. Now she was putting out, now she was giving in — come on, come on you bastards, take me — come on, come on you bastards, give me what I want! She jerked her pubis upwards, she spurted across the stage towards a group of men seated as close as they could be to it. She bent down and shook her breasts at them. She pulled back and angled her pelvis at them, as she ground it round and round, wriggling every few turns as if with spasms of pleasure. One of them reached his hands out and touched her leg. She jumped smartly back, laughing, and carried on.

Alice did not know where to look. She was aroused and embarrassed, and hoped nobody was watching her and noticing. The kindly hostess had wandered off to continue her duties after giving Alice a pat on the hand. She was alone, exposed. She truly felt as if she were in an anteroom of hell.

She stood up abruptly and made her way to the Ladies. When she looked in the mirror she could hardly recognise herself. She had put on pale make-up to hide her normally wholesome complexion and tied her hair back as neatly and severly as she could, but it was not these superficial changes that astonished her. It was the look in her eyes — fierce, serious, austere, a look she had never seen in herself before, a look that frightened her. There was something of the implacable warrior in it, something that would make you hesitate to cross her path too lightly. Where on earth had it come from?

When she got back to the table Anaxa was sitting at it, wrapped in a great black cloak. She smelt musky and musty, but that was not unpleasant to Alice, in fact she felt a rush of unconditional warmth for her companion. She knew she was in good hands somehow.

"I didn't notice any sacred bit," she said, with an effort at lightness.

"I wasn't feeling in a holy mood tonight."

"No. So where do we go from here?"

"My spies tell me he's gone underground."

"Literally or metaphorically?"

"Under the earth, I mean. I'm not given to poetic phrases. There's a whole city down there, almost an empire. Some people live down there all the time, some just pay a visit when there's something they want. You pay a price for entrance, unless you're a messenger like me. They tolerate me because I'm necessary, but they won't want you in. They don't like rescuers — they call it 'interfering with another's fate' — and they'd probably make you pay twice over, if they caught you. But they aren't going to catch you, I'll see to that. I'll pay the price if necessary."

"What kind of price? What kind of things go on down there?"

"Oh, you have to sign a paper handing over your will and agreeing to let them extract a recompense equal to the value of the pain or pleasure you've requested. Some people just want a bit of naughtiness — then the price is not high — but some of the things that go on down there are really heavy, really vile I mean. They turn your stomach. Of course, I won't sign any paper, but if they find out what we've done they'll make me pay anyway. But who cares? Maybe they won't find out. Let's move on to practicalities: I'm going to get a big hat and a cloak so that you can pass as a boy. My guess is that Lewis isn't with women down there and it would be difficult for us to make contact with him as women."

"But I'll never pass as a boy! I'm too curvy."

"You wouldn't up here, but you will down there! People don't see clearly, they see what they want or what they're told. Soon as I tell them you're a boy, they'll believe it. Just act shy and dumb and nervous if anyone talks to you. As well you might be if I was really taking you down for such purposes," she ended grimly.

"It sounds like a terrible place. Why has Lewis gone there?"

"It's terrible. But it's also fascinating. Just you remember that everyone down there has *chosen* what's happening to them — don't feel sorry for them, don't get involved. If you do, you're lost. That applies to Lewis too. I don't know why he's gone there. Looking for something I suppose. Not mine to reason why. But I have my fears and I

132

have my suspicions, so we'd better get going or we might be too late."

"Too late?" Alice repeated.

"I mean he might have gone in too deep for us to follow. Now practicalities: have you got your knife and are you prepared to use it if you must.

"Yes, I have, and yes, I think I am."

"Good. let's go and get you a cloak and find an entrance to the place. They're changing all the time, but I've got a pretty good idea where there will be one tonight . . . you can tell when you're near because you feel a kind of buzzing in your pelvis, as if someone was running a chain-saw in the room under your feet . . . "

★ ★ ★

Alice wrapped her cloak firmly around herself against the artificial chill. They were standing in a pink-carpeted, blank-walled corridor, the hum of the air-conditioning in their ears. It reminded her of the BBC in Manchester, which she had visited once with a film director friend who was trying to get her work in the costume department. The entrance had been hidden behind an old fridge in some poor woman's kitchen. It seemed her husband was a "punter" and had "gone under" for a month's break. His "price" had been to have the entrance in his house for a month. Alice thought this was most unfair to his wife, but Anaxa pointed out wearily that in this game there were no innocents. Now Alice was registering a most disturbing sensation: the buzzing which had swept them so easily into the underworld had turned into an insistent, melodious throbbing in the region of her genitals. She felt as if the lips of her vulva were becoming gigantic, swollen and moist. She could feel the ripe, juicy walls of her vagina rubbing against each other as she shifted her weight from one leg to the other. The sensation was agonisingly pleas-urable, and was building up to a point that would demand release. Her heart began to beat wildly, as if she were about to be penetrated in some cosmic act of sex.
sex.

"You didn't tell me about this!" she said.

Anaxa glanced at her flushed cheeks and gasped.

"I'd forgotten! I'm so used to it. Right, before we get into trouble, listen! Concentrate on your breathing, watch your breath come in and out. Imagine that it's coming down, right into your vagina, taking the energy up and out, by way of your heart, and then your head. Got that? Now try it. Remember that it's the energy you'll have to use when it comes to the crunch with Lewis, and if you squander it in sexual fantasy it won't be there to help you when you need it. OK?"

Alice closed her eyes and tried. It was not so difficult after the initial struggle to forget the imminent possibility of sexual release, and after a while it felt as if a channel had opened up between her genitals and her heart which was feeding the rest of her body with a kind of radiant energy, a secret heat. When they set off again she felt she was gliding even floating, not walking along the rose-pink floor.

There were doors on either side of the corridor, ordinary office doors with reinforced glass panels in them. Alice was wondering what was going on beyond them, when Anaxa stopped and peered through one. After a couple of seconds she drew back, chuckling and stepped aside to let Alice take a look. Behind a very large, empty desk, a man was sitting with a plump girl on his knee. She wore a tight black ciré dress with a low-cut, boned bodice, over which her ample breasts were flowing. The long slit up the side of the dress revealed suspenders and a stripe of white thigh before the black stockings they held up began. The girl's head was buried in the man's neck while his left hand was burrowing into the white flesh of the thigh, evidently trying to push the dress up over her hips. But it was very tight and was not yielding easily to persuasion. His other hand was uncomfortably strained over one of the girl's shoulders, occasionally managing to knead a breast when the position allowed it. Alice burst out laughing too.

"Don't they mind being watched?"

"I suppose that's part of the fantasy."

"But it's just like a cartoon out of 'Playboy'!"

"Of course! It's sad, isn't it? Some people have so little imagination. And remember, it has to be *her* fantasy too . . . yes, this sort of thing is typical at this level. Pretty feeble stuff really. Makes you laugh more than anything.

It's a different cup of tea down at level seven, I can tell you."

"Which level will Lewis be on?"

"I don't know. No lower than level five, I hope, but I fear he's gone in fairly deep. He'd be anxious to avoid the ludicrous, you see."

"But why are we rescuing him? Surely he'll just come out when he's had enough, even if he has to pay the price."

"From level five downwards the pull is terribly strong. Few people leave once they've gone that far. Of course it can be done, but it takes a super-human effort, and often some kind of intercession, I mean intervention, from the surface world. Anyway, let's get to the gallery and find my spy. There's no point in subjecting ourselves to unnecessary stimulus and temptation."

As they headed inwards they began to meet other people; some ordinary-looking except that they either kept their eyes cast down or swept them around ravenously with no shame or moderation; some cloaked and anonymous; some, who seemed to have authority in the place, dressed in black leather with chains, pistols and whips hanging about them. Everyone walked fast and purposefully. There was no conversation or laughter. Alice took Anaxa's arm and whispered "Why the chains, the whips? Surely there are no laws down here to be enforced?"

"Ninety percent of people's fantasies are punitive," said Anaxa wearily. "Punishing or being punished. In various hilarious or gruesome ways. The guards are part of it. People still want the hackneyed black-leather bit."

They walked on. Eventually they came to a gigantic revolving door made of glass and whirled through it to find themselves in a space that reminded Alice of the top gallery of the Royal Albert Hall. Here the atmosphere was more social — people strolled aound in twos and threes drinking coffee and chattering, for all the world like a concert-interval audience. Anaxa explained that it was the main meeting-place for all the levels, a place for recuperation between 'experiences'.

"But don't worry," she added, "level one is pretty innocuous, even though the other levels use it as a breathing-space and hunting ground. You can see the whole range of punters with their gloves off here."

Indeed Alice was obliged to forget her 'eyes down policy. The naked faces surrounding her were just too fascinating to ignore. It was like being at a party where everyone else was very drunk and indiscreet while you were clear-headed and sober. Women who, in the upper world might have been idealistic social workers or teachers, walked around flaunting themselves in tee-shirts which barely covered their buttocks, or swathed in towels which fell open to reveal more than they covered. Their faces showed that they knew exactly what they were doing, and that they were enjoying it.

"You're allowed to show but not do out here," commented Anaxa, "just in case you hadn't guessed."

And the men! Men who in the surface world no doubt wore suits or jogged in earnest jogging gear had allowed their fantasy to flower quite freely — they wore frocks, make-up, silk dressing gowns or velvet pantaloons. One big hairy man was in a nappy, smoking a cigarette and talking to another man who was naked except for his flat cap and walking boots with thick, speckled socks.

"Don't laugh!" said Anaxa firmly in her ear. "They'll throw us straight away if they think we're not participants."

"It's wonderful!" said Alice, fighting back the tears of laughter.

"Everything that lives is wonderful, but this sort of wonderfulness wears thin after a while, I can tell you!"

She pushed the limp, astonished Alice to the edge of the gallery where the actual size of the place confronted them for the first time. As she looked over the edge, the galleries beneath her seemed to swirl around, boring down into the earth in a calamitous spiral. The hall was very high or deep depending from where you looked at it, but it was also very narrow so that you were not very far away from the people hanging over the rails on the opposite side. On the floor, far below, Alice could make out a fountain and one or two greyish figures flitting about.

"They look like shadows," she said.

"They are," replied Anaxa shortly.

The place seemed light and dark at the same time; when you looked across any distance the air in front of you was smoky, irridescent, and it was difficult to focus, to penetrate the glittery fog. And as you stood on the floor you could feel the mighty throb of the place vibrating upwards through your legs. It took a strong effort of will and concentration to let the energy run through and out instead of letting it collect in the loins and build up into a delicious unbearable tension. Alice was beginning to understand how the place worked and why people stayed there instead of going home to do their duty and control their passions.

While Anaxa scanned the other galleries for her 'spy', Alice turned back to sneak another look at the denizens of level one, and found a large black man standing in her line of vision, staring fixedly at her. He was naked, his body was oiled and shining, and his penis hung half-erect between powerful footballer's thighs. Alice felt the lips of her vagina swell and bump together. It was difficult to resist such a direct stimulus. She allowed her eyes to travel up to his face. His eyes were already penetrating her. She felt hot and loose. She wanted to go up to him, put her hands around him and knead his undoubtedly magnificent buttocks.

Then she felt a sharp jap in her ribs and Anaxa's cool lips were gabbling in her ear.

"Don't be stupid, Alice! Remember, he thinks you are a boy! He wouldn't be interested in what you have to offer . . ."

Alice flung her eyes down and turned back to Anaxa. She was trembling. It was so difficult to keep control.

"Trouble is," she said miserably, "at this rate I'm going to smell like a bitch on heat."

But the black man was not so easily put off. He tapped Anaxa politely on the shoulder.

"You a chaperone, lady, or what?"

"I am," said Anaxa running her eyes up and down his body with cold amusement. "He's promised, I'm afraid. A juicy morsel for the kings of level five. Bought and paid for. I'm sure you wouldn't want to interfere."

"Sure enough," said the black man, laughing good-naturedly. "I just hope the little bunny knows what he's in for with those guys."

"He does," said Anaxa tersely, and he loped away, rubbing his hands on his glossy, hard-muscled rump as he went.

"Bunny?" said Alice.

"Don't bother your pretty little head about it. Ah, here comes my spy. Look relaxed. Don't look like a conspirator."

The 'spy' was a skinny man in a mohair suit the colour of weak tea and a complexion the colour of stewed veal. He slung his arms around Anaxa in a nonchalent, brotherly gesture.

"Found him," he said. "Or it sounds like him. Heard two old tarts talking — new meat on level five."

"Thank God it's five, not six," said Anaxa. "I was praying. I've been to six once and I could hardly move in it, but five is workable."

"People can be moved," said the man glumly.

"So we'd better move. Can you tell us more?"

"I think he's been bought by a party of old poofters, so those tarts were saying — not nice boys I'm afraid. Into the heavy stuff. But they can't have done much damage so far, they'll want him to last a while."

"You mean they're going to kill him?" Alice chipped in horrified.

"It depends what he wants," said Anaxa, "but the trouble with this place is that you can't hide what you really want. You get it anyway. I think we'd better get going. Any other notes, Paul?"

"There's a deep levels party on level six tonight, should last until about four. Now it's possible they'll have taken him with them to show him off. But they *might* be keeping him at home as a kind of treat for later on. And if that's the case, you might get to him before they come back. But then you'd have to wait and get a key off one of them and God knows how you'd do that."

"We'll kill the buggers if necessary," said Anaxa matter-of-factly.

The man flapped his jacket to cool himself off.

"Hot in here tonight. I'm going off duty now, so I think I'll have a little indulge, if you don't mind. Good luck and excuse me, ladies."

"Is he a messenger too?" asked Alice after he had gone. "Or a punter?"

"He's a messenger, but he has a weakness for gossip, and

138

sometimes he has to pretend to be a punter to get information out of people."

But Alice had stopped listening. She was thinking of Lewis, bruised, bleeding, degraded, locked up in some filthy cell. She was struggling to understand why he wanted to have such things done to him. 'Thanatos,' she thought. 'Eros and Thanatos. He wants to be broken down, destroyed, flung against a wall, torn into shreds and little pieces. Burst like a boil. He wants to die, she thought and Bernard, my brother wanted to live. He will be thwarted, just as Bernard was. Bernard, Bernie. Try to reach me from wherever you are. Protect me from all this filth and sin. Deliver me from evil . . . '

They stepped out of the lift and into level five. There was dead silence in the corridor. Even the hum of the air-conditioning was gone. Alice felt immediately drowsy and heavy in her limbs. She supposed it was the 'atmosphere' that Anaxa had been talking about. She resolved to conserve her energy.

"They're all at the party!" Anaxa was saying. "That's a stroke of luck for us. Come on, let's find the lock-ups."

Anaxa strode down the corridor peering into rooms or pushing doors open like an angry schoolmistress looking for an errant boy. Alice tried half-heartedly to glimpse what was behind the doors. In one room she caught sight of a boy strapped face down over a swing contraption, so that his buttocks were presented to two men who stood idly pushing him backwards and forwards while smoking cigarettes.

"That's what's called 'having a fag'," said Anaxa callously.

"It's horrible!" said Alice.

"Keep your powder dry. Harden yourself. It's nothing to what we might see. Don't look, Alice, it will only weaken you. Hang onto your knife and concentrate on breathing."

She set off down the corridor again, decisive as an avenging angel. Alice followed, head down, eyes fixed on her grey boots as they marched along the floor.

"Aha," said Anaxa suddenly, "this smells promising!"

She walked right into one of the rooms, holding the door open for Alice. It was a drab, square classroom with a blackboard at one end and a few ink-stained school desks clustered at the other. It smelt of ink and chalk and boys' sweat. In the corner opposite the desks was a green door with a big iron key sticking out of its lock.

"It all seems to come down to the schoolroom, with these men," said Anaxa. She flicked her pearly blackbird hair back from her face and Alice saw that for the first time she was frightened.

"You're frightened, Anaxa."

"Yes. This is not my element."

"Nor mine."

"I think he's near here. I can smell him in the air."

"My heart feels very cold and heavy."

"What's that on the board?"

"Latin. I can't make it out. I only did 'O' level."

"I suppose we should unlock the door."

"Uhu."

"We mustn't let the languour overtake us. Let's go. Be very quiet now."

Gently Anaxa turned the key in the lock and eased the door open. They found themselves in a narrow corridor on either side of which were barred cells. The silence beyond the door was even deeper than that outside, and it was deathly cold. In the first two cells there was no-one. In the third, on the left-hand side, they could make out a figure crumpled agains the far wall. They stood patiently, waiting for their eyes to get used to the dim light. The first thing to burn into Alice's retina was the glow of his silvery-gold hair. Then she could make out that he was sitting on the ground hugging his knees, his face buried in them, rocking himself backwards and forwards. 'Just like the child in the cellar," she thought. 'Crying and crying and nobody comes and then he gives up and rocks himself to death . . . .'

He was wearing just a pair of ragged jeans, and she could discern weals with crusty scabs on his back, a patch of dried blood on his fair hair. She turned to Anaxa who was already looking away. She took her arm and steered her back into the schoolroom.

They sat on the desks and brought out their cigarettes. Both their hearts were pumping wildly. Alice had never shared an emotion so completely with another human

140

being, not even Bernard's girlfriend the night he died when they had wept in each other's arms. They smoked their cigarettes in silence.

"Right!" said Anaxa.

"Right!" said Alice.

"The plan is: you should wait here until someone comes. I'll hide in an empty cell, in case you need help, but you'll basically have to manage it on your own. Let's pray to God that just one of them comes. I they come mob-handed we're all lost. You tell him, whoever he is, that you're Lewis's brother. Don't worry about the disguise not being too convincing — down at this level people see what they want to see, and once you've said it there will be no problem. Tell him you've come with a message for Lewis. He won't like that but, with any luck, the idea of two brothers will turn him on. Then hopefully he'll want to lock you up with Lewis, while he goes to tell his cronies. You'll have to get him the moment he opens up, but before he locks you in. Stab him in the back or the neck. It's the only way. OK?"

There was a long silence while Alice tried to visualise the action and her part in it.

"I don't think I can do it, Anaxa."

"You must."

"I couldn't live with myself if I killed another human being."

"But all you will be doing is to provide the blade upon which he will impale himself! At another level, he wants it, he's probably asked for it in fact."

"I don't believe that stuff. It's like saying people choose to starve to death in the third world. I can't do it."

"Then Lewis must be sacrificed."

"*No!*"

"That's the way it is. Those are the rules of the game."

"But supposing you don't play the game? Can't we just threaten the man and tie him up?"

"That won't work, Alice. If he senses any softness he will outwit us. He will prefer to die, rather than be humiliated by women like us."

"Surely there's another way!"

"Like what?"

"I don't know, but maybe something will come to me."

Alice took the long knife out of her bag and ran her thumb down the blade. It was definitely a knife that intended itself to be used. She imagined how easily it would sink into soft, unexpecting flesh.

"Perhaps I don't love him enough."

"Perhaps not."

"I would have killed to save my brother."

"Your brother?"

"My brother's dead, there was no way I could save him, but I would have killed to save him, if I could have . . . oh my mind is getting cloudy, I don't know what I'm saying. What shall we do?"

"The atmosphere is getting to you. Save your strength. All we can do is to leave it to chance. Do as I've told you up to the stabbing part. Maybe you will be able to do it after all, or maybe something else will come to you."

"It can't be right, to kill somebody in cold blood, it can't be right . . . "

The conversation died and they sat and waited in silence. Anaxa picked split ends off her hair; Alice prayed to her dead brother and tried to still her beating heart.

But they were not taken unawares when they heard the jangle of keys in the corridor: Anaxa slipped quickly behind the green door and Alice locked it after her. She was turning to face the other door when it opened.

The man who entered was not the jack-booted, iron-muscled torturer that she had been expecting. He was a plump, fortyish character dressed in crumpled oatmeal-coloured suit with soft viyella shirt and tweedie tie slightly loosened at the neck. He twirled the keys nonchalently on one chubby forefinger and looked for all the world like the genial host of a late-night TV chat show. His cheerful intelligent eyes registered mild surprise at Alice's presence. She felt hot and foolish. There must be some mistake — maybe this was not the jailer but a kindly, sensible administrator come to release Lewis and send him home to bed. Apologetic, explanatory phrases bumbled behind her lips, but she repressed them. She would let him speak first.

"Can I help you?" he asked, advancing towards her tentatively like a considerate bank-manager towards a nervous client.

"I'm Lewis's brother," she said. "I believe you're keep-

142

ing him here. I've brought him a message from his mother."

"I see. If you give me the message, I will be glad to pass it on."

"I'd like to talk to him in person, if you don't mind."

"Ah, well, that could be difficult. Sit down a minute and let me explain something to you." He put his arm on her shoulder and led her gently back to the desks where she and Anaxa had been sitting. "What's your name, if you don't mind me asking?"

"Al," said Alice throatily.

"Well, look, Al, I'm afraid it's not as simple as you think, to give a message to your brother. You see, he's been a very, very bad boy and at the moment he's being punished for it. In solitary confinement. Now, that might sound very harsh to you, but the thing is that Lewis has actually *asked* to be punished. He's even agreed as to what the punishment should be, and signed a paper consenting to it. So you can imagine that he would be very cross indeed to have his punishment interrupted by a visit from his brother. After all, that would mean he'd have to start it all again right from the beginning, wouldn't it?"

"But I must see him! My mother will kill me if I don't. I promised!" Alice felt genuine tears of panic and terror rising in her eyes. This turn of events was completely unexpected. That they should be defeated by bland, smooth reasoning was too absurd.

"Supposing I was prepared to share his punishment?" she said suddenly. "Supposing I signed the paper too? Would you let me see him then?"

The man drew a little away and studied her. Alice knew he scented something false about her and was trying to work out what it was. She could sense that he was puzzled by what he saw in her eyes, something that would not be present in the eyes of a boy of the age that she was supposed to be. And yet he smelt no actual threat in her. She must hope that his curiosity would outweight his wariness, that he would rationalise away his unease and let her in.

"All right," he said finally. "I'll lock you up with Lewis while I go and fetch the contract. But once you're in the cell there's no going back. Do you understand?"

"Yes, of course," said Alice, gripping the dagger tightly

within her bag.

He led the way through to the cells, his podgy body swaying confidently. At Lewis's door he jangled the keys playfully against the bar. Lewis looked up. In the dim light Alice could not see the expression on his face, and doubted whether he could see that she was there.

"Well, Louie-Louie, your little brother's come to visit. What do you think of that? Come and say hello."

Lewis rose to his feet and came unsteadily to the cell-door. He held Alice's eyes for a moment and then cast his down. His face was streaked with dirt, his eyes were filmy, half-open, as if he were drugged or dreaming. Blood from the wound in his head had dripped down his neck and dried on the golden chain he wore round it. They had had to cut Bernard's chain off after he died, because the fastening was broken.

"Oh no," Lewis was saying quietly, "Oh no, no, no, no, no . . ."

The fat man was watching them closely. Alice felt she must speak.

"I've got a message for you, from our mother." She stopped and coughed, her throat was full of phlegm. "Something she wanted you to know before you go . . . or whatever. If this gentleman will let me in I can tell you. I'd rather tell you on my own."

Lewis stood stockstill. A tear trickled from his eye down his dirty cheek.

"Why did you come? Now they'll get you too. What was the point? This is terrible, terrible, terrible . . . "

The jailer must have been intrigued by their mutual distress because he began slowly to unlock the cell, pushed Alice in and came in after her. The three of them stood in a wary triangle: Lewis swaying, shaking his head as if trying to wake up from a bad dream; the fat man watching as an epicurean cat watches a struggling bird; Alice, battling not to succumb to her pity for Lewis, trying to keep awake.

Lewis staggered backwards and sat down heavily on the floor. The fat man went over to him, bent down to tilt his face up. Alice sidled sideways, to put herself between him and the door.

"What's the matter, honey?" he was saying to Lewis. "This is the first time I've seen you crying. This is what you wanted, isn't it? And now you'll have your little brother to keep you company. That will liven things up a bit now, won't it?"

"OK, give me the keys!"

Alice looked round to see whose strong steady voice had spoken. It was her own. The dagger was out, in front of her, pointing at the fat man.

"And don't shout! You make a noise and you're dead immediately. Don't think I'll hesitate to use this thing."

The fat man stood up and turned to face her. He smiled, as if delighted and amused at the turn events had taken.

"I see," he said softly. "A rescuer. How exciting. Does your little brother know what happens to rescuers when they're caught down here, which they always are of course, Lewis? Does he know the price they have to pay?"

Lewis shook his head.

"Come on! Give me the keys, fat man! Lewis, find something to tie him up with! Listen, fatso, give me the keys!"

The man was advancing slowly towards her.

"I'm afraid that's quite impossible. You'll have to kill me if you want them."

"I don't need to kill you," said Alice from a dry throat. "I don't even believe you're real!"

The room began to revolve slowly around them. Lewis was still sitting on the floor and Alice knew that that was bad. But luckily time had slowed up to give her room to make a decision. She braced herself to shove the knife deep into the man's chest. But as he got close to her his eyes sought hers like a lover and she knew he was trying to hypnotise her, to dominate her with his will. She breathed deep down into her belly, called up all the energy stored inside her, and felt it flow from her loins, through her heart and into her head. But she could not avoid meeting his eyes. 'It doesn't matter,' they were saying. 'Don't you see? It's all a game, it's all one, nothing matters, nothing lasts, nothing is serious or for real. There is only the pursuit of pleasure in all its forms, that's all, so kill me, kill me if you want, it's all the same to me . . . '

Suddenly Alice understood the place Lewis had come to and why he had given in. She also knew if she killed the fat man she would never escape from the underworld, that it would become inescapably and for ever her main reality, the centre of her being.

"You're nothing but a pack of cards!" she yelled. "You're nothing but a pack of cards!"

The fat man gripped her arms and flung her against the wall. The dagger clattered to the floor. He hoisted her by the shoulders and flung her against the wall again. If he did it one more time she would shatter, break into a hundred, thousand pieces. But he did not. She was sliding slowly to the floor, her limbs watery, her head swimming, and this time she was picked up and quite gently leant against the wall. The fat man ran his hands down the length of her body, underneath the cloak.

"A girl!" he said with great satisfaction. "Even better. We're not keen on girls down here, but we find uses for them, yes we do."

Alice knew exactly what he was talking about. Part of her consented and said 'OK. Let's do it! A coward must be punished for her crimes.' But then she filled her mouth with saliva and spat right in the fat man's face.

"Fat creep!" she shouted. "You pay for boys because no woman would ever have you, you unimaginable pile of stinking shit!"

He slapped her hard across the face. Everything jarred and jumped out of focus. She was tumbling onto the floor, her head hitting something hard, she was jettisoning into white space, she was travelling very fast, then she was cradled in some giant arms, lifted, and set gently back again on earth.

When she opened her eyes she saw Lewis, standing, cuddled in the fat man's arms. He stepped back and there was blood all over both their chests. But the dagger was in Lewis' hand, he was plunging it in again as the fat man staggered back against the wall, as if to make it easier for Lewis to drive the long blade right into his flesh. Then the fat man was sliding heavily to the floor, Lewis was stepping back again like a morris dancer returning to his place, Anaxa was in the room flinging her cloak around his shoulders, they were walking fast together down the endless corridors, they were standing in a purring lift, they were out in the wet streets, whirling back towards the centre of the camp.

146

"Will they come after us?" asked Alice, as Anaxa fumbled on the landing for her key and Lewis leant against the wall, his eyes shut tightly against the neon light.

"Not us," said Anaxa. "Lewis. But he has learnt something tonight that they can never take away. He has a chance now, before he hadn't. This is not a fairy-story, Alice. Thing will go on being hard."

★ ★ ★

Later, while Alice drank whisky from a dirty tumbler, Anaxa washed Lewis, disinfected his wounds and put him to bed in her bed. He lay, staring at the ceiling, refusing to answer when they spoke to him. When the two woman had finished the whisky, they lay down in their clothes and fell asleep on either side of him. Alice woke at dawn with a dry mouth and got up to get a drink of water. She sat on the end of the bed and watched the two of them sleeping — the innocent fair man and the debauched dark woman. And yet it was not as it seemed: the fair man was not innocent and the dark woman had not been debauched. 'How are things then?' thought Alice, 'If they are never as they seem?' All she knew was she saw a dark head and a fair head on the pillow, and that they belonged together. She was not needed any more. She had served her purpose, even though she had failed in the moment of crisis to use the knife.

She washed her face in cold water at Anaxa's evil-smelling sink, dried it on a dishcloth and slipped out of the room. Downstairs in the shop Tom, the shopkeeper, sat behind his counter, sipping Russian tea and reading from a big book which could have been a ledger or a book of ancient wisdom. He did not look up at her approach, but she dragged a stool over to the counter and sat down opposite him anyway.

"What was all that about?" she asked.

He looked up at her. His grey eyes were neither warm nor cold; they were clear, full of space and light. She felt properly *seen* by them and it was a comforting sensation. She tried to hold his gaze but could not. Her eyes fell down and rested on a little pile of precious stones sparkling on the counter.

"You ought to know," he said. "You were there."

His voice was gruff and matter-of-fact, not laden with portent as somehow she had expected it would be.

"I know I failed," she said. "I was supposed to be the warrior, but I couldn't kill him. Lewis had to do it and now he won't speak to us. Perhaps we did more harm than good."

"Maybe you weren't meant to kill him."

"Anaxa told me that I must."

"Anaxa is Anaxa, not God. Do you always do what you are told?"

"No. Well, not very often. But what she said had a feeling of rightness about it, I felt that I should obey."

"You felt you should, but you didn't."

He raised his eyebrows and grinned at her. She realised he was not as old as she had thought.

"Hmm," he said, "what you don't seem to take into consideration is that you're a woman. A woman-warrior maybe, but a woman nevertheless. And a woman can be courageous without killing. It can be more corageous not to kill. Or did you feel that your courage failed you?"

Alice took herself back to the scene of the night before. Although the whisky made her head ache there was an astonishing clarity in her remembering.

"I was frightened up to the point where things started to happen. After that it all went of itself. It just happened. I wasn't either cowardly or brave. I was just there. But now I'm back here, it seems just like a bit of imagination, a bit of wishful thinking, I suppose."

"And you want me to tell you how to evaluate it? You want me to tell you how to think? Why don't you trust your own experience? Why do you want to think there's always a right and a wrong, a good and a bad, a real and an unreal?"

Alice sat back feeling elated and crushed at the same time. Her head was hammering, but she did not mind. The world seemed suddenly spacious, substantial, exhilarating — she felt she could plunge into it and it would bouy her up, bounce her — that even if she fell ever so low something would pull her out and up again, into the sunshine.

"You're right," she said. "I'm a fool. I'd better get back

148

now. My friend will be worrying. They won't come after us, will they, those men from the underground?''

Tom leaned back in his seat and lit a cigarette. Alice was surprised that he smoked. She had imagined that wise people did not need such props.

"You're not out of danger," he said abruptly. "But they won't harm you unless you let them. You must guard your senses. Avoid too much drink, drugs, parasitic people, ambiguous situations. They can all make cracks in your armour, and then you're vulnerable. I worked down there for a time, not in the sex business, I was an addict of the void, a void junkie . . . '' here he shook himself all over like a dog. "it took me a long time to recover from the damage I had done . . . ''

Suddenly Alice felt very, very tired and stopped listening to Tom. She wanted the shop, the camp, Anaxa, Lewis and all the rest to disappear and to find herself back home in her own bed with the neighbours' kids squalling outside the window, the pipes squooshing as the lodger made himself his morning tea. She wanted to get up and wander in her baggy overalls into her workroom with the ailing plants and plaintive face of the neighbour's cat at the window, wanting to be let into the warm. She felt a tremendous nostalgia for her *own place*. She wanted to slump on the sofa and stare at her old drawings, the voluptuous odalisques, the dusky men, the running and jumping children with which she'd peopled her world. She wanted to sit and stare at the swathes of cotton, silk, sparkling gauze and sombre velvet hanging on her wall until a shape came into her mind and she started *making* . . . 'That's *my* place,' she thought, 'that's where I belong. Why did I ever leave it?'

Then she began to remember the time she had forgotten: the arid, empty days just before she had come to the camp. Days spent in laborious, obsessive fantasies about Lewis. Days spent mechanically churning out piles of drawstring trousers to sell on the market. Days when she smoked and sipped Martini from twelve o'clock, read no books, not even her beloved 'Middlemarch', allowed her friends to drift in and out of her life, but never asked about their lives. Days when the only food she had in the house was tinned rice-pudding which she ate in front of

'Crossroads' in a daze or lying on the floor listening to Billie Holliday wailing about her man who was so mean . . . Days when she consoled herself with fantasies of Lewis suddenly 'realising' and 'recognising her worth', and grew fat from lack of exercise and pale from lack of sun . . . a whole stream of endless identical days which ended when Maria appeared on the doorstep with her sensible travelling bag and demanded to know where were the biscuits and tins of lump-fish roe and bottles of wine that Alice normally kept in stock to entertain her friends. And suspected that something was wrong and went out busily buying chicken and paté and tomatoes and wine to take out on a special picnic in the country, designed to cheer them both up, because she herself was far from happy . . .

Alice fell into a deep sleep. She dreamed a while and then sank down into the darkness, the soft, insinuating darkness where everything is made, and, for a while it bouyed her up like a baby in a cradle, rocking her on a choppy sea, until the weary spark of consciousness that was attaching itself to the person of Alice J Cunningham relinquished its hold on her and she was swept far out to sea, beyond the sandbar where the dolphins and the porpoises were playing.

★ ★ ★

PART TWO: The Kingdom

"My beloved spake, and said unto me, Rise up,
my love, my fair one, and come away.
For, lo, the winter is past, the rain is over
and gone;
The flowers appear on the earth; the time of the
singing of birds is come, and the voice of the
turtle is heard in our land;

The fig tree putteth forth her green figs,
and the vines with the tender grape give a
good smell. Arise, my love, my fair one, and
come away.

O my dove, that art in the clefts of the rock,
in the secret places of the stairs, let me see
the countenance, let me hear thy voice; for
sweet is thy voice, and thy countenance is
comely."

From Chapter Two of
Solomon's Song.

CHAPTER EIGHT

Waking Up

CHAPTER EIGHT

Alice was walking along the street towards the market when she came upon Maria with a flat stomach.

"You've had the baby!" she exclaimed, putting her hand on her friend's belly to check the evidence of her eyes. Then suddenly the baby was there, struggling in Maria's arms — a big, chubby, red-faced and orange-haired boy with a mouth stretched open in a black 'O' like a baby in the 'Dandy', from which issued a clarion call of yells.

Alice catapulted out of bed as if someone had suddenly shouted her name, and stood for a moment, naked in the middle of the room, blinking and rocking on her heels. A cascade of images effervesced in her head and behind them all was the calamitous noise of a baby crying. 'I've been dreaming,' she thought, 'I dreamed that Maria had a boy!' She flung on her dressing-gown and ran downstairs to put the kettle on. While it was coming to the boil she dialled the number of Maria's house in Sheffield. A gruff voice unfamiliar to her answered.

"How's Maria?" she asked.

The man chuckled embarrassedly.

"She's fine. It's a boy, a monster, eight and a half pounds. Difficult birth but they're both OK now. Are you Alice by any chance? I was going to ring you after breakfast, she asked me to let you know."

"And are you, are you . . . " Alice was searching for the name of Maria's number two lover, the one who had sired the child, but couldn't find it. "Are you the father?"

"I am."

"Congratulations then."

"Oh I didn't have much to do with it really," he responded sheepishly. "Although I must admit I am more chuffed about it than I thought I would be."

"Good, good," said Alice abstractedly and sat down to her Weetabix with big tears rolling down her cheeks. Maria was all right now; she could stop worrying about her, the boy-child would surely pave the way to grace and mellow the extremely sharp and hurtful edges of her feminism. She noticed that although her heart was big and heavy, swollen with a mixture of emotions, around it there seemed to be a lot of space, and her body felt light, willowy, as if she had magically lost two stone in the night and shed some other heavy burden . . . but what sort of burden could it be? It was most strange — something had changed, but she had not the faintest idea what it was. She did not feel particularly happy, in fact she was restless and jangled and wondered what on earth to do with the remainder of the day, but undeniably there was some kind of extra light in the kitchen, some subtle glow inside her chest which had not been there before.

And Lewis? She had a feeling she must have dreamed about him because the image of his face was vividly present in her mind. But something else was incredibly present too — a sense of having *given Lewis up* the way she had given up smoking a few months before. But she had not! Only the night before she had gone with a girlfriend to the pub where he often drank in the hope of bumping into him. He had not turned up and she had come home late having drunk too much vinegary white wine which she could ill afford and fallen bad-temperedly into bed. She had comforted herself before falling asleep with the thought of returning to the pub the next day to try again. She must see him because he was due to leave soon on a long trip abroad. But now she knew she wouldn't go. Now she knew it would be better for her not to see him. It made her sad but she knew that she could bear it. She felt a kind of relief that she would now be permitted to resume her normal life. Perhaps she would properly begin on the big tapestry of the Greenham women, perhaps she would paint the upstairs rooms and clean the house from top to bottom . . .

In fact, from that day onwards Alice's life began to improve. She was not happy, but neither was she either actively unhappy or glumly tranquil. She found surfacing within herself various lost but useful qualities, such as a stubborn ruthlessness which, once set in motion, enabled her to evict her melancholic PhD student lodger who had permanent cystitis, stayed in bed most of the day and had given up paying rent, and replace her with a cheerful young businessman who needed a pied-a-terre while doing his Yorkshire rounds, paid a decent rent promptly and mended all the broken things in the house. He also heard from one of his contacts that the 'Three Ridings' TV company were looking urgently for a costume assistant to work on a big-money series about wartime Leeds. She applied and, to her astonishment, was offered the job.

Soon her overdraft diminished and the early rising and long hard hours on location worked the lazy fat off her body. She went swimming at lunchtimes and designed herself new clothes at the weekend so that her old flamboyant image was restored. She was particularly happy in a flamingo-pink ensemble: pink boots, pink shorts and a big pink mohair jumper which she knitted in a week. The nagging sadness, the sense of loss she had woken up with on the day she had dreamed of Maria's child, never left her, but she learnt to live with it. Some evening she would even allow it to sit alongside her on her voluptuous settee and she would stroke it like a nervous cat who needs to be made to feel at home. Other evenings she sat in her neglected garden, often in the dark, talking to the elves and devas who had taken refuge there from more well-ordered places.

She knew it was an eccentric and, worse, a wet and sentimental activity which would have been scathingly condemned by Maria had she known about it, but something stubborn in Alice was determined now to have its day, do as *it* pleased not as others would, and if talking to windy spirits in an overgrown back garden was its predeliction then that was that!

Even so she was looking forward to seeing Maria — the baby was a month old now and unless he was feeding would probably be sleeping most of the day, she reasoned. There would be plenty of time and quiet to talk and Maria would be pleased to see that Alice had recovered from her depression.

But the baby did not sleep. He remained clasped to his mother's bosom all the three long hours of Alice's visit, either suckling, snivelling or snoozing fitfully. As soon as Maria put him down the baby started to cry, and Maria could not bear to hear him cry . . .

"Surely he's got to lie on his own sometime, Ria" said

Alice timidly, "surely it wouldn't hurt him to cry for a few minutes before he goes to sleep. He's only exercising his lungs . . . "

Maria looked at Alice with angry tears flashing in her eyes.

"But he's distressed! He was badly traumatised by the birth, he nearly didn't survive! He needs reassuring that it's all right to be alive and ask for comfort. How can I just let him lie and suffer while I sit here drinking coffee and enjoying myself?"

Alice shut up. Her private opinion was that although no doubt we all find being born traumatic we get over it pretty quickly and learn to cry, not out of agony, but to get something we want delivered to us pretty smartly. The baby looked vigorous and wily to her — it was very much the baby of her dreams although it showed no sign yet of having red hair — in fact, it seemed oddly out of scale with its tiny mother. Alice presumed that the father, not in evidence today, must be a big man. A big man who won't support his own child! 'Wonderful!' she thought sourly, as she tried to be good and helpful, making cups of tea and healthful salad sandwiches for lunch and resentfully doing the washing-up she thought the other occupants of the house should have done already, especially considering two of them were unemployed. In the early afteroon the baby finally fell asleep, its hot red cheeks burning with unwilling exhaustion, and Maria closed her eyes and fell asleep beside him. Alice sat for a while, indignation and tenderness warring in her breast, and finally covered them both carefully with a blanket, wrote a lying note about having to get back to do some work, and left.

Then she began to have strange dreams. She recalled them in short sequences or even single images: Lewis hunched in a dark room with blood welling from his hair; she and Maria walking through a dark old wood and into a big Victorian building with corridors that went on and on, and a beautiful garden (they *had* been in a wood like that once when they had gone out for a picnic to cheer themselves up, but had actually turned back at an old gateway in the wood because Maria was not feeling very well), a white-skinned dark-haired woman dancing on a stage, a concert given in a kind of Crystal palace by a weird group of women dressed in outlandish space-suits . . . and so on.

Alice pondered these dreams, she even wrote them down in a book bound in Chinese silk Maria had given her for her birthday, but she did not exactly take them seriously. They seemed to belong to the same realm as her drawing and painting, the best of her dress-designing, and of course she did not take *these* things seriously, that would be laughable! Except that one day of course she *would* work hard at something and prove that she had it in her to create, but not yet, because she had to earn a living, and sort herself out, and get over the thing with Lewis properly. Her mother did not agree.

"Alice, God will reproach you in the next world for your indolence! You have an eye others would give their arms and legs for, and you will not use it! Bernard used to be so proud of you, remember? That time we came to the art school and your paintings shone out with a radiance the others couldn't even shadow!"

Alice ground her teeth and wondered how she could love and hate her mother so vehemently at one and the same time. So clever, so astute, so big-mouthed, flowery and uncompromising in her language!

Mrs. Rosa Sieminska-Cunningham wanted more than anything for her daughter to be a real artist. A failed one she wouldn't mind. A penniless one she would support. But a half-hearted dilettante, who at this moment was wasting her life hanging forties dresses on the thin, elegant shoulders of TV actresses who treated her like a servant! This was more than Alice's mother could tolerate.

But Alice glared right back, fiddled mutinously with her flopping hair and felt queasily brutal and triumphant. Beyond that she and her mother spent their time together grieving for Poland under martial law, making up food parcels for the distant relatives and talking of Bernard, what he might have been and what he might have done. Had he not died so surprisingly in the cool Maytime of the previous year.

So, for quite a while then Alice lived on in a bright open plane of existence, writing down her dreams, squalling with her mother, working exhausting but remunerative overtime at 'Three Ridings', and feeling a kind of sour-sweet sadness when she read Lewis's finely-written reports from behind the lines in Afghanistan, which appeared from time to time in a radical journal along with his photographs. Then a new actress appeared on the set of 'Yorkshire's War', a haughty sultry woman with black hair, and tumults of outrageous imitation silver jewellery cascading about her person, who would not gossip with the other actresses or even to Alice, but either coolly vamped the men or sat alone painting her nails or staring witch-like into space. She was to play a Sephardi Jewess who has fled Europe and arrives penniless and provocative in Leeds to set up as an up-market prostitute and wreak havoc amongst the Yorkshire airmen and their wives.

Alice was fascinated by the woman's arrogant bad taste, and in fact admired it far more than the leg-warmer narcissism of the other women on the set. They all disliked the newcomer of course, but Alice was not sure. She suspected than Anaxa, as she was called, was simply one of those actresses who immerse themselves so completely in the part they are playing that they cannot shrug it off while they are not performing. And Jessica, the Eastern-European Jewess, *was* supposed to be sexy, spiky, hostile to her own sex, insolent and ungrateful to the solid Yorkshire families who were sheltering her from Hilter's wrath. It was just so with Anaxa: she kept herself deliberately apart, never came to the pub at lunchtime, and in general comported herself like a Queen in exile from her rightful kingdom.

So Alice did not react to Anaxa's cool with coldness. She chattered sunnily to the actress while she dressed her, at first telling her ironic stories about the rest of the cast, then moving on to ask her about herself: was she married? Did she like Leeds? Was she herself Jewish? At first Alice got nowhere: Anaxa answered her questions in impatient monosyllables and expressed no interest in Alice's life or gratitude for the friendliness being shown her. Then one day, when they broke at six o'clock she appeared in the dressers' caravan, carrying a bottle of vodka and a brown paper bag, from which she proceeded to unpack a tin of caviar, a jar of pickled mushrooms, biscuits, sour cream and two dirty glasses probably stolen from the bar.

"I know you think that I am unfriendly," she announced, pouring a large measure of vodka into one glass and thrusting it at Alice. "But this is not the case. It's only that I don't like to talk about myself, I don't like being asked questions. But this is my way of being friends with you. The father of my child has been here on a visit — he brought all of this. I want you to share it with me. Are we safe in here for half an hour?"

They were. Alice, in charge that day because the head designer had the 'flu, was in possession of the key and could lock up when she wanted to. She viewed the delicacies Anaxa had brought with glee: they were just the treats she had grown up with, longed for (her mother being that most rare of creatures — a Polish Russophile!) and could never find in supposedly cosmopolitan Leeds.

"Alice, you are the only real human being here, and now that I have drunk with you I will trust you and tell you everything. I only ask that you will tell the others *nothing* about my life. They understand nothing, they are fools, and I do not wish to be known by them. They do not understand the simple fact that before an actor can begin to act she must abase herself to *nothing* before God and keep in mind always her real unworthiness to play the part of a more honourable human being. By that, I mean a human being who suffers her own sorrows, does not act out other people's!"

Alice was captivated by this speech. She had always fallen in love easily and Anaxa fulfilled her every dream of outrageous sensuality and eccentricity. That night she went back to Anaxa's flat with her and met her five year old daughter, Masha, just the kind of girl-child Maria had longed for, thought Alice ruefully, a sturdy, masterful little girl with round black eyes and a dusty, embroidered dress that was forever being hitched up so that her brown, knickerless bottom could be scratched.

They drank more vodka, ate pickled herrings, olives, honey cake. Alice discovered that Anaxa's mother had been an Armenian Jewess, her father probably a Russian soldier who had availed himself of her mother's services the night before she and her own mother fled away across the border into Turkey.

"I come from a long line of courtesans," said Anaxa seriously. "My mother was not a prostitute, but a dancer, who lived a dignified life with her mother and sold herself occasionally to men who appreciated her art and her beauty and were willing to pay the right price to possess them for an hour or two. Only an hour or two, mind you, my mother never allowed, in the whole of her life, a man to spend a whole night with her. She was a woman's woman through and through. I would like to say the same of myself, but unfortunately I am a weaker animal . . . "

At this moment there was a timid knock at the door, which opened to reveal a pale young man in a grey tee-shirt and sweat pants, whom Alice recognised as the boy who was playing Anaxa's younger brother, an escapee from a Polish work-camp who crosses Europe to find his sister and make a respectable Jewish woman of her.

"Davie, not tonight, darling, can't you see I'm busy," drawled Anaxa langourously from her reclining position on the bed. "Maybe tomorrow, but I don't know, I may be too tired after the seduction scene with Rabbi Gutman going on all day . . . "

The young man's eyes drank in the vodka, the plates of food, the two half-drunken women lolling odalisque-like amidst the festive debris. He looked for all the world like a concentration-camp survivor seeing real food and women for the first time for years, although Alice knew he was an accountant-fathered Cambridge graduate from Golders Green. He retired submissively and Anaxa laughed.

"I love men," she said, "but they must not be given too much respect, we must keep them in their place." She paused to rub her hands over her white thighs to clean them from the grease of a tumbled buttered biscuit of Masha's which had landed in her lap. "Men are all right, they are useful, they are necessary. But women are magic. That's what my grandmother used to say. She meant real women of course, not stuck-up, scraggy creatures like those we work with every day."

Later Masha, who could not be expected to go to bed while Anaxa and Alice were having fun, jumped up on the table and began to demonstrate her belly-dancing skills for the guest's benefit. The two grown-ups clapped out an erratic rhythm to accompany her as she stamped and shimmied, her dress held up around her head, and Alice found herself confessing to Anaxa that she was not just a costume assistant at 'Three Ridings' but also an artist, albeit a lazy, unaccomplished one. On her new friend's heated insistence she began to sketch Masha as she danced, inventing as she went along an exotic costume for the little girl. She made four separate sketches in the end, loosened by alcohol, making up a different set of clothes each time. Anaxa picked them up and retired to her bed to study them. After a minute she looked up at Alice with hard eyes and a belligerent accent in her voice.

"Tomorrow, Aleechka, I will take you to my friend. He has a shop here — interesting clothes for dancers and other people who don't want to look like all the rest. Very exclusive. People come from all over the north to buy from him, but he won't move to London. He likes it here in Leeds. He will pay you to design for him. You will see. Tomorrow after we finish, I will take you to him."

And so it was that the next day Alice found herself walking with Anaxa, outrageous as ever in black mini skirt and high heels, through the decaying Chapeltown area of Leeds, past Pakistani take-aways and lewd enormous pubs promising topless lunchtime gogo dancers, into a small cool shop where everything was white, except the long mirrors standing in each corner and the sparse racks of skimpy exotic clothing ranged along the walls. A tall, slender man also dressed entirely in white appeared soundlessly from the back and folded Anaxa in his arms. His eyes flashed onto Alice with a kind of avid yet courteous interest which made her feel bashful. She smiled at him but he did not smile back, just looked. She noticed that his own clothes were as unaffected as to be almost affected — an ordinary white shirt rolled up to the elbow, loose white trousers and the cheaper sort of tennis shoe, worn without socks. His straight, dark hair had streaks of grey in it and was badly cut around the ears so that it stuck out. Alice thought he was the most elegant and yet the most natural man she had ever seen. He took them through into the back shop and made tea.

"No booze, I suppose," ventured Anaxa boldly.

"Not for you, wanton — it will do you good to be sober for a change. But for your friend of course, if she would like . . ."

Alice declined anxiously, not wanting to have what Anaxa could not. But as Anaxa rose and rummaged in a cupboard to find a nearly empty bottle of gin and the man held out a glass to her, laughing, she realised it was just a game.

Anaxa told her friend, whose name was Tom, that she, Alice was a buried genius and then abruptly produced the playful sketches of the day before from her bag and smoothed them out on the table.

Alice was surprised to see how accurately she had caught the flow of Masha's vigorous little body as it bounced and shimmied, how the colours of the exotic dancing clothes which she'd exuberantly shaded in with Masha's colouring crayons, jumped off the page. They were colours she would never have thought of using together in her 'real' work, but they worked! She was astonished.

The man studied the drawings in silence for a full minute, then looked up at Alice, again staring her right in the eyes, but in a way that was not invasive or challenging, simply direct.

"They're quite good," he said. "But I bet your serious work is rather mannered, rather pretty-pretty. Am I right?"

Alice nodded, chagrined by his perspicacity. She saw before her the swirling ladies, the stiff jagged men of her sketch books and was ashamed. Why had she never seen that before?

"If you can hold the playfulness, if you can work on these just out of the corner of your mind, not trying too hard, not struggling for any particular effect, they could work. Look, I'm doing some costumes very cheap for an Asian children's dancing group. This sort of thing would be fine, if you tone the sexuality down a bit. I'll give you fifty pounds for a set of six different matching outfits. If they like them I'll have them made up and maybe we can business on something serious . . . oh, and see if you can develop that flowing, swirling feeling in the clothes without making them wispy, insubstantial . . . and think of the fabrics. Must be cheap. I don't mind doing this for nothing, but I'm not going out of pocket."

Alice just kept smiling and nodding. She could not think of anything to say.

"I've met you before, haven't I?" said Tom suddenly.

"I don't think so . . . unless . . . which art school did you go to?"

"I didn't go to art school."

"Well perhaps you just saw me at a party or something . . ."

As she spoke Alice felt a deep blush spread through her as if her body were reproaching her for telling a lie. But she was not lying, she was telling the truth — she had never seen Tom before! It was absurd, as if her body had a memory that was closed off to her mind.

"Never mind," said Tom, "maybe it will come back to you. Some things are difficult to remember, if they don't fit in with what we think we know."

"Hah!" said Anaxa loudly. "Don't confuse the poor girl with your nonense, Tom. Ignore him, Alice. He's just a small-time junior magus on the make."

"All the same," said Tom carefully, sidestepping Anaxa's attempt to send him up, "If you do remember, come back and see me again some time. Quite apart from the business of the dresses."

"Yes," said Alice, not quite knowing what he was talking about, but impressed by the solemnity of his tone. Good God, perhaps he thought they had met each other in a previous life! Alice did not like the idea of that at all!

They were back in the street, Anaxa fumbling in her bag to see if she had enough money to pay them a taxi home, while Alice, herself utterly out of cash, stared into a delicatessen window and thought how nice it would be to spend the money instead on some hot samosas and walk.

"Is Tom a lover of yours, Anaxa?" she asked tangentially as her friend counted ten pence pieces into her hand. "I just wondered because you seem to know each other pretty well."

"Certainly not!" Anaxa said sharply. "I like to keep things separate."

Alice did not ask what things it was Anaxa liked to keep separate because she was seeing something most surprising in her mind's eye — Anaxa and Lewis lying in bed together, a dark head and a blonde head touching on a dirty pillow . . .

"Anaxa, do you know a man called Lewis Jarman?"

"No darling, and will you stop asking me stupid questions? I have to tell you that I don't, but I also have to tell you that I don't necessarily know the names of all the men I sleep with."

"I'm sorry, it's just my imagination playing tricks again. But what did Tom mean with all that stuff about meeting me before?"

"He was playing with you, darling. Dangling the bait to see if you were interested."

"Interested in what?"

"Interested in remembering."

"Remembering what?"

"If I told you that I'd be remembering for you wouldn't I?"

★ ★ ★

When Alice thought about the incident afterwards it seemed to her as if Anaxa and Tom were involved in some secret from which she was excluded, as if they were in a conspiracy together which had to do with her. And yet she trusted Anaxa completely. It was all most odd.

She went home and read through her dreams in the Chinese book. No, it did not seem that she had met either Tom or Anaxa in her dreams. She felt ashamed of having entertained the idea that she might. But there was something else that *was* striking in the series of fragments: Maria was often present — pregnant Maria, vulnerable Maria, infuriating Maria. Alice wondered if Maria ever dreamed of her. It was not something they had discussed. She decided to visit Maria again and ask her.

However it was still not easy to talk to Maria alone and uninterrupted. Roderick was three months old now, and indisputably hearty, but Maria was still connected to him by unbreakable, invisible threads. He had only to contract his small red face, or whimper in his sleep, and she would bound to his side, and press him to her bosom. She had started work again now and left him with a baby-minder during the day, so that she was even more anxious to fulfil his every need in the evenings and weekends. And if Roderick was not the problem, the other occupants of the house were. While the baby slept in Maria's room, the only warm place (they were economising on heating of course) was a corner of the kitchen table, where they were hopelessly prey to table-layers, cup-of-tea makers and bummers of cigarettes.

Finally Alice persuaded Maria to borrow an electric fire from someone's room and plug it in in the lounge so that they could go in there and talk in peace. Maria sat neat and cross-legged on the floor, drinking milk to build herself up, and staring at a point just behind Alice's left ear. 'She's glazed with tiredness,' thought Alice. 'Where's that big fellow who fathered the child? Can't he take some of the burden off her?' But Maria's lucid brain was not tainted by exhaustion.

"I did have a lot of anxiety dreams," she said, "about the baby being born dead and so on. But nothing with you in. Except — wait a minute — there was one where you seemed to be *talking* to the baby. It was weird. I was angry with you for upsetting him. Yes, he was a *he* in this dream, not a she like in the others. How *funny*!"

Something flickered at the back of Alice's brain. She remembered lying under a tree, the day they had gone out for that depressing picnic. She remembered Maria falling asleep and herself daydreaming a fantastic conversation with the foetus in Maria's womb. Illicit excitement flared in her stomach.

"It *is* funny," she began, "because on the day we went for that picnic I *daydreamed* I was talking to your baby, and that it was actually a boy. An angry boy."

"But that wasn't when I had the dream," said Maria pleasantly. "That was much later, when I was resting up with my incompetent cervix. It's just a coincidence."

"W-e-e-ll," said Alice, aware of a great frozen avalanche of conflicting concepts hanging over her head, ready to crash down and drown her fragile clarity, "time isn't such a fixed thing as we think it is. Maybe. Couldn't it be that the time you dreamed the dream had some inner connection with the time I daydreamed the same thing?"

"Alice," said Maria patiently, blinking as the smoke from Alice's cigarette wafted too close to her, "it's an appealing theory, but surely it's more likely that we were both experiencing an unconscious desire for me to actually *have* a boy, not a girl baby? A *positive* animus projection if you like, but tainted with both our fears of male violence.

and, in my case, an ambivalence about the *invasion* of my body by a male. More plausible really, don't you think?"

"Y-e-e-s." said Alice tentatively, "it's more plausible, but not necessarily true. Maybe both our theories could be true! And a few others besides. Maybe the universe is much more unpredictable than we think. And more open!"

At that moment came the sound of wailing. And while Alice was wondering what creature it was crying out so piteously, Maria was already on her feet and half-way up the stairs, undoing her blouse as she ran, so that Roderick would not have to bear another instant's frustration.

* * *

She lay on Anaxa's bed, drunk. She had done quite well for a fortnight, laying off the booze and the cigarettes. But then she started having bad dreams, dreams that made her wake up screaming. She started sleeping with the light on, and waking in the morning with a sore head and a foul taste in her mouth. She started feeling frightened to go to bed, especially if the lodger wasn't in. And so she went out and bought a packet of cigarettes, a bottle of brandy, a tin of Greek olives, and headed round to Anaxa's place, causing the ejection of a hopeful suitor. For once Anaxa was not drinking, for a reason she was not prepared to name, and instead prowled around the room restlessly, putting old "forty-five" records on the gramophone.

"You're annoyed with me for chasing away your young man, aren't you, Anaxa?"

"Certainly not. He was far from thrilling me. I'm perfectly OK. It's you I'm worried about. You don't normally drink like this. What's the matter?"

"I don't know. I just hate myself."

"I don't think you do, Alice. Self-disgust is not your problem."

"What is my problem then, oh far-seeing one?"

"You're messing up your head with something, that's what I think. I'm sure it's not drugs, you say it's not men. Apart from tonight I don't think it can be alcohol. What is it, Alice? Come on, give me a break."

"It's dreams," said Alice suddenly and melodramatically. "I keep having these bad dreams. And before them, strange ones, when I knew I was dreaming but I didn't wake up. I don't know what they mean, but I'm not happy about them, they are spoiling my good life."

"Ah," said Anaxa gently. "Dreams. OK, I'll get the cards out and have a look at things for you."

Alice propped herself up on her elbow and watched as Anaxa laid out a dirty pack of Tarot cards on the floor. She picked out a blonde lady with a wooden rod and placed it on its own.

"That one's to signify you. I'm using it because she signifies spiritual things, and perhaps your problems are spiritual."

"Spiritual?" blurted Alice. "I haven't got a spirit, Anaxa. I'm just blood and guts and randiness and stuff and nonsense me. There's probably nothing wrong with me that a good screw wouldn't cure."

"A good screw cures nothing, Alice, as well you know. And anyway they're very hard to find."

"A good screw cures nothing, Alice!" Alice repeated in a Polly-Parrot voice. "Well, I don't know — I thought sex was supposed to be the panacea for all miseries."

"The beginning of all miseries more like," said Anaxa sombrely, handing the cards to Alice for her to shuffle.

"I've decided actually to have nothing more to do with terrible men," said Alice comfortably. "I shall no longer cast my pearls before swine. I shall be celibate and wait for the father of my children to turn up. If he doesn't I shall just have to buckle down and become a great painter and . . ."

"That's enough!" interrupted Anaxa, reaching for the cards. She was not her usual tolerant self tonight. She seemed to have lost patience with Alice and to be leaning wearily against a shut door behind which fulminated some great trouble of her own. Alice shut up and sat quite still while she dealt out the cards. The room was full of pungent odours, each battling against the other for ascendancy: she picked out garlic and onions, bleach, Turkish tobacco, a musky perfume tinged with sweat, and even the sweet smell of wet, dead leaves from the blocked gutter by the window. For a split second she caught herself in the act of paying attention to the outside world. It was a strange, unfamiliar sensation — to be actually *there*, not floating somewhere in her head . . .

"Alice!" Anaxa's voice cut into her reverie. She had not noticed that the cards were all spread out ready to be turned up.

"Sorry!" she said and frowned ostentatiously to signal her deep concentration.

Anaxa turned up the first card, which lay over the stiff golden queen which represented Alice. It showed a big red heart with three swords sticking out of it.

"Erghh!" exclaimed Alice. "How horrible! My heart is to be pierced by swords. Oh, I don't like that! What does it mean Anaxa, what does it mean?"

"Steady!" said Anaxa. "It's not something that's *going* to happen. It's something that's happening already. It's the heart of the matter, if you like. Suggests a certain masochism, Alice. You put yourself in the way of being hurt. You offer your heart to be pierced. It hurts but it makes you feel, it makes you feel alive just before you die . . . a rather drastic way of living, don't you think?"

"I don't think I'm like that," said Alice, bewildered, pushing from the back of her throat the faint taste of blood, the memory of pain.

"It's not so bad. A lot of energy there, which doesn't have to go on being squandered." She turned up the next card which lay across the pierced heart at right angles. "This crosses it," she said. "That means that the force of this card opposes the force of the first card." The card showed a lady in blue, sitting on a throne with a crescent moon improbably balanced on her head. Anaxa cocked an eye up at Alice and looked at her with a surprised air.

"Interesting," she said. "The High Priestess."

Alice started to giggle.

"No relation, honest! I've never seen the woman before."

"It doesn't refer to a person! It's part of you. On one level, it's your intuition, the sense of things you have, which you can't put into words, the sense that makes you an artist — a lazy one maybe, but still an artist . . . On a higher level, it's the higher feminine in you . . . "

"The *what*?"

Slowly, steadily, Anaxa turned up the other cards. It was a bright, garish modern pack. Alice found the design crude and distasteful and the sentimental idealisation of the human form when it appeared annoyed her. But she scarcely had time to move on from her aesthetic displeasure to a sense of their meaning when Anaxa turned them all face down again, messed them up and returned them to their box.

"Hey, what are you doing?" she said indignantly. "That's my future and I want to know it! Is it as bad as that?"

"No, no," said Anaxa soothingly. "It's just that I don't need them any more. They're only a cue, a trigger. I don't know why I didn't see it before. But now I've seen it, I don't need the cards to guide me."

"Seen what?"

"What confused me was . . . you are so nice, so well-balanced. I took you at face value. It's understandable: I like your face value! But now I see that something is happening to you. Tom was right to ask you to remember."

'And I was right,' thought Alice, 'when I guessed that you and Tom were in some kind of conspiracy against me. Or *for* me maybe. I mustn't give in to paranoia . . . '

"You're a witch, aren't you, Anaxa?" she found herself saying suddenly. "And you and Tom are in it together, whatever it is. And now you're going to tell me I'm really one of you. I knew it! I knew something like this was going to happen!"

Anaxa didn't laugh, as Alice had expected she would. She gave Alice a hard, searching look, which Alice didn't like at all. After an uncomfortable pause, she spoke.

"You can call me a witch if you like. Tom does. But I don't belong to any coven. I'm a one-off. I work alone. My mother taught me what I know, and my grandmother."

"What do you mean 'work'? Are you talking about magic? Because if you are, I don't believe in it . . . "

Alice's voice wavered. Her lips trembled, and her heart was drumming at her ribs. She wanted to get up and go home but dared not in case the impact of what Anaxa was saying exploded disastrously in her when she was all alone.

"Don't talk nonsense, Alice! You don't even know what magic is, so how can you not believe in it? The point is: you've *seen* something. You've been shown something. The dreams prove it. You're beginning to remember, and you're scared. It's not surprising. But now you have a choice: go forward and explore what's waiting for you, or turn back to the old safe world you know so well. Which are you going to choose?"

"I don't know. I don't know what you mean."

"I think you do."

"In a way I do, but . . . "

"Listen!" Anaxa interrupted tersely. "Let me explain it another way: I think of myself as a traveller. So does Tom. Now, actually, everybody travels all the time, between levels of consciousness, between worlds, but mostly they don't know they're doing it. They are not awake. We try to keep awake, that's all. It's difficult, but possible . . . you're just finding that it's possible but your bad dreams are trying to scare you off. You mustn't be frightened of them, these dwellers of the threshold, they're not real you know."

"I know" said Alice in a voice that turned out as a croaky whisper, "but I must go home now. I'm not feeling very well."

She stood up, her knees wobbling, the pleasant drunkenness irrevocably gone.

"You see," she said, "I don't really know what I want."

"You should think about it."

"I think I'm willing to just take what comes."

"But where do you think it comes from?"

"I don't know. Nobody knows."

"There are people who know."

"Who think they know."

"Who know."

"If I believed you, I would have to find out too."

"But you don't believe me?"

"I don't know . . . "

Anaxa rose abruptly and started tidying the room, a thing Alice had never seen her do before.

"You'd better go now, I'm tired. We won't mention this again, unless you want to. We'll just carry on being friends, OK?"

Alice kissed her, ashamed of herself, and turned to go.

"There's something amiss with you too, isn't there?" she asked, standing by the door.

"Yes," said Anaxa. "Something too deep for tears. The

only help is not to think of it. Goodnight."

★ ★ ★

Alice did not go to bed when she got home. She made tea, put Chopin's Preludes on the record player in her workroom and slumped down on the settee. She picked up a pad and pencil that were lying there and started drawing dancing figures. After a while she put down the pencil and felt her brow. It was hot and tacky with sweat. Was she running a fever? Was she going to be ill again, like last year? Was she going to have to fight *that* battle all over again? She shuddered. No! Surely she had sorted *that* out, surely she had come to some sort of understanding with the force that wanted to kill her? Surely she had agreed to some sort of undertaking . . . No! What was this nonsense she was remembering?

Fever gives you such weird hallucinatory experiences. They are not meant to be remembered afterwards . . . 'But Alice,' she asked herself, 'if you gave your word sometime, even in a feverish fantasy, are you not obliged, by honour, to hold to it? To stick to the agreement, whatever it was?' 'All right then,' she answered, 'let's bite the bullet here and now. I'm going to bed, I'm going to sleep. The force which got at me when I was ill must still be around in there somewhere: let it come out and get me again, let it tell me what to do, and I'll do it, come what may!'

She threw her sketchbook down and threw herself into bed without washing, tearing her clothes off and letting them lie where they fell in disarray. She covered her head with the blankets and ordered herself to fall asleep immediately, which she did.

★ ★ ★

In the morning she remembered nothing. She had slept a sweet and dreamless sleep and woken cheerful and full of beans. She was half way downstairs, singing, to make her breakfast when she recalled her impetuous 'arrangement' of the night before. 'Well that settles it once and for all,' she thought, banging the kettle down boisterously on the

173

cooker and cutting bread with a flair and panache normally only found in the musicals of Ginger Rodgers and Fred Astaire. 'It's all stuff and nonsense, and there isn't any 'force'. Anaxa was talking through a hole in her head and I don't need to talk to Tom about anything at all. I'm going to have a lovely day because it's Saturday and I'm going to give myself every kind of treat and break I've been hankering for!'

She began by stealing two rashers of the lodger's bacon and sliding them under the grill.

★ ★ ★

Later that morning she took a cup of real coffee in an elegant green and gold coffee cup up to her workroom and arranged herself comfortably on the old settee with its exquisite lady's boudoir pink-and-white-glazed-cotton cover, the cover she had made in the early days of her infatuation with Lewis, imagining how he would come and recline on it with her while they talked half the night of art and love and mysteries . . . Such a thing had never happened of course, but this morning it was agreeable to recline there on her own and stare at the swathes of material she had hung all over the opposite wall, strips and shards of cotton and silk, patterned with flowers, stars, sparkles, striations, mainly deep blues, bright fuschia pinks and irridescent emerald greens . . .

As she stared she became pleasantly aware of her comely, no longer over-fleshy body as it sank down into the sofa's own soft pink flesh. She felt happy with herself, at home in her skin; a Saturday relaxation stole over her and told her there was no need to feel guilty that she was not doing something useful, it was time to play . . . Thomas, the next door cat squeezed in at the window and came to sit on her lap. The two of them dozed off in the sunshine.

Some time later she opened her eyes.

The cat was heavy on her lap. She would have liked a cup of coffee, a cigarette, a piece of toast and jam, but she dared not move. Thomas was imposing his will on her. This small, scraggy tomcat had more will than she did, an intelligent, morally developed human being! 'I've mucked around for thirty years,' she thought, 'scattering myself, frittering myself, trying to avoid being like my mother, trying to avoid having a 'career', trying to avoid sacrificing myself to a man, trying to avoid being a 'real' artist, in case I might not be good enough, might fail and be humiliated . . .'

Her eyes fell on the sketches she had been fiddling with the night before. They were just doodles really, of something that had been flickering on her interior screen for a day or two and needed playing with. The idea was of three women dancing, or was it one woman dancing caught at different moments? She was doing a kind of belly-dance: in the first picture she held her hands up high, her wrists snaking around each other, and had just flicked one hip out to the side. She was watching her own hip attentively, her balance was just a little uncertain, because she was a beginner, dancing for herself. In the next image, the central one, her feet were planted on the ground, quite wide apart and her belly and hips jutted forward, so that her pelvis made a bowl shape, as if offering itself. You could feel the vigorous thrust that had pushed it forward. Her arms were raised up in the air, making a cup shape in which her fingers flipped outwards as the lip. And her eyes stared straight out at you, cool, direct, arrogant, proud of her own power. Perhaps she was dancing for a man, a man whom she desired or who desired her. In the third picture she was spinning, using the flick of her hips to propel herself round, turning faster and faster, one hand swirling in the air while the other one held balance at her waist. And her eyes were turned inward, looking at the void. She was dancing for God. . . .

Alice tipped the cat off her lap and crossed the room to find a cigarette. Her heart was thumping and she felt aroused and agitated. There was in her absent-minded sketches a swirl, a boldness, a sparkle of energy and . . . what was the word? Happiness? No — *joy*! That was it, a thing that she had never seen before in her work. Gone were the stilted decorous figures in their wispy gowns and doublets who lingered plaintively on the fringe of woods and meadows, dipping their slender toes into genteely glittering rivers! This little dancer's feet were square and solid, they were flattened from much stamping on the earth. You could smell the meaty sweat trickling from her armpits. You could sense that after her dance was finished she would be going home to suckle her baby or make love . . .

The dancer had a life outside the picture! She moved into it from a past crowded with incident and adventure, into a future which was not yet settled. She might find herself a prostitute, a fallen woman; she might become a respectable mother of children, married to one of the men she had captivated by her dancing; she might sacrifice her dancing to God and become a contemplative, living in the desert and meditating all day long. Nobody could know. The little dancer was free, no-one could constrain her spirit as she danced, spiralling herself finally into the heart of God. Nobody could capture her spirit with a net, kill it with a knife, no heart intent on rape, debauchment, lechery could soil her!

Suddenly Alice saw the immense potential of the triptych structure: past present and future all given in one moment. The abolition of time! Hell, purgatory, and heaven, bursting through into the now! The worlds of body, psyche and spirit streaming through each other into being, making a spacious present in the eye of the beholder, so that he or she could smell that poignant, precious odour of endless creativity. . . .

'It would have to be a big, big picture,' thought Alice, dropping ash accidentally on the disgruntled cat as she fumbled through her portfolio for the largest sheet of paper. 'Maybe I could surround her with images of Inferno, Purgatorio, Paradiso, like in Dante . . . limbo could be a crowd of people lying around some communal household smoking dope and watching old Frankenstein movies on a black and white tele . . . but what the hell would heaven be like? That was Dante's problem too, if I remember from the book — hell was so much more interesting than anywhere else. But maybe I could crack it!'

Her bowels shuddering with too much excitement she raced to the toilet and sat, staring at the curious Thomas the Smudgeface who watched her closely with bright, wide-open eyes. 'No-one has done this before,' she told him triumphantly. 'Everyone is into gloom and apocalypse, and elegance and sex and simplicity and half-baked

176

symbolism. People don't paint pictures which tell a story any more, not nowadays . . . oh, and I could put all sorts of secret messages in, *rebuses* like in Holbein's Ambassadors, or that nice picture book about the search for a golden rabbit that people liked so much, and ordinary, people who don't normally care for pictures could have great fun looking for the secret messages, and unravelling the meaning of the thing . . . '

'But,' she realised heavily, jerking the chain and kicking the importunate Thomas out of the way, 'my technique is not really up to it. I'm good at movement, colour, clothes, atmosphere, but what about the background landscapes? The expressions on people's faces? I've never been very good at those. Maybe I could do it just with the eyes? But how to convey depth of feeling just in the painting of the eyes? I shall have to start looking at people's eyes more carefully, I shall have to start practising, noticing how people's state of mind, or rather, state of being is registered in their eyes . . . but it will be so hard, I'm so lazy and I'm not used to concentrating. I've been a dilettante for thirty years!'

'And who,' she asked herself, smearing some muddy, mixed-fruit jam onto a left-over piece of toast (for Alice never entirely forgot her stomach however enthralled she might be by higher things), 'will pay for it? It will take all my energy for six months at least, probably longer, and I have no money saved to support myself. There's no way I could combine it with working at 'Three Ridings', I'd have to give that up even though they're promising me another contract and it's so nice to have some money for a change. . . . But perhaps I could work harder with my things for Tom, and get back that job teaching 'people's art' at the WEA, and clear the junk room out and get another lodger in. . . . '

'I suppose,' thought Alice, skipping upstairs to the shower, 'that I can use Anaxa as the model for the dancer, if she doesn't mind, the dancer who dances all the way from heaven through purgatory to try and save the soul of her beloved who is locked up in the lowest reaches of hell — that's Lewis, of course. . . . But Anaxa and Lewis haven't met each other yet . . . I think I'll introduce them when he comes back from Afghanistan . . . I'll

have a dinner party and invite Maria and Tom and the lodger and Masha can sleep upstairs in my bed, and maybe the two of them will like each other and there will be some kind of reconciliation between me and Lewis too . . . '
The fantasy melted into a vague cloud of glowing Christmas warmth as Alice rubbed shampoo into her wayward hair.

Clean and dressed, she found herself at a loose end. It was Saturday and usually she started off by going shopping, but she felt on this special day she should take some small step towards the fulfillment of her new undertaking. Should she go out and buy some paints and paper? No, there was much preliminary sketching to be done before she would need those. Should she jump on a train to London and go and visit Holbein's 'Ambassadors' at the National Gallery? No, she would be spending money she might need in a few months time, and besides, she had a good reproduction of it hanging in the kitchen. Should she go and see Tom and ask him what he thought of the idea? No, an artist doesn't discuss her inspiration with other people and dilute its force with common sense. . . .

There was nothing else for it: she must get to work! She spread out a large piece of paper on her easel and took a piece of charcoal from the box. She drew the torso of a woman dancing, twisting, turning, trying to find her balance . . . but it wasn't right! She tried again, starting this time with the line of the arms, reaching up above the dancer's head. No! They were stick arms, they didn't pulse with the irresistable force of life flowing back towards its beloved, longed for source . . . She put the charcoal down and wiped her hands on her overalls. It was irritating to get dirty so quickly after getting herself clean. Perhaps she should just nip down the road to Morrisons before they got too busy, and call in on Pauline on the way back. . . . *No!* Just one more try to get the feeling right before giving up and living an ordinary Saturday. . . .

This time she kept her attention light, half thinking about what she would buy to eat for dinner later on. When she stepped back fearfully and looked at the finished figure, she had to admit that she had caught *something* of the little dancer's struggle to perfect her movement. Around the hips it was just perfect and that was in many ways, the most difficult bit. . .

Two hours later the figure was only marginally more alive and her overdrawing had almost destroyed the fine initial sketching of the hips. She ground her teeth and replaced the piece of paper with another one. 'Let's try purgatory next,' she thought, 'it's easier on the nerves than hell!'

★ ★ ★

CHAPTER NINE

The Snowqueen's Daughter

CHAPTER NINE

The Snowgoose's Daughter

CHAPTER NINE

It was late summer now, nine months from the day of Alice's inspiration, and she had finally decided to go and visit Tom. To visit him *properly* that was, not with the drawings of fabrics or questions about work, but only with herself. It was evening when she set out on her bicycle, and after a hot, sulky day it had just rained, so that the streets steamed and a tired red sun was sagging behind the winding lines of terraces on the hill as she flew down from Woodhouse Moor to Chapeltown.

Alice longed for a wind, a wind to blow away the staleness and stickiness in her head, to flush out the grinding anxiety that was in her at the moment, the fear that was melting in her bowels every morning when she woke up. But the hot summer hung on ruthlessly and her legs, as they churned the pedals of her sensible bicycle, felt weak and heavy as lead.

At first things had gone very well. She had spent weeks just sketching, inventing characters and situations, working hard on her drawing, striving to catch the fugitive expression in the eyes which will reveal the soul or lack of it, the telling disposition of limbs, the subtle spacing of groups. She had refused the offer of another contract at 'Three Ridings' and disciplined herself to get up early in the morning to start working. She had studied the painters she thought of as her masters: Holbein, Chagall, Dürer, Brueghel, Picasso, and read about their troubled lives; pored over Dante, Blake (whose paintings repelled her) Rilke and Wordsworth, and devoured lots of clever science fiction, which cowed her with its cruel brilliance but taught her a lot about scale.

But now she was stuck. Her drawing was adequate, but her painting technique still fell hopelessly short of what was necessary to transfer her glamorous visions onto paper. She was too vague. Her use of colour was good — she could, in a few strokes, create a cloudy, evocative landscape behind her figures which conveyed clearly what region of heaven or hell they were in. But she had imagined *detail*, brilliant, exquisite *detail*, which would reflect *outside* the suffering protagonists what was going on *inside* them. And she could not do it.

Thus she found herself in that most agonising of states for any artist, of holding in her head a brilliant and shocking vision which she was not equipped to express. At certain moments she panicked entirely and wondered how she was going to fill the rest of her life, now that she was failing at the great test she had set herself.

And then there was her 'emotional life'. Since Lewis's departure there had been a vacuum and since Alice abhorred vacuums Alice had hastened to fill it. She filled it for a while with a graduate plumber who smoked a lot of dope, watched a lot of television, but had a kind heart and a good mind on those rare occasions when he was not too stoned to use it. His relaxed, easy-going manner had driven Alice into paroxysms of rage.

Then there was Donald the divorcée, an old schoolfriend of the lodger's who made a great deal of money being a computer expert in a bank. He was an ugly, lanky man who meditated and ran in marathons and spoke eloquently about the lack of a 'warm intelligent woman' in his life. He had a thin, sensitive eight year old son who was to be sent away to boarding school and who wrung Alice's heart utterly each time she looked at him. She knew he needed a mother and that she did not want to be it. So Donald too had to be renounced in favour of the fresh, maddening air of celibacy. Alice was once again alone and not particularly liking it.

And so her life's ticklish unsatisfactoriness had pushed her finally to pick up the 'phone and ask Tom if she could come and talk to him. *Seriously*, she said. He laughed his discomforting, ironic laugh and said "of course". Now she was banging on the shop door (he lived above the premises), waiting to wheel her bicycle into the brilliant, white-painted hall.

She had presumed he would know exactly what she had come for, but when they were facing one another across his kitchen table, glasses of strong sweet tea before them, she found herself embarrassed and uncertain, and him stony-quiet, unhelpful, stirring his tea and slowly stripping the cellophane from a new packet of Benson and Hedges.

Apart from the brass samovar in which he had brewed the tea the kitchen was very ordinary. It was clean, much cleaner than Alice's kitchen by a long way, and it contained coffee pots and biscuit tins and glass jars of beans and muesli just like everybody else's kitchen. 'What had I expected?' she asked herself. 'An alchemist's laboratory? A magic circle painted on the floor?' Tom himself also looked very clean. His silvery hair was translucent in the last beams of sunshine and there were sparkles of gold and ginger in the beard he had started to grow. He wore a simple red and white striped tee-shirt and the same white trousers he always wore in the summer, but his skin was pale. 'So pale,' she thought, 'it's as if he never goes outside.' His dark grey eyes held hers very calmly without flicking away. 'Were it not for his eyes, she reflected, he would not look at all like a magus, even a junior one. But the eyes, the eyes are the eyes of someone who knows something. . . . '

"Anaxa said I ought to talk to you," she began.

"Oh yes? What did she think you ought to talk to me about?"

"My dreams."

"Dreams? Women always want to talk about dreams. What is this fad for dreams and dreaming? Does nobody live in the real world nowadays?"

Alice felt wrong-footed. She offered him her usual glancing, self-deprecating smile and saw something flicker in his eyes. 'He's not totally impervious to my charm,' she thought, relieved.

She told him about her block. She told him about her dreams and she told him about her conversation with Anaxa about the 'work' and 'travelling' and witchery. Then she sat back and waited to see what he would say.

He did not say anything at first. He sat back too and lit a cigarette and purposefully sipped his tea. Alice reflected that, although pale, he was an attractive man — his mystery became him.

"Well?" he said finally. "So what can I do for you? What is it you want exactly?"

"I want to know if there's a way out."

"Of what?"

"Of this mess. This situation. This paralysis, this maze,

this impasse. . . . "

"There is a way-out," he interjected. "Of course there is."

"And are you going to tell me what it is?"

"You want me to tell you, rather than let you find it for yourself?"

"I *can't* find it for myself, otherwise I wouldn't be here."

"You won't like the way I can offer Alice — it's the way of hard work! On the self in the first inst. But no fascinating therapeutic sessions, no dream-analysis, no gurus, no nirvanas. And it doesn't necessarily make you happy either."

"What makes you think I wouldn't like hard work?" said Alice, genuinely wounded.

"All right. I read you wrong. If you are interested, a group meets on Sunday nights at eight at this address." He leaned over to a drawer and pulled out a slip of paper which he pushed towards her.

"What kind of group is it? Will you be there?"

"Go and experience it. I'm not telling you any more. And no, I won't be there."

She was disappointed. There was a glamour about him which made 'hard work' seem exciting as long as it happened in his presence.

"But there are other ways, aren't there?"

"Of course. If you can find them."

Here his solemnity broke and he grinned almost conspiratorially at her. She was puzzled but warmed. His eyes skated off her face and onto her rather ample cleavage, exposed as it was by a low-cut tee-shirt which had shrunk in the wash. Suddenly she was confused. Was he playing with her? Winding her up? Did he fancy her carnally, and in that case, did she fancy him? Was the energy she could feel eddying between them sexual or something finer, wilder, stronger. . . ? She wasn't sure. She left soon after with the slip of paper folded in her pocket, her hands shaking a little as she fumbled with the carrier on the back of her bicycle, trying to stuff her handbag in.

She was nearly home when the rain started in earnest. The dusty streets, just dried off from the last shower, gasped and sizzled under this downpour's battery. She was dismounting at her gate when the first lightning flashed and for a split second the whole downwards-tending cobbled street stood clearly before her in the astonishing day-and-night light of a dream. 'If I could hold that image,' thought Alice, 'hold still that image and study it, I would have all the detail I need for my backgrounds. But how to get inside that flash? How to freeze that image? How to live inside that moment and leave this confusing, scattering continuum? How to stop the world so as to know it?' Thinking of this she hefted the dripping bicycle into her hall. The telephone rang. 'Here's trouble,' she thought. 'The storm has found its victim!'

"Alice?" It was with relief that she recognised Anaxa's voice. "I'll pick you up in half an hour. We've got to go to a club. I've got to see a man. I need you with me. OK? I'm leaving Masha with Mrs. Dravomera downstairs. I'll see you soon. OK?"

"But Anaxa, it's late!"

"Alice, it's important."

"All right. What do I wear? What sort of place is it?"

"Wear what you damn well like. No, on second thoughts, better look like a woman. I'll explain later. 'Bye."

She put on her daft red dress. 'Going into the unknown, meet it with bravado,' she thought. It was a fifties party frock with a full skirt and a ruff around the neck. A smaller, finer woman would have looked ludicrous in it. Alice, with her long limbs, wide hips and big bosom, looked like a tipsy ballroom queen fallen on hard times but hanging on to her dignity. She quite liked that look. She primped her hair up into a back-combed mushroom and selected a red handbag and red, boat-like plastic shoes. There she was, half Amazon, half Hollywood love-goddess, all together larger than life. She smiled at her reflection in the mirror. Dressing up always cheered her up.

Anaxa arrived shockingly on time, dressed in her customary black but with a face white with tension, not make-up, and her mouth a flat red slit from which poked a long brown cigarette. The taxi-driver was a haughty spade who shot them reproving glances in the mirror. 'I expect he things we're a couple of whores out for a night's work,' thought Alice.

"I said look like a woman, not a Spanish dancing doll," said Anaxa tightly.

Alice shrugged.

"Aren't we going out to enjoy ourselves?"

"Certainly not."

"So what's the story? What's up with you? You look like something out of Lorca."

"It's a serious matter. No joking. Not a piece of fun."

"I know. I feared as much. Tell me."

"We've got to meet a man. Not a very nice man. He sent word for me to come. I don't know what he's got on me, but he's got something, that's for sure."

"What sort of man?"

"Pimp. Big, powerful pimp."

"And what does he want with you?"

"I'm guessing that he thinks I've been working solo. Wants to bring me in. Make me pay. For the privilege of being protected by him."

"But why? . . . " Alice was confused for the second time that night. "Why does he think that?"

"He thinks that," Anaxa cut in crisply, "because I have been. Working solo, I mean. That shocks you, doesn't it?"

"You mean you've been working as a prostitute?"

"Yes. Well, not as a prostitute, more a courtesan, like my mother. Look, Alice, when I'm not acting, what can I do? I can't live on the SS. I'm not trained for anything else. The money's so good! Good God, I don't go on the streets — they come to me. Only one or two, not bad men. More screwed up really. The sort who've been fucked up by their mothers. You know the sort."

"I know the sort," Alice said. She was thinking of Lewis.

"Alice, don't judge me — help me! If this bloke breaks me I'm lost! I've got to convince him I'm not working, that I'm just a woman who likes to change her sexual partners quite a lot. But before that I've got to find out what he's got on me so that I can plan my actions. Do you see?"

For a moment Alice felt complete revulsion at the enterprise and wanted to ask Anaxa why she didn't cast a spell to save herself, since she claimed to be a witch. Then she remembered how the soldiers had taunted Jesus on the cross and felt ashamed. "Then why have you dressed like that?" she asked gruffly. "You look just like a whore."

"There's no point in me looking different from normal is there? Just arouse his suspicions. I've got to act as if I don't suspect what he wants with me, innocent, and yet not too innocent, if you know what I mean."

"And how can I help you?"

"Alice, you're my only hope! Because you *are* innocent. Once he clocks that you're my friend, he won't be so sure about me. Whores don't have nice, well-brought-up girls like you as friends, and even in that stupid dress you look nice and well-brought-up."

"Thanks a million. Actually I'm very proud of this dress. . . "

The taxi stopped. Anaxa jumped out, paying the grim spade off with a cold look and no tip. Alice followed her up some dusty, green-carpeted stairs to a shut, blistered door with a peephole in it. Anaxa rang the bell. A fat Irishman with gravy stains on a broad kipper tie opened to them. It was one twenty-five to get in, which included a snack of either chips with curry sauce or salad barmcake.

Alice got her chips immediately (she was hungry) and began to feel cheerful and at home. She was overdressed of course but in this place it did not matter — in the crowd of Irish housewives out for a girls' night out, ageing hippies and drab sub-punk kids, she was just another quaint anachronism. There was nowhere to sit because the people who had come to hear the R and B band had bagged their places early, so they stood up near the bar, Alice drinking beer, Anaxa whisky, nervously lighting each other's cigarettes, while Anaxa scanned the door. After a while a tall young man came in and went to the bar. Alice felt Anaxa's attention light on him and fix.

"Is that him?" she asked. "He looks too young."

"Not him. His assistant. The acceptable face of prostitution. Hang on while I go over . . . "

Alice watched her approach and accost the man. She could only see his back which was supple and willowy in a creased white jacket, and his hair which was curly and black, but she had a feeling that when he turned round she would recognise him, know him as an old art-school mate, or primary school contemporary maybe . . .

Quite soon Anaxa brought him over. He was carrying

another round of drinks for them and his eyes met Alice's in courtly obeisance. No, she did not know him — it was just that he had the perfect good looks of the men in 'Dynasty'.

"This is Bill, Alice," said Anaxa. "He's come with an offer for me from a friend of his, an offer he thinks I'd be crazy to refuse."

Alice was taken aback. She did not know how Anaxa wanted her to act. Shocked? Bored? Baffled? She decided 'baffled' would be most realistic and opened her eyes in puzzled expectation.

"And Anaxa doesn't seem at all keen," said Bill in a dry Eton n' Sandhurst drawl, "But then I haven't shown her these yet. They were shown to me by a bloke I met at a party and they fell unaccountably into my pocket as I left." He skiffed a couple of polaroid photos onto the table next to them. Anaxa picked them up and glanced at them cursorily before handing them to Alice.

Alice looked: the first showed Anaxa, in black underwear, brandishing a whip and grimacing meanly, while in the foreground bobbed a blurry blonde head. It looked like a picture taken for a laugh in some drunken moment, but she guessed that Bill had produced it as evidence of Anaxa's professionalism. The second photo managed to be all in focus. In it, Anaxa, now wearing only a pair of bikini pants, straddled the fair man, who lay full-clad on the bed, his eyes shut, his mouth open, as if in exclamation. The man was clearly and unmistakeably Lewis Jarman.

Alice felt Bill's eyes stinging on her cheek. She knew her reaction was critical. She held her shock at arm's length but did not manage to repress an initial flicker of recognition.

"Well?" he said.

"Well!" she repeated. "I know this man!"

"Really? How curious!"

"Yes," she heard herself say, "he's my cousin! And what's more I know where these photos were taken — at a fancy-dress party at one of those posh health clubs in town. I went as a boy — Peter Pan actually — and Lewis said he wished he'd thought of it."

It was a gamble. If Bill knew Lewis well he could check the cousinship and find out she was lying. If he didn't he might well be convinced because there was more than a passing resemblance between herself and Lewis — many people had remarked on it. She lifted her eyes and looked straight into Bill's. She felt strangely mirthful and invulnerable. He flinched away from her look and took a draught of beer.

"Is *that* the evidence against me?" asked Anaxa scornfully. "You'll have to do better than that."

Bill's eyes skated away from them, as if he had suddenly lost interest and was looking for someone more exciting to talk to.

"I shan't trouble you ladies any further tonight" he said, still not looking at them. "And I'll pass on your good wishes to my employer, Anaxa. He'll be delighted to hear you're sticking to the straight and narrow. At long last, eh?"

As he drifted away from them Alice watched her real reaction to the photos gather itself up to hit her: Anaxa a whore and Lewis her client! Hah! It was unbelievable, and yet she was not really surprised. The happy world in which she had been going to introduce the two of them to each other, was exploding in slow motion around her, and she did not expect to be thrown clear by the blast. Down here in hell everything was connected up in a sticky, slimey net of coincidence. It was revolting, it was nauseating, it was heart-breaking, but it was *true*. She would have to live with it. She turned to Anaxa.

"So we convinced him then? We convinced him you're not a whore? I must admit I'm surprised." She wanted to punish, she wanted to hurt.

"Not at all," replied Anaxa crisply. "We just frightened him. Our power together is more than his."

"Oh God, what rubbish!"

"Don't Alice! I know you're angry. Lewis is obviously a good friend of yours. I'm sorry. But you were really good, really superb just now. You scared him off, the little shit! You'd think he could find something better to do with his education, wouldn't you, then be a runner for a pimp?"

But Alice was not to be mollified. She borrowed the money for a taxi from Anaxa and sailed self-righteously home.

* * *

The next morning she had difficulty waking up. It was as if she were caught in the atmosphere of a dream, although she could not remember the dream. Sunshine flooded her workroom. Dust-motes danced over her easel. The trees outside sighed and wrestled with the lively autumn wind. Her bare legs felt cold but she did not want to cover them up: she wanted to feel the air on her skin a bit longer. The three giant canvasses stood breathing cool, collected emptiness into the room. She found herself sitting, literally paralysed, in front of them.

She sat for an hour without making a mark. The floor was littered with sketches. It was time to start on the real thing. There was no more preparatory work to do. But she couldn't. Her heart banged. Her mouth was dry. She needed to go to the toilet. But she daren't move. If she left the room she might never come back again. She might escape back into her ordinary life. It was too big a step to take. She'd better sit tight until the spirit moved her and she started . . .

At eleven o'clock she gave up and trailed downstairs, thinking to make herself a cup of coffee. But instead she found herself out in the bright gusty streets on her green bicycle. She had no idea where she was heading — she just rode, through the wet leaves, the hard buffets of wind, the heart-breaking odours of dissolution, until she came to a place she recognised.

The allotments. That is what it was and what people called it, but Alice called it, to herself, 'the wilderness'. A tract of land, part cultivated, part wild, which lay in a bowl-shaped valley between two housing estates, one of Victorian terraces, one of modern council houses, criss-crossed by little paths and mud-tracks down which boys rode their motorcycles, it had always held for Alice a sharp, melancholy appeal. On mid-week afternoons, when the children were at school, she would wander there, usually heading for the banks of the muddy little river which meandered through it, and often ending up at the 'house', which sat oddly, but somehow quite properly, at its centre.

It was a three-storey Victorian villa, empty but not entirely uncared-for in appearance, which must have been built at around the same time as the terraces, of the same red brick, by some individualist who did not care for neighbours but did not want to live far from the centre of the thriving city. Children had climbed the walls into its garden, broken open its sturdy green gate, plundered its apple trees, but not so far succeeded in violating the building itself. The windows were all still miraculously intact. Perhaps someone was keeping an eye on it. Or perhaps its sturdy isolation and integrity evoked subliminal ripples of respect in the breasts of the Yorkshire ragamuffins who played around it.

Today Alice wheeled her bicycle into the garden, propped it agains the wall and stood absorbing its pleasant fin de siècle atmosphere. There were blackberries nearly ripened along the wall and some very late blossoming Rose Bay Willow herb just hanging on to its last feathery seeds. As she stood a big gust of wind flung in through the gate, tore the last of them free and filled the garden with dancing snow-fairies. At least that's what Alice had called them when she was a child. Tears started up into her eyes.

After the wind it was very still. She sat on the remains of a low wall round what had once been a vegetable patch and pondered. Why did she like this garden, this house so much? Why did just being here remind her of something, some place, utterly familiar yet utterly alien, a world where something was going on, something she was part of and yet not part of, something she could not quite remember and yet she knew to be real, fascinating, enthralling . . . why did she feel so *at home* here?

She wandered down the steps which led from the flag-stoned patio down into the cellar and kicked desultorily at the door. It opened. She was astonished but prodded it further open with her foot so that she could see inside the cellar without going in. Blackness. She edged down onto the last step and peered in. Darkness visible. Then, very far away, at the distant left-hand corner of the room, an oblong of light appeared. A door had opened and a white beam slanted across the glistening stone floor.

"Quick, quick!" A woman's voice skittered across it at her. "Quick, quick! There isn't much time!"

Alice stood, frozen, on the threshold.

"Quick!" the woman's voice came again. "I can't hold this door open much longer!"

Alice found herself rushing at breakneck speed across the smooth floor and through the far door. Who or what rushed her she did not know, but it felt as if her feet hardly touched the ground. Once through to the lighted area she was aware of someone rushing on ahead of her and herself following after as fast as she could.

"Where are we going?" she shouted breathlessly after the retreating figure.

"We're going to see the king," the voice came echoing back at her.

Alice tried to stop herself, to dig her heels in and halt the irresistable progression, but she could not get a grip on the polished floor. She was propelled ever onwards by some force she could not see or know.

"I can't!" she shouted, gasping, quivering, in the grip of the worst panic of her thirty two years. "I can't come! I'm not ready! I'm just not ready to see the king!"

* * *

She was in a waiting room. She hated waiting rooms — they were linked in her mind with the anticipation of pain and job interviews. There were other people there, about fifteen of them, and Alice knew without asking that they were in the same predicament as herself. They studied their shoes and wandered aimlessly about. One or two stood stockstill, their eyes blank with fear. Alice shivered. A dark, strong-looking woman appeared at her side.

"Come with me," she said. "I've got something to show you."

She took Alice's arm and guided her into the room next door which was much darker, lit only by a mass of candles crowded together on a low table in the centre.

"Look!" said the woman, and Alice saw that the walls of the room were covered with a tapestry, which glowed and sparkled as if somehow illuminated from within. Her first thought was: 'What the hell is it made of?' It seemed brighter, clearer, more *animate* than reality itself. The colours, textures, the shades of light and dark, were so subtle that you could hardly find a name for them and yet they shone with a dewy clarity that pierced Alice to the heart. She had never seen anything like it before. Her 'favourite' pictures were dull and lifeless in comparison.

The tapestry seemed to contain everything — flowers, birds, animals, butterflies, grasses, waterfalls, every kind of elemental and animate creature, except man. You felt you could walk right into it and live there, were it not that the delicate web that held it together would be too fine to hold your gross, hard-breathing body and would expell it violently as a child coughs up a crumb of cake that has taken the wrong turning down its throat.

It was all so exquisite that it was difficult to concentrate on any one part of it, but Alice was particularly enchanted by the figure of a young doe who stood on the threshold of a magic woodland and gazed out at her with lambent, speaking eyes.

"Did *you* do this?" she asked the woman, conscious of the disgraceful thought passing through her mind that no mere *woman* could be capable of such artistry. She felt the woman behind her shake with mild laughter.

"If you think this is good," she said softly, "wait until we get upstairs."

They were climbing a narrow staircase and the other people who had been waiting were with them now. At the top they were ushered into an enormous room with a ceiling so high you could barely sense the end of it, a vast empty council chamber ringed with bank after bank of red leather seats. Diffidently they all began to wander around it, watched by the dark woman and a man who had come in with her, who stood shadowed by the door so that they could not see him. Alice realised, with a movement of dread, that these people were initiators. She was not at all sure that she wanted to be initiated.

They continued to walk around the room in a big circle. After a while she felt her face stiffening and when she touched it with her hand it seemed to have set and hardened into a mask. When she looked into the mirrors which surrounded them she saw that the mask was gold and that her face was twisted into a grimace of anger. It was both horrible and shocking to see herself like that, but suddenly she understood. *That* was what it was all about then, *this* was what the initiators wanted to show them! Fear and joy welled up inside her in uncontrollable spasms like seasickness. 'Oh God,' she thought, 'I can't take much more of this! I'll scream and scream in a moment, I really will!'

Then suddenly someone was handing her a cup of tea and a digestive biscuit. She was sitting with the others in an untidy, makeshift living room, on sagging couches and threadbare armchairs which looked as if they had been rescued from a skip. Someone was talking about having to get back to Liverpool and how they had just missed the last train. Someone else was offering to put them up for the night. Alice felt dazed and her brain did not seem to be functioning any more. It was empty and she could not find its usual furniture. Where was it she was going? What did she have to get back to? Who were these other people sitting in the room who were so strange to her and yet so familiar? And who were the couple, the dark lady and her shadowy companion, who had brought them here for this initiation?

Shortly afterwards they broke up and she found herself standing outside in what seemed to be the desolate inner suburbs of a strange city. It was raining, she had no raincoat and she could not think where she was going to spend the night. There had once been a bicycle of course, but that was long ago — it was probably lost beyond all recovery and not worth searching for . . .

Night was falling and lights began to wink on in the houses on the hills around the city. Alice was cold and wet and alone and had nowhere to go. 'There must be a place for me somewhere here,' she thought. 'They wouldn't just cast me out like this into the wilderness surely . . . ?'

She came to a bus shelter where one small lady stood waiting, enshrouded in a transparent pink plastic mac too big for her.

"Do buses go from here to town?" she asked timidly. The small figure turned towards her: it wore thick pebble glasses which magnified its bright hamster eyes grotesquely.

"Yes, they all do . . . " The woman's voice petered out and she stared unblinkingly at Alice.

"I know you," she said firmly.

"Yes," said Alice. "You look familiar to me."

"Are you by any chance involved in the Space Virgins project?"

"The Space Virgins?" Alice felt that this was something

she had heard of a long time ago, but it was as vague and misty to her as everything else in her life at the moment. "No, I'm not. Are you?"

The little woman took off her glasses, which were blurred with rain, and studied Alice hard again without them.

"I know where I met you! You came to the surgery once! In the camp. Do you remember?"

The camp? Yes, Alice remembered. It was that place she had lived for a while with Maria, where strange things had happened and they had been trapped.

"You got out, then?" she asked the woman.

"Yes. By accident. And you?"

"I don't remember. I suppose I must have. Unless this is the camp. It isn't, is it?"

The woman shook her head emphatically. A big double-decker bus loomed up through the twilight and they boarded it.

"You're a bit disorientated, aren't you?" said the woman kindly. "You must come with me to the rehearsal. There'll be food and wine there and you can join in if you want to. I'm Lettie by the way, since you've probably forgotten, and I'm the lead singer of Lettie and the Space Virgins. Not that we're just a band. We do all sorts — singing, dancing, spectacles, and transformations. We're all women of course."

"And all virgins?"

"No, not all. Only me. That's why I'm the lead singer."

"How strange," said Alice, "how very strange."

She felt suddenly light-hearted. Childish excitement fizzed in her belly.

"I'm looking forward to meeting your Space Virgins," she said. "I can't imagine what they will be like!"

The Virgins were just changing into their costumes when Alice and Lettie arrived at the church hall. Alice was gob-smacked! Here were ten or so women of all ages, shapes and sizes dressing themselves up as beings from outer space! The small fat woman with the feathered hat who had harangued her at the police station was zipping herself into a home-made robot suit which had things which looked like and probably were bed-springs pranging out dangerously from every side of it. A pale chain-

197

smoking person was winding herself one-handedly into sheets of polythene so as to be invisible. A black girl was hanging pieces of tiger-skin onto the chains that dangled around her oiled, nearly naked body and said she was a primitive space-tiger-shamaan. Alice wondered how she could join in since she had no costume to wear, but Lettie said, 'later, later' and sat her down to a plate of spaghetti and a tumbler of red wine.

The Space Virgins started their rehearsal. Lettie was still wearing her ordinary clothes — a grey pleated skirt and Shetland jumper — and looking just like Alice's old latin mistress from school. She explained that she was the earth-person among the Space Virgins and therefore did not require any special costume in order to look the part.

It seemed the Virgins did not need instruments in order to make music: they used their voices.

"Koorrawoorra, koorrawoorra, koorawoora — acha!" went the bird creature from Arcturus.

"Haga, jabbawha, hagga, na-*na*!" thudded the hefty robot.

"Meeringway, meeringway — allahstattasashay . . . " whined the tiger-shamaan.

"Eeeeeeerrrin, eeeeeeeessarray . . . " howled a couple of jackal priestesses who moved always together, sometimes making identical patterns, sometimes exactly mirroring each other. And all this in syncopation, every utterance weaving itself like a thread (or in the robot's case, like a rope) into the fabric of a vibrating wall of sound. Alice loved it. She wanted it to go on for ever.

Then Lettie insinuated herself into the mass of glittering, ululating creatures and began to sing. Alice had heard *this* sound before somewhere. Was it her mother humming old Polish lullabyes to her? Was it the weird girls who had rocked the swing boat in her bad dreams? Anyway it was the kind of sound that hits you right in the belly, making the pelvic bowl ring, making your whole body resonate like a bell. Alice felt that the sound was calling her home. She listened spellbound to the words:

> "My mother was the snow queen,
> And I the snow queen's daughter,
> Reared in the icy palaces

Far from love and laughter . . . "

Lettie paused and began to turn slowly round and round on the spot, while the Space Virgins keened and moaned out the chords of a deep, ineffably melancholy melody to accompany her.

> "My brother was the bleeding boy
> Washed up on stony beaches
> And I alone to comfort him
> Where sunshine never reaches.
>
> My sister lived beyond the glass
> On the far side of the mirror
> Though I could never hear her voice
> I knew she felt my terror . . ."

Silence fell around Alice. She was in a bell-jar and the Virgins were outside it, surrounding her, mouthing their music on the other side of the glass. Cotton-wool silence pressed on her ears. Then suddenly the sound exploded into her again, with a new, dark vibration of anger and longing in it, and she felt herself sitting at the very centre, the eye of a racing storm, while Lettie's high, pure voice reached her across the waves.

> "My sister, my sister,
> My sister inside the mirror,
> If I could only meet and touch
> My lost sister behind the
>   mirror . . . "

Alice's heart began to ache so violently she felt she would surely die of it. Her clothes were soaking wet, whether from the rain, the storm, the sea or the tears that were pouring down her face she did not know. She only knew she could not endure the longing that was reverberating through her body for one second longer . . . Then the waves of sound receded and she found herself washed up on an island where a misty sun was bringing warmth back into her freezing limbs.

"Alice! Alice! Alice!" A myriad of tiny elfin voices were calling to her from somewhere both near and far away. The notes chimed and hung in the air like humming birds so that she felt she could almost reach out and touch them, burst them like bubbles with her fingernails. Then other voices came:

> "Swinging between two worlds,
> One the world of forms,
> The other the world of shells . . .
> Swinging between the worlds . . . "

and these voices were cold and ethereal, voices of demon-women who wanted to chill her heart and lure her away from life. Then, thankfully, there was Lettie's voice again, lilting and sensible, the voice of the mother who tells the bedtime story to the fearful child, the story which frightens and yet soothes the child to sleep . . .

> My mother, the snow queen, has won!
> My brother the snow queen's wounded son,
> Lies flung out on a stony beach,
> Water coursing under his hair,
> Blood on the pebbles, blood in the air,
> The splinter of ice like a star in his heart,
> Dreaming of voyages into the dark,
> While his life seeps slowly into the sand,
> He's dying of cold by his mother's hand.
>
> Sea, take my brother into your arms,
> Carry him out to the desolate lands
> Where the thin bell calls the lost boys home
> To play in the garden after the storm . . .
>
> I will watch until he's gone,
> Until the big ship takcs me on.
> I can cross the water, dive under the sea,
> My brother will never come back to me."

200

Alice felt a terrible, absolute grief. It was her story and yet it was not. Her mother was not the snow queen and her brother was simply, undramatically dead of cancer, not of cold. And yet she *was* the snow queen's daughter and Lewis *was* her son, there could be no mistaking that. She ached with grief and a sense of loss — her brother and Lewis, both lost, her sister far away inside the mirror, quite cut off from her. Where could she turn? Who could she turn to? How could she put one foot in front of the other, now that she had nowhere to go?

She looked up. The Space Virgins stood immobile around her, ludicrous, disciplined, impeccable. Lettie took her hand and led her back to her seat. She could not remember leaving it, neither were her clothes wet at all.

"Sit down and finish your wine," said Lettie. She pulled a chair up close to Alice's and waited.

"That was amazing!" said Alice, when she had got her wits back. "But I don't understand — what was happening when . . . "

"Shhhhhh . . . " interrupted Lettie. "Don't talk of it. Our songs affect people in strange ways but we don't discuss it, we don't analyse. Otherwise we might end up back in the camp!"

"How did you get out of the camp? I recognise some of the women here from the sergeant's waiting-room, don't I?"

"Ah well . . . one day an Irishwoman started to sing in the waiting-room to pass the time, and it took off from there. I tried to put a stop to it at first — may God forgive me — but then I tried it myself and found that I had the most extraordinary gift for singing other peoples' lives. I just *knew* them without asking. It's probably because I'm a virgin. So we started a group, we worked and we rehearsed, and the night of our first performance we came out of the hall and found ourselves here, not in the camp! We asked no awkward questions, I can tell you! We were just so glad to be out."

"I bet you were! So was I!"

"But Alice, I'm so glad you're here! You must have done something too, made something perhaps . . . "

"Oh, but I haven't come straight here. I've been back to . . . to . . . " Alice tried to remember where she had been since she left the camp, but there was an obstruction in her mind which blocked her vision backwards in time. "I've been somewhere else anyway," she finished lamely.

"But now you're here, you can stay! There's nothing to stop you!"

"It's lovely here, Lettie, I'm overwhelmed! But I don't belong. It's not my place. I was brought here for some kind of initiation, along with a group of other people . . ."

Pearly tears glittered in Lettie's hugely magnified eyes, transforming themselves into a trickle of ordinary water as they escaped the confines of her glasses and made tracks across her powdered cheeks.

"I had hoped that maybe you could stay with us, and become a Virgin . . ."

"I could never be a Virgin, Lettie," she responded, jamming the impulse to laugh at her own words in case Lettie thought she was laughing at her, "not even a Space Virgin. I've got something else to do. I don't remember what it is but I suppose I'd better keep on looking . . ."

She shook herself, trying to keep the sadness at bay. This was a new kind of loneliness: to be welcomed, loved, understood by your sisters, but to have to leave them. Not to be able to act. To be obliged to float, to wait (Alice had always hated waiting for anything) without any promise of reward or comfort. The waiting room. Waiting to see the king. Well she had not seen him, and she was glad — she was not ready for such experiences, and such experiences were surely not intended for lazy, unregenerate, self-indulgent creatures such as herself. She was not even a proper, enthusiastic sinner who could repent and be redeemed . . .

She woke abruptly at dawn with a hammering heart. 'Messages beaten out on the heart,' she thought, 'Who is trying to communicate with me?' The sky was full of astonishing golden-yellow light, the rising sun diffused behind thin clouds. The air was still and cold and as she breathed it in her heartbeat grew lighter, finer until it was ringing like a tiny bell in the enormous cavern of her chest. She dressed and went outside into the empty streets. It was like walking in the middle of a flame, everything danced and shimmered. She felt she could easily step into one of the upward-flaming currents and soar into the air.

'Am I dreaming?' she asked herself but immediately knew that it did not matter whether she was or not. She would not have been surprised to come upon a lion or a unicorn strolling down the street, but she met no other beings on her way, only heard the distant rattle of the milkman and the low hum of traffic from the motorway that ringed the town.

She walked round the block twice, staring into the curtained windows of the houses, hearing a baby's waking cry, hearing the milkman come closer, feeling certain that she was about to encounter someone, that she would turn a corner and come suddenly upon them . . . waiting for her, that something absolutely extraordinary was about to happen, any minute now. . . .

But nothing extraordinary happened. Nobody was waiting round any of the corners. And by the time she passed her own house for the second time she was feeling tired and very hungry, so she doubled back, went in, switched on the radio and filled the kettle. Thomas the Smudgeface sidled in and she gave him some milk. She began to realise that the only thing that awaited her was the usual hard day's painting, the usual infuriating encounter with her own inadequacies, palliated by the occasional flutter of inspiration which she might well be too dazed, too preoccupied with trivialities to notice.

Lewis. He had jumped into her mind again. Had she dreamed of him? She palped his image gently: she saw his face flushed, excited, his eyes glittering. She felt his knee pressing hard against hers. He was telling her something . . . She took her coffee and her toast and mashed banana up into her workroom and sat down on the sofa.

She picked up her charcoal and began making sketches, from memory, of Lewis. She drew him animated, arms in the air, arguing about the middle-east problem with someone in a pub. She drew him sleeping, his body curled up, protecting himself, his face contracted, tormented by bad dreams. She drew him lying half-naked on a desolate beach, half-in half-out of the water, blood welling from his ash-blonde hair. But then she remembered his look of ecstacy from her imaginings and tried to draw it. But she only succeeded in evoking the face of a madman, an imbecile, a baby. 'Where does this ecstacy come from, Lewis?' she asked his phantom on her page. 'What has thrown you out of your self with such momentum?' And she felt herself drawn down again into the threshold of sleep, that bright twilight state where you can wander between the worlds, half-creating, half-receiving, the ego as plastic and permeable as an amoeba's skin, letting you move in and out of a myriad possible identities and adventures, but always bringing you back gently to yourself.

The last time she slipped out (allowing herself 'ten more minutes' before getting back to work) she found herself standing outside the house in the middle of the allotment-wilderness, at the front this time, wondering whether to knock on the door and see if anybody was in. She climbed the three steps and peered through the letterbox. The hall was quite empty. She examined the flower pattern on the smoked glass panels set in the door. When you looked closely at it you could see, not just flowers, but birds and animals twining themselves around in the flow of shapes. She was wishing she had a notebook with her to jot down one or two of the figures for possible use in her painting, when the door suddenly opened and her eyes travelled up to encounter the quizzical eyes of a big broad man with a shock of untidy red-brown hair. He stepped back politely to let her in.

"Next time, knock! We can't always read your mind!"

He led her through the hall into the big back room, where about fifteen people were assembled, sitting on the floor in a circle. A dark woman stood leaning on the mantlepiece, smoking.

"Ah," she said as Alice entered, "good, we wondered if you were coming. Now we can begin."

Embarrassed to be late Alice squeezed herself onto a cushion between two hunched men and cast her eyes down onto the floor.

"OK," said the woman, sliding into her place in the circle, "There's no need for formalities with you lot, so forgive me if I plunge right in . . . "

She paused and Alice flicked her eyes up to look at the other people the circle. But it was difficult to make out their individual features, or even to study the clothes that they were wearing — it was as if a fine mist was hanging in the room, made of water and weak sunlight, that somehow obscured the view and puzzled the eye. The woman spoke again, in a different, more resonant tone:

"All you who have come here in answer to our call, know now why you were chosen, why you came . . . "

A flicker in the corner of her eye made Alice turn her head to look out towards the window. And there, rearing up, as if from the garden underneath, she saw the immense contours of a great whale! Then each of the people in the circle stood up in turn and, crossing to the window, jumped out into his gaping mouth. When her turn came Alice found herself following suit, launching herself into the black hole and sailing down labyrinthine tunnels into the great creature's belly. But only part of her jumped, the other part sat calmly watching from the floor.

"OK?" said the woman again, and without fuss Alice felt the two parts of herself reuniting. The woman smiled round at them. She was plump, brown-skinned, and her eyes glimmered with humour and resolution.

"Jonah and the Whale. You remember, I hope: 'Oh Lord, not me, I want a quiet life, please, not me, I'm not worthy . . . ' Well, you're here because, whether you like it or not, the whale has swallowed you. Because finally, the thing you have spent all your energies turning away from, has caught you and engulfed you. And yet, in your daytime lives, you don't know this and persist in carrying on as if 'something else' was the most important thing. Now, you all have a different 'something else'. An idea, a person, a vocation, an obsession, a work of art, but one factor that you all have in common is that you believe this 'something else' to be bigger and more important than yourself.

"This is the beginning. It does not matter that you think your 'great work', your 'something else' is the most important thing. Unless of course you make the mistake of thinking that you share your great work's greatness! Because like the compass needle which points to magnetic north, not true north, your aim, being true unto itself, can still help you find the direction of the true north, the place of the Crystal Palace, the icy wastes you dream of in your deepest dreams. And when you hear, in the daytime world, the words 'North Pole' or 'Pole star' or any reference to the north and going northwards you will remember this group, this place, this purpose. Not consciously at first, because you are absolute beginners, but subliminally, in the secret places of the heart. For the moment that is enough."

Alice sat, suspended between sleeping and waking, belief and disbelief, listening to the woman's words, which were like the words she sometimes heard in dreams, but more coherent, more digestible. She had her eyes shut. She was not at all sure, if she opened them, whether she would see the silent group sitting around her or the walls of her own workroom. She kept them shut and the voice continued:

"Now, go. Go and try, a little at least, to remember. Some of you may be able to bring this session up into consciousness . . . " Here the woman caught Alice's eyes and smiled into them, so that her own eyes squeezed into an almond shape like Masha's. Alice had always loved these sort of eyes and for a moment was badly distracted by her admiration. "But remember," the woman continued — "whatever you recall consciously is bound to be somewhat distorted. Don't take it too literally. Don't think about it too much. Just let the memory rest in your hearts, and take root there . . . "

Alice opened her eyes. The workroom stood quietly around her, waiting in the neutral afternoon light. She had not been sleeping, she had not been dreaming. She had been . . . thinking? . . . imagining? . . . listening? . . . receiving? . . . fantasising? Her mind raced, trying to grab up all the details of the experience before they faded, to work out what 'the purpose' might be, who the other members of the group might be, whether there was any way of using the whole thing in her painting . . .

She stopped. Some instinct told her to leave it alone, not tamper with it or force it into any category. She got up and went downstairs to make tea. She felt completely alone, and yet very happy and calm. Everything was going to be all right.

After tea she started blocking in the central figure and the groups around her on the left-hand canvas, which was hell. She worked steadily, absorbed, concentrated, confident. By seven it was done — the proportions looked right, bar minor adjustments which could be made while going along. She pinned the sketches of Lewis in ecstacy next to it. Into which panel would they fit? It would depend, she supposed, on what the cause of his ecstasy was . . . Anyway tomorrow she could start on the real painting, creating atmosphere via contour, movement, colour . . . doing the things she was good at and could not help but enjoy.

Suddenly she realised that she was over the threshold. She had started! Her block, her paralysis had gone and she hadn't even noticed! She felt a burst of the kind of violent physical joy which can only be absorbed by drink or communication. She raced downstairs, grabbed a can of lager from the fridge and dialled her mother's number.

She had not yet told her mother about the painting, the dancer, the journey through the worlds. She had held back partly through diffidence, partly through meanness, not wanting to give her mother the joy of being pleased with her. But now it was time: Roza must know that all those years spent struggling with her stubborn, aimless daughter had not been entirely in vain.

"Hello, mamma, it's me! Before you speak, let me tell you the good news — I'm working! No, I don't mean for money, I mean for real! I'm painting — something *big*! No, it's impossible to tell you about it on the 'phone — I just wanted you to know in principle . . . I'll tell you the idea behind it when I see you . . . It will be soon, I promise — I'll bring some sketches to show you if you like. Now listen, did I see you had a book about Swedenborg out of the library the other day? Yes, I want to read it, I want to see what he's got to say about heaven . . . for my painting, yes . . . do you think you could send it on to me?"

★ ★ ★

CHAPTER TEN

The Snowqueen's Son

CHAPTER TEN

Alice was exhausted by the day's events, went to bed early and slept heavily through the night, dreaming deep elusive dreams which she would not remember in the morning. She was wakened at nine o'clock by the repeated ringing of her doorbell followed by an impatient banging on the door.

She thumped downstairs and flung open the door to find Masha there, panting and puffing in melodramatic urgency, hair sticking up uncombed on her head, one red sock up and one down around her ankles.

"Mum says you're to come over to her *immediately*," the child announced, reproducing her mother's note of firmness impeccably.

"Why didn't she 'phone, Masha?"

"We've been cut off. I'll be late for school but she said it doesn't matter, just to tell them my mother's ill."

"And is she?"

"I don't know. She's in bed. She's not very happy really."

"And she couldn't come to me?"

"She said you were to come. That it was very important."

Alice sighed, irritated, having planned a day of intensive painting, but promised she would get there as quickly as she could.

Anaxa was still in bed when she arrived half an hour later. The room stank of smoke and there was a brandy bottle on the bedside table. There was no bread in the bread-bin, and the two inches of milk left in the bottle had little buttery rafts floating on it. She felt another spasm of irritation — apart from anything else she was hungry and there was nothing to eat. She filled the kettle and lit the gas. She pulled the curtains back and opened the window. Anaxa, who had scarcely moved since Alice came in, drew herself up from under the covers and fixed Alice with blank, mournful eyes.

"Lewis is back," she said.

"Is he?" responded Alice lightly. She should have known of course from her daydreamings, but she had not yet learnt to distinguish intuition from wish-fulfillment. "When?"

"Yesterday. He was in the 'Rose' last night."

"Oh," said Alice neutrally. She had not told Anaxa about her own infatuation with Lewis. There had seemed no need — it was all over now and it made her feel queasy to think of it.

"You're not thinking of taking up with him again are you?" she asked.

"Taking up with him?" repeated Anaxa heavily. "What kind of crap are you talking now? The truth is that I love him. I am in love with him. Didn't you realise that? Didn't you *see*?"

Alice felt as if she had been tipped into a tank of stagnant water. When she bobbed up, breathless, to the surface, she found tht she was shocked but not surprised by Anaxa's revelation.

"Oh God!" she said wearily. "Wouldn't you just know it. Sod's law in operation once again!"

"I saw him in the 'Rose'." Anaxa continued, "I was with an Arab boy I know, but I pissed him off and went to talk to Lewis. He has changed, Alice. There is something strange in him. He was kind to me, but he wouldn't come home with me, not even for nothing. He says that sort of thing is all over for him now."

"Perhaps he's turned. He always was a bit ambivalent, I've often thought . . . "

"It's not that!"

"Well, what is it then? You tell me. You're the witch, the psychic one."

"I would be glad — if it is what I think, I fear — I would be glad about what has happened to him, if only I were not in love with him. But I know that he cannot be allowed to come to God without taking me too! I know this sounds big-headed, Alice, but I don't mean it that way. But Lewis has to *see* me, *take* me, as a woman not a whore. While he thinks he can just cast me off and go to God, he is very wrong!"

"Wait a minute, 'Naxa, I don't understand. Are you saying that Lewis has had some kind of religious conversion?"

"Yes! Now, I am not holy, not religious. You know that. But I understand these things, more than the average person, as he does not. Oh, he has met some man, some magician in the mountains there, and now he thinks he will become an enlightened man! Oh, Alice, I cannot bear it! I cannot bear it, and I cannot give him up. You must help me, you're the only one who can."

Anaxa sobbed with complete abandon. Alice made tea. She was shocked to see her brave, wild friend in this state and she did not know what to do. She had loved Lewis herself. She knew his fatal imperviousness. She knew his wound and she knew that she could not heal it. Would Anaxa succeed where she had failed? After a long struggle she had been able to give him up, detach herself from him. Could Anaxa do the same? She doubted it. Anaxa was not a canny self-preserver like herself, who knew how to get out of the water when the waves were getting too big.

"Anaxa, what can I do?" she asked softly, handing her friend a mug of milkless sugary tea. "He is his own man. He is not a man who thinks a lot of women. It's sad, but there it is — there's nothing to be done about it."

"He thinks he can rise above human love! He thinks it is a lower sort of thing! Perhaps the man he met in Afghanistan did not speak English properly. Perhaps he did not explain that human love is the first step. Or perhaps he was a bad, false teacher who will lead Lewis into hell!"

"But perhaps you are jumping to conclusions! Perhaps he just needs a breathing space — if sex has always been a problem for him, perhaps he needs to give it a rest for a while."

Anaxa dragged herself abruptly out of bed and poured the dregs of the brandy into her tea. Her sweat carried the rank odour of pain which Alice recognised from her brother's last weeks in the cancer hospital. Now, as then, she was gripped by the agony of impotence. There was nothing, nothing she could do.

"But Alice, you haven't seen his eyes," continued Anaxa feverishly. "He has seen something and it is standing in his eyes! His eyes are not looking out any more. When he saw me last night he didn't see me. His eyes are filled with something that is blinding him."

"Ecstacy?" asked Alice dryly.

"You should see it for yourself."

"I have seen it."

"You mean you dreamed it?"

"Sort of."

"You see! You are connected up with him! You can reach him, you can find out what's going on."

"What does Tom say?"

"Tom? I haven't talked to Tom about it. He would not understand — he is a man. He would talk about obsession and how bad it is for you. Like eating too much butter or drinking too much gin!"

"Shall I go out and get bread and make some toast?"

"No, thank you. I don't want to eat, but you can get me another bottle if you've got any money on you at all."

"Anaxa, I'm not doing that! That's stupid — it's not going to help anything. Look, why don't we ask the cards about it? I've been practising and I can do them now. Maybe they will have some good advice for you."

It was a blind stab in the dark. Alice was aware that common sense dressed up in a Tarot reading was often more palatable than common sense imparted directly by a sensible friend.

"No, no, no! I don't want to know if I'm doing wrong! I can't do any other thing. I don't want to change and be sensible. I want you to go and see Lewis. I want you to find out what happened to him. I want to know where this ecstacy comes from, so that I can fight it with weapons of my own."

Alice sighed. Her stomach rumbled. Here she was, trapped by Anaxa again. But this time she would not be bullied. She would make a deal.

"OK. I'll see him. I'll try to find out what you want to know. But only on one condition: that you get out of bed now, go to the shops and get some food and eat it. And that you don't start drinking again until tonight. OK?"

Anaxa nodded with uncharacteristic submissiveness and began, unsteadily, to get out of bed. Alice took her by the shoulders and squeezed them, as if to tighten her up and give her strength.

"Go out and buy yourself some special treats. I can lend you a fiver. I'll come round and see you as soon as I've anything to report. And remember what my mother says: 'No man is worth it.' What she means by 'it' I'm not sure. Suffering I suppose. Anyway, she's right you know . . . "

Her words fizzled out. She let go of Anaxa who set off stumbling around the room to find her clothes.

"Wash first," said Alice, "it'll make you feel better."

She set off home with a heavy heart, fearful of what, in Lewis, she might find.

★ ★ ★

In truth the last thing Alice wanted was to see Lewis. She was using his phantasm as a model in her painting and she feared that meeting him in flesh and blood, after a year of abstinence, would destroy the painfully achieved equilibrium between her art and her life. But perhaps the fact that she was doing it for Anaxa would protect her. She dialled his number.

"Lewis? It's Alice . . . " she curbed her inclination to babble, to apologise, to say 'don't worry, I'm not after you, I'm not going to make your life a misery again'.

"Alice!" he sounded genuinely pleased, but then he was always a consummate actor and dissembler. "How are you doing? Someone was telling me you're leading a hermit-like existence, devoting yourself to a great work."

"Yes," she said buoyantly," and someone was telling me you've come back from Afghanistan a changed man, having accidentally discovered the meaning of life."

"I wish it were true! But I did meet somebody. I had an extraordinary experience."

"I'd love to hear about it . . . "

"It's difficult to talk about, but how are you anyway? It's such a long time since I saw you."

"Could you by any chance manage a drink this lunchtime?" she asked him quickly. She felt him hesitate. In the old days he would have found an excuse not to, but now he was trying to be good.

"All right. It couldn't be a long one, but why not? How about the 'Rose' at half past one?"

"If we go in the back room we'll be able to talk in peace."

"Sure. See you then."

She walked to the 'Rose' which was about a mile away instead of bicycling so as not to spoil her hair. She was looking sublimely normal, having fought off the temptation to dress outrageously or exotically, since the meeting was not for her own benefit. She wore baggy khaki trousers and a red pullover. She tied her hair up in an austere French pleat and pulled a beret over it. She wanted to have the appearance of a true seeker for whom the adornments of the world are quite irrelevant. Lewis was not there when she arrived so she sat in the back room with a half of Guinness and practised looking around her in a cool, discouraging manner. It was a tough pub and a woman on her own had to do something to be left alone.

When he entered, ten minutes late, her heart jumped up as she had thought it would not. He wore his usual short-sleeved check shirt and jeans, his face was tanned dark brown, he had aged five years in one, but he was still outstandingly beautiful! He kissed her warmly on both cheeks and fetched her another half of Guinness.

He smiled at her in silence for thirty seconds or so and she returned the compliment, scanning his eyes for signs of ecstasy. Other people, watching them, would have thought they must be lovers, so intense and affectionate was Lewis's look. But Alice knew the truth: it was a trick of his to keep you at arm's length.

Yes, she could see what Anaxa meant about his eyes: there was a new light in them, a milky, filmy, bluey-whiteness, such as you see sometimes in the eyes of elderly people, beautiful in its way, but also sad because it generally signals the onset of some kind of blindness. And his hair! Almost white from the sun, but greenish-brown at the roots, magic hair, both dark and light at the same time! His body, leaning forward ardently at her, breathed health and vigour, and yet his usual sturdiness was gone — there was something fragile and convalescent about the way he held himself and organised his limbs.

For ten minutes they chattered. Alice was in no rush to press him for his story — she knew he would not be able to stop himself from telling it . He had always had a strong confessional impulse, as if to put his sins into the right words somehow absolved him from them. So now she relaxed and gave his a censored, ironic account of her inspiration and absorption into a life of tormented creativity. He was intrigued and mildly envious.

"I'd much rather be a painter than a poet, if I could choose. Worlds are so heavy, limiting — there's no elation, no exhilaration in the business of working on a poem. But with painting there must be times when you just lose yourself in the sensuous pleasure of the craft."

She agreed there was but told him of the recurrent dry times when inspiration and energy faded away and she was left beached like a whale on her sofa, longing for the telephone to ring, to break the drear monotony.

"I usually fall asleep," she said. "Or drift around on the border of sleep, playing with different levels, different worlds, having adventures in consciousness which I hardly remember when I come to . . . " She watched him closely to see if he recognised what she was talking about.

"Yes," he said slowly. "I know what you mean. I was ill while I was out there, and spent quite a lot of time in that sort of state . . . "

"Was then when your incredible experience happened?"

He laughed.

"Yes. It was the beginning of it anyway . . . I'll tell you the whole story, Alice. I haven't spoken about it to anyone so far, but you will probably understand why it stirred me up so much, and I trust you not to gossip about it to other people . . . "

Alice blushed to hear her integrity so mistakenly praised and hoped he would just attribute her tomato colour to the alcohol.

"Go on then, tell me. Your secrets are safe with me."

"Well, I was living in a village in the mountains, waiting for the men, the guerrillas who were training there, to set off on an expedition. I was lodging in the house of a woman, a late middle-aged woman who spoke a little English. She told me she'd lived a while in Birmingham in her youth. It seems unlikely, I know, but I had no reason to disbelieve her, and she was a very intelligent lady — she understood a lot of things that were not put into words.

So, I'd been sleeping on a mattress in her living room, taking meals with her and her daughters in the evening and wandering around during the day trying to make myself understood and taking pictures of village and family life to fill in the time. I could see it making a nice spin-off book.

Then I fell ill. At first it was just the usual gut-rot you always get on holiday — you know — diarrheoa, stomach cramps, a bit of a temperature at night. My landlady was very kind — she insisted I have her bed and she slept with her two daughters. But then, at the point when your system is quite cleared out and you usually get better, I got worse!

My temperature rocketted. There were no thermometers there of course so I have no idea how high it actually was, but I have never sweated like that in my life before — everything, my sheets, the mattress, the tee-shirt I wore for decency's sake, were all soaked through. At night I was delirious. I couldn't eat at all, and eventually my stomach was so sensitive I could not keep down water either. Even a couple of sips made me vomit. I was very frightened. There were no antibiotics to be found in the village and no hope of getting any. I knew that if I couldn't drink I would quickly get dehydrated and die!

My landlady was worried too. She fetched a couple of local wise-women who stood around the bed and muttered to each other. When they left my landlady came to me and said:

'They say you are going to die and all you can do is to prepare your spirit to meet your God.'

I burst into tears! She rocked my head against her bosom and wept with me. When I was too weak to cry any more she said:

'They said more. They said that you are freezing to death. That the fever is your body's way of trying to save you, by melting the ice inside before it freezes you to death. But your heat is not enough. It will kill you before it saves you. You cannot melt yourself. But there is one thing we can do. They did not suggest it because they are decent women, but I know a little about healing myself — I studied it many years ago. You will not like it, but there is a chance you can be saved. But you must do exactly what I say. No questions. If you disobey in any way, you will use up your strength and die. Do you want to do it? Or shall I leave you in peace to prepare for your journey to that place where we all must go someday?'

I told her I would do whatever she said. She went out of the room and came back fifteen minutes later, dressed in black. Her kindness had gone, she was cool and impersonal with me. But I was in no position to object. She sat down by the bed and ordered me to stare into her face and pay attention to what I saw.

At first there was nothing different, just the face of a severe woman in her fifties, with greying hair and hard black eyes. But after a minute or two something extraordinary started to happen: her face changed into the face of a young girl, beautiful, flirtatious, with moist round eyes as big as saucers. Then it changed again — it was my mother's face, not loving but cold and angry, as if she was disgusted with me . . . but it didn't stop there — the face went on changing and changing and I swear I saw in it all the faces of all the women who'd ever meant anything to me in my life, the women I'd slept with, hurt, been hurt by, loved and stopped loving . . . every sort of woman, but all either angry or tearful or cold with disgust and contempt for me. Then finally her face became her own again. The plain, impassive mountain woman's face.

The next moment she was pulling the sheet back and laying her hands on my penis. She told me sternly to keep looking into her eyes and not to look away for any reason whatsoever. She told me I must grow big and have an orgasm, and she started masturbating me. Well, if you've ever been very ill you'll know how far sex is from your mind. It seemed an impossible thing for me to do, but fear spurred me: I really believed that I would die if I did not have an erection, so I had one, and she carried on stroking and pulling at my penis, all the time staring coldly into my eyes.

There was no pleasure in it of course, only a tearing, burning sensation — not just in my penis but all up and down the central column of my body, right the way from tip to tail. I wanted to turn away, to bear the pain in darkness, to concentrate on just getting through with it, but I knew I must keep my eyes on hers or die, and believe me, Alice, I did it!

Finally after aeons of wretched agony, I came. It was not like an orgasm at all, but as if my whole body were a boil that burst and covered everything around with disgusting pus and venom. It was the last thing on earth I wanted to happen, it tore me up at the roots — it was an eruption of everything foul and mean and vicious in me, every voluptuous delight in hurting or being hurt coalescing together and bursting itself against me, in me, out of me . . . I don't know. And at that moment I had the most exrtraordinary perception: it was as if the woman sitting by me reached into my body via my eyes and wrenched something out of me, something, long, sharp, ragged, like a dagger, a raw-edged piece of steel."

"A splinter of ice?"

"Yes, yes, that was it exactly, that was just the feeling of it. I thought my eyes would burst too, then, thank God, I lost all sense of what was happening in a terrible convulsion of nausea. My guts erupted and I threw up everything that was left in me . . . I passed out then, I must have, and I was away, floating very far away, somewhere else completely with no sense of anything except an extraordinary, bright, dazzling white light that filled every corner of my consciousness. It was enveloping me, overwhelming me, and I felt relaxed, quiescent and calm, as if I knew that everything was going to be all right. But then I heard her voice again, very harsh and stern saying:

'Turn round Lewis, *turn round*! Turn away from the light and face the darkness. You are at the gate of life and death. You *must* turn round and come back now, you *must* turn round!'

I didn't want to, I wanted to stretch out and rest in the lovely sunshine but I wrenched myself round and found I was looking, not into darkness but down a long, grey corridor, with doors on either side of it. A dull, insurance-office sort of corridor. It was hard to walk along it, something was trying to suck me back, but I made myself put one foot in front of the other until I sensed the street-door was in front of me and I leaned against it and fell out into the open air, and fell asleep, I think, at the same time . . .

When I woke up I was weak as a kitten, but the fever was gone and I managed to drink some water. I was in a different house, the house of the man I told you about. I never saw the woman again. It seemed it had to be that way.

From that day on I began to get better. I drank, I ate, I

was soon on my feet and given jobs to do in the house, women's jobs really because it seemed that the man lived alone and was out during the day training or organising or something.

When I was really quite well again he took me outside and explained, gesturing, that he wanted to play fighting sticks with me. I tried to say no, that I couldn't do it, that I was a non-violent, non-fighting sort of person, but you try explaining something like that to someone who doesn't speak your language! It's impossible to do it without seeming rude. In the end he got angry and since I had accepted his hospitality, his care of me, I had to acquiesce.

I tried to fight with him. I was hopeless of course and he was a trained soldier, but what shocked me was that he wasn't gentle with me! When I lost concentration he knocked me down! He bruised me, he mashed my knuckles quite badly once, and then wouldn't let me stop and call it a day — he made me carry on though I could hardly hold the stick. He made no allowances for my weakness after being ill. It was a horrible, baffling thing to do to me, and he made me do it every day as well!

It was funny though: I hated it and yet I liked it. Part of me enjoyed being able to be aggressive, violent even, didn't mind being hurt, being bloodied in return.

Finally I learnt that if I paid attention for every moment while he was fighting with me I could at least stop myself getting hurt, and, just occasionally, catch him off his guard. He loved it when that happened and used to roar with laughter, pleased I suppose that his hard work was having results. It was exhausting stuff. At the end of each session I was fit for nothing. But it did help me get well quickly — I could feel energy flowing back into me and in the morning I woke up feeling happy, vigorous, looking forward to the day. Alice, for years I have woken up with a dry mouth and fluttering heart, woken up with a dread in me for what I'd have to face in the course of the day. But that was all gone — it was like being a kid again, an innocent kid.

The rest of the story is the bit that I've been telling everyone else. The exciting bit with the guns and fighting and Russians in it, because after I had proved myself with the sticks the man took me with him into the mountains.

They made me carry my fair share of equipment as well as my own gear, but I refused to carry a gun. They understood that and let me be. Anyway you can read the story of that time and see the photos in the Sunday Times colour supp. in a few weeks time so I'll skip on a month and come to the days before I was due to start the journey back, with a couple of French doctors who were going home to have a rest.

The man who looked after me offered me a choice — his name was Sami actually, I don't know why I keep calling him 'the man' — he'd found a boy who knew some English who translated for him and he told me that, if I wanted, I could stay with him, forget the camera and take up the gun. If I did that he would be prepared to be my teacher, not only in things of war but also in what the boy translated as the 'moving of the heart'. I took it to mean some kind of esoteric discipline, perhaps Sufi stuff. If I did not want that, I could return to England with his blessing, but I would have to pay the price for being saved from death: I would have to throw away my camera and my notebooks and find another way to earn a living.

Naturally I was horrified. As you know I make a good living from these things. I asked him if I had to give up writing poetry too, and he guffawed and said of course not as long as it was good poetry. Bad poetry he said would give me terrible trouble with my bowels! I asked him what would happen to me if I didn't give up journalism. He wouldn't answer, just shrugged his shoulders and looked bored. Then he softened and said it was the camera that made me ill and I could draw my own conclusions as to what would happen if I kept on using it. 'Oh,' he said, as if just remembering something he'd forgotten, 'and I've got a message for you from the woman who looked after you. She says you must abstain from all sexual activity for a year.' That set him off laughing again, but eventually he stopped, embraced me and said if I looked I would surely find a teacher in England who could instruct me on the 'moving of the heart'.

I chose to come back of course. I'm no Lawrence of Arabia. When I got back here I put my camera away, to give me time to think. I've got money obviously from the job which will keep me for months, maybe a year. But

222

when it runs out the same dilemma will be here. Do I destroy my camera? Or was it all just magical nonsense? To give up what I do best and what I most enjoy seems like craziness. And yet I remember how I felt, marching with those men, they with their guns, me with my camera. I felt ignoble, Alice. I *was* ignoble. What would you do, Alice, if someone told you to give up painting?"

"It's not the same. He didn't tell you to give up writing poetry. If I was told to give up designing dresses I'd do it like a shot. But I wouldn't give up painting, not for anyone."

Lewis put his head in his hands and massaged his brown face wearily.

"If I were you," said Alice suddenly, "I'd do it! I'd throw the camera away, and stop the writing. But then I've always been a credulous creature, not like you. I mean I believe in things like astrology and Tarot cards. I suppose that's why it's happened to you, all this stuff."

"I must say I don't see what my experiences have got to do with astrology and Tarot cards."

"No, well you wouldn't!" said Alice feeling the old argumentativeness rise up between them. "But anyway if you want a teacher there's a man called Tom who you could talk to. He's sort of a friend of mine. He knows about these things."

"I think I'll leave it for a bit. I need a rest, time to think things through . . . "

"I'm not sure thinking will get you anywhere." Alice was quite unable to resist sniping at him. She knew it did no good, and would only put him off the things she talked about — like Tom — but she could not deny herself the satisfaction of putting him right.

He grinned at her.

"I don't want to argue with you about it. Anyway, enough of me. Tell me the gossip, Alice. Tell me who's been doing what to whom, since I've been away!"

★ ★ ★

Two thirty in the morning and Alice was bicycling home from babysitting Masha, Anaxa having found a new job hostessing at a night-club in town. A month had passed since Lewis's return, and now the sturdy October winds fought hard against her as she laboured up the bill next to the allotment wilderness. In fact, the winds were so fierce that she had to dismount half-way up and push her bicycle to the top. Up there she paused to draw breath and stared down into the valley. Lights all round, lamps winding up the opposite hill and car headlights gusting past her where she stood, but no lights down there, in the abysmal valley where the old house was. 'Shall I go down and visit the house?' she thought. The idea of stumbling along the dark path with only her failing bicycle lamp to guide her was not appealing, and yet she felt a strong impulse to go there, knock on the door and see if anyone was in. But of course they would not be — those strange meetings had happened in another world, the world of dreaming and imagination, not this one. If she went down she would surely find only a locked door and courting couples in the walled garden sheltering from the wind. On the other hand, there *were* places where the worlds crossed, inter-section points . . . she felt badly in need of guidance from the people of the house — it was possible that she might find them there . . .

She needed guidance because she did not know what to do next. She was waiting, waiting but not sure whether she should be waiting, or whether there was something she should be doing, some action that she should undertake to bring about the future that she wanted. In her outer life things were reasonably in order: Anaxa had accepted that Lewis needed time to think and settle down. Alice had told her the bare bones of his story, leaving out the lurid details, and assured her friend vehemently that he did not seem like a man who wanted to escape from life but much more like one who had never really lived and was now, slowly and painfully, trying to learn how to do so.

"Be his friend!" she had urged Anaxa. "Invite him to dinner. Talk to him. Don't think of him only as a lover . . . that will make him run away!"

"Being friends with men is not my strong point," replied Anaxa sulkily. "I'd rather wait till he grows up and sees the light. I mean, how should I be friends with him? I wouldn't know what to say, how to keep the conversation going!"

Lewis she seldom saw. She heard that he was working as a labourer on a building site on the outskirts of town. When she did glimpse him, in the 'Rose' or buying vegetables in the market on Saturday, he looked troubled but excited — there was an energy fizzing through him that he did not seem able to properly control. She left him alone and he did not seek her out.

Maria she was guiltily neglecting. Since her painting had got truly under way, since her contact with the group in the old house, she felt full of experiences which Maria would scorn and reject as hallucinations of a weak and self-indulgent mind. Maybe she was right. For her part Alice felt that the contradictory elements in Maria's life must be putting a near intolerable strain on her; the complete sacrifice of her every non-working moment to Roderick and motherhood, her fight to be a one-woman feminist-therapy centre within a hospital that viewed her with deep distrust, her sudden decision to become a celibate separatist, her evening class teaching women's studies from a marxist perspective at the WEA . . . it all jangled discordantly in Alice's ears. And now she was planning to enter therapy, for the second time, to 'try and sort out my own internal contradictions in the context of a patriarchal system hostile to the whole concept of women's autonomy!'

So she swung giddily, uneasily between Anaxa's magical world and Maria's rational one, not knowing in which she really belonged. In fact she felt wrong, restless in both — they were somehow not the *right place to be*. There was somewhere else she had to get to, something else she had to do . . . Something wonderful had happened to her in one of those other worlds, she had been somewhere rich and strange with people who belonged to her . . . but she couldn't remember where it was or who they were . . . She couldn't connect up any of her 'imaginary' experiences with her ordinary life, and the only time she felt at home and at peace was when she was painting.

And Tom was no help. She had not gone to the group he'd recommended, but he still came to visit her late at night, to drink sweet tea and tell her pointed stories about false seekers on the path. When she told him about her strange dreams, fantasies, memories — whatever they were — he just snorted and remarked that she had a most

vivid imagination and would do well to avoid over-simu-
lating company and intoxicating liquor for a while. When
she kissed him goodbye he made sure her lips never got
anywhere near his own, presenting always a cool cheek.

The dark house waited at the centre of the wilderness.
Was it empty or full of voices, presences and portents?
Alice hesitated at the gate, leaning her bike against her
legs, wondering how to overcome her fear of darkness, of
strange men lurking, of creatures far worse than rapists
who might be waiting there to jump out and wreak revenge
on her. With great effort she heaved her heavy bike over
the fence (the gate was locked) and hid it in the peripheral
undergrowth. She jerked the front lamp off its bracket and
set off with beating heart towards the house.

Half-way along the path, her eyes getting used now to
the intermittent, cloudy moonlight, she realised that she
was being very foolish. She knew that the house would be
empty, derelict. She was confusing levels — a dangerous
thing to do, as Tom had warned her. Perhaps staying up so
late without the intake of alcohol which normally accom-
panies late nights had kicked her into an altered state of
consciousness, in which she had forgotten for a moment
where she was, that she was not 'dreaming' at home on the
voluptuous settee, but biking home from babysitting in a
ferocious wind, needing to get back and go to bed quickly
so that she would not be too tired to put in a full day's work
the next day.

She turned back, embarrassed, and relieved that she
had come to her senses. She reached the locked gate and
fumbled in the undergrowth for her bicycle. It was difficult to find — she must have dumped it further along. She
groped gingerly down the wall, kicking out with her feet to
locate it. Then she made her way back again towards the
gate. It was stupid, but the bicycle simply wasn't there!
Her heart skipped. This was ridiculous — of course the
bicycle was there! It was scarcely a couple of minutes since
she had left it, not time enough for anyone to climb over
the fence and steal it, even supposing there was anyone
around. She glanced around her fearfully. The wind
whisked over the tops of the bushes. A battered taxi
whizzed past on the road. 'Don't panic!' she told herself,
'Search carefully.' And she began to comb the long grass

methodically, telling herself the bike must have slipped down to the ground with an unheard thump as she walked away and that she would be making contact with its icy skeleton any minute now.

She did not. After five minutes she stood up. 'O Christ,' she thought, 'I'm trapped on the wrong side again! What will I find out there, along that street? The camp? The strange city? Or just Leeds at three o'clock in the morning drifting in and out of sleep?'

She had a choice now: to turn back and go to the house after all to find what was waiting there (perhaps the disappearance of the bicycle was intended to force her to do just that!) or to strike out into the city to find a landmark that she recognised. If this were Leeds then she was not far away from Tom's shop — it was just down the hill and round the corner, a ten minute walk. If she was somewhere else, not Leeds, then no doubt the walking would take her to another suitable destination.

She decided to go for Tom's place, preferring the open streets to the dark pathway. As she swung down the hill she began to relax: the place looked exactly like Leeds — allotments on one side with their funny old home-made sheds, building site on the other, dark terraces climbing up the hillside . . . Perhaps her bike had been stolen after all and she was still in her normal waking world!

She turned the corner into Tom's street. All the other shops were dark, their windows shuttered and barred against break-ins, but Tom's window blazed with light. 'Maybe he is up late working,',thought Alice, 'in which case he can make me a cup of tea while I 'phone for a taxi and everything will be all right after all.'

Tom answered her knock almost immediately. He was fully dressed, in his white trousers and shirt, looking as fresh and elegant as if he were about to give a cocktail party.

"At last!" he said. "I've been expecting you. Now, no time to waste in explanations. Come upstairs and let's get on with it before the moment goes."

She followed him up the stairs. The whole place was ablaze with light. The air effervesced like champagne; there was an atmosphere of excitement, anticipation in the house. And although she could not hear voices she sensed the presence of other people in other rooms.

He led her up past the kitchen to the top floor where she had never been before. Outside a closed door he paused and turned to her.

"Alice, after this point I can no longer help you. So before you go in let me say one thing. Your methods are unorthodox, perhaps also dangerous. But you seem determined to do things your own way and that must be respected. You've begun, so now continue. You could have done it all so differently — but you didn't. Now all I can say is, for God's sake, have faith in yourself, in your own perceptions. Try to keep your heart still, your breathing light and even, and remember, you really are *here*, in my house, nowhere else. Now go in. Your friend is waiting. Thank God you didn't go to the other place. That would have been most complicated."

He pushed the door open and stood back so that Alice could walk into the square, white room. As soon as she was in, the door closed gently behind her and she realised that a man was sitting on the floor by the window, his head down on his arms as if asleep. She knew without needing to see the face beneath the fair hair that it was Lewis.

He looked up. She was surprised that there was no blood on his hair, no wound in his head. He just looked like one who has been dozing and daydreaming to pass away the time. He did not seem surprised to see her.

"It's all so simple really, isn't it?" she said, thinking of the way everyone in her life seemed to know each other or get to know each other without her having the bother of introducing them.

"What do you mean?" asked Lewis in his polite well-brought-up-boy voice, with iciness just under the surface.

"I mean . . . well, how do you come to be here? I didn't know you knew Tom."

"I don't."

"So what are you doing here?"

"I don't know, Alice, and what does it matter?" She felt he was on the brink of getting very annoyed indeed with her.

"Sorry." As soon as she said the word she regretted it. Why should she apologise for asking normal questions?

"Actually I'm here against my will. Try the door — go

on — you'll find your friend has locked it from the outside."

The door was indeed locked. Alice wondered what the hell was going on.

"Did you throw away your camera?" she asked, to fill the embarrassing silence.

"Yes, I have actually. That surprises you, doesn't it? But I've bought another one, with the Sunday Times money. Did you see the piece — it was in last week?"

"No, I'm afraid I didn't. I've had to cancel the papers to save money. Buying another one doesn't seem very much in the spirit of the instructions they gave you."

"The 'instructions'? Who has the right to give another human being 'instructions'? Who are 'they' anyway? It's all hocus-pocus." His eyes as he spoke were as hard as diamonds, boring through Alice's soft exterior and bruising her at the core. She stretched a nervous smile across her face. "For goodness sake, how am I going to earn my living, if not by taking pictures and writing articles? I've been doing building work for a month and it's destroying me — I've got no money left for anything else. If I have a talent for photography, for journalism, Alice, don't you think I have a duty to use it?"

In truth Alice did. She could not bring herself to argue against him. He held his eyes locked onto hers, maintaining his hard, defiant look. Eventually she had to look away, her eyes watering. The fluttering she had noticed in him since he had come back was gone. He seemed to have stiffened and set. Things were not in balance any more, the astonishing radiance and energy had gone. He was now just a nice-looking, ruddy-cheeked man who sat on the floor angrily justifying himself. He was not going to succumb to the fever again and die. He was going to be successful and normal. He had grown up, that's all. He had found a focus and lost all his blurry edges, his flares and spills of brilliance and cruelty. Now he would meet a pretty and intelligent girl quite a few years younger than himself and settle down with her. He would never be capable of deep love, real intimacy, but his young wife would idolise him and forgive him. Anaxa could forget it. She hadn't a chance.

"Lewis . . . " she said suddenly, pronouncing his

name with dream-like intensity, and he smiled at her in his old, dreamy, ecstatic manner. She laughed with shock at the change in him. What was this? Was he playing a game with her?

"I'm all right," he said gently. "The building work was a good idea. It reminded me of something. Building, digging, putting brick on brick. Until I was sixteen, you know, and I got a camera for my birthday, my real passion was archeology. I'd already started going on digs . . . but it all faded away when I discovered taking pictures. It was too arduous, too dirty. And it would have taken me years to make a name for myself. But when I was in Turkey on my way home I met an old mate from school, who was organising a dig in Capadoccia. Excavating the ancient cavern systems there. Did you know whole tribes of people used to live there, underground? He said they were always glad of extra people on a dig, would give you food and shelter, even if they couldn't give you money. I was thinking I might go and work there for a while . . . "

"But you just said you were going back to photography!"

"Did I? Of course I've thought of it, but I've lost the taste somehow."

This was a different Lewis again! The radiance had transformed itself from a sparkle to a glow. He seemed younger. He seemed to have gone back and connected himself up to a younger self who was naïve, enthusiastic, curious. He was talking like a passionate schoolboy. Alice liked this Lewis: his humility disarmed her.

Now she knew that it was not Lewis who was playing a game. It seemed they were in some sort of world that was close to the source of all possibilities, where different futures were tried out, different pasts contacted. Where you could be for a while the person you would be if you made a certain choice, followed a certain path . . .

"Lewis," she began tentatively. "Do you remember the camp? The underground pleasure palaces? The cell where they imprisoned you? The knife, the killing, the escape?"

Lewis's eyes blanked like a video screen while its computer is searching for a different programme. Alice meanwhile wondered what this *was* she was remembering. But yes, she did recall it all in pristine, reverberating detail —

the blood pumping all over the fat man's nice viyella shirt, his voluptuous fall to the earth, their terrified flight with Anaxa back to the upper world . . .

"I remember killing someone, because I had to . . . and that I'd tried to forget it but couldn't and was very frightened that they would come after me . . . but that was in a dream, a dream I had while I was ill, but which I think I've had ever since I was a kid . . . it didn't really happen. It was just a dream."

"Just a dream . . . " said Alice dreamily, "why do we think the experiences we have in dreams are less real than the things which happen to us in our waking lives? You killed, it seems to me, you really killed, even if there is not a material corpse rotting somewhere in the earth to prove it . . ."

She looked at Lewis and saw the sweat stains on the underarms of his shirt, the coarseness of the skin on his cheeks where he must have had acne as a youth. She looked into his eyes and way deep in, way back beyond their colour and their sparkle, she caught the sombre glitter of the old dagger of ice. 'Is it still in there then?' she thought. 'He said the woman in Afghanistan had plucked it out! . . . How terrible to be tied in love to a man who cannot love! Oh Jesus Christ, surely I had gotten over this!'

Suddenly she remembered Anaxa.

"Lewis, what about Anaxa?"

"What about her?"

"What are you going to do about her?"

"Why should I do anything?"

"Well, we're all responsible for one another and . . . "

"Alice, don't give me your soppy mystic crap! I had a business arrangement with Anaxa which is now terminated and that's that."

"A business arrangement?"

"I hired her services. As a whore. And a very good one she is too. But she won't leave me alone. She's hounding me. I don't know what it is she wants from me — only that I can't give it."

"I should have thought it was obvious what she wants."

"Well she can't have it!"

"You were happy enough to have her when you wanted

sex."

"Oh, Alice, don't take that weary pious holy-righteous tone with me! To tell you the truth I'm sick of sex. I'm sick of crawling into bed with women. I'm sick of fucking, sick of ejaculating, sick of wanking, sick of female company!"

Alice sat there, her body thrumming with outrage, anger, the pressing need to put the boot in, hurt him just as viciously as she could. The only thing that stopped her was a want of phrases; she was having trouble with her brain again. It was churning out the same old hopeless melodies like a pianola and she knew, in the present situation, none of them would do.

The silence locked them up each in their own misery. The bright light in the room began to hurt Alice's eyes. She got up and tried the door; it was still locked. Stale-mate. Stagnation. Her heart ached savagely for *something*, something different to happen. She shut her eyes. Down in her guts something moved. She had not eaten for hours — was it hunger? Waves of queasiness washed up her throat and filled her mouth with bitter-tasting saliva. She felt slightly sick. She opened her eyes. She was still stand-ing in the room, leaning against the wall. Lewis was still sitting hunched up on the floor. She shut her eyes again, to escape, and seemed now to be travelling, spiralling up and up into a vast, empty region. She was moving too fast for comfort but she dared not stop — she would be sick. She was travelling in somewhere and nowhere. She was in a place which could not be described or named, which exist-ed and yet did not exist, a place where there were no mir-rors and you could never see yourself, although she knew you *were* yourself and there was no rubbing out of you . . . she might have been there before, a long time ago, or she might just have imagined it, it might be a place she had invented in her painting — it might be a part of hell or pur-gatory . . . or heaven?

Up and up she spiralled. The air, if air it was, sparkled and fizzed . . .

Then something ripped across the screen of heaven! A crackling whiplash of electric current that bounced Alice right off the wall and sprung her wide awake and tremb-ling into the centre of the room. Lewis had coughed! She stood, bewildered a moment, her eyes fluttering and flashing, her heart galvanised, ready for action, ready to take on anything that came!

Lewis had coughed because he was sobbing! He was sobbing as she had never seen anyone sob before, sitting bolt upright, not moving to cover his face, not trying to wipe the tears with a hand or mop them with a sleeve, his shoulders jerking up and down convulsively just like the laughing policeman's. He was not giving in to it, and at moments actually managed to control the shuddering of his chest by holding his breath, but then as if kicked in the belly, he would start again, with hoarse, racking spasms that seemed to torture not relieve him.

Alice did not move to embrace him — it was not the kind of crying that could be comforted by a hug. Neither did she want to stand and watch him suffering. She felt that the sobbing, like the ecstacy, had nothing at all to do with her. She backed away from him and tried the door again. This time it opened easily. Quietly she left the room, shutting the door after her, and went downstairs. In the kitchen a harsh fluorescent light illuminated the figure of Tom seated at the table in immaculate pyjamas, caught in the act of dropping a sugar-cube into a glass of Russian tea.

He looked up and fixed her with his usual penetrating stare. She walked towards him and stood right over him, intent on reflecting his penetrating stare right back at him.

"What the hell was in that room?"

"Nothing. Just energy. Yours and his."

"Not yours?"

"Not necessary. I was just the go-between, the fixer."

"He's crying now, you know, sobbing his heart out."

"Good."

"How can you say that? He's breaking his heart."

"And what do you think he's crying for?"

"I haven't the faintest idea."

"For himself of course. We always do."

"I think it's dangerous, the sudden discharge of all that emotion."

"A lot of things are dangerous, Alice. Sometimes it's necessary to take risks. What happened to him in Afghanistan touched him deeply, pushed him right to the edge, but not over it. He was in a dangerous condition anyway, teetering on the brink."

"And you took it upon yourself to push him over?"

"No! We talked for some hours before you came. He was very tired but very keyed up. You were in some sort of state — I could see that. It was the small hours of the morning, the time when people are born and die. Just a certain set of circumstances, that's all."

"But why? What for?"

"Why live in prison? Why live in fear? Why not travel across the boundaries? What is the virtue of living like a slave?"

Alice did not respond. Her head was still spinning slightly from her own encounter. She sat down abruptly at the table and took a sip of Tom's tea.

"It was an opportunity, that's all. Did you take it?"

"I suppose so," said Alice gruffly.

"What happened?"

"I don't want to talk about it."

"All right."

He got up and poured her a glass of tea. He looked very tired. Her anger with him was evaporating. They heard the creak of slow steps on the stairs.

"I suggest you go before he comes down. I need to speak to him and he won't speak freely if you are here."

She stood up and made her way to the door. Suddenly she felt unutterably tired."

"My bicycle," she muttered, "what about my bicycle?"

"I think you'll find, Alice, that your bicycle is exactly where you left it. Now, go on, quickly, before he comes."

★ ★ ★

Outside in the damp streets smelling of curry and burnt oil and beer, day was dawning. A fine drizzle had thoroughly chilled her by the time she reached the allotment gates, but already, glinting dutifully in the long grass, leaning sedately against the wall, she made out the hulking contours of her bicycle. An early digger glared at her as she wheeled it towards the gate. The saddle was wet, the brakes slippery, but it certainly felt like a bicycle of this world not the next as it zizzed her home over the wet streets to Weetabix and 'This Week's Composer' and a long tedious story from the lodger about how he had locked himself out the night before and waited ages, shivering in the porch, for her to come home before being obliged, in view of the desperate situation, to break the kitchen window and climb in . . . She wondered, as his truculent Yorkshire voice drawled on, if Tom would now invite Lewis to the mysterious 'group' which she had neglected to attend . . . so that Lewis would become an enlightened man, and realise that Anaxa was worthy of his love, and marry her and take Masha away from their life of poverty and booze and pragmatic prostitution . . . But she supposed that was a scenario only found on the wilder shores of Mills and Boon not in the urban wilderness of Leeds' half-hearted demi-monde. Her head swam with tiredness. She would have to go to bed for a few hours. Heaven would have to wait until after lunch.

CHAPTER ELEVEN

The Sulky Princess

CHAPTER ELEVEN

Anger. That was what it was. That was the name of the emotion Alice was registering now. She was angry with herself, angry with Anaxa and Maria, angry with Lewis, angry with men! Particularly with men. Oh yes, yesterday she'd been on the 'phone to Maria for half an hour arguing against separatism, but today she wondered whether perhaps Maria was right — that the only way was to leave them entirely alone. Because she was sick of being sorry for them, making allowances and excuses for them, being exaggeratedly pleased when they behaved for once like human beings, not like brats . . . and this in the aftermath of her night in the upstairs room with Lewis! Instead of feeling warm, reconciled, accepting, like she ought to have done, she felt furious! She luxuriated in her contempt for them — Lewis, Tom, Roderick's absent father — these immature, self-indulgent, narcissistic, woman-hating, masturbating, infuriating men!

Her eyes swerved onto her uncompleted canvas. She had been so pleased with it last night, when she had rung Maria up, but now she could see that it was too insipid. Her style was *still* too pretty-pretty! The truth was that there was not enough harsh, reverberant, *masculine* energy in it! And that was pretty bloody ironic in view of her present state of mind regarding men! And where, pray, was she to find that 'harsh, reverberant masculine energy'? No matter what she had said to Maria about not wanting to hide in a cosy, sisterly nest, she *was* doing just that. And her animus, who ought to be a shining, ruthless warrior, was instead flaked out across the threshold, blocking the exit, a fat, domesticated dragon, whose teeth and testicles had been drawn out or cut off years ago. It was most depressing. She could not get out. She was trapped in the nest, tricked into impotence, cheated of her prince, her muse, her inspiration!

Thomas the Smudgeface mewed to be let in at the window but she ignored him. A neutered Tom-cat would not do. She needed the real thing. But how could she find it? By searching and scouring the world for it? Or simply by summoning it, by holding in her mind the intention of having it and calling it steadily towards her? She liked the idea — it had a wood-smoky scent of witchery about it. But Alice was not very good at concentrating on such abstract things. She drew her scribbling pad towards her and continued the adventures of Maria, the sulky princess.

This was a character she had invented for Masha, a rebellious little brat of a princess who didn't want to be a queen when she grew up. Alice was drawing pictures to illustrate the story, which was a serial she told Masha every time she babysat. The story-so-far was that Maria's elder brother had been killed in a hunting accident, so that the sulky princess was due to be crowned queen. Luckily she had been saved just in the nick of time by a giant bird who had carried her off to a high mountain cave, with strict instructions to remain there until her prince turned up to rescue her. However Alice and Masha had together decided that the princess would not wait but would learn to fly herself and set off to seek her fortune. So she tore up her posh coronation dress to make wings, and set off.

At first things had been fine, her flight wild and exhilarating, but now Alice found herself drawing the little princess rudely crashed to earth, crawling alone through a dusty desert, bruised, bedraggled and alone. Now maybe, she was regretting her decision to launch off on her own so recklessly . . .

Yes, thought Alice, that's me — crawling along in the desert, suffering stubbornly because I've rejected the masculine, but longing for it just the same . . . and as she stared at her poignant sketch, she felt her anger turn to lust and a shaft of sexual hunger lanced into her vagina and lingered there, vibrating.

"Oh *no*!" she said out loud. Sex was the worst and wickedest distraction when the painting was going badly. But she was not going to give in to it today! She jumped up, let the cat in, and ran down to the kitchen to fetch her cigarettes. When she came back the atmosphere of the room had changed. It was as if her dangerous energies had been discharged and transformed by the sunshine into a clear and thrilling medium in which all sorts of things could be made, all sorts of things could happen. And she felt quite calm and ready for work — all lust and anger spent.

* * *

That night, when Alice arrived at Anaxa's to babysit, she found her friend flopped in her dressing-gown in front of the old black and white tele, instead of being tarted up and ready to go out to work.

"I've given it up," she told Alice listlessly. "I was fed up with all the groping and the slapping that went on. We'll just have to manage on the SS for a while."

But, SS or not, there was a nearly full bottle of brandy on the mantelpiece.

"So you didn't need me?" said Alice wearily. "You might have rung up and told me you weren't going out!"

"I need you, I need you, Alice! I need you to help me drink this bottle of brandy and Masha wants to hear the next installment of her story."

Alice felt suddenly sad. She sat down on the bed. She remembered Lewis, what he had said about Anaxa. How there was no hope for her. She wondered whether she should tell her so, whether her present dull-eyed listlessness was due to her continuing obsession with him . . .

"Have you seen Lewis?" asked Anaxa.

"I bumped into him the other day."

"And?"

"And nothing. We just talked about this and that."

"He despises me, doesn't he?"

"Oh Anaxa, how can you say that?"

"Because I feel it. How do you know I'm wrong?"

Alice was trapped. She could either lie and comfort Anaxa with some fabricated quote from Lewis designed to show he did not despise her, or she could tell the truth, in a gentle, bowdlerised version, the truth that Lewis did indeed despise her.

"He's not worthy of you, you know."

"That's not the point. What does he think of me? Come on, Alice, tell me. I know you know."

"He says he's sick of sex, 'Naxa, that he doesn't want to know."

"Sick of sex or sick of me?"

"Oh God, don't interrogate me! I don't know!"

"You do, you bloody do know, woman! Tell me or I'll never speak to you again!"

Anaxa was on her feet now, her torn dressing-gown swinging open to reveal her white, unhealthy skin, standing over Alice with her glass held high as if to threaten her.

"He said he didn't know what you wanted from him but he wasn't going to give it to you anyway!"

Anaxa brought her glass down slowly to her mouth and drained it. She sat down calmly in her seat.

"Thank you," she said politely. "That's all I wanted to know. I just wanted to know if there was any hope at all. It seems there isn't, and that's all right."

"It's not all right," said Alice quietly, "it's not all right at all."

"Oh, Alice, don't make a fuss! Tell Masha her story, will you? I want to watch the end of Coronation Street — there's someone I know in it." She turned away from Alice and fixed her eyes determinedly on the TV screen. Alice knew she should not let the issue slide like this, but she also knew there was no point in bullying Anaxa to discuss it further if she did not want to. 'I'll bring it up again later,' she thought, 'when she's had a few more brandies and Masha has gone to bed.'

She and Masha arranged themselves comfortably on the sofa, Masha as usual with her head buried in the cushions and her bottom in the air, (she liked to listen in the magical isolation of darkness so that no-one could see the expression on her face) Alice with her sketchbook laid out across her knees. Alice explained how Maria's wings had failed, how she had crashed to earth, and how, just as she was weeping with despair, she had felt a cool shadow descend on her and looked up to see a golden lion sitting gazing down at her. She'd thought he was her saviour, and would carry her home to the palace, but instead he stared hypnotically into her eyes and said:

"Dance, little princess, dance! Dance or perish in this desert like a dog!"

Here Alice gave Masha a nudge and she bounced up to look at the picture of Princess and lion in deadlock, eye to eye.

"And Maria felt it was the last thing in the world she could do at that moment — dance," continued Alice, "so she cried and sobbed and told the lion she was bitterly tired and thirsty and hungry, and stamped her foot and did everything she could to make the lion change his mind. But it was no good: the lion would not give in."

Alice paused and found Masha's round pontefract-cake eyes looking up at her, the pupils enormously dilated.

"And what do you think Maria did now" she asked the spell-bound child.

"I should think," said Masha, in a tiny whispering voice, "that she danced."

"She did indeed" said Alice, "because she really didn't want to die.

Impatiently Masha leaned over and flipped to the next page of the sketchbook. It was blank.

"Oh *no*!" she shouted indignantly. "There's no picture of the princess dancing with the lion."

"Ah, well that's where you've got to help me! You've got to do some belly-dancing for me so that I can draw the princess doing it too."

Masha jumped up with alacrity. She had none of the bashfulness of an all-English little girl. Coronation Street ended, Anaxa put some clashing, wailing Turkish music on her record-player. Masha climbed up onto the table and pulled her pyjama trousers down onto her hips. Smiling for the first time that night Anaxa started clapping while Alice got her crayons out and prepared to sketch.

With an expression of fierce concentration on her face the child bent her sturdy legs and began to swing her pelvis round and round. Alice laughed to see the kid so self-forgetful and so vigorous. Masha's jubilant energy and pride in her dancing shot arrows of longing into her body. She wanted to dance too, not draw.

"Where did you learn to dance like that?" she asked when Masha had finished and jumped down off the table into her mother's arms.

"Me mum taught me," said Masha, bouncing off Anaxa's bosom into Alice's lap, and arranging herself in a comfortable straddling position. "But you've not drawn anything! What about the next picture?"

"I'll do it in a minute, Mash. I just wanted to watch you dancing. You're ever so good. I wish I could dance like that."

"You could," said Anaxa shortly. "I'll teach you. I used to do it for a living. Bloody hard work — three sessions a night, every night, seven nights a week. Good money though. They used to stuff pounds notes down the front of my costume, sometimes even fivers and tenners. I did the proper sort — none of this cleaned up nonsense I've seen these feminists do on tele. The real McCoy. My mother taught me. Her mother taught her.

"But there's nobody I want at the moment."

"There isn't? What about Tom? You see him quite a bit."

"Tom? His mind is on higher things. He comes to see me to talk about God. There's nothing sexual between us."

"Alice," began Anaxa in the amused, forbearing tone that many of Alice's women friends tended to use with her, "you think a man *ever* comes to see a woman to talk about God? Really? A man comes to see a woman always, *always* because she is a woman, because he needs a woman. Can't you see that? You are stupid sometimes.

"Tom and I are platonic friends," said Alice earnestly. "And he has girl-friends. They don't last long but he has them. He likes to keep the turnover high so they don't get too attached. He's not at all interested in me."

And yet she had a picture of him standing at her door, arms folded protectively across his chest, engaged in self-conscious valedictory banter at three o'clock in the morning. She could feel the cursory peck on the cheek with which he had said goodnight to her. There was certainly more than casual friendship between them. She had thought of it before as a fraternal kind of love. But perhaps Anaxa was right — perhaps the tension she had felt at those moments was a suppressed erotic longing . . .

Anaxa unfolded her limbs and began to clear the floor ot its debris.

"Alice — you taught me how to make conversation. So I will teach you how to dance, how to speak to a man with your body before you've even been introduced! Stand up. Mash, put the music on at the beginning again."

She showed Alice how to stand with her feet wide apart, firmly planted on the ground, her knees bent, and to thrust her hips out, round to the side, right back and round to the front again. She told her to imagine that she was drawing the outline of a big bowl with a pencil held between the lips of her vagina, a bowl full of shining, sparkling water which might slop and splash and spill but which could never be exhausted. The movement made Alice feel both lewd and exposed. After a while it made her sad, but Anaxa would not let her rest. After the bowl they did the figure-of-eight and some hip-loosening exercises, then balancing on the toes and seeing how far back you could stretch. By the time the record ended she was exhausted, but still Anaxa pushed her on.

"Come — now — dance for me and Masha! Push yourself, open yourself, enjoy yourself! There is nothing to hold back, nothing to deny! Give! Give! Push! Push! . . . OK, now you can rest and I will tell the secret of making it work with men."

Alice fell backwards on to the bed and lay there with her legs apart. She could feel her vagina wet and open and the blood pulsing urgently up and down the spongey hills and valleys of its walls, juices trickling down their slopes like mountain streams . . . but still she wanted to cry, to bury her head in the pillows and weep, to weep for the wasted power and vitality of womanhood, the hopelessness of love, the heartlessness of men, the stupidity of women . . . but she felt that it would be an unseemly thing to do in front of Masha so she controlled herself and sat up straight again.

Anaxa dropped down beside her and took her hand.

"Now, if you are dancing, and there is a man watching you, a man you want, you must do two things to bring him to you. The first is easy: catch his eye whenever you can and hold it for a second. Then, you take your eyes away for a while and carry on, but keep coming back to check that he is still waiting, looking. Then when you have got him fascinated you imagine long white threads of light streaming out from your body, particularly your pelvis, right in *here*, and here you imagine a very bright, very strong ball of flames, burning like a bonfire in the night. You send out the threads to him and wrap them round him, wrap them round all the organs of his body that you can feel — the heart, the backbone, the belly, everything. And when he is all wrapped up in your web of fibres, you start, very slowly and surely pulling him in to you. You let the threads tighten — they are very strong — you tighten your buttocks, you keep your hips rotating and you suck him in, you wind him in to you. Remember, if you do it properly, you cannot fail. You are the Goddess, he the God, and in this, in matters of love and sex the Goddess is stronger than the God!"

"Is it OK for Masha to hear all this?" asked Alice anxiously. "Isn't it a bit early for her to be thinking of these things?"

"Nonsense! She is going to be a woman when she grows up, so she might as well grow up a proper woman who knows how to deal with men, not frigid and polite and paralysed like you Englishwomen. Sorry, Alice, I don't mean to be rude — I mean only in the matters of sex. Anyway, you like listening, Masha, don't you?"

Masha wriggled her bottom against Alice's lap and giggled fruitily. Then there was silence in the room. Except for the whooping and chattering of the neighbours's television. Except for the scuffling of drunken boys in the street below. Except for a sudden poignant phrase of Bach, chimed by a distant ice-cream van and cut off just before its culmination . . .

"It's very late for an ice-cream van," said Alice absently.

"Repent, repent, it's later than you think!" said Anaxa flippantly.

"Oh," said Alice with a sigh. "I feel so very sad tonight."

"Nothing to be sad about. Life is hard and it will go on being hard. Nothing more to say."

". . . But I feel so cut off from you! As if you were behind a glass, a glass I could never break to get to you . . ."

"It will pass. It's only a feeling, only a mood."

". . . and I don't believe your terrific 'philosophicalness' tonight. I think you're bleeding, but you won't admit it!"

"Masha, go to bed now, will you? It's late and you've got school tomorrow. And close the door behind you."

They sat in silence until the child had brushed her teeth at the sink, and obediently shut the door of the kitchen after her.

Alice took a deep breath. Now was the time to speak. Now was the time to spill the beans about her own adventure with Lewis. It was the only way she might break Anaxa's obsession. She poured herself a little brandy and began.

"Anaxa, I have to tell you something. You know that Lewis is a friend of mine, but what you don't know is that I loved him too. Once. For quite a long time actually. Well, I say I loved him, but in fact it was an obsession, an infatuation, a terrible, uncontrollable craving. I was really quite peculiar for a while . . . "

Anaxa turned dull black eyes onto Alice, eyes without expression, without intelligence, without humour or commonsense. Alice felt suddenly out of her depth, in a dark, hopeless place with no edges.

"So?" Anaxa said.

"So . . . well, what I have to tell you is that I discovered the same thing as you did — that there's something frozen in him that can't love. Like the little boy in the snowqueen story. Oh, sure — he can write poetry about love, he can take pictures of people that are full of love, but he can't love an individual woman. He just can't. And if you think he can then you're on a hiding to nothing. For God's sake, Anaxa, save yourself! Give him up! Get out! Stop loving him! Please! Do it for me. Do it now!"

"I can't," said Anaxa simply. "No, it doesn't surprise me that you loved him too. I suppose I knew. But I didn't ask because I didn't want to know I knew."

"What are you going to *do*?"

"I *will* have him, Alice! I will do everything that's necessary to have him. He can't escape me. I know he still wants me, sexually. He's just fighting it. But once I can get him into bed with me, the battle's over, he can't resist."

"But that's just sex, Anaxa! Sex is just sex. That doesn't mean he has to love you!"

"Poor Alice, you don't understand these things, do you? No wonder you make such a mess of it with men. You believe what they tell you, you listen to their words — but that's not the real thing, that's not how men and women are meant to communicate! A woman can always win a man, if she is prepared to wait, to concentrate, to sacrifice.

I am. I will. I will have him Alice. You just wait and see."

Alice looked at her friend and saw that she was crazy, saw that there was nothing she, Alice, could do to break the glass and save her. The ice-cream van chimed its crystalline bars of Bach again, this time much closer. Again the symmetrical cadences of the music were cut off abruptly by the timing mechanism. Again Alice felt anxiety out of all proportion to the incident: why was the ice-cream man playing his chime so late? Was he so desperately in need of money that he had to risk breaking the law by sounding his chimes at this hour? Or was he crazy also? Was he sounding his mutilated phrase of Bach as a signal to all crazy people in the city, that the hour had come for them to declare themselves and take over the world?

"I think I'd better go," she said finally.

"Don't! There's all this bottle to get through and you haven't even started it yet!"

"What's the point Anaxa? I'm not in the mood. I can't cope with you when you go all witchy and glassy-eyed like this."

"Alice! We don't have to talk. I could do the cards for you, or we could watch the tele. Don't leave me yet — I feel like company!"

But the ice-cream chimes had chilled Alice's heart. She felt stony revulsion at the thought of lolling in front of the tele all night, getting completely drunk and ruining her clarity of mind for the next day's work. She decided on a cool white lie.

"I'm sorry, I'd like to stay, but I think I've got a migraine coming on. I mustn't drink. I think I should go straight home and straight to bed. If you don't mind."

Panic and sympathy warred in Anaxa's eyes. She got up and escorted Alice to the door.

"You're sulking because I won't take your advice," she said. "You don't realise that I can't. It's just not in me to give up."

"In a way I admire your stubborness. I can't even be sure your're wrong. Miracles do happen. Maybe you will be able to melt his frozen heart . . . will you be all right?"

"Of course."

"You won't drink too much?"

"Piss off — you're not my chaperone!"

"I'll see you at the weekend then?"

"Probably."

"Bye."

"Byee, Alice, Goody Two Shoes!"

She whizzed home on her bicycle as fast as she could, pumping her legs to make herself feel alive.

Once home she went straight up to her workroom and worked solidly for two hours on the outer shadings of the purgatorial skies, which were actually watery rather than airy in texture, for some reason she chose not to look into. At midnight she went to bed, and lay there for a while feeling cold and blank, dazzled by visions of sheets of glittering water hanging in front of her eyes. Eventually she opened her eyes to try and make the image go, but it seemed as if the air in her room had turned to water too, cold, still water in a deep, clear pool . . . She shut her eyes again. Now she was looking down at the water, now she was standing on the brink of it, her arms swung back, ready to dive. She hesitated. The water was uncannily clear. It reflected an infinite depth. She was frightened and fascinated. She knew she could go no further unless she jumped, but if she jumped could she be sure she would ever bob up to the surface again?

The calamitous, brutal ringing of the telephone! Brring, Brring! Brring, Brring! Alice raced to the hallway and scooped the receiver up. There was no voice at the other end, just prickling noises which could be static or anxious breathing.

"Hello. A.J. Cunningham here." She spoke in a deep, bass voice in case it was a rapist or a burglar ringing to see if she was in.

"Alice?" The voice was tremulous, see-sawing around the syllables of her name.

"Yes, this is Alice."

"Mummy went out for just a half hour ages and ages ago and I tried to be brave and I thought she was coming back any minute now but she wasn't . . . and . . . and I don't know where is is!" Masha's voice disintegrated into spasms of sobbing.

"Masha," said Alice gently. "Look at the clock. It's just after half past two now. By the time the little hand in on the three and the big hand on the twelve I'll be with you.

Don't cry now. Go to the fridge and get some orange juice and biscuits ready for me to have when I arrive."

"We don't put biscuits in the fridge."

"Well, get them out of wherever you keep them then. See you very soon, bye-bye."

It was raining hard outside. Flinging her bicycle cape over her head Alice pushed off from the kerb and swung out into the street, a ludicrous yellow avenging angel bundling herself into the perilous currents of space and time. She knew beyond doubt that 'they' had got Anaxa. Who 'they' were and why 'they' should want her she did not know, but she had sensed the miasma of listless blackness gathering round her friend for some time now, ready to jump in and engulf her when she had reached her lowest ebb. Anaxa's perdition was close, the smell of it caught her throat like smoke from a bonfire. Her own jump was quite forgotten, but although she did not know it, she was travelling, she was descending through the inky water, to a place she had never visited before.

* * *

Alice sat on the edge of Lewis's battered red Chesterfield and bit her fingers. She did not look at the glossy photograhic journals strewn over the coffee table. She did not admire the ethnic objects on the mantelpiece. She did not poke the smartly burning fire. She just sat systematically ripping slivers of flesh off the side of her fingers with her teeth and swallowing them. She was waiting, with mounting impatience, for Lewis to finish making the coffee. She felt sure he was fiddling with grinders, filters, and packets of delicatessen biscuits deliberately to drag the process out and put off the moment of being interrogated by her.

At last he entered, carrying a tray of coffee which he dumped on top of the glossy magazines.

"I'm sorry I've been so long," he said. "It's displacement activity of course. I'm very distressed. I'm really very distressed. But I can't think what the bloody hell to do."

He did look distressed, she had to admit that. His eyes were puffy, his face shiny and unshaven, his hair uncombed, his shirt not properly tucked into his trousers. But these were merely outward and visible signs — what was going on in his heart?

"Lewis, wait a minute! Go back, go back! Tell me what happened last night. What did you talk about? What did she say? Where do you think she went when she left you? Was she very upset? You've got to tell me! I've got to have some idea of where she might be."

He poured the coffee. The room filled up with its delectable, civilised odour.

"She turned up at about eleven," said Lewis, histrionically rumpling his hair. "I was writing, but I invited her in, made her some coffee. She seemed pretty calm, though I think she had been drinking. We talked for a while, about Armenia actually. I believe her mother's family came from there. Then she suddenly announced that she was staying, that she wasn't intending to go home! I told her I had work to do. I told her I was being celibate at the moment. I told her I was expecting some friends to arrive at any minute . . . but it wasn't any use. She just said calmly that whatever happened she would stay.

"And then, suddenly, it seemed to me that I *had* better let her stay. After all, what was this chastity which I was so anxious to protect? It was not something that was of use to anybody else but me — just a safety precaution for my soul. So I decided to let her stay, to have sex with her, if that was what she wanted . . . and that is what I did."

'Oh *no*!' thought Alice. 'He thought she wanted *sex*. He decided she could have it. He thought he was being thoughtful and magnanimous. Oh *no*! And then, and then, and then?'

"You see," he leant forward in his old animated style, eyes sparkling, hands gesturing, justifying himself brilliantly before a board of invisible judges, convinced that they could never find him guilty when they had heard his plea. "You see, I remembered the woman who cured me of that terrible fever! I know what she was trying to do when she made me promise I would not sleep with any woman for a year: she was trying to teach me respect for women and their sexuality. But what she couldn't know is that I would be faced by this kind of dilemma, where a woman whom I had callously used in the past comes to me and *begs* me to sleep with her. It seemed to me that, in this situation, the correct action was to do the generous thing, to give the thing that could be given. But the terrible fact is, Alice, that I *couldn't*. When it came to it I couldn't — couldn't get it up! I just couldn't! I tried, I really tried, Alice, to see her as a person, a woman who should be loved with tenderness and a humane affectionate sort of passion. But Eros and Agape just don't mix for me. I just felt cold, cold, disinterested, and even, after I'd tried hard for quite a while to get myself going, even quite revolted by the whole performance!

"I tried to tell her that it was no reflection on her, but rather a damning reflection on me, my hollowness, my emotional incapacity . . . I don't know if she understood. After a while I fell asleep. When I woke up — at about eight o'clock this morning — she was gone. I don't know when she left. Are you absolutely sure she didn't go home? Perhaps she took a walk and got back just after you had left. It's possible isn't it?"

"I stayed until eight thirty. Took Masha to school. Went back. Left a message that I was coming here, asking her to ring immediately when she got home. It's — what? — ten o'clock now. Of course I'll go back there and check, but, Lewis, I don't think so. I think she's probably feeling desperate. God knows where she's gone or what she's done. That's why we must think so hard about it. Try to get inside her head and imagine who or what she might turn to."

"But Alice, why, *why* should a miserable incident in bed with an impotent fool like me make her desperate?"

"Lewis, don't you understand anything? She is in love with you, hopelessly in love with you! It wasn't sex she wanted last night when she came to you, but sex is the only way she knows to get close to men!"

Lewis buried his head in his hands. The coffee steamed untasted on the table. Alice picked up her cup and drained it hungrily. She had expected to feel angry with Lewis, to be disgusted by his cruel dismissal of her friend, but instead she was confronted by an abyss of emotional ignorance in him which excited her pity, maybe even her contempt, and made her realise how little she had known him. She felt an impulse to go over to him and put her arms around him, just as she had done that night long ago when he had said he was cold, so cold, but she dismissed it and gathered up her common sense.

"Lewis," she said briskly, "let's be practical. Let's think of all the clubs she might have gone to — to get a drink, to find some friends to talk to. She may just be kipped down on somebody or other's floor, sleeping off an all-night binge. Oh God, if only I had stayed with her instead of going home to sulk. But no matter, let's start."

"But her daughter . . . surely she wouldn't just desert her child like that, leave her alone while she went out drinking?"

"Masha told me that a long time ago Anaxa made her memorise the telephone number and practise how to dial it and told her that if ever she did not come home when expected she was to ring me straight away. And she did. Anaxa knew that I would look after Masha. All the same, you're right — it was an irresponsible thing to do."

Her frustrated anger turned itself towards Anaxa. Another day's work down the drain because of her incontinent craziness! She would probably turn up at Alice's around lunchtime, bedraggled but unrepentant, swearing that she would never sleep with a man again except for money in the whole of her life to come . . .

Suddenly Lewis sprang up from his chair.

"There is one thing I can do. Come with me, Alice, come next door!"

He led her through to his little dark room. On the table lay a disordered pile of black and white enlargements — images of war — boys with machine guns, disfigured corpses, the usual fare of Sunday supplement journalism. Alice picked up a picture of a woman staring into the camera with grave, penetrating eyes.

"Yes, that's her," said Lewis, shortly. "Wait here, will you, there's something else I need."

The look in the woman's eyes reminded Alice of something, someone . . . who was it? Could it be the photograph of Akhmatova on the front cover of her Selected Poems . . . or maybe the photo inside of her lying on a sofa, taken after they had stopped publishing her poems, where she looks so baleful and aquiline and proud . . . ? Or was it Anaxa the photo reminded her of, not

Akhmatova? Certainly, if she did not know the woman in the photograph, she knew the expression in her eyes — it was an expression all women who do not flinch away from loneliness must come to have. Alice wondered if she too would have it one day.

"Right!" said Lewis, bursting into the room again. "Where's my camera?"

It stood on the table, mounted on a mini-tripod. He snatched it up and flung it onto the floor. Alice gasped. The impact was a blow to the heart. Then he took the axe he had brought in with him and began hacking the camera to pieces there on the carpet.. The tripod's fragile little legs buckled, the intricate mechanisms of aperture and focusing were crunched to jagged fragments. But the body, the solid, humble body of the thing would not be smashed. It bounced jerkily out from under the axe's heavy stroke and landed somewhere under the table. Lewis got down on his hands and knees to retrieve it and placed it back with the other fragments, ready to be smashed again. Again it resisted the blow's impact and rolled sideways, dinted but still basically intact.

"Bastard!" he shoted furiously and swung the axe up yet again.

"No!" screamed Alice. "You've done enough. Leave it, leave it be — it's not meant to be completely humiliated!"

Lewis brought the axe down slowly and looked at Alice in disbelief.

"It's only an object! It's not feeling any pain!"

"Then why are you killing it?"

He stood for a moment, his face crumpled up in childish perplexity.

"Because it's the only thing I know how to do," he said finally and laid the axe down upon a chair.

Alice hesitated for a moment, snatched up the photo of the grave-faced woman and walked out of the room and out of the flat without saying another word to Lewis. She was not angry with him — she just knew that in her search for Anaxa he could only hold her back.

★ ★ ★

CHAPTER TWELVE

The House in the Wilderness

CHAPTER TWELVE

By two o'clock in the afternoon Alice was back home, having drawn a blank at every club she had visited. After the clubs she had called on Tom who had shrugged and said, "she's done it before, you know; she'll be back, bleary-eyed by teatime," and then on to the exquisite young actor who had once had a heavy crush on Anaxa, who shuddered and said he had not seen her for some months, *thank God* . . . and now she was slumped over the kitchen table, her eyes shut, her heart fluttering with exhaustion, praying for inspiration. Surely somewhere within her was the knowledge of where Anaxa was!

Nothing came. Her mind was a chaos of grotesque images — Lewis flushed with desperate, fruitless sexual exertions, Anaxa white and empty-eyed beneath him; the involuntary tightening of the young actor's face when she mentioned Anaxa's name to him; Masha in a tantrum of inconsolable tears all the way to school that morning; Lewis again, his face innocent, wounded, so damned *intelligent*, standing over his wrecked camera, living in a world where the loving of a woman was an almost inconceivable thing . . .

Wretchedly she rose and flopped down on the settee. She shut her eyes. She must not fall asleep of course because she had to pick up Masha from school in half an hour, but surely she could allow herself a few minutes respite from the cacophony of images, the circling wheel of painful thoughts and fears . . . She let herself drop down into the space that was waiting under her and was instantly swept away, balancing on the iridescent wave edge that runs between the worlds — 'surfing' she called it — yielding and bracing herself by turns, surging easily toward the big light, the glamorous sparkle of space, but keeping one foot on the floor so that she should not be utterly swept away . . .

When she jerked herself up and awake a few minutes later she could not remember where she had been or what she had seen, except that a name was left stranded in the interstices of her memory, the name 'Lettie', associated somehow with 'space' and a word like 'virtue' or 'virgo'. She was sure she knew no-one of that name, unless she had recently read it, or dreamed it, or encountered it in one of those thrilling, treacherous worlds which cut at right angles across every moment of her own, but whose immanence vanished as soon as she swung back onto the usual axis of her being.

"Lettie, Lettie, Lettie . . . Space . . . Virgo," she murmured, "Please come and help me out . . . tell me where Anaxa is so that I can save her . . . try to put the right thing in my mind to do . . . "

Masha was waiting at the school gates, solemn and dis-approving of Alice's lateness, clutching a string of paper dollies to her chest. Alice realised with shock that the child was very dirty, her face streaked with dust and snot, a faint scene of urine coming off her as Alice bent down to hug her in greeting.

"A bath for you, Masha, as soon as we get home, and into the washing machine with your dungarees, OK?"

"OK," said Masha in a small voice which struck at Alice's heart far more than any whining protestations would have done.

"I've been looking for your mum, kid, and I'm sure we'll find her very soon. Or maybe she'll be back already and is trying to ring us up. Shall we put our skates on and run to get there quicker?"

They tore up the hill, the big blonde woman in the wobbly high-heeled red boots and the small girl square and dusty-headed in her duffle-coat. But the house was silent as they entered it and Masha burst instantly into tears, having been nearly certain that her mother would be waiting for her there.

Alice quickly filled the bath with bubbles and hot water and put Masha into it. Thomas the cat came in and began to walk tight-rope around the rim, trying to catch the crea-tures of foam that Masha kicked up. Masha stopped crying and started hooting with exaggerated laughter. Alice put her fingers in her ears and went downstairs. She stood at the front window staring out into the street. As soon as she stopped acting she fell into a daze that was something be-tween sleep and daydream where the outer world receded from her and she was aware only of an inner roaring and concatenation of images that she could neither grasp nor hold. With great effort she pulled herself out of it and made a decision to call the police at five o'clock if Anaxa had not come home by then. She continued staring out of the window and noticed the little lady over the road coming out with an enormous pair of garden shears to cut her hedge. Alice waved at her and she waved back. Then she seemed to think of something, sprang out of her gate and came trotting over the road to Alice's door. 'Oh *no*,' thought Alice. 'Not mindless gossip from Lily at this hour. I just can't take it, I really can't!''

"I meant to tell you," puffed Lily, wrapping her thin arms around her chest against the cold. "There was a man looking for you while you were out just now. Blond, nice looking. He hung about for a while, so I came over to ask if I could take a message. He just said to tell you 'no luck' and that he'll be at home till seven o'clock in case there's any news."

"Oh, thank you, Lily . . . thank you, it was quite an important message."

Lily hesitated on the doorstep, noticing Alice's agitation, but being too polite to ask the cause of it. Alice was on the point of pleading business and shutting the door, when she realised she wanted to talk to someone and that Lily would do.

"Come in and have a cup of tea! I'm in a bit of a crisis actually . . . got the daughter of a friend of mine staying — friend's just disappeared . . . been looking for her all day . . . " As Alice led Lily through to the kitchen she realised she was babbling, but she was too tired to be coherent and suddenly she wanted to tell Lily everything.

"I've left my ciggies at home," said Lily feeling in the pockets of her cardigan.

"Smoke mine, smoke mine," Alice said passing her the crumpled packet she had been clutching and squeezing in her hand all day. "I'll just put the kettle on and dry Masha and I'll be right back."

When Alice returned from drying Masha and sending her out to play with Salma, the little Asian girl next door, she found that Lily had made the tea and was sitting sucking the burnt-out stub of her cigarette and staring bleakly into Alice's back garden. She wore crimplene bell-bottom pants and a Courtelle cardigan with hairs from her Alsation straggling all down the front of it. When Alice started to tell the story of Anaxa's disappearance the blue-bell eyes behind their thick-lensed glasses brightened with sympathy and alarm. After she had finished there was a long pause while she fiddled with her hair and bit her fingers and Lily timidly extracted another cigarette from the packet and lit it. Alice could feel something bumping up her neighbour's throat, demanding to be said.

"Alice . . . " she began tentatively, "I wouldn't say anything but I can see that you're desperate. It's just that sometimes I can see things. I mean; before they happen. Only sometimes mind. I could try, if you like . . . "

"You mean try and see where my friend is?"

"Well, I could try . . . I can see death sometimes. I see it as a great, black, bird-like thing hovering over their heads. You know Mr. Leatherbarrow from number seventeen? Well, I saw it hovering over him on the day he collapsed with that stroke!"

Alice's eyes smarted.

"Did you really? Sounds like you've got a strange gift there, Lettie!"

"My name's not Lettie?" laughed Lily, tugging her cardigan across her bosom. "Funny though, it was my mother's name."

The inner roaring started again. Images flashed past her eyes like a shower of playing cards. She looked into Lily's out-of-focus blue-bell eyes and for the first time recognised her.

"I'm sorry — I once knew someone called Lettie! She was nice, you should be flattered. But *Lily*, perhaps you *might* be able to get a sense of where she is or what she's doing, my friend. Would you be willing to try, for me?"

Lily trembled like an old tree struck by an unkindly blast of wind.

"I don't know. I can try, but it's a terrible responsibility. Tell me what your friend looks like and I'll see if anything comes into my mind."

Alice described Anaxa and gave Lily a scarf of hers which she had borrowed. Lily listened intently, stroking the scarf, but looked miserable.

"I've never done anything like this, Alice. I really don't think it's going to work."

She put her hand out tentatively and took Alice's. She held it lightly for a moment and then let it drop. She sighed and shook her head. Alice sighed and lit another cigarette. Then Masha came rocketting into he house, sobbing vehemently and threw herself into Alice's lap, claiming in a loud, wailing voice that Salma's brother had threatened to hit her with the clothes pole if she did not get out of their garden immediately.

Lily and Alice laughed in spite of themselves while Alice cuddled Masha and wiped her tears. Then, as Masha turned to cast a covert glance at her extra audience to see how the performance was going down, Alice noticed a tremor across Lily's paper-skinned face.

"Is this your friend's daughter?" she asked.

"It is."

"I had a flash then! Just came and went. Of a woman, under a blanket in a room. A big room, with sunshine pouring in from a big, wide window. Nothing else in the room, just the woman, her black hair showing, and the sun."

"Was the woman sleeping? Was she all right? Could you see that?"

"Nothing more, Alice. It was just a picture, like a slide flashed up on a wall for a second and then gone. It may mean nothing, but when I saw the child it came, and of course the child's links with her mother must be very strong."

Alice leant her cheek on Masha's and tried to see the room too. Sunlight . . . a big window . . . a woman lying on the floor under a blanket . . . A big window? Where had she seen a big window recently? A big bay window looking out onto a neglected garden, not unlike her own? She *had* seen it. It *was* familiar . . . but where? In real life? In dreams? Or in another world? A big window, a giant whale, and people jumping ludicrously, nonchalently into its mouth . . . what nonsense was this she was remembering? And yet it was not quite nonsense because afterwards the woman had spoken and said that their aim was as magnetic north to true north but that it did not matter too much because they still could hit the mark . . . yes, and it had been happening in the back room of the old house in the wilderness, the house she had never entered in her waking life, but which she knew . . .

Could Anaxa be there? Was it possible? She opened her eyes and found two pairs of round, serious eyes staring at her, one pair blue and one pair black.

"I think I may know the room," she said, "so I suppose I'd better go and see. Lily, would you mind keeping an eye on Masha? Masha, will you be very good until I come back?"

The old woman and the little girl nodded solemnly. Alice walked out into the hall, lifted her bike out into the street and set off for the allotments with all possible speed.

* * *

The house stood sombre in its desolate garden, its red bricks soaking up the last rays of the setting sun so that it looked like a darkly glowing ember at the back of a dying fire. In her vision access had always been reasonably straightforward, but now she found the front and back doors firmly locked, the cellar door likewise, and though she banged and banged on the smoked glass panel at the front no-one came to answer her. She walked round to the back again. The big window she remembered was at mezzanine level and too high to be looked into but the sun shot its beams straight and low across the neat vegetable plots of the allotments right into it. Alice hoped, if Anaxa was indeed inside the house, that the glass of the window had transformed the light into warmth for her. She lingered in the back garden, pacing back and forwards like a cat waiting to be let in, but the building seemed impenetrable. The only thing would be to smash one of the windows with a brick, but supposing the noise brought curious gardeners running, and supposing Anaxa was not inside to justify her vandalism . . . how foolish and criminal she would look.

Then she noticed that there was one faint possibility she had overlooked — an encrusted cellar window, obscured by dead leaves and dandelions, which reached about a foot above ground level. It was shut, but looked as if it might be dunted open with a pole or a piece of wood. Alice felt little relish at the thought of sliding into a dark, unknown cellar, but there seemed no alternative, so she looked around for something to serve her as a battering ram. Her eyes lighted on a sagging post which had once been used to support a washing line, and she managed to wrench it up from the flower bed in which it was planted. The window resisted the first blow but at the second it snapped open.

The red leather skirt she was wearing was too tight to allow free movement so she slid out of it and stuffed it in her bag. The high-heeled boots were not ideal but she hated the thought of slithering on the wet dead leaves in her stockinged feet, so she kept them on. Then gingerly she dropped one foot down onto the sill of the waiting aperture. It seemed solid enough so she let her other foot join it. Now all she had to do was lean backwards and jump through into the room beneath. She did so and landed safely. The floor of the place was quite dry and clean and in the dim light from the open window she could see that the cellar room was empty and neutral — nothing frightening about it at all. Emboldened, she put her skirt on again and moved out of the room into a hallway she could see beyond an open door. There was just enough light here to allow her to make out the contours of a stairway leading upwards.

"Oh God, let the door be open at the top, please let the door be open at the top!" she prayed as she edged her way up the stairs. At the top she pushed hard at the surface in front of her. It was quite unyielding. She felt around for a door-knob. There it was — loose, rattling on its spindle, an old-fashioned Bakelite knob. It turned easily in her hand . . . and fell off! Trembling she rammed it back on, feeling for the screw. No screw! She pressed it hard leftwards and twitched it down. The door sprang open, and she fell forwards into a bright, white-painted room.

She stood for a moment in shock. Although obviously not in use, this kitchen was far from derelict. There was quite a modern gas cooker, and cabinets and a long pine shelf supporting a set of enamel pots and pans. The house had not been so long uninhabited as she had thought.

Respectfully she moved through into the hallway. It was strange to see the front door with its intricate smoked glass panel from the other side. Her heart hammering, she turned left and opened the door which must lead to the big back room.

At first she was simply dazzled by the sunshine. Diffused by the grimy windows, it filled the room with a dull red glare which Alice think immediately of the wrath of God. Then she registered the smell — the sour, fruity tang of recent vomit, and before she even looked she knew what she would see next — the blanket with the humped up shape of a body under it, the splayed-out black hair, the brandy bottle, the discarded pair of stiletto shoes with the familiar mucky piece of elastoplast holding the sling-back of one together.

She flung back the blanket and lifted the white face out of the pool of vomit in which it was resting. She wiped the mouth with her sleeve and pushed her own face down as close to it as she could without touching, listening for breath. She thought she could just hear a small wheezy rattling in the chest. There were two half-empty bottles of pills — one of them Paracetamol — hiding under the blanket. She scooped them up and stuffed them into her bag. Then she pulled Anaxa up into a sitting position and tried to wrap the stinking blanket round her so that she could carry her down the road. But the limp body was so heavy she could barely support it while standing up, never mind walking. Would it be better to leave her and run quickly to 'phone for an ambulance? Or drag her outside and find a late gardener to help carry her? Everything would take far too long! If only she had rung Lewis and asked him to come with his car!

She laid the heavy body down for an instant and turned desperately towards the door, as if expecting a ministering angel to materialise there in answer to her agonised prayer. There was a beat-pause and then the front door banged. Footsteps slammed purposefully down the hall, and her involuntary exclamation of astonishment brought the intruder quickly into the room. He stood for a moment, dazzled as she had been, a tall, sturdy man in a great-coat, hair dishevelled, an enormous rucksack on his shoulder which descended with ominous slowness to the floor as he said his first words.

"What the fuck are you doing in my house?"

"Oh!" said Alice, feeling, in spite of her grief, the familiar sense of wrong-footedness which had her all her life. "I can explain! Please don't be ang friend here is very ill, unconscious. She's taken all pills and even Paracetamol. We must get her to the pital straightaway. Do you think you can carry her?"

The man loomed urgently towards them. Alice saw that his face was pale, his eyes sparkling as people's do when they have a fever. He bent down and put his hand on Anaxa's brow.

"Christ!" he said, and without further comment picked the limp body up and carried it out of the house.

"I have a car," he said, as they strode, as near running as he could manage with his load, along the allotment path. "We must get her to the infirmary as fast as possible. Is she breathing? You'll have to try and give her some mouth to mouth in the car if she's not."

Alice told him gasping that she thought her friend was still breathing. She felt the uneven path bucking under her as she scrambled after him in her stupid high-heeled boots. It was as if they were being carried along in the current of a great river which seemed set to smash them against a solid curtain of rock that lay ahead, and yet she hoped against all reason that it would suddenly turn a corner and set them free instead into the sea. If only, if *only* Anaxa could live, then, *then* she would really change her life and try to stay awake like this all the time, try to live her life as it was meant to be lived . . .

* * *

At the hospital they said they could give no odds yet on Anaxa's chances of survival. The Paracetamol was the most serious problem but it so happened that they were just starting trials with a newly discovered antidote, so she might be lucky and be saved without kidney damage.

When she heard this Alice knew that Anaxa would live.

"Such luck, such coincidence comes only to the deserving wicked!" she said to her companion. "Someone up there's determined she should pay for her sins in this world not the next."

.ey stood awkwardly in the hospital foyer, glancing ⅃ideways at each other. Alice gripped the stranger's dusty arm and said, "Come on, rescuer, we need a drink!"

In the pub, her companion, who said his name was Gene, bought them whiskies while she telephoned Lily and told her what had happened. Lily did not seem surprised that her vision had been so accurate, and was more concerned to assure Alice that she would put Masha to bed and stay with her and that there was no reason for Alice to hurry home.

"I'll go back to the hospital in half an hour," she said as she sat down next to the big, dusty presence. For the first time she looked carefully at his haggard face.

"You don't look so well yourself," she said. "I'm sorry your homecoming has been so traumatic."

"I'm fine," he said. "It's just the old fever. I get it once a year, regular as clockwork. Nothing much to be done — I try to carry on business as usual. I picked it up in Iran years ago. But I hope your friend will be all right. Tell me about her. What brought her to this pass?"

Alice would much rather have asked him about himself, but she dutifully outlined Anaxa's story, leaving out her own connection with Lewis and other lurid details, domesticating their strange friendship into something ordinary to discourage further questioning.

"But you said just now that she was wicked," he interjected, and she noticed he had soft amber-coloured eyes which crystallised into sharp focus as he threw in his question. He was not an easy man to throw off the scent.

"I was joking. Well — no — I meant it, but only in that she is wicked to herself."

"How so?"

She wriggled on her stool. She did not want to tell this stranger everything, but how to explain that without explaining everything?

"You're very curious."

"I'm interested," he said with his first real smile which revealed that he had an oddly buckled tooth which made him look at the same time babyish and piratical. "I'm interested in everything."

"Well so am I? So tell me about you. Where have you been? How come that house belongs to you?"

"It's only recently mine. It belonged to my grand-mother. She died last year and left it to me. She'd lived there like a recluse for years — a lot of people didn't even know that the house was inhabited. This is the first time I've been back since she died. I'm astonished it's not been more vandalised. Oh yes, I've been abroad. I dig for a living."

"You're an archeologist?"

"A grandiose title! Yes, I suppose I am. Another drink?""

Alice insisted on buying the next round, thinking that she and Gene with their stubborn mutual curiosity would soon reach stalemate. She realised that she had not thought of Anaxa for a whole five minutes. Perhaps because she knew that things were going to be all right . . . When she got back to their seats Gene had stood up and was making ready to go.

"Excuse me," he said. "I must knock this back and go. Please let me know about your friend. I would stay a bit longer and keep you company, but I know the signs. In half an hour I'll be out cold. Then you'd have to carry me home too."

"But will you be all right? Are you going to sleep in that house? You can stay at my place if you like. I can . . . "

"No," he interrupted her. "No thank you. I'll be fine in my sleeping bag on the floor in there. I like the place. I'd rather be ill in my own home, if you don't mind."

They parted and Alice returned to the hospital to be told that Anaxa's stomach had been pumped and that she was sleeping. She was allowed to see her for a moment. The immaculate hospital bed made her look even more mucky and exotic and wicked than usual. The dusty hair with its iridescent blackbird sheen, the white bruised face, the shapely dancer's arms, laid out gracefully on the coverlet, drinking in blood from the drip that stood next to the bed — she had all the voluptuous innocence of the completely fallen. You wanted to touch her, to kiss her, to stroke the soft, bare flesh that she offered.

"God wouldn't let you die, 'Naxa," said Alice fiercely under her breath. "So don't you defy Him again!"

Under the purplish skin of the eyelids Alice could see troubled dreams flitting: Anaxa was still travelling between the worlds, looking for her lost lover under the earth, calling him and receiving no answer. But her life's glow was not escaping her. The freak November sunshine had kept her warm in the old house, and now it seemed to Alice that her own flame was flickering quite steadily again.

"You will ring me as soon as there's any news?" she asked the little nurse.

"Are you the next of kin?"

"She has none. Only her little daughter, who's with me. I am her closest friend."

★ ★ ★

At home a note waited from Lily saying that she had taken Masha over to her house and put her to bed because she had to be there with the dog who got restive if left alone too long. She instructed Alice to go to bed and get some rest. Alice went up to her workroom instead and poured herself out the last of the gin. There was no tonic to go with it but she did not care. Before she slept she must let the shudderings in her chest and legs still themselves. The fierce energy she had had to summon in order to find Anaxa would have to be dispersed. But it didn't want to go. It did not want to quietly slip out by the back door like a good fairy who had humbly done her work. It wanted to push her further on and upwards, or rather downwards, into a dark, awesome place that she had never been before, at least not waking . . .

And there were all the infuriating questions flying around in her head: what had Anaxa been doing in that house? By what means had Lily 'seen' her there? Who was Gene? Had Anaxa really, *really* meant to die? Did she know that there was a newly discovered antidote to Paracetamol which might be available to save her life? What would Lewis feel when he knew what Anaxa had done and why?

She stood at her uncurtained window and stared out into the night. Suddenly she remembered her bicycle. She had left it leaning against the wall in the garden of the old house. It was unchained, unlocked, exposed to the roving eye of any passing kid. Gene, she presumed, would not notice it. Would it still be there in the morning? She looked at her watch. It was just after ten. Twenty minutes of fast walking would take her to the house, and it was only a five minute whizz back again on the bike. It might be just the energetic interlude she needed before she tried to sleep, and she could ring the hospital to check if there was any news as soon as she got back. She slugged back the rest of the gin, changed into sensible boots, put on the big, moth-eaten fur coat she wore at the coldest times and left the house.

The allotment-wilderness formed a kind of shallow bowl, sloping up on all sides to the perimeter fence, and Gene's house stood on a little rise in the centre so that you could just see the top windows as you walked up the path leading to it above a row of sycamores which had perhaps been planted by Gene's grandmother to give her some protection from the curious eyes of allotment gardeners. As Alice entered the back gate she noticed that a dim light was burning in the downstairs room where she had found Anaxa earlier that day, which must mean that Gene was still awake. She would have thought his fever and weariness would have knocked him out by now. She found her bicycle, wet from rain, but entire, and stood with it propped against her hip, pondering. Should she call in and check on him? After all he was alone and he was ill. But what if she woke him from a restful sleep? She decided to knock very gently on the door and go away without disturbing him if there was no immediate response.

She leant the bike up against the wall again and walked round to the front. No light at all was visible through the smoked glass panel. She knocked firmly but quietly, and waited. For several seconds nothing happened and she was about to turn and leave when she heard a tumbling, crashing noise, followed by muffled exclamations and the appearance of a stooped, enshrouded figure behind the glass.

'Wrong-footed again,' thought Alice as the door opened and Gene's contorted face confronted her. He was wrapped in a blanket and looked as if he had been asleep.

"I'm sorry, I've woken you up! I came to collect my bicycle and I thought I'd just check that you were all right, since I was here."

"I just tripped over this damned blanket in the hall! I was half asleep. What time is it?"

"Oh I *am* sorry. I shouldn't have disturbed you. Are you all right?"

"Of course I'm all right! And stop apologising. It was kind of you to look in."

"Good. There's no news of my friend yet, I'm afraid. I think it's about half past ten. Thank you very much for helping me today. Look after yourself. Goodbye."

"Where are you going?"

"Home."

"Don't be stupid. Now you're here, come in and have a drink. I've got some whisky. Worst thing for a fever of course, but I'm feeling better already thanks to a glass or two earlier on."

Alice could think of no reason not to consent so she followed the blanketed figure into the big back room. A fire of logs was burning in the grate. That and a couple of candles stuck in saucers provided the only light. A big mattress had been dragged up close to the fire and was covered with blankets and an opened-out sleeping-bag.

"Is this the same mattress that Anaxa was sick all over?" asked Alice.

"Yes, but it's scrubbed and turned over. I didn't have any choice. Sit down. You'll have to share my glass I'm afraid. I've got some bread and cheese somewhere if you're hungry."

"No, no, I'm fine." She realised she had not eaten all day, but her stomach felt at once numb and on fire and she felt she would be sick if she put anything into it.

They sat side by side on the mattress, sharing the glass. Gene said nothing and she could think of nothing sensible to say herself. The flames hissed and spat around the damp logs but the fire was hot and made her feel very warm and drowsy in front whilst leaving her freezing cold at the back. She turned a little to avoid its full force and found herself able to study Gene's face in profile unobserved.

He had a beaky semitic nose and eyes that sloped downwards a little at the corners giving him a melancholy expression in repose. His skin was sallow, waxy from the fever, and his wiry dark-orange hair sprang up and out from his face as it if had been pushed back and out of the way all his life but was still trying to get back into a normal position for hair. Alice could not decide whether he was good-looking or not. He was big and vigorous, and, she guessed, given to fits of bad-temper. There was a kind of familiarity between them already which stopped the silence being awkward and made her feel good in her skin. She reached in her bag for a cigarette.

"Do you mind if I smoke?"

"As long as you've got one for me."

She lit his cigarette for him and noticed that his hands were shaking, but did not dare ask him yet again if he was really all right. She glanced around the floor — jeans, pullovers, books lay scattered about. She noticed "Conference of the Birds" and a Turkish-English dictionary.

"Did you meet any dervishes in Turkey? Do you speak the language well?"

He turned and looked at her heavily.

"Don't talk. It's not the moment. Do you mind if I get back into bed?"

"Of course not."

She edged off the mattress to let him get in. He threw off his blanket and revealed himself to be naked except for a pair of ragged, airtex underpants. His body was strong and well-fleshed, but without the muscle that would indicate a person who tried hard to keep fit. He wriggled into the nest of blankets and threshed around, arranging himself in the warmest position.

"I'd better go and let you get some sleep," she said.

"I'm cold."

Alice was gripped with an acute sense of déjà vu. 'I'm cold, — that's what Lewis had said that first night she went to bed with him, and she'd gone over to him and rubbed him to make him warm. And had failed, because his coldness went too deep for her to reach. Her heart hardened. All these cold, narcissistic, selfish, bloody men!

"Do you need more blankets?" she asked politely.

"For God's sake, get in and warm me up!"

"But I hardly know you."

"What's that got to do with it?"

She did not reply. She sat on her haunches in front of the fire, undecided. She did not know him. He smelt of feverish sweat. He was gruff, grumpy and demanding, telling her not asking her to warm him up. Most men would not have dared to speak to her like that. She was intrigued. He sat up abruptly and stared at her angrily.

"Come on! You're a woman. I'm a man. I'm not going to rape you. You came here to find me and here I am. Get in!"

Stiffly she started to move her outer clothes. When she got down to socks, knickers and vest she stopped and wriggled in between the covers with him. His skin was hot and damp, not pleasant to the touch, but he gave her no time to pussy-foot around before clamping his long arms and legs around her like an ardent child. Then he lay quite still, panting a little, as a furious irresistable warmth rippled up through both of them. Alice felt herself giving up the fight, sinking down and down into the earth, feeling herself heavy, soft, vast and accommodating as the sea.

"I didn't come here to find you anyway. I came to find my bike," she heard herself remark conversationally.

He raised himelf up on one elbow and smiled his snaggle-toothed, piratical smile at her. Then he kissed her carefully but forcefully on the mouth before clamping himself around her once again.

"I thought my libido was dead," he said loudly in her ear. "You must be a remarkable woman to get me going while I'm in this pathetic state." He shifted again to allow his stiffening penis room. Alice gasped at his effontery. Did he expect her to be *flattered*?

He began to caress her body, but it was cursory, hot and quick. He pushed up her vest and her knickers down. Something somersaulted in her loins. She let him open her legs with his and sink into her. "Oh Christ," he said, "how long I've wanted this!"

She started to move with him, to let him thrust deeper in. The walls of her vagina were burning — it was as painful as it was pleasurable to feel him pushing into her. She writhed her breasts against him to try and push him a little away, his weight was crushing, hurting her. But he wouldn't shift.

"Oh God!" he said. "You're so lovely, you're so beautiful . . . keep still a minute, will you?"

Astonished she kept still and he began to fling himself

into her, faster and faster, sometimes deep and sometimes shallow, but hard and harder, pushing the borders out and out and out.

"I'm nearly there," he panted. "I'm nearly coming . . . Oh God, I can't hold back . . . and you, and you, and you?"

"I'm OK, don't worry about me."

"But . . . " his back arched and he threw himself down into her for the last time, with a wild exclamatory cry.

"Aaaah!" he bellowed again and again, as if he were stabbing the air with the knife of his voice, killing it, killing it. Alice lay still, trembling infinitesimally until he finished and sank down into her, panting at first, then relaxing into the deep, even breathing of sleep.

'I have been used,' she thought, but as soon as the words appeared in her head she was ashamed of them. She had yielded all the way. She had consented to everything that happened. Anaxa lay between life and death, just as she lay between Gene's heavy, hot body and the damp, cold bed. She had wanted *this* just as Anaxa had wanted *that*. Everything was still, and yet it was moving, and it seemed that the movement was *towards* the stillness. She was warmed through by Gene's body. Everything in her relaxed.

After a moment she pushed him off and he subsided beside her without waking, his arms and legs still wrapped around her. She felt them beckoning. She dropped down. The waters closed around her. She was gone.

Later they were preparing her to receive. The preparations were not so bad — she did not mind the opening up because they did it gently, and with care not to jar or hurt her in any way. But when she was ready she began to feel frightened, and when it approached her and she realised what it was they were preparing her to receive she lashed out blindly and in panic shouting 'No!' with all the vehemence she could muster.

She woke up sitting upright on the mattress, her heart pounding, the room flashing, making and unmaking itself in front of her eyes. The peace she had experienced before had gone. Gene turned over in his sleep, miles and miles away and dropped down deeper into his exhaustion. She felt cold, terrified, certain that everything was bad and was going rapidly from bad to worse at every moment.

In the light of the dying fire she found her clothes and pulled them on with fumbling hands, aware of his semen trickling stickily out of her as she raised herself unsteadily to her feet and pulled on her boots. She searched for a cigarette and lit it on an ember. In the vanishing light the room seemed to recede into vastness like a cathedral or an enormous cavern. Outside the window a nearly full moon was battling with clouds and sometimes sailed free of them for a moment, filling the room with silvery light.

'His grandmother's house,' though Alice. 'I bet she was a monstrous old matriarch. It is a bit too powerful, this atmosphere, a bit too much really . . . Perhaps it's to do with the position of the house — in the centre of a bowl. Maybe that's what I felt, just now, in sleep, some fearful surge of power towards a centre, which was me. Perhaps that's what came through Gene, why he had such a shattering orgasm . . . '

She looked at him lying on the mattress. He was face up now and his arms and legs were cast about him, frozen in a flailing motion, like Dionysus dancing on a hill. His features were sharp as if cut from flint and his mouth was open, uttering a silent cry. As she stared the moon was obscured by clouds and the plains and hollows of his face were filled with shadows, with shadows that moved, making and unmaking, changing him before her eyes from boy to man to lion, to a goat, to a dervish whirling in close-lidded ecstacy, a boy laughing hysterically at the sea, her dying brother radiating his life away, and lastly, Old Nick himself, the devil — vehement, triumphant, mocking, jumping, ogling, leering right up off the mattress into her dazed, exhausted eyes!

She sprang up, shaking her head to dispell the image. She must go! There was no place for her here. She must run away to escape this formless, dreadful thing that was out to get her, fill her, stop her breathing with its heavy, glutinous weight . . .

Outside she steamrolled her bicycle out of the garden and down the lumpy path into the street. The grammar school clock struck four, the dead hour of the night. It was now impossible to sleep. She decided to go to the hospital. She would make a vigil for Anaxa. She knew from Bernard's illness that in the night-time nurses sit around smoking and drinking cups of coffee, their day-time sternness gone. They would not mind her turning up, and too bad if they did!

But when she reached the ward there was no serenity or muted night-time jollity (on the night of Bernard's death she had discussed with the Sister the merits of the different night-clubs in Liverpool), but instead the rat-like scurry of footsteps, the rasping dialling of a telephone, and around Anaxa's bed three nurses and a doctor, who was leaning over pressing hard and rhythmically on her chest.

The small nurse of the afternoon flew past Alice snapping "Her heart's stopped" on the way. Alice was pushed back to let a large piece of equipment on a trolley be wheeled in. Electrodes were unhooked and fixed. As people moved she had glimpses of Anaxa's white body, so used to love and lechery, her small breasts with their big purple nipples juddering as she was roughly handled and readied for her final chance to live. Alice felt sick. The aggressive, jolting thrusts of love her own body had so recently known came back to her; a horrible, irresistable sexual excitment filled her; the orgasm she had not had seemed to be trying to shape itself convulsively in her and find expression at this dreadul, tragic time!

The machine was ready and switched on. The doctor and nurses stook back respectfully. Alice braced herself against the door-jamb.

"Anaxa, you bitch, don't die! You *must* live — he was never worthy of you — didn't I tell you that?"

The words jangled tinnily in her head. Anaxa's body galvanised, arched, and fell heavily to earth again. In a dark corridor somewhere Alice saw Anaxa turn and look angrily, bitterly into the light. "*No!*" she said. "I'm not coming back. There's nothing for me there!" Alice gripped her viciously by the wrist, her nails biting hard into the soft flesh, and dragged her, with every ounce of strength she had, back up the corridor toward the light. She was much bigger than Anaxa but her friend fought and scratched with all the fury that small people learn to use instead of force, fighting for her own death, her inviolable right to die, in the face of Alice's gross, animal liveliness.

"You bitch!" screamed Alice. "Would you desert me

275

too? Don't you know that I need you? How do I explain to Masha that her mother was a coward who killed herself for love of a man who wasn't fit to lick her boots? You betrayer of women, you cow, you whore, you fucking prostitute!"

Anaxa stopped struggling and looked into Alice's eyes. Alice saw that her eyes were completely filled with darkness, no longer reflecting even a spark of light. Her body had gone limp too. So now it was easy to pull her onwards towards the door. But once there the light burnt out Alice's consciousness and she remembered nothing more.

When she came to, a short while later, the small nurse ('barely eighteen,' thought Alice, 'what does she know of life and death?') was kneeling next to her, holding her hand, and telling her with careful, professional tenderness that Anaxa was dead. 'So I didn't manage it,' thought Alice, 'I didn't manage to pull her back over the threshold! My strength was not enough and she has got her own way. So be it! Bring on the dancing girls — let's mourn the Queen of the Night in style . . . '

★ ★ ★

CHAPTER THIRTEEN

"The Secret Places of the Stairs"

CHAPTER THIRTEEN

Alice pulled the trays of pizza out of the oven and laid them on the work surface to be sliced. More people had come than she had expected and she hoped there would be enough food. She hated not giving people enough to eat, and since her guests had already drunk her dry, had a whip-round, and been to the Indian Off-Licence for more supplies, it was imperative that something hit their stomachs soon. She cut the pizzas into eight and stood back to take a gulp of wine. She was enjoying herself. She loved parties and this was a good excuse for one. That it was a funeral was somehow irrelevant — the mourning could wait — it was more important to get back up to the workroom where the music was, and make sure that everyone was introduced. She did not want the two sides of Anaxa's life to stay separated in her death. She wanted Maria to meet Masha, Tom to tell his black jokes to the hostess-girls from the club where Anaxa had worked, Lewis to be charming to Lily and Gene to flirt with everyone. 'A wedding or a funeral', 'a wedding or a funeral' she kept repeating to herself. What did it matter which of them it was — either way there was a certain consummation which had been devoutly wished for . . .

In the workroom Laurie Anderson was panting from the stereo. Outside a high wind had risen and was pattering rain hard but fitfully against the window-panes. Her great picture was turned with its face to the wall, wedged securely behind the table. Everybody was standing up, animated, talking. It looked as if introductions would not be necessary.

One of the club girls, a scraggy redhead with sharp knees under a velvet mini-skirt, came up and put her arms around Alice's neck.

"The food's ready," said Alice brightly, "it's in the kitchen if you are interested." But the redhead would not let go of her. She shook her by the shoulders so that Alice had eventually to meet her eyes.

"She loved you, you know." said the woman drunkenly.

"She loved you more than anyone. Sh' was awright, sh' was awright wi' us, but you was the real friend to her. She always talked about you when she'd had a few, but this bloke, this bloke she was so hooked on — she never mentioned him at all. Only the odd time, when we pushed her . . ."

Alice rocked on her heels, feeling the heat condense in her face and the tears of rage forming in her eyes.

"But she wouldn't live for me, would she?" she said bitterly, "She preferred to kill herself for him. Some love! Some sisterhood!"

"Scum!" spat the redhead, trying to pull Alice closer to her. "Is he here? You tell me an' I'll deal with him . . . bastard, fucking scummy men . . . God never forgive me if I don't deal with him tonight!"

"No, he's not here! And anyway he's not worth dealing with. And Anaxa is dead, so please enjoy yourself. She wouldn't have wanted any revenge."

She separated herself and went to the table to refill her glass. She had lied of course — Lewis was there, leaning on the mantelpiece charming Lily as she had hoped he would. Could he be blamed for Anaxa's death? Was it his fault he could not love her? Could not love anyone? Could not love himself even, but only punish? Alice looked at him, glowing, explaining, gesticulating, and could not find it in her heart to hate him.

The doorbell rang. Someone just arriving? Yes, she had sensed someone missing but not who. At the door stood Tom, grey-faced, dressed in a black suit with a dazzling white shirt. He stepped in without a word. As Alice took his umbrella from him she felt that he was trembling. She put her arms around him and pulled him firmly towards her. It was the first time she had properly hugged him in their long acquaintance and it was a surprising experience: his body was frail as a child's. At first he resisted her but then gave in and rested himself against her. He let out a big sigh.

"I didn't want to come. I've come for your sake, not hers."

"Why not hers?"

"She's dead," he said harshly, "And that's that."

"What do you feel about it?"

"Nothing. Or just angry. Angry with her for not coming to me. She knew I would argue her out of it. She didn't want to be persuaded. Silly cow."

Alice pushed him away from her gently, reminding herself that grief expresses itself in strange, incongruous ways.

"What are you dressed like that for?" he asked abruptly.

"Like what?"

"Like a tart."

Alice looked down at herself. She had put on the only black things she had possessed — a black cotton pullover that fell off her shoulders, a short black leather skirt and black stilettoes. She had never worn all these items together before, and with the black Turkish earrings Anaxa had given her and the black ribbon she had tied round her neck, she supposed she did look like a woman of the streets.

"What does it matter? Sex and death are close companions. Besides, come upstairs — there's plenty more like me up there!"

Now someone had changed the record, to the Sex Pistols' "Never Mind the Bollocks" and a few of the club girls were dancing, bobbing up and down like crazy adolescents, breasts jiggling, silly shoes unbalancing them, falling against each other and knocking over people's drinks. One of them, a statuesque African woman with enormous bosoms, picked up Masha, wound her legs around her waist and started bouncing her up and down in time with the furious music. Masha yelled and screamed to be put down but was glad that the big lady ignored her protestations. Alice looked round for Gene, the only important person unaccounted for.

There he was, on the lascivious settee, each arm around a girl, his long body slumped and splayed out, taking up too much space. Alice watched him for a moment, half outraged, half delighted, until he caught her eye and winked at her. She turned away, blushing, and went over to the record-player to see what was to be put on next. As she bent down she felt arms grabbing her from behind just below her breasts, pulling her up and back. She turned round indignantly.

"You're looking very sexy tonight, Alice! Don't think I

haven't noticed. You're certainly the belle of the ball."

"It's not a ball, it's a wake!"

"My heart grieves for you, but my body aches for you, o mistress!"

"Does it indeed?" said Alice, wrong-footed again, wishing she had spent her last few pounds after the funeral expenses on some sexless black sack to hide her body in.

"Besides," he said, still holding her round the waist, kneading her flesh with his thumbs between the skirt and the pullover, "I didn't know your friend. I only met her when she was dying, which was tragic in itself, but it is difficult to grieve sincerely for someone you don't know. I came tonight for you, Alice, because I know you loved her. I wanted to keep an eye on you."

She looked up at him. His amber eyes were clear, sharply focussed, at odds with his restless, sensual handling of her. She took hold of his hands and removed them from her waist.

"Thank you, Gene, I'm truly grateful. But I'm all right. Tonight is a celebration of Anaxa's life, and I intend to celebrate. I shall do my grieving in private, later on."

She knew she sounded curt and schoolmistressy but she could not help that. Gene's sexuality was too much tonight. 'He'd like to fuck me into forgetfulness,' she thought bitterly, 'but I'm not having it. This night is for you Anaxa, and no man is going to come between us. I know what must be done.'

Some more people arrived, a couple of bouncers from the club: a big, genial black man and a squat tuxedoed bruiser with a squashed-tomato face. They both kissed her graciously and presented her with more whisky and some flowers. She felt comforted by their presence, as if the powers of darkness had lost their will to hurt for a night and were reduced to baffled innocence. Tom was standing at the door holding a very small glass of whisky, listening to Lewis expatiating enthusiastically about something. Alice hesitated. She wanted to talk to each of them, on their own, but together it would not work. Lily appeared at her elbow, and held a cigarette out to her, in the northern way, filter end pointing at her, ready to go straight into the mouth.

"Are you all right?" she asked.

"Yes, oh yes," said Alice, feeling suddenly weak at the knees and light in the head. "I think I'll sit down though. They know where the food is, don't they?"

They sat down side by side on the sofa. Alice lay back and shut her eyes. Her head was swimming. It seemed such a long time since she had had a full night's sleep.

"Do you remember, Alice?" said Lily softly.

"Remember?" said Alice, vaguely, opening her eyes just a little to see if Tom and Lewis had broken up yet. She was aware of Lily breathing deeply beside her. Did she suffer from asthma or something? Alice had never noticed it before. She shut her eyes again.

"Try to remember, to remember the secret places you have been."

"That's in the bible," said Alice sleepily. "I always loved that bit, — 'O my dove, that art in the clefts of the rock, in the secret places of the stairs, let me see thy countenance, let me hear they voice . . . "

" 'For sweet is thy voice, and thy countenance is comely . . . ' "

"What did you say just now about secret places?" said Alice, waking up a little with a sense that something slightly odd was going on.

"We were quoting from the Song of Songs."

"No, before that . . . you said something about remembering secret places. Didn't you?"

Someone had put Turkish belly-dancing music on the stereo. Alice had a momentary flash of another place — close but far away; warm, fiery, welcoming; real, but hopelessly imaginary . . . then the music jangled commandingly and she found herself on her feet, lifting Masha onto the table to dance her belly-dance. She felt giddy, as if she had just fallen asleep for a second or two. Perhaps she had. Perhaps she had dreamed that Lily asked her if she could remember the secret places she had been . . .

The room was full of clapping, shouting women, egging on the little girl as she stamped and shimmied on the table. The men were all pressed to the wall, retreated into corners, shadowy, unreal. Some of the women were moving with Masha, rotating their hips, jangling their bracelets, thrusting their pelvises forwards in time with the masterful music. Alice joined in, feeling the familiar tremor and thrill ride through her as she raised her arms slowly above her head and gave in to the pleasure of it . . .

Masha jumped down off the table.

"You next, Alice!"

Alice flicked off her shoes and, hitching the leather skirt up, climbed via the arm of the settee, onto the table. The atmosphere changed. A little girl was one thing, but a grown woman — that had possibilities! Alice stood, hand on hip, surveying the crowd . . . Tom's thin white face floating near the door, ready to leave if it all got too much; Maria wry and embarrassed on the sofa with her arms crossed, looking away; Masha, bored already, steaming across the room on her way to the kitchen in search of more crisps . . . She tried to remember Anaxa's instructions. 'Be proud, be arrogant — you are a queen! Control them with your body, Alice! Don't hold back, don't hold back!'

She started very, very subtly, making tiny circles with her hips, circles, figures-of-eight both up and down and side to side, then revolving round in a circle, carried by the momentum of her flicking hips . . . then shimmying, throwing the body back and dropping down onto her knees, snaking upwards with the arms like pillars of fire, shimmying the shoulders — how strange that it was so much easier to do all this in front of an audience than alone — then up again onto her feet and this time making the circles big, pushing them up and out at them, throwing hoops of scalding energy out into the audience, over Tom, over Lewis, over Gene, binding them to her so that they could never escape . . .

At first she had to concentrate quite hard, willing herself into boldness, bright performance. Then suddenly it was easy! She saw Anaxa dancing, she remembered the feel Anaxa gave to it — the effortless, flicking, flowing, undulating rhythm of it. She felt Anaxa in her, her limbs enlivened by the other's dark vitality, her heart full of boundless, lonely arrogance . . . for a moment her consciousness of herself lapsed and she *was* Anaxa, dancing her own death at her own funeral, dancing and laughing and pitying the living their ignorance, their idiotic pursuit of that which is not real . . .

. . . When her vision cleared she saw that she was still holding them rapt, even Tom who watched her sideways, as if unwilling to be tempted, Lewis who was flushed and talked to someone feverishly while he watched to mask his interest, and Gene, who clapped and swung his own hips and shouted words of appreciation when the feeling took him. Working on a slow side flick Alice caught his eye. He was laughing but his eyes were steady as usual, looking straight into hers. Alice registered the beam of desire for her that was shooting from them — it zinged through her and bounced lightly somewhere deep in her belly, bounced and reverberated, nearly breaking the rhythm of her dancing. She had to wrench her eyes away from him and cast them unfocussed on the mass of sympathetic women.

Soon she jumped down, to a spatter of jovial applause and the girls helped up the African woman who jiggled her bosoms enthusiastically and burlesqued the dance with suggestive movements of her own invention. Alice reached for a serviette and wiped her face. She was trembling and soaked with sweat. Nobody was paying any attention to her: there was no Anaxa to lay her hand along her backbone, to squeeze her at the nape and say 'well done for being arrogant, well done for dancing like I taught you to . . . ' She made her way towards the door.

In the kitchen Tom was getting water from the tap to drink.

"One whisky, Thomas, that's your lot, eh?" she asked shakily.

"I thought I might drink tonight," he drained his glass of water, "but now I think not. I think I'll be going home, if you don't mind."

Alice stared at him blankly. She had visualised that he would stay till the end, being Anaxa's other confidante, and share the burden of the endless dionysiac party with her, that they would sit on the lascivious settee together and talk all night and remember her. And perhaps at dawn they would put their arms around each other and fall asleep, or even go to bed like brother and sister and hold each other through the night.

"Did I shock you in there, with my dancing?"

He shrugged.

"Good God, no. It was fine. I'm just tired."

"You loved her, I think."

"Let's not over-dramatise! She was a crazy woman and I'm an eccentric man. We recognised each other, that's all."

"It seems quite a lot to me."

He raised his eyebrows.

"I'm not denying it."

Alice felt desperate. She wanted him to stay. Half an hour ago she had brushed off Gene, feeling she must mourn Anaxa alone. Now she was terrified at the thought of being left alone with her grief. But she was too proud to appeal to him directly.

"I'm too proud to appeal to you directly, Tom," she said, "But won't you stay and keep me company until they go? Maria can't stay — she's got to get back to her mother-in-law's for the baby. And I don't know most of the people here — it's all a bit too much for me."

Tom looked at her steadily.

"What is it you want from me, Alice?"

Alice blushed.

"I want you to become my friend and support me in my hour of need."

"Isn't there something more you want from me?"

"Maybe."

"Well, I can't give it. I'm damaged goods. You deserve better, or different, at any rate."

"What's damaged you?" she asked, choking on the dregs of whisky in her glass, wishing she were upstairs in bed, sleeping, away from all the waves of pain she could sense were on their way.

"You idealise me, Alice. You only see my good side. Sure, if you're talking about lust, sex, screwing — I could do that for you. I don't find you unnattractive. But you don't just want that. You want more. You want intimacy and love."

"And you don't want that?"

"I can't do it. Something was broken which won't mend. Something was wounded which won't heal. I hope it will one day but it hasn't yet, and that's that."

"But what was it that wounded you? Was it a woman? Your wife maybe?"

"I don't want to discuss it. It's boring. I'm a lame dog, Alice, and that turns you on for a start. But why don't you leave us lame dogs alone and go for Eros, go for someone who'll give you what you want, or rather what you need? *You're* not damaged! You're daft, impulsive, disorganised maybe, but not wounded. Don't you understand Alice, you're a lucky one!"

"A lucky one?" Alice repeated with a deep breath. It did not seem so to her. It seemed to her tht she had always been frustrated; that either she had not got what she wanted or she had got it and then realised she did not want it any more. How could that be lucky?

"I have tried to give you what I could," continued Tom, glancing longingly towards the front door. "I told you about the group. You didn't go. I pulled you in that night when you were lost and about to get yourself into serious trouble. You were angry about that. Well, that's all right, I don't want gratitude, of course I don't, but you must learn to take what people can give, Alice, not what they can't."

"Everyone's always trying to teach me things," said Alice sulkily. "But I could teach you things too you know. I could teach you that all your great relationsips with God is pretty useless unless you also have the ability to give in to human intimacy, to let someone love you and love them back. After all Abraham loved Sara and Isaac an awful lot, even if he did love God more. You could try being a human being for a change instead of a magician — how about that?"

"Sounds nice."

"It's not particularly nice! Don't put it down like that — I'm not being sentimental. I had that sort of intimacy with Anaxa and she drove me crazy! Then killed herself! Not very nice at all."

"I know, I know . . . " began Tom soothingly.

Gene crashed into the room, tripping over Thomas the Smudgeface who was sitting pugnaciously on the threshold and knocking Tom's glass of water to the floor as he steadied himself on his shoulder. Alice saw Tom shudder involuntarily at the contact and then order himself to relax. Gene left his hand resting on Tom's shoulder while he laughed and swept his chaotic hair back with his other hand.

"Well, Dionysus rules OK up there, but it all seems Apollonian calm down here."

"We were just talking about intimacy," said Alice dourly, furious that Gene had interrupted just when she felt she was getting through to Tom. "Tom's no good at it. I'm not much better but occasionally I do manage it and then the person usually dies. Not much of an advert really."

The two men looked at each other in the pause that followed. Gene's bigness, his animal high spirits, made Tom seem slight and peaky, but there was a hardness in Tom which could check the other's power. They were equals, Alice could feel that. But they did not fight with the same weapons. Fight? Must men always fight? It must be so tiring, so boring, having to assert yourself all the time. Alice felt suddenly glad to be female. She let her body go soft and yielding, let herself fall back against Gene, cuddling into his bigness. But it was not right. His maleness splashed over her, invading her, disturbing her dreamy odalisque fullness. She pushed herself away again.

"I'm going," said Tom suddenly. "Gene will stay and look after you, I'm sure."

And he was gone, quick as a cat who leaves for an urgent rendezvous with food or sex or wildness. Gene stood, balancing on one foot, measuring his chances.

"He's not big enough for you, Alice," he said quietly. "He'd squeeze all the juices out of you and kill your joy of life. Not for you these sombre characters — you were made for happiness and sensuality."

Alice stared at the fridge, discountenanced.

"Anaxa thought it would be a good idea," she said with studied vagueness.

"Then she didn't understand men."

"She thought she did."

"Poor woman! To die for a delusion. You must make up for it. You mustn't cast your pearsl before swine. Come here to me."

Alice's mouth trembled. She was near to smiling, but her resolve held her.

"No. I have to see to the party. I have to look after Masha. It's not right at the moment, Gene."

"Not right? What could be more right."

"I have to mourn my friend."

"You mean you have to protect yourself."

"Bit late for that, isn't it?"

"I'm sorry. It was nasty, brutish and short last time. We were both in a strange state. Let me make it up to you."

Alice wrapped her arms tightly round herself.

"Please understand, *please*! I've got to look after the *people*," and she walked, neat and decisive as a traffic warden past him out of the kitchen and up the stairs. A moment later she heard the front door slam. 'I don't care,' she thought, 'He is insensitive and importunate. He must learn about the right time for things!' She marched into the workroom and straight up to the big black bouncer who took her in his arms and wheeled her around the room in a giddy foxtrot-frottant.

Now she was alone, completely alone, whirling in the crowded room in a landscape of utter desolation. Desolation. She liked the word. She had heard it that morning, in a poem of Blake's they had read out on Radio Three: "Wisdom is sold in the desolate marketplace where few come to buy." 'That's what I'll do,' she thought, 'I'll go to the desolate marketplace and buy some wisdom. I'll buy, I'll buy, I'll buy . . . '

Much later and drunker she went to bed alone and fell instantly asleep. In the morning she found that Thomas the cat, having accidentally been shut in and unable to wake her by miaowing, had delivered a big pile of shit onto the kitchen floor. She took one look at it and was heartily sick on top of the piles of washing-up waiting in the kitchen sink.

★ ★ ★

Soon Alice's life, which had temporarily taken on a tragic dignity, degenerated once again into the stuff of comedy. Three things happened in quick succession: the bank refused to extend her overdraft any further and she found herself forced to borrow money from her mother, who was delighted to lend it, feeling that penury proved that her daughter was trying to be a real artist at last. Next, the social worker who had been reviewing Masha's case, decided that Alice could become the child's official foster-mother, in spite of being penniless, unmarried and bohemian in her life-style. Alice, brainwashed by too many documentaries about the cruelties of the social services, was astonished and delighted and insisted on sharing the last of the whisky left over from Anaxa's wake with the haggard lady who looked near-overwhelmed by problems of her own. Thirdly, she discovered that she was pregnant. There was no doubt about it: she missed her period, had tender breasts and felt queasy in the mornings. She began to spend a great deal of time lying on the lascivious settee listening to Kathleen Ferrier and weeping.

But to say that she felt thoroughly miserable would be misleading. It would be more accurate to say that she felt *helpless*, which for her was such an unusual state that it caused her a kind of wild, existential discomfort, an itching in the soul from which floods of tears were the only relief. She felt 'bad in her skin' but quite unable to jump out of it — the growing foetus weighed her down to earth. She slept heavily, but could not remember her dreams. She could not make the simplest decision (such as whether to allow Masha to eat sultana pancakes with syrup every morning for breakfast) without vacillation and anxiety. When Masha cried for her mother Alice cried too. When Masha was sunny and forgetful of her loss the child's courage stabbed her and she had to choke back the tears rising in her throat so as not to burden Masha with her own grief.

She knew she should be 'doing something' about this ridiculous pregnancy, but every course of action seemed mined with fearful possibilities. If she told her mother, her mother would probably insist on moving in and taking her and Masha over for the duration. If she told Gene (whom she had not seen since the night of the wake) he would think her a scheming, demanding creature who was trying to weigh him down with unfair responsibilities after one night of reckless lust. If she had an abortion . . . but no, she couldn't do it. The baby had been conceived in some kind of joy — or at least enjoyment, albeit muddled and muddied by other sorts of emotion — it deserved a chance to live.

So there was nothing to be done except live day by day, forget the painting for a while, and try to earn some money. Here she was lucky. Tom needed someone three days a week in his shop, and since she possessed a certain eccentric style, he took her on. But the money was not enough, so swallowing her pride, she presented herself at the Poly as a nude model for the life-class, and because she was big, voluptuous and an old art-school friend of the tutor, she got the work. That the job required complete immobility suited her admirably and with the money she was given for fostering Masha, she could just manage to keep them both.

Meanwhile, as the skies darkened towards Christmas, Alice knew that she was living cosily and foolishly in a tiny vestibule of her self while the vast, echoing mansion of the rest of her being stretched neglected beyond it. She knew that pregnancy in itself was no excuse to stop painting entirely and cut herself off from the world, but she was frightened to move or act, frightened as she had never been in her life before, and she did not know why. She was paralysed. She dared not move for fear of waking up the frightened beast that slept within. If she stayed still, so would it. If she moved it would engulf and devour her.

But something *was* eating her anyway. Something was vibrating, crackling, burning . . . something was using up her energies and making the spaces in her resonate. She was reminded of her fever the year before, the struggles that had gone on during those delirious nights, when she had felt as if there was almost nothing of her left, as if she were just a tormented blob of consciousness being tossed around on a boiling sea.

But now the burning had started again. She tried to ignore it, to dampen it by eating good food and re-reading 'Middlemarch' for the fifth time, but it outwitted her, it found a crafty new means of expression, one which Alice was, constitutionally, not fitted to resist — sexual desire! She was not expecting this and it hit her all the harder. She found herself aching for sexual contact with an intensity she had not known since adolescence and first love. It was not a genital ache, but a painful knot of needfulness which clenched up her womb, sent spasms up into her belly and down into her loins, that made her heart bang viciously and her legs twitch. It did not succumb to feverish bouts of masturbation. It was not general — it could not, she knew, be assuaged by a casual night of sex with a friend. It was directed quite specifically towards one man, and that man was Gene, the father of her child.

Oh, how Alice hated this bitter realisation! She had thought frequently and resentfully of Gene, of his arrogance, his easy, confident masculinity, his good humour and his sparky surliness, his cavalier assumption that she would be pleased to jump into bed with him again on the night of Anaxa's wake. Alice did not like men like that. She like them gentle, doe-eyed, melancholic. Or, (and this was Maria's version) narcissistic, elusive, magical in their ambivalence. And yet she had to admit that Gene had not been brutal or unkind to her, that his body pleased her, his bright eyes had seen her, that the anger he had triggered in her was exciting and enlivening, that, if she were only not pregnant, she would swallow her pride and present herself at his door, apologise and start from the beginning again . . .

'And why should I not do that anyway?' she asked herself one Monday morning after Masha was packed off to school. 'If I call on him at this hour there will be no sexual overtones, and I need not tell him I am pregnant. We can have a cup of coffee and talk and he can see that I'm over Anaxa's death and back to normal again. Maybe we can be friends and take things easy for a while.'. . . She dressed in her most ordinary, unseductive clothes — grey track suit with pink boots and a battered leather flying jacket — and set off for the allotments with a calm and innocent air.

At first there was no response to her bangings on the door, and she thought he was not in or perhaps had gone away again, but suddenly he appeared, holding a small towel in place around his waist, looking surly and ironic and not even slightly or subliminally pleased to see her.

"What do you want?" he asked coldly, not putting any special stress on the 'you' to indicate that she was any kind of special 'you' to him.

"Just to apologise," she said, blushing with mortification, "for my behaviour at the funeral."

"I accept your apologies. What else?"

"Well, could I perhaps come in for a moment?"

"No."

"Why not?"

"It's not convenient."

"Just for five minutes."

"I'm in bed with someone, if you must know."

"Oh. Will you come and see me later then?"

"Why should I?"

"Because I want to talk to you."

"About what?"

"About . . . well . . . I wondered if we could be friends."

"Friends? I've got friends. I need a woman. And I've got one in there waiting for me, so if you don't mind . . ."

"But surely you understand? I needed some space to mourn my friend."

" 'Space to mourn your friend'? Sounds like something from the Guardian Women's Page. You were frightened, that's all. That's why you threw me out. You're a coward, and I can't be bothered with women who've got no guts."

"What do you know about me and what I am?"

"Listen, I'm freezing on this doorstep. What do you want to talk to me about?"

"We can't talk here."

"Here or nowhere."

Alice stamped fretfully on the doorstep in her pink boots. This was not going right for her at all. This was not what she had expected or planned. Gene was being utterly unreasonable, and so unreasonableness was the only weapon she could fight back with. She took one deep breath, stamped again and thrust her hands toughly into the pockets of her flying jacket.

"I'm pregnant," she said.

"Hah!" said Gene and stepped back abruptly as if she had shoved him in the chest.

"And it must be yours. I haven't slept with anyone else for ages. So!"

He looked down at his towel and tightened his hold on it. He cast a panicked glance down the hallway and shifted his weight from one foot to the other. He opened his mouth as if to speak and then shut it again.

"I'm sorry! I didn't intend to spring this on you. But you were being so unreasonable. I always take precautions, always. But that night I didn't have my cap with me. I wasn't expecting to have sex with you."

"My foot you weren't! That's why you came round. Don't you realise that? Bicycle my foot!"

"That's absolutely not true! My bicycle is important to me. I didn't want it stolen by some kid. I felt sorry for you, you were ill. I was in a state about Anaxa . . . anyway, don't worry, I shan't trouble you again. I shan't be asking you to support it or anything. I just thought you ought to know. No, I don't mean that — I didn't mean to tell you at all, you forced me to! I just wanted to come and see you and apologise and be friends with you again . . . "

Her words dried up. There was nothing more to say. It was going to happen again — the ultimate disappointment. The big cold. The turning away. The battling on and just having to bear it. But it would be all right. She was a woman of the north. She could bear the cold as well as the warm. She stepped back from the door and turned away without looking at him. A long, hairy, arm yanked her back again.

"Go into the kitchen and wait. I'll be five minutes."

She sat on a dirty chair in the cold kitchen and heard the low voices and shuffling that bespoke the dressing and leaving of the other woman. She imagined a tender embrace and an explanation. "This hysterical woman, she won't go away. I'm sorry, but I'll have to talk to her. I'll ring you later OK?" The thing was that she was not at all hysterical. She was calm and curious to see what was going to happen. The front door slammed and Gene appeared in a mangey blue dressing-gown too small for him.

"Are you going to have an abortion?" he asked in the tone of voice in which one enquires if someone is going to take a bath.

"No."

"Why not?"

"There's no reason to. My mental health is fine. I have work. I have a house."

"Have you at least considered the possibility?"

"Not really."

"Has this happened to you before?"

"No."

"What do you want me to do about it?"

"Nothing. I don't know. Do you want me to have an

abortion?"

"No."

"Well then, what do you want?"

"I want to make love to you. Here. Now."

"Why?"

"To see what it's like . . . "

"You know what it's like."

"When I'm sober and not ill."

"But you've just been screwing some other woman."

"So? I'm in practice. I'll wash."

Alice looked at him across the table. His face was shiny with early morning grease. His tangled hair was also greasy and he smelt of sweat and sex. His big skinny wrists stuck out of the short arms of his dressing-gown. But he did not look ugly or ridiculous. He had a dignity that never deserted him. Her eyes drifted up to his face and she saw he was looking at her. His eyes were neither cold nor warm. He was giving nothing away. Perhaps she would be better to pick up her shopping-bag, her bike lamp and walk out. Cut her losses. Take no risks. Quit before the real trouble started. But her womb was burning, it was already too late. She had been opened up against her will (or rather while her will was looking the other way) and something had been planted in her that could not be uprooted. Besides she was already on her feet and walking behind him into the back room.

There was no fire in the grate today although the mattress was still in place in front of it. The fitful December sun had only edged round enough to throw a bleak, greyish light into the room. Alice stood unsteadily between the piles of dirty clothes and dirty plates and watched while Gene plugged in an old electric fire and went out, without speaking, to the bathroom. She sat down on the edge of the mattress and removed her boots. She could not quite believe in what she was about to do. 'Perhaps that's my trouble,' she thought, 'I'm never really there when I do things. I'm always beind or ahead of myself. But I can't get out of this one. I suppose I don't want to. I suppose I do want Gene to make love to me again.'

He crashed back into the room, jarring her out of her delicate meditations. She shivered. He flung off his dressing-gown and wriggled between the disordered sheets and blankets.

"Hurry up!" he said. "It's cold."

With what was probably infuriating slowness Alice removed her clothes and folded them neatly into a pile on a relatively clean bit of floor. She knew without checking that Gene was watching her closely and felt uncomfortably conscious of how her big breasts swung as she moved and of the large space between her hips. But after all, he was big too. Perhaps he would not mind.

They lay for a moment facing each other.

"You *are* beautiful," he said.

She was surprised. She had not expected compliments. She had forgotten his generosity. She noticed he had washed his face and combed his hair and was touched by these acts of consideration.

"How are you?" he asked.

"Fine," she said and laughed.

"Good," he said. "Don't let's take all this too seriously."

She was jarred again. So now it was all a joke?

"I mean," he continued, "let's not make a life or death issue of it. Since we've already made a life, let's relax and enjoy ourselves."

"I'll try, but I'm not sure it's that easy."

"It can't hurt the baby can it?"

"I don't think so. Orgasms are supposed to be good for them, I believe."

"Then you must be sure to have an orgasm."

He kissed her neck, rubbing his bristly chin into the cup of her shoulder. She shuddered and turned to him. Their mouths met clumsily, roughly, parted again, each surprised by the assertive reality of the other. They tried again. This time he asserted *his* idea of a kiss and pressed hard with mouth and body against her. She yielded, waited till his impetus was spent and then flickered her tongue between his lips, feeling with her hands down his long back to reach the swell of his buttocks and cup them in her hands.

Then darkness fell in their minds and it was easy, rolling together, backwards and forwards, now rough and fast, now smooth and slow and sweet . . . something tight in her belly found itself dissolving and he hardened in response to it, penetrating her in slow motion, gasping as he fell right into her and touched the neck of her womb.

"Careful, careful," he said. "It's just so easy for me to come too soon."

"Don't worry, don't worry," she whispered.

"But I don't want to come without you."

"Oh . . . Oh . . . Oh . . . " she panted as he pushed into her and her labia puffed out to receive him, but she knew she was not going to come.

"I don't think I'm going to come," she said.

He paused for a moment and then thrust hard into her.

"You are, you are! You bloody are! You must!"

"I can't force it."

Now he stopped dead and withdrew himself from her.

"I'm not coming unless you do," he said. "I'd rather get up and read the paper."

'Ho!' thought Alice. 'Once again my life turns from high drama to low comedy in one deft stroke.'

"That's silly," she said, in a quiet, embarrassed voice.

"Is it?" he said, pulling himself off her so that he could grip her shoulders hard. "Is it really, Alice in Wonderland? Well, if so, tell me why I should give to you if you won't give to me? Or rather, why I should let you pleasure me if you won't let me pleasure you?"

Alice turned her head to one side so that her eyes could escape the glare of his.

"It's not a question of that. I hardly know you. I don't know whether I can trust you."

"What crap!" he said abruptly. "You're just holding back because you're scared. If you can't trust the father of your child, who can you trust?"

"Jesus Christ! Who do you think you are?"

"I know who I am, Alice, that's for sure. But do you?"

An image sailed through Alice's mind like a breath of wind through a tunnel. A big, dark man opening a door, smiling ironically, turning, walking away in front of her, opening another door, turning again, showing her courteously into a large room, where a group of people were assembled, seated on the floor.

"Is this some kind of conspiracy" she asked in a voice that seemed to come from another Alice, very far away but also unbearably near, an Alice she sensed without seeing behind a veil of glutinous, swirling glass.

"No, it's all your own doing, Alice. But don't stop now — keep going! You called, you came for me, and I was here, waiting. Don't turn back now . . . keep going . . . don't you see, you're nearly there . . . "

Her sister was behind the glass, very close, but it was as if rain was washing over the glass, obscuring her image, and the sound, the gutteral roaring of the water made it difficult to hear. Alice was terrified. They had been preparing her, setting her up for this, they had lured her into a trap! It seemed they thought that she was ready, but she *wasn't*, because she was pregnant by a stranger, and had Masha to look after and Anaxa was dead and everything was turned into nightmare, and she couldn't open because she knew that what would come in would destroy her, she was sure of it . . . But still the image, clear and obscure, of her sister waiting on the other side for her . . . the other woman, waiting, waiting to be recognised by her . . .

Gene had penetrated her again and was moving stealthily inside her, and that was good and comfortable, but her attention was elsewhere. She knew there was something she had to remember, remember quickly before the moment came round again, the moment of receiving . . . then she felt a weight behind her, a pressure building up behind her chest or *inside* her chest, that wanted to throw her forwards and out of herself with tremendous force . . . The ground was slipping from under her feet and soon there would be nowhere to stand and she would be forced either to jump or fall . . . but what was it she would be jumping into? Would the glass break as she flung herself through it or bounce her horribly back upon herself? Would the woman on the other side catch her as she came or disappear and leave her alone in nothingness? Again she didn't know, but something was being touched and stirred in her, making her feel very uncomfortable, indeed it was beginning to sear and burn her quite unbearably . . . A cry was coming out of her, her voice was going out before her . . . it seemed the moment had come to jump, to let herself be pulled through to the other side, hoping desperately that there was something waiting to receive her there and hold her, because if there wasn't then that would be the end of everything . . . she jumped.

A great shout went up, as if a football crowd roared its approval of a goal, and she was through! She was *there*! Balancing precariously, breathless, teetering over nothingness still, but definitely *there*! The rainy glass had yielded easily to her weight and now she was confronting the face that had been obscured. Now, *now* it was that she must remember the knowledge she had been given in those other worlds, those secret places of the stair, now it was that she must *recognise* . . . and, *yes*, she knew the woman reaching out her hand to her. A tremendous, deafening calm enveloped them.

"Come on," said the woman, "come quickly!"

They passed a deep cool pool with naked boys sitting immobile at its edge, turned a corner, and entered a little room. There was a fire, candles and an amazing brightness which dazzled her so that she couldn't make out the faces of the beings there.

"This is the palace of essence, Alice" said a voice. "Can you feel it?"

Alice could feel the silence, the tremulous intensity of the air, and also a freedom and space around the area of her heart which she could never have imagined hitherto. She turned to try and see the woman, but an arm constrained her.

"This is what lies at the back of nothingness," they said. "Try to remember when it's over and seek essence, Alice, trust in the invisible . . . "

But the silence was being broken up now by a terrible roaring. The scene before her was flashing painfully in her eyes, and the vibrations, the deep vibrations, shook her to the core. She tried not to resist them, she tried to go along with them and let them buoy her up and take her somewhere, but before she could see, the spark of panic in her glittered and flared up. She cast round wildly for her companion . . . her face was just there . . . or was it a reflection in the crystal palace wall? The face was . . . she recognised it quite clearly as her own face and yet somehow different . . . the face of the woman who had been waiting, waiting to be recognised for all those million years . . .

The roaring, disintegrating noises had got too much for her. The crystal walls were falling past her, very fast. It was time to jump the other way, and yes, OK, she was exhausted but could still do it, do it *now*! A violent tug in the guts, a belabouring of the heart . . . lights out and down the clattering wooden stairs to kingdom come . . . the baby listening for her mother in the nursery . . . the idea of Alice Cunningham flickers and dies down . . . not dead but sleeping, sleeping at the bottom of the deeps . . .

A long time afterwards. A dark green place. Silence. Stillness. Infinite but comforting deepness. Everything yielded but the very idea of yielding wiped away. Seeing nothing, feeling nothing, just being, balancing between the longing to stay within the silence and the longing to give in again to the sweet contralto note of sleep that was calling her . . .

"Alice?" She opened her eyes and Gene was looking down at her, his face wet with sweat or tears, she did not know which. For a moment they held each other's eyes. She knew him. He knew her. Everything else was far away, in the world of pure imagination.

"Well done, well done, kid," he said softly and rolled off her so that they parted with a slurping sound.

Alice was laughing. Gene was laughing. But underneath, in the still-present stillness she was thinking: 'Ah yes, *now* my throat is opened! *Now* I know what my voice is supposed to sound like. *Now* I can really begin to learn how to sing . . . '

* * *

Epilogue

But no, patient reader, I am not going to leave you with such an unsatisfactory, up-in-the-air sort of ending! It is only right that we should complete the cycle and follow Alice and Maria back to the picnic place they first visited two years ago, although this time of course, the roles are reversed: it is Alice who is in her sixth month of pregnancy and Maria's (new red) car they have travelled in. But otherwise things look very much the same. They lie in the grass under the chestnut tree. The sun beats down. The tall grasses sway. Alice rubs her pollen-reddened eyes and tugs the maternity frock she hates down to cover her freckled knees and stop them burning. Maria munches her way daintily through a monstrous doorstep of a salami sandwich and sucks the juices from a fat, overripe tomato. The elf looks down, hopeful perhaps that this time something exciting *will* happen.

And yes, Alice is once again depressed. She has not lived happily ever after. Gene has returned to Turkey, taking Lewis with him to find labouring work on one of the sites. Alice feels angry and abandoned, even though it was in fact *her* idea that she should finish her painting and Gene his excavations before they contemplated a steadier life together. But that was before the great-hearted (but thick-skinned) Gene had offered to take Lewis under his wing and introduce him to the right people out there. 'It must have been at Anaxa's wake that they met and talked about it,' thought Alice, gritting her teeth in rage. 'It's just not fair that I should be left here to stew on my own while Lewis has possibilities of redemption handed to him on a silver salver, and skips away unscathed from all the griefs and responsibilities left behind by Anaxa's death.' She had been so anxious to behave like a proper, liberated, unpossessive woman that she had not dared ask for what she really wanted, which was for Gene to marry her immediately and take her with him to Turkey. She could see now that, for his part, he had wanted to respect her desire, as an artist, to complete her great work before having the baby, and had hesitated to suggest that they might just possibly put their need to be with each other above other considerations. And so they had opted to do as they ought not as they wished and were now suffering the consequences, which were, in Alice's case, that she had once again turned her giant canvas firmly to the wall. She would not or could not see Heaven, and therefore could not complete the third part of the triptych. Stubbornly unhappy, she wrote Gene brave letters and made outlandish garments for her own and other people's babies.

Now sweating under the ruthless sun, she sighed and dragged her heavy body over into a patch of shade. How she longed for a cigarette or another glass of wine! But now that both of those were out of bounds there was only the distraction of talking to relieve the pressing irritation of daily life against her sore heart. She opened her mouth and, without thinking, spoke:

"I had thought, Maria, that pregnancy would make me cowlike, serene and radiant with unearthly beauty, but instead I'm fretful, grumpy, queasy, ungainly, fat and hot! If I'm like this now, God knows what I'll be like in three months time!"

"Cut the self-pity, Alice!" said Maria in the hard but caressing drawl she had learnt from her formidable mother. "I had a much worse time of it and I didn't moan on about it like you do. Your mystic friends say that suffering is the most difficult thing of all to give up and, looking at you, I'd say they're right."

"Oh, I wouldn't mind if I was *suffering* properly. It's these petty irritations that get me down. Hayfever, heat, Masha's tantrums, the thought of Lewis and Gene sitting up half the night in their tent somewhere discussing Sufism and thinking what noble seekers after truth they are while I sit here blowing up like a balloon, incapable of doing anything except drinking tea and whining!"

"Well that's your own choice," said Maria tartly. A cloud sailed across the sun and she shivered, suddenly feeling bored and chilled. "Come on, let's have a walk in the wood before we go home. Just to complete the pattern."

And so it was that once again the disappointed elf saw them pack up their picnic things and make their way down the side of the field towards the wood, Maria marching on ahead, a tiny, resolute Amazon; Alice straggling behind to hitch up her bra and her knickers down to ease their pressure on her expansive flesh.

And once again they passed through the stone gateposts which marked the beginning of a drive which led, evidently, to somewhere, and stopped to rest just before the track curved round to the left. Only this time it was Alice, not Maria, who remarked that she was tired and wanted to go home. They stood for a moment under the high, over-arching trees, and smelt the freezing perfume of the bluebells.

"This is where we turned back before," said Maria. "Don't you want to go on this time and see what's round the bend?"

"I don't know," said Alice. She felt uneasy, aware of the reasonableness of Maria's suggestion and the unreasonableness of her desire to turn on her heels and walk quickly back to the car. "It's funny — I feel I know what's round there, but I don't want to see it . . . if you know what I mean."

"Well, you sit down for a minute and rest and I'll just walk on a bit and see what's there. I'm curious to know."

"No, no, I'll come," said Alice reluctantly. "I'm just being silly, I suppose."

They walked round the bend and soon saw the house before them, a genial red-brick Victorian mansion with white-painted window-frames and a lilac tree drooping at its porch.

"Well, there you are, that's it," Alice began to say, but Maria had skipped off and was darting round the house, peering into the windows and finally disappearing around the corner.

"Hey, come and see this garden!" she shouted.

"It's trespassing!" yelled Alice testily.

"No, no, the house is empty. There's nobody living here. Come on — it's lovely!"

Alice stomped round the path, past a vegetable patch where grotesque, overgrown cabbages breathed out a putrid stench at her, through a green door in a high brick wall and into an enclosed garden where blowzy roses bloomed and Maria stood by a dry fountain staring back towards the shuttered house.

"I bet they had great garden parties here," Maria was saying, "It must have been a lovely place to live . . . "

But Alice was not listening. A profound lassitude swept through her and plumped her down on a mossy bench shaded by honeysuckle. After a moment Maria came to join her. They did not speak. There was a deep silence in the garden which sucked up thought before it had found expression. A sleepy bee bumbled past Alice's face, brushing her nose on its way to the honeysuckle.

"Ah yes," she said suddenly, "Last time the fountain was working, wasn't it?"

"We've never been here before, Alice," said Maria sternly. "We turned back half way up the drive. Don't you remember?"

"Remember?" Alice remembered all right. She remembered the other drive, which led to the camp, the room, the Aquarium, the underground pleasure palaces . . . everything. But it was like seeing someone vanish round the corner in a dream and knowing you would never catch them and you might as well wake up. Within a second she had stopped remembering. All that remained was the memory of having remembered something and forgotten it.

She look round sharply at Maria. Maria was looking at her. Her dark eyes were flicking over Alice's face with something like anger, but her pupils were big, oddly dilated in spite of the bright sun. Alice realised she was not angry but frightened. She too had remembered and forgotten and remembered that she had known something for an instant before forgetting it.

She looked down at her lap to escape Maria's eyes. She thought of all the dreams, adventures, coincidences, fantasies, strange meetings, births and deaths that had swept her from the picnic of two years ago to this one, left her pregnant, impoverished, separated from the man who had seemed to be the one she had always been looking for . . . What the hell did it all *mean*? What was the point of making these eery journeys into the worlds which cut across the 'moment now', to see the awesome machinery which churns behind the clockface of reality, when after all you always had to come back to the ordinary world of working, sleeping, eating boiled eggs, falling in and out of love and failing to complete ambitious works of art?

Then Alice looked up and looked hard at the garden. She saw a willow-tree sway and bend under a strong gust of wind. She heard the bee buzz angrily around a blossoming rose. She felt the bench damp and hot under her thigh. She smelt the odour of rotting cabbage mixing itself with honeysuckle and the astringent, lemony soap that Maria used, and she tasted the liquorice sweetness of her own saliva as it filled her throat and mouth. She realised that she was seeing the garden, or rather *experiencing* the garden for the very first time. Those vaguely recalled times when she had seen it before, she had not *seen* it, she had *remembered* seeing it now. But if those times were in the past, how could she have remembered this *now*, this present, which was surely in the future then? It made her dizzy to think like this but she knew she must not stop. She was nearly there, nearly on the right track . . .

'OK, so this is *real*,' she thought. 'This place that I perceive with all my senses is real. But what of all those other places, those secret places I have been?' 'Well, they're real too, Alice,' she told herself. 'It's just that they exist in other worlds which other people may not remember or pay attention to, even though they certainly go there. Everybody does. The only difference between you and most of the others is that you are a rememberer, a messenger, a traveller between the worlds — like Anaxa was, like Tom is — that's all there is to it!'

Alice stared hard into the green garden and all at once heard a noise, a roar, as if the sky was cranking open and the engines of God were coming out. As she looked the garden darkened but grew brighter at the same time, more and more real and inescapable, and the roar intensified into a mighty soaring note of thunder until it made her eardrums beat and the garden flamed and flared up into her retina!

And then: a moment's utter silence before she heard the singing: Aaaaaaah . . . Aaaaaaah . . . Aaaaaaah! Voices of angels singing as they made the world, as they charged it up with immense, resonating energies! Alice flung her head back and looked up into the sky in pure delight. She wanted to reach her arms up and have them pull her up to them like a little girl who is swung up in her father's strong arms . . . and she knew she could, she could do it if she wanted to!

Her head opened like a daffodil and was filled with the rushing and fluttering of a world of wings. She was almost blinded with the joy of it, the ecstacy of imminent liberation . . . and then she remembered that Maria was sitting next to her and said:

"Maria, can you hear it? The angels singing?"

"Alice!" Maria's voice was sharp but teetering on the verge of tears.

'Tears of joy?' wondered Alice. 'How wonderful if she can hear them too!"

"Alice, it's just the echo of the jets when they flew over us just now! It's just a sonic boom, or something. What are you talking about, you idiot?"

Alice turned and saw her friend staring at her, cross and startled and a little bit alarmed. But she could still hear the angels' voices, their deep bass note just beginning to die, to fade away into the substance of the world. She waited until they had gone completely before she spoke.

"Never mind," she said, "you're right. I am an idiot. But it's all right, it's all right now. We can go home."

Maria still stared at her, perplexed, so Alice leaned across and kissed her on the cheek. Maria smiled, pleased in spite of herself, then jumped up to her feet.

"You and your illuminations, Alice! Where will it all end, I ask myself?"

"Oh, it doesn't matter where it ends," said Alice, reaching her hand to Maria to be pulled up. "But I must get home and finish the picture before I forget."

"Forget what?"

"What heaven is like of course."

★ ★ ★